Katz Box

Bob Henneberger

Copyright 2010 Bob Henneberger

www. temptpress. com

Books by Bob Henneberger

Crackstone Chronicles – Extinction

Crackstone Chronicles – Connections

Crackstone Chronicles – Extraordinary Solution

Katz Pajamas

Katz Cradle

Hunting Paradise

Tempt Press
PO Box 77
Colchester, VT 05446

Published by **Tempt Press**
P.O. Box 77, Colchester, VT 05446

First Print Edition, 2010

Copyright © 2010 Bob Henneberger

ISBN: 978-0-9830118-5-9
Library of Congress Control Number: 2010936746

To Sandy

Things done well and with a care, exempt themselves from fear.

CONTENTS

1. THINK FAST, NOT DEEP
2. BYE, BYE LOVE
3. BUSINESS IS BUSINESS
4. HOME IS WHERE THE RENT'S FREE
5. WHO'S THAT KNOCKING AT MY DOOR?
6. OFF TO SEE THE WIZARD.
7. ALL YOU CAN EAT
8. ALL'S QUIET ON THE WATER FRONT
9. KATZ' CALL
10. THE HARE AND HOUND
11. AS BEST AS I CAN REMEMBER
12. THE BOX REBELLION
13. HAVE IT YOUR WAY
14. A HARE'S BREATH AWAY
15. REUNION
16. NO REST FOR THE WEARY
17. JUST ONE MORE LITTLE THING
18. SOUTH OF THE BORDER
19. WHAT'S UP, DOLT?
20. THE TIE THAT BINDS
21. A SHOT IN THE DARK
22. WHO WAS THAT MASKED MAN?
23. WHO'S THAT KNOCKING AT MY HEAD?
24. COME OUT, COME OUT WHOEVER YOU ARE.
25. NO REST FOR THE WEARY
26. CAN THE FAT LADY SING YET?
27. THE KATZ BOX
28. I DO, AND THEN I DON'T
29. GUESS WHO'S KNOCKING ON MY DOOR?
30. IT COULD HAVE BEEN WORSE
31. I TOLD YOU IT COULD GET WORSE
32. LIFE IS GOOD

1

Think fast, not deep

It was half way through the year, August, 1980 to be exact. I was on a container ship so this wasn't the cruise of a life time, it was just business. This was another one of those jobs I'd rather not think about until a week after it was over. I'm a private investigator and I do a lot of different jobs each year, but those that take turns like this kind of leave me scratching my head in amazement.

In times like this, I've realized I should take stock of my life and asked the question, have I chosen the right career? Did I miss an opportunity that could have changed my life for the better, or at least something safer? But, not having the time to debate the relative merits of this situation, I attributed it to my predilection to act with gargantuan gobs of chutzpa.

Right next door to me, the Japanese couple's cabin mirrored mine. Obviously the couple had settled in for a much longer haul than I was in for since they had way more personal stuff crammed into their space.

I'm only six foot one, but the doors were so low that I had to stoop over slightly to stand in the entrance of their disheveled room. Deciding not to go in yet, I scanned the area for something not trashed; nothing leapt out at me. All the books had been searched, then thrown in a pile on the floor.

The shaving cream can lay emptied into the sink, where someone had cut the can with a large knife, something with enough strength to splay open the moderately thick metal. The toothpaste, deodorant and makeup containers had suffered the same fate as the shaving cream.

Stacked in the corner of the shallow closet, six empty suitcases made quite a tower. Actually the closet formed only an indentation in the wall with two metal bars to hang cloths on, one bar near the ceiling and the other half way down. Two dressers stood on either side of the double bed the only bed in the room. My room had two narrow single beds and I swear those beds in my room were at least three inches narrower than a real single bed.

The dressers were small, with only four short drawers, but they looked large in that small an area. Like the ones in my room, these dressers were constructed with solid wood and finished with a high gloss varnish; I think they were made from white pine. I noticed that the drawer was constructed of solid wood with dovetail joints at the front and back; the construction was quite fine for a place like this. All eight drawers had been not so meticulously emptied on the floor then stacked in the small shower stall. Whether to call it a shower stall, a toilet room or a wash room since all three occupied the exact same diminutive space, I never could figure out. Whoever had done the hurried rearranging, also did a through job of searching the contents of the drawers and all the hanging clothes; seams were ripped, and shoe soles cut off while someone had looked for something.

A faint smell of sandalwood hung in the air, although I didn't remember smelling that before as I passed the door several times in the past day. My cabin held a slight musty odor to it, accented by the scent of a lemon wood polish. Behind all these up front smells was the faint odor of diesel fuel, the life blood of this ship. I wondered if they had burned incense the night before while they were keeping me awake, bumping the wall next to me. Perhaps they were smoking tobacco, either wacky or real, in their cabin in violation of ship rules and needed a cover-up. Perhaps one of them had a killer gas attack and didn't want the embarrassment. It no longer mattered.

I did notice the silence, the louder engine noises were now absent since we were in port. I couldn't hear any voices, nor loud banging from containers being moved about on deck. Ten minutes earlier, some noises had come from the stern of the ship, as if the crew were shuffling boxes in preparation for a major off loading, but nothing now. The whole time I was on that ship, I noticed that no one listened to music. Even bad music would have been appreciated once and a while.

About the only thing in the room that hadn't been slit open was the body on the floor.

I looked more carefully at this poor guy's head wound; the dark red flow almost stopped, blood had begun to coagulate. A heart beat would make the fluid spurt with a pulse, but the wound oozed so I guessed the murder had taken place within the last half hour or so. I didn't see any breathing, and I debated if I should actually enter the murder scene to check for a pulse. I had a strong sense that I should not go into that room, I also had a strong sense that the man was quite dead. He had to have been there for the destruction of all his material goods, or shortly thereafter, because he lay on top of all the junk on the floor. Unless he still hid behind the partially opened door, the killer had to be long gone since one could see almost the entire cabin from my vantage point; as I've said over and over, these cabins were quite small. I had not heard any loud gunshot, so it had to be a silenced automatic.

Yoshihiro was a pleasant man, he didn't deserve to be killed. His pockets were turned inside out and some of his clothes were torn. I wondered if whoever had tossed his room found what they wanted before killing him. I kind of doubted it.

"Mr. Katz ." Wolfgang slid around the corner of the hallway behind me. I guessed my decision to enter the cabin was made for me; I would not be going in. "Drop your gun slowly to the ground."

I cautiously turned to face the crisply dressed officer who was pointing a shotgun at me; it was a nicely engraved Beretta over and under twelve gauge.

"I don't have a gun, I didn't shoot him," I insisted.

"I think the police should decide that." Wolfgang lowered the shotgun to his waist, still pointing it at my chest.

"Just think about it." I raised my hands slowly in the air. "My gun is in your safe. I walked here, in fact I haven't yet walked all the way into the room; did you hear a gunshot?"

"No." He thought about that for a second. "But the ship is quite noisy, that might mask a shot."

"Not in a metal room with lots of hard surfaces for the sound to bounce off of," I observed quickly. "It had to be a gun with a silencer, and for the silencer to work it had to be an automatic. I have a revolver which hasn't been fired in a while, as well as it being in your safe, if I haven't already mentioned that."

"It's not my place to investigate anything like this once we're docked in port." Wolfgang shook his head, as if he had made up his mind that I was some mass murderer who deserved hanging in that disheveled small room. "I'd rather handle it myself, but that's impossible now. We'll wait right in this hallway until the police get here to arrest you for murder."

"It could be you who killed this man, or one of your crew." I pointed to the body. "Have you considered that?"

"I'm sure the police will question all of us before they are through."

The Captain tried to appear grim but couldn't. He appeared happy that I was the one he found staring at the dead man.

"But I'm sure they will question you more than any of the rest of us," he added.

Damn, things like this put a real crimp in an investigation, you know. This whole thing started more than a week ago when Cassandra left me, and Billy Sullivan showed up on my front porch a few days later. I should have known that two bad things are usually followed by a third.

2

Bye, bye love

"And, why am I supposed to like this?" I asked, looking as much like a hurt puppy as I could.

"Well." Cassandra sighed, not wanting to injure my feelings any more than she already had. "I still think I need to finish what I started. We've talked about this for over a year, since before we moved here."

Mostly she talked about it; I agreed with her in the long run, although I felt like a dog locked in the run at that moment. It's that I didn't look forward to her doing the deed.

"But, why now?" I asked.

I hate to whine, but I was now more in love with her than ever. I didn't want her to leave me, or Atlanta now, not after our move to the East coast and right after I thought we were starting a closer phase in our life together. It wasn't a bad premonition, I didn't want to be Cassandra-less for the next four months.

"If I don't go back and finish my dissertation I'll lose all the years I worked for it." She sat back down on the edge of our bed. "The whole time I worked with you in Los Angeles, I took classes. Sometimes only one a quarter, but I kept at it; I want to finish what I started."

"I know, I agree with the logic."

I knew I was acting hurt. On one level I was pissed at myself for acting that way, I couldn't help myself.

"Can you turn that music down." Cassandra glanced at me. "Ever since you've gotten on that opera jag, you've been playing it a little too loud."

"Okay."

I got up and turned the volume down some. This was my favorite version of Verdi's Rigoletto, with Callas, Di Stefano and Gobbi. Opera was meant to be heard loud and our neighbors were gone. Besides, it was better than the incessant drone of the air conditioner, but I guess she wanted to concentrate on our conversation.

"I'll only be gone for four months," she said, sounding kind of happy I was going to miss her so much. "You can visit me a lot if you like."

"I guess I could move back there while you finish."

"You could, but since we decided to sell our Los Angeles office, where would the money come from to pay all our bills? Remember, as private investigators, we work cases to make money." Cassandra didn't sound pissed, just somewhat annoyed. "You have to stay here unless you want to close this place down and move permanently back to California."

"I know we're going to sell the Los Angeles branch soon, at least I hope our buyer stays interested," I said.

I liked Atlanta slightly more than the City of Angels, and we were settling down here better than I had expected. Our Los Angeles office was doing great and I was happy for that. Our cut of the profits turned out to be over four thousand dollars last month, but that's not what my life is all about. I calculated that if we could sell the business for at least three hundred thousand, we could bank around two hundred thousand after taxes and expenses and that could be our retirement, or it could be one hell of a honeymoon. Or, it could be I was hatching eggs before I laid them.

"Exactly, so you have to stay in Atlanta or there'll be nothing here when I finish. I can't work cases, finish my dissertation and teach a class all at the same time. What if we sell the Los Angeles business and there's no income from Atlanta?" Cassandra put her hand on my arm. "We can't live on what they

12

pay a graduate assistant, besides I won't stay in California that long."

"We could live well off the income from the Los Angeles branch. My real question is, are you sure you want to sell the Los Angeles branch right now?"

Maybe if we waited, I could go back out there and stay with her. I know, I know, I was thinking impulsively.

"We've talked about this a lot since we moved here to Atlanta."

She glanced away from me for a moment.

She was getting impatient. We had sort of agreed on all this before, so I understood why she was annoyed. If I became a serious businessman, we would have no time for fun, let alone any time for cases. My government friends wouldn't approve anyway, so I had to sell and keep our operation small, just the two of us. The Company had asked that I be the only one running this detective agency, but it was too late for that, Cassandra was too important to me now. I wanted to tell her then and there the real reason I needed to ditch the growing business on the West coast, but I couldn't, not yet.

"One quarter." I looked down at her sitting on the bed. "Four months, no longer?"

"I can finish it in one quarter, it's almost done now but they require I be enrolled and on campus for the quarter I defend."

"Damned, I'm going to miss you." I sat next to her on the edge of our bed. "I want you to promise me something."

"What?" She looked at me like she knew I was up to something.

"When you finish your degree, you'll move back here and we'll get married."

"That again?"

"Yes, that again."

"Okay." Cassandra smiled as she squeezed my hand.

I knew that smile, it was different from her 'you moron' smile. This was the 'I love you' smile.

"Is that an okay, you will?" I quickly asked. "Or, is than an okay, you bother me but I still love you?"

"It's just an okay, I will marry you."

"You finally mean it?" I couldn't believe she agreed.

"Why not? We've solved a lot of conflicts on this working together thing." Cassandra shook her head slightly. "So I don't see anything wrong in running the agency as an official, legal couple."

I sat there dumbfounded for a second. I had hoped for this, but now I had to reassess more than filing joint taxes. How would my government handlers take this? I felt like a dog on a choke chain.

"This is great. So, right after you finish? When is the quarter over?"

"Wait just a minute, mister." Cassandra held up her hand. "Assuming it does take only one quarter for me to get my diploma, how big a deal is our wedding going to be, and who's going to plan it?"

"Are you looking at me?" I pointed to my chest.

"Suppose I am?"

"A Justice of the Peace as soon as you get back here."

"I don't think my mother would put up with that, do you?"

"I guess not; do we have to tell her?"

"I guess we do." Cassandra stood up. "I think Dad would like a word in this also. I suppose I could plan something small, Mom would like to help too."

"That's the spirit."

"Yeah, right." Cassandra shot me one of those looks that was something between 'you're so cute' and 'you're so dead'. "I have to get to the airport now."

"I'll get the big suitcase and meet you at the car." I stood up and followed her out of the bedroom.

"So," Cassandra's demeanor changed as she focused on her trip back to California and all the work she would have to do. And, at least I hoped so, she would regret all the time we would be apart. "What do you plan to do with yourself until you come out to visit?"

"I don't know." I picked up on the need for light conversation. "I guess I'll try out my new gym."

"Yeah." She looked around the living room, as if to take a mental picture before leaving. "Did it look good?"

"It looked more than good." I nodded in agreement. "They teach Taekwondo. The guy I talked to down there said they have a female teacher too."

"Maybe when I get back." Cassandra glanced at me, then at the front door. "I'd gotten used to that gym in Los Angeles."

"I'm glad you started some training." I picked back up the two suitcases and headed to the door. "When you get back, maybe you could try out the new fitness center."

"What cases do you have pending?" Cassandra asked, as we muscled her several suitcases down to the car.

We had too many suitcases and not enough car; I had to do something about that.

Looking down Euclid, towards the neighborhood and away from Little Five Points, I took in a deep breath. At ten in the morning, temperatures were reasonably warm but not the humidity. By now, in late summer, our windows stayed shut, two wall unit air conditioners busily humming away cooling and drying out our apartment. They also blocked stagnant car fumes from the street. Still, outside air pollution was a hell of a lot better here than what I breathed in Los Angeles.

"I don't have many cases left," I answered. "I did get a call yesterday from a friend of mine from the Marines."

"What did he want?" Cassandra dropped one big and two small suitcases next to our car. "That's something I wish you'd talk about more. I know it's a sensitive subject, but if we're getting married you need to confide in me more."

I had been honest with her about most aspects of my existence, but she hit the nail on the head this time. Cassandra not only knew things about me that most others didn't, but she had helped me deal with the darker parts of my childhood, like my life growing up on a farm in Pennsylvania, my mother killing herself and the deadly emotional distance of my father after that. She knew all about my summers in Brooklyn with my aunt and uncle and my two cousins. But, my time in the military and the life long changes brought about in those years, I had not confided at all. I wanted to, but more than my trauma was stopping me; I had to push along a chain of events with my government employers.

"Earth to Benjamin." Cassandra patted my shoulder.

"Sorry, I got lost in thought."

"I love you much." Her expression softened. "I'd like to get lost in there with you."

"Now's not a good time, you're due at the airport soon."

I had to have that discussion with her soon and I had to have a discussion with Billy Sullivan sooner.

As I stared around the neighborhood again, I focused on the trees; I sort of needed to soften my focus for the goodbye scene. Two red oaks rose from our front yard, as well as a magnolia tree, that species was required in Atlanta; there must be one per block at least and we were the lucky ones here. The wisteria in the back yard apparently thought it was kudzu and had taken possession of most of the small parking lot behind our building.

Since moving here, I had enjoyed watching the different greens of summer. By August, the leaves turned a darker green, to prepare briefly turning colors before falling. Shade from the poplars in our side yard had grown more intense; the reflected green color from all the foliage on our block also darkened. A light breeze blowing the leaves felt good on my face, even though days were getting hotter as the summer wore on. I supposed it could be worse. A faint honeysuckle scent intermingled with the odors of deep fat fried whatever from the several eating establishments up the block from us.

"I guess we'd better get to the airport," she said. "Maybe you could visit me around the beginning of the quarter? "

"I'll try." I opened the door for her. "When is that?"

"A few weeks from now." She sat in the passenger seat. "What about your friend from the Marines, does he have a job for you?"

"I don't know, He might have a corporate job for me."

I hadn't seen him in a while. But, every time I did see him it wasn't fun.

"Have I met him?" Cassandra opened the window.

"No," I replied as I slid into the driver's seat. "I don't think so."

"I hope he has a big paying job for you." Cassandra settled into the passenger seat.

"I think he does, judging from the way he sounded." I started the car. "I think it has to do with the company he now works for."

"What company?"

"I forgot the name." No, I knew it well. "His firm provides services for several large insurance companies." I shot her an ambiguous grin. "He's sort of an insurance pimp."

"Well." Cassandra put her hand in my lap and stroked my leg. "Don't get involved in anything too risky; I love you. Be careful and call me every day."

I wish I had followed her advice.

3
Business is business

Business is business, so without Cassandra around, paid snooping is business and I only had one of those type jobs left to do.

Jack Williams was paying me two hundred a day to snoop on his office manager, Kathy Malcolm. Jack thought Kathy was stealing money from him. Since she kept the books for his company, he needed help to uncover the truth.

Jack's office was in Smyrna, which is north west of Atlanta. He owned an excavation company, a business that sprawled over eight acres. He owned a lot of large earth moving equipment as well as several large mounds of various grades of dirt, from rough fill dirt to rich top soil. Atlanta was an emergent area, and Jack's business was growing along with it.

The morning after I dropped Cassandra off at the airport, I drove into the parking lot of Williams Excavating; now, that's an imaginative company name. A better choice didn't have to be complicated, something like 'Dig It' would work as a company name, but he didn't hire me for PR work. The parking lot used loose gravel, something called crush and run. "Crush and run' sounded like a felony offense, but I knew better since that's what I had to put in the small parking area behind our building in Atlanta. Parked out in front of Williams Excavating, I got out of my car knowing that I'd have to run it through a car wash later that day. Gravel failed to cover worn spots on the ground, where the red clay oozed through. The smell of stale, musty dirt filled my nostrils.

A woman sat typing busily behind one of two desks in the large front office. "Yes, Mr Williams is in." She stopped typing and looked up at me "Is he expecting you?"

" Yes. My name is Benjamin Katz ," I answered while studying the woman.

No one else was in the office, so she probably was the one he suspected of stealing.

Seconds later, Jack Williams quickly walked out carrying a clip board thick with papers. We greeted each other, then he looked sideways at his typist who had returned to her work.

"Let's get going so I can look over your property and give you an estimate." He motioned for me to exit ahead of him.

"I take it that woman is your office manager?" I asked as the door closed behind him.

"Yes, that's Kathy, my office manager." He shook his head. "Let's get into my truck and take a ride to the diner up the road where we can talk."

"What makes you think she's stealing money?" I asked.

"One of my contractors called me about a double billing he got, and when I went back into our records and looked for the first billing, I couldn't find it." Jack took in a steady, but sad, breath. "I got a copy of both bills for the job from the contractor and damned if he wasn't right. Both billings were for the same job, but only one copy was in our records."

"It could be an error." I shrugged my shoulders.

"I should be making more money," Jack insisted.

"So should I, but what are you driving at?"

"Even though my business has doubled in the past three years, my gross receipts haven't," Jack insisted again. "I've raised my rates to keep up with fuel and labor, but my gross profits are only a few percent higher than three years ago."

"So, you think your manager is skimming off the profits?"

"Only two of us mess with the books and billing, and I know it isn't me."

"Why don't you fire her and see if the money coming in gets better?" I asked.

"I couldn't."

"Why not?"

This began to sound like a dysfunctional family rather than simple embezzlement.

"Kathy's been with me for twelve years."

Jack stared at me, waiting for something while I remained silent.

"We've gone through my marriage, my kids, her kid, and the death of her husband together; I can't believe she'd steal from me, we're more like family."

"You'd be surprised how little difference that makes," I observed. As a private investigator, I knew that was true. Hell, after my first case I knew that was true.

"How do you mean?" He asked.

"Family steals from family as often as strangers steal from strangers."

Sugar coating doesn't help with that truth.

"Oh." His face, which was weather worn, suddenly looked more weathered.

"You said that her husband died?" I had a hunch. "What did he die from?"

"Someone shot him." Jack didn't look at me when he answered.

"I see."

There had to be a lot more to that answer but I decided to let that slide for now.

"You had breakfast yet?" Jack pulled into the parking lot of a Waffle House.

"No." I looked at him and shrugged my shoulders. "Just a cup of coffee or two."

"So, you charge two hundred a day plus expenses?" Jack asked as we both slid into a booth.

"That's right." I pulled a menu from behind the napkin holder. "Like I told you over the phone, this shouldn't take much more than three days to complete."

"That pay scale's like a lawyer." He buried his face in the menu.

"Not when you consider that I work up to ten hours for that two hundred, and sometimes I get shot at."

"I guess you're right." Jack laughed for the first time. "Sometimes I'd like to shoot my lawyer, though."

"Do you have an accountant? Who does your payroll and taxes?" I needed someone else to take responsibility for snooping into the books, that task could eat up weeks of time.

"Yeah." Jack put his menu down. "My wife's cousin works for a firm in Atlanta and he does the company taxes and payroll. But, he works with Kathy, she's the one who keeps my company's books."

"Maybe you could give me his phone number."

"Yeah."

"It might be good if you could call him and give him warning about me looking into your problem."

"Yeah."

The waitress took our order. The food was warm and quick, that's the best I can say about it.

"Is there anything else you need from me?" Jack asked. I sensed he wanted to be alone for awhile.

"I need you to sign a contract."

I pulled out one I had typed his name on before I took off that morning.

"I need to read it first."

He took it from my hand, carefully studying it for five minutes. I asked for his manager's social security number as he signed the contract.

"Yeah." He picked up the clip board he had set next to him on the bench. "I've got all the stuff from her records as well as some of the billings I can't figure out."

"Could you meet me at your office this evening after Kathy has left?" I did want to briefly check the billing and the books; nothing in depth, just enough to get the general idea.

Jack agreed readily enough. He didn't say much more as he drove me back to his business and dropped me off at my car. A layer of red dust covered my whole Porsche. Before I returned to the office, I had to run it through a car wash for sure.

. . . .

Using the Social Security number Jack had given me, I ran a credit check. Running a legitimate state sanctioned detective agency gave me the right to run a credit check on anyone. It takes only an hour at most to get an answer, usually only ten minutes; fax machines are expensive, but wonderful.

Her FICO score of 425 revealed that Kathy Malcolm had dozens of late payments, four maxed out credit cards. A call to her bank proved more depressing; I called in as a merchant needing to know if she had sufficient funds to cover a three hundred dollar check. She had only thirty dollars in her checking account and the clerk was kind enough to volunteer that Kathy didn't have a savings account nor a CD, nor any other accounts there. This painted a picture for me, it sort of also painted her in a corner. I needed to see where she lived and talk to some of her neighbors.

. . . .

Damn, Kathy Malcolm lived with her eight year old daughter in a trailer park two miles out of Hiram; not even a double wide. Being a trailer park, lots of neighbors were home in the middle of the day; I know that's economically bigoted, but it's true. Kathy's trailer was in the same condition as most of the others in that trailer park, perhaps ten years old, but in good repair. She had put a skirt around the base of it, but I could still see it was on four flat tires. She must have planted most of the shrubs and flowers around the trailer. I recognized a long stretch of Cherokee Rose along the front, held up by four trellises. Must be trimmed each year to keep them that low. I knew tornadoes loved trailers and this area has a fair share of tornadoes each year, but I didn't notice any tie downs.

"Hello."

I approached a woman in her mid forties, hanging laundry on a clothes line two trailers south of Kathy's

"If you're sellin' somthin', I ain't interested." She didn't stop hanging clothes.

"No, Ma'am." I smiled my smarmy smile. "I'm with the C&S Bank, and I was sent here to look into a large loan application from one of your neighbors."

"I don't like the chicken shit bank no how." She still didn't look at me.

"Ma'am, I'm trying to do my job." I stared directly at her. "I ain't a banker, I just do background checks for 'em, that's all."

"Who ya spying on for them?" She looked at me for the first time.

"Kathy Malcolm." I glanced at the ground for a second, then back up at her.

"Oh, her." The woman sighed loudly. "You ain't the first suit lookin' after her doin's ."

"Who else has been out here?"

"The county social workers."

"Why?"

"Nobody likes her much no how."

"Why?" I asked again

"You'd best ask the old man who lives next to her." The woman pointed to the trailer between her and Kathy's. I saw someone staring at us through the living room window of that trailer.

"What's his name?" I asked.

"Richard." She returned to hanging clothes.

. . . .

"Come on in." Richard opened the door before I knocked.

"Hi." I replied. I stepped into the trailer. Two window air conditioners ran full blast, so the space was at least cool but the scent of years of mold growth hit me like a hammer as I walked into the darkened living room.

"Saw you talking to the bitch next door." Richard sat in the overstuffed sofa.

"I'm working for the bank doing a background check on your neighbor." I remained standing.

"Kathy?"

"Yes."

"Don't loan her nothing." Richard's expression fell. "Money ain't what she needs."

"Excuse me?" I was intrigued.

23

"Her husband was shot four years ago, and Kathy has tried as best she can, but she's in way too deep for her best interest."

"Okay." I sat down in an old wooden rocking chair. "I get the point, sir. What's the problem, though?"

"County welfare people are looking into the way she's raising her daughter and I'm afraid she's going to get in way over her head to keep her girl." Richard sounded nervous.

"Are you connected to her somehow?" I looked concerned. "Not that it matters, but I was just curious."

"Her late husband was kin to me."

"So, what does she need, if she doesn't need money?"

"Can't rightly say." Richard looked cautiously at me. "Least ways, not to the likes of a banker," he hesitated. "No offense, man."

"I see." I stood up. "I don't think I need any more information."

If Cathy was embezzling tons of money from her work, she sure wasn't spending it on her housing. I thought a visit to the local sheriff might help.

....

The local police office was the back two rooms of the long squat building housing the city offices. This town had only one cop, but he got two whole rooms; I guess I know who's the important politician here.

"Hi." I stuck my hand out. "I called you a short while ago, I'm the one who's investigating Kathy Malcolm."

"Why you carryin' a gun?" He pointed to my coat.

"I'm a licensed private investigator." I sighed as I pulled out my wallet. Every time one of these pot bellied sheriffs gives me a hard time, I hear the song, 'workin' on the chain gang' play in my head.

"I don't doubt that." He studied my ID card. "What you want to know?"

"Who shot Mrs. Malcolm's husband?" I asked.

"Don't know." He remained in his seat. "The Cobb County Sheriff's Department could tell you better than me."

"I suppose they might, but I think you know more than they do." I looked carefully at him.

"Could be he was mixed up in a stolen car parts ring up Gainesville way." The policeman leaned back in his chair. "Could be he got on their bad side and got hisself shot."

"I believe you." I nodded my head. "What about his wife?"

"What do you mean?" He looked up at me.

"Was she involved in his car parts business?"

"No."

"Do you know her well?"

"Who are you working for?" The cop asked.

"I can't tell you." I shook my head slowly. "I'm sure he wouldn't want me to say."

"Don't matter." He stood up, hitching his pants up to cover the vast expanse of belly hanging out; there wasn't enough pants available to cover the bulge. "I probably know who hired you anyway."

"What about the Malcolm woman?" I persisted. "Do you know her well?"

"We's kin." He leaned on the edge of his desk, looking down at a stack of papers.

"What's her story?" I asked.

He didn't want to tell me much, even though he had already told me a lot.

"Ain't much most folks around here don't already know." He glanced at me then continued speaking. "Her daddy was the town drunk, she left home at fifteen and married Billy to get away. She still don't drink no liquor nor beer because of how much she hates what it did to her mom and dad."

"But, she's in trouble for drugs now, isn't she?" I began to connect the dots. "That's where all the money's going, right?"

"Can't prove nothin' yet, but, yeah." The policeman sighed. "She's gonna lose that cute girl of hers."

"Thanks for the information, sir." I stuck out my hand again, this time he shook it.

"Only reason I told you anythin' is cause I know damned well who hired you and he needs to try to fix this best he can." The policeman nodded.

"Can I have one of your cards?" I reached for a tray full of cards with his name and phone number on them.

"Take a few of 'em." He finally sort of grinned as I opened the door and left.

. . . .

The next stop was the accounting offices of Smith and Waller. Earl Bellamy was Jack's cousin-in-law and a junior partner in a medium sized accounting firm. The office was on Peachtree-Dunwoody near the perimeter. I noticed that it was near two hospitals.

"Yes, Jack called me this morning and told me what you're investigating for him." Earl shook my hand. "I wish he had told me about it sooner."

"Why?" I asked. "Did you suspect something?"

"Just that he wasn't bringing in as much in profits as I thought he should have." Earl motioned for me to take a seat.

"What did you think was the problem?"

"I don't know." He shrugged. "I guess I didn't want to poke my nose into his business; family, you know."

"Well, apparently he isn't skimming from his own business."

I was almost one hundred percent sure of that.

"That's more of a relief than you'd guess."

"No, I can see that it is." I kept my grin.

"So, now I can help him locate the lost money?" Earl smiled back at me.

"You work with his office manager," I replied. "Have you noticed a change in her the last few years?"

"Come to think of it, yes I have. She seems to be getting slacker in her bookkeeping."

Earl cocked his head to one side. He too was beginning to connect some dots, although I don't know if he saw the same picture as I did.

"How so?"

"Some of the receipts don't show up in the billable ledger." Earl appeared to be piecing this all together in his head as he spoke to me. "That might indicate that she would bill a contractor, take the money for herself and not put an entry for the bill or the receipt."

"Why would some entries show a receipt and not a bill?"

"If Jack opens the mail and gets the check from the contractor, he'd make an entry in the ledger showing he received the money, but Kathy wouldn't necessarily make a corresponding entry for a bill."

"So, unless Jack goes back to all the contractors he dealt with for the last few years and looks at the money they sent him, he won't know how much money is missing."

"Right."

"How hard would that be?"

"If we could get a list of the contractors, it shouldn't be that hard." Earl was happy again. It was obvious that this was right up his alley. Weeks and weeks of looking at financial records was not my idea of fun, even though I've done it before. I guessed that Jack's cousin would charge a lot less than two hundred a day to do it, so I felt some sense of relief about that.

"You know." Earl appeared to have another idea. "If she's stealing money from Jack, maybe you should look hard for unpaid bills."

"Maybe she's writing the checks for services to herself?"

"It's harder to hide since the folks will keep billing Jack's company until they take him to court, but, yes she could be doing that also."

"Thanks." I stood up. "I'll tell Jack to get in touch with you about all this soon."

. . . .

"Thanks for meeting me here." I nodded towards Jack as I walked into his office at seven that evening. The sun wouldn't set for another hour or so, but the shadows were long. Even though the sun was low, the temperature wasn't; Atlanta's humidity was going to take some time to get used to.

Pennsylvania had been as humid in the summer, but that was a long time ago. At least Jack kept the air conditioner going.

"Not a problem." Jack was in better spirits. "Kathy went home at four thirty and I've been going over her books since then."

"Anything interesting?"

"Not that I can see right away, but look at all this I found in the bottom file drawer." Jack held up a fist full of bills.

"Bills you never paid?" I asked.

"How did you know?"

"Your wife's cousin said it might be another way she could steal your money." I sighed; this was becoming more of a downer than I liked.

"So what did you do so far?"

"You mean, to earn the two hundred?"

"Not that insensitive," Jack answered. "I was just interested."

"Your office manager has terrible credit, seems to be broke, and doesn't appear to be living any kind of high life by the looks of her home and car." I waited for some reaction.

"So, maybe she isn't stealing?"

Jack was hopeful; I guess he liked the woman.

"No." I sat down in front of the desk and moved several ledger books over to me. "I think she's robbing you blind and snorting or puffing all the money away."

"Drugs?" He sounded surprised as he stood up.

"That's my guess." I looked up at him. "Haven't you noticed a difference in the past few years?"

"Yeah." Jack sat back down and slumped into his chair. "I figured that she was still grieving her husband. It has to be hard to pick up and carry on with just herself and her daughter."

"I suppose."

I got lost in the books for about thirty minutes while Jack paced around the room, and his office; occasionally he'd glance over my shoulder. I used a yellow highlighter to point out the rather large inconsistencies. In the past month, Jack's firm had done eight large jobs. Entries for the day labor and fuel existed, but the billing was for a little over half of what it should have

28

been. Jack guessed that he was out twenty thousand on those eight jobs.

"Damn it." Jack sat on the edge of the desk. "What else has she done?"

"My guess is that she is having to buy more and more of the coke to get high so she's been taking more money lately."

"So, what am I supposed to do?"

"That's what you're paying me for." I sighed and sat back in my chair. "My professional advice is that you take these books to the police and file charges against Kathy."

"How can I do that?" Jack protested. "Who would take care of her child if she went to jail?"

"She's being investigated by the state welfare folks." I had to broach this subject with him. "She might lose the child anyway."

"What?"

"I'll type up the whole case tonight and deliver it to you tomorrow morning so you can think about all this." I felt sorry for him right then, Kathy was a family friend as well as a worker.

"You need to turn her in for her own good, she needs help with her addiction."

"But, what about her daughter?" Jack insisted.

"Talk to this man." I handed him the card I took from the small police station near Kathy Malcolm's house. "I think he might be able to handle this matter initially, with a little more compassion than the Cobb County authorities. Also, he'll be in a position to make sure Kathy's daughter won't get lost in the child welfare system."

"Okay."

Jack was at a loss, I could see the wheels turning in his head. I had the impression he did have good intentions for that family, even though the mother was robbing him.

"You clearly have to remove her from this position." I stared straight at him, hoping to emphasize my point. "She can't keep your books anymore."

"Right," he acknowledged. "Who can?"

"I think you'll need to have a long discussion about all this with your wife's cousin, maybe he can suggest a solution that won't put your business at risk."

"Man!" Exasperation was obvious all over his face. "This is a hell of a mess."

"It's not all that bad." I tried to lower his anxiousness a bit. "You hired someone to find the problem and suggest a solution."

"I guess I did."

"There's more at stake here than your losing some cash, you know." I felt I had to reinforce the collateral damage in this case. "You need to talk to that sheriff about Kathy and her daughter, he's related to Kathy."

"Right." He was lost again in thought. "I will."

"I'll be here at eight thirty tomorrow with the final report."

"Okay."

"Look at the good side." I smiled as I walked to the door. "It only took one day, so the bill from me will be small."

4

Home is where the rent's free

Cassandra's flight from Hartsfield to LAX was uneventful. She even got a few winks of sleep, although the overweight salesman next to her snored and spread out a bit too much to allow her much comfort. She pondered the true meaning of success in the detective business: first class plane tickets. Maybe in the next life.

Her friends, Mark and Mary Hatton waited at the airport to pick her up. Mark had been friends with Benjamin from the time they were both lieutenants in the Marines, and had finished tours in Viet Nam, although not in the same places.

Four years ago, Cassandra had met Mark in the course of detective work in Los Angeles; by that time, Mark worked as a lieutenant in the Los Angeles Police Department. One year later, he married Mary; at their wedding Cassandra served as one of the several bridesmaids and Benjamin as an usher. Yes, Cassandra had had to wear a peach colored dress that made her look like she came directly from the set of Gone with the Wind. Maybe that was a bit of synchronicity, since a few years later she moved to Atlanta.

As she arrived in California, L. A's smog only slightly grayed the blue skies. Inside the terminal, a myriad of loud voices assaulted the individual, as well as cause a slight headache. A vast army of travelers rushed in every direction, streaming past her in a blend of business travelers, vacationers, and foreign

31

visitors. Altogether an eye pleasing, crowded human vista. Then she spotted her friends.

"It's good to see you again, Cassandra." Marry Hatton hugged her.

"I'm glad you're back, if only for a few months." Mark smiled. "When is Benjamin coming out here for a visit?"

"He said he'd try to get out here before the quarter begins." Cassandra hugged Mark. "That should be in the next few weeks."

"Let's get your bags, then we can celebrate." Mary pointed towards the exit, and the long way to baggage claim. "Do you feel like going out to eat?

"Yes, I do," Cassandra replied emphatically. "Could you drop me of at my folks' house first?"

"Of course, is that where you're staying?" Mark followed the two women ahead of him as all three joined the mass of humans coming and going from and to flights.

Cassandra nodded. The trio chatted, catching up on each other's lives. Cassandra's most recent news was about her father. They had not yet heard that Glaxo, the drug company, had hired him as VP for European sales." When he got reassigned to France that Spring, her parents found an apartment in Paris to live in. The Huntington Beach house was empty.
. . . .

Cassandra almost immediately fell into the comfort of her old home as her memories had been enjoyable. Given the future she had chosen, Cassandra felt she needed the four month calm in the last home she had shared with her parents. Her memories were pleasant, calming, and boring; it would be a nice vacation. She hoped Benjamin could spend some time there with her, later.

"What a great house." Mary had walked in the front door of Cassandra's parents home in Huntington Beach. "What are those trees by the driveway?"

"Chilopsis." Cassandra glanced back over her shoulder. "They came with the house."

"So many different scents, coming from all over. All the flowers, trees and bushes, do they bloom all summer?" Mary asked.

"Yes, something is in bloom from spring to fall."

Mary looked at Cassandra, then craned her neck in the direction of the side yard. "It looks like one of your parents is a gardener."

"That'd be my Mom." Cassandra warmly remembered her childhood.

Pointing out different trees, she took her guests on a brief tour of the small gardens nestled around the front of the house.

"Let's see," Cassandra said, "I know Mom has a few Tea Trees, and she likes Eriogonum fascicalatum, or California buckwheat, as a filler around the few maples. The grass is Bermuda, it grows real well even if you forget to turn the sprinklers on sometimes."

Mary took in a deep breath through her nose. "What is that delightful smell I caught as we came in?"

"I bet it's the Lily-of-the-Nile." Cassandra became lost in a memory for a second. "Mom planted those years ago and it blooms this time of year. I love those long blue flowers."

"I have to have a tour of your whole yard," Mary said. She and Mark still lived in an apartment; they were saving for a house.

"Let's set up a time." Cassandra smiled back at her. "When we have more daylight to do it justice."

"I'd love that."

Cassandra's folks had bought that house fifteen years ago when house prices hadn't yet reached the stratosphere. The house was late fifties California modern, outside façade half brick and half clapboard painted a muted off-white. Inside, it was over three thousand square feet with four bedrooms and four baths all on one floor.

Built on the uphill slope from the road, not on the ocean side, the home offered wide views. The living room was about twenty five feet wide with a bank of five large picture windows looking out on the Pacific ocean. Three center windows rose to the top of the vaulted ceiling, giving an open feeling to the big room, as if it were a cave in the hill with an unobstructed view of the sea. The home was high enough from the road to ignore pedestrians and traffic. Cassandra's mom had planted even more low shrubs to help hide the street. Neighborhood covenants prohibited tall trees, so their view of the ocean and some of the beach was unobstructed.

"Do you want to stay for the sunset? That's quite a show for any new visitors to the house."

Cassandra began to haul the larger suitcase back towards the bedroom she had stayed in as a teenager.

"Let me help you." Mark grabbed an equally large suitcase. "And, yes, I'd love to stay here for the sunset."

"Could you see what the folks left us in the fridge?" Cassandra pointed to the back of the living room. "The kitchen is back there, through the dining room."

"Did they move to France recently?" Mark asked. Apparently he never turned off his detective mind.

"No." Cassandra shook her head. She didn't mind all the questions. "They came back here to check up on the house and visit friends; they left last week."

"Too bad they couldn't have overlapped to visit with you." Mark struggled with the larger of the suitcases.

"Yeah," Cassandra sighed. "He had to be back there for a series of meetings with a British health minister." She was disappointed that she couldn't see her folks for at least a day, but they had invited her to spend Christmas with them in France that year.

The large living room had two doorways besides the one from the entrance hallway. A passageway in the back wall, far left, lead to the dining room and the kitchen, and another one leading to the long hallway to the right, as one entered the living room from the entrance hallway. The passageways weren't small openings, they were large archways; the architect obviously liked open, flowing designs. The bedrooms and three bathrooms were down the long hallway. The fourth bathroom was tucked into the family room area behind the dining room and kitchen. Swinging around the right side of the house, the driveway led to a carport outside the family room. Although the family room should have been the major access point into and out of the house, Cassandra had Mark park his car in the driveway and come in through the front door. It was a habit everyone in her family had, and she didn't know exactly why.

The three of them stood chatting for a few moments, making plans to go out after sunset. Cassandra took a sharp right and dragged her suitcase down the hall, followed by Mark carrying the others. Cassandra headed to her old room, the one she used all through high school; she had picked the first back bedroom to the left. She liked the view of the back garden from the window, plus this bedroom had its own bathroom.

"Doesn't it seem strange, moving back home after all these years?" Mark asked.

He looked around Cassandra's old room which her father had converted into a study; several old photographs of himself and friends from thirty years ago still hung on the wall. Her father was an Army officer in World War Two, having served in Europe and North Africa. Cassandra noticed that her folks had taken up the wall to wall carpet and restored the hardwood floor in this part of the house; it appeared much nicer than the multicolored carpet she remembered. Her father had moved Cassandra's old double bed back in, along with a small dresser and bedside table as a temporary accommodation.

"I know I'd feel strange if I moved back in with my folks," Mark added.

"It's not so bad, the folks aren't here and there's plenty to keep me busy." Cassandra dumped the suitcase in the far corner of the bedroom. "Besides, you'd feel weird moving back in with your parents because you're married now."

"Speaking of that." Mark looked serious for a moment. "When are you and Benjamin going to take the next step?"

"I actually agreed to marry him when I get back to Atlanta in four months." Cassandra smiled broadly at Mark.

"They're finally getting married," Mark stuck his head out of the bedroom door and shouted down the hallway.

"It's about time," Mary shouted back. "There's not much in the way of food and drinks out there."

"That doesn't matter," Cassandra remarked as she walked back into the hall and headed to the living room.

Mary met Cassandra and Mark in the living room and hugged her.

"Before we leave, you have to see my parents' room." Cassandra looked out the front window, noticing that sunset had begun. Hanging near the horizon, a few clouds shone as if they had caught fire.

"What's so special about it?" Mark also stared through the window.

"The bathroom has one of those private patios with a hot tub." Cassandra pointed in the general direction of the back bedroom. She was looking forward to setting the hot tub back up and using it. "Mom had done a great job of planting a garden in that space. Right before I went to college, the patio there had drainage problems so dad tore it all out and started from scratch building a slightly larger patio with a higher fence and better drainage, then he installed a four person hot tub with all the horns and whistles."

"Wow." Mary was impressed now. "I'd like to see that."

"See it?" Mark chuckled. "I'd like to use it."

"After we admire the hot tub, I want to treat you two to a great dinner for all your help," Cassandra said.

. . . .

"Are you sure you can afford this?" Mary looked at the menu. "I've never been here before."

"Le Chardonnay has the best French food; at least I think it does, but Benjamin always disagrees with me. He's not here now, so it's my call." Cassandra lowered her menu. "Besides, Melrose Avenue isn't that far from your apartment."

The herbs, the cream bubbling in sauces, and the smell of garlic put a smile back on Cassandra's face. Although she didn't lament the move to Atlanta, places like this could give her regrets.

"It's kind of expensive." Mark felt he had to say at least something.

"Don't worry about it." Cassandra put her hand on Mary's shoulder. "I have the company credit card, and the office out here is doing great."

"I heard it is." Mark looked serious. "Then, why do you want to sell it?"

"It's mostly Benjamin's idea." Cassandra put her menu down. "I don't think he wants to run a big business."

"I assume you're right." Mark glanced at his menu, determined to get something not too expensive. "Benjamin never did strike me as a mogul."

"I suppose I have to agree with him. We'd spend more and more time managing a business and not working cases," Cassandra mused out loud.

She picked her menu back up. She was looking less at prices, and more at entrees she couldn't get in Atlanta.

"I think that might be better," Mary interjected. "I mean I'd rather sit around an office all day and worry about a bottom line than run around the streets getting shot at."

"Benjamin's the target in this company," Cassandra smiled at Mary. "Besides, I kind of like working cases. I didn't think I'd like it that much at first, but the work is a lot more fun than anything else I've done yet."

"I guess I don't understand it," Mary said nervously. She blinked a few times and looked away.

"I understand both of them perfectly." Mark put his hand on top of Mary's knee. "I'm with Benjamin on this one, I'd sell the business out here too."

"We have an offer on the table." Cassandra nodded.

"Who?" Mark asked quickly. "Not that it's any of my business, though."

"I don't mind." Cassandra sipped her water. "You're like family anyway; the guy who took over as manager wants to buy it."

"Peter?" Mark thought about the man for a second. "I don't know him that well. He always seems pleasant."

"He's worked out well as manager," Cassandra answered. "Peter's father owns a chain of appliance stores in the valley and is willing to front the money to buy the agency, but now we have to haggle about the price."

"What do detective agencies go for these days?" Mary's curiosity got the best of her.

"The asking price is three hundred and fifty thousand, but our agent tells us we'll have to settle for less, then there's the debt for equipment and a portion of the long term lease on the office space to deduct from the price, then there's the agent's fee, so, I guess we'll find out how much it's worth in a few weeks."

"Wow." Mary left her mouth open a little. "That's still a lot of money."

"Will the new owner keep the same name?" Mark asked.

"Benjamin wants to keep the name, Cheshire Katz , but he said they could call it Cheshire Investigators, or Cheshire Agency, or anything like that." Cassandra picked her menu back up.

"So, you two are going to stay in Atlanta?" Mary sounded sad.

"I think so," Cassandra said, wistfully. "Benjamin grew up in Pennsylvania and his only family consists of an aunt and uncle in New York and a brother and his family back in Pennsylvania. I grew up around the Washington DC area and most of my family is there. I'm an only child and my parents are now in France so I suppose we belong back on the East Coast."

"We'll still miss you two a lot," Mark said.

"And, you'll have to invite us to your wedding, even if it is so far away." Mary went back to her menu, undecided.

"You bet we will." Cassandra felt at home with these friends. "It's not that far away, anyway."

5

Who's that knocking at my door?

This case wrapped up quickly, Cassandra had been gone for only three days when I gave Jack Williams all the information he'd need to pass on to the police, if he wanted to press charges against his office manager, Kathy. In cases like this, half the employers don't tell the police even though I recommend that they do. I guess they hire me to avoid going through official channels. In Jack's case he had no other option than to turn in his bookkeeper and friend for stealing. Too much money was involved, and he would have to press the case, to keep his subcontractors off his back for the unpaid bills and to require that his insurance company pay for some of his losses. I shouldn't care, it's just a job. But sadly, I did care.

Anyway, my old Marine buddy was supposed to contact me; he was supposed to call me yesterday, but our answering service didn't have a call from him.

The lonely ride from Smyrna back to our new abode in Little Five Points was quiet, I didn't even have the radio on. That was another thing I hadn't quite gotten used to here, not enough variety in radio stations. I liked most kinds of music, but preferred classical; there weren't enough classical music stations here. The Atlanta market had too many country music stations, and that was the only kind of music I didn't like. Maybe a cassette player needed to get put in my Porsche, sometime soon. Traffic was heavy on 85 this mid morning. Usually it wasn't so bad, which is why I go straight through town instead of using the perimeter, typically, all the heavy stuff is on 285 almost all day. I pulled off the interstate and rode down Ponce to Moreland and on to home.

Cassandra and I got our building on Euclid Avenue, off Little Five Points as a gift from a former client slightly over a year ago. The two story brick building, divided into six apartments, was ours, free and clear; half was mine, and half was Cassandra's. Our Atlanta home and office building looked like a big brick box to me, but Cassandra thought it had plenty of character.

It was around the corner from Little Five Points. Right after we moved in we found out that our new neighborhood had been, for the last eight or so years, the infamous center of hippy doings in Atlanta. I had a feeling that the South hadn't a clue as to real hippy doings, compared to Los Angeles, but Little Five Points was proving to be an interesting location none the less. It also held a fine assortment of bars, restaurants, food stores, head shops and gay and lesbian book stores; I was growing to love the diversity.

We moved into the apartment on the top floor, left rear. We didn't rent the lower front left apartment so we could put our office into that space. Major renovations had been completed less than five years ago, which meant that all the plumbing and wiring was new, up to code. The other four apartments were rented out to a wide assortment of people. I thought the tenants in the building possessed a lot more character than the building itself.

Being the landlord gave me the right to park my Porsche in the dilapidated double garage, the only garage space for the building.

"Hello, Benjamin."

I didn't see Billy sitting on the only piece of furniture on the front porch until I walked around the side of the house from the garage. The only chair on the porch was a half rusted, metal lawn chair Cassandra had bought at a local garage sale. The chair was about twenty years old, but still useable and cost us only ten cents; we left it looking shabby so no one would steal it.

"What're you doing here?" I replied. "You were supposed to call me yesterday."

"Well, I had to see your new place for myself." Billy Sullivan grinned as he rose from the old chair.

"I don't think so." I glared at him. "You only came to see my place in Los Angeles once, four years ago and it wasn't pleasant."

"Come on now." Billy's smile faded. "It wasn't me, it was the job I sent you on."

"How can I forget," I replied.

I waved at Mrs. Smith through her front window as she waved back at me.

"She's a nice lady, Benjamin," Billy said.

"Who? Mrs. Smith?"

I assumed he hadn't met the two girls living in the back apartment; they had told us they were going to move out at the end of the month and neither Cassandra nor I were disappointed to see the last of them. I had a bet with Cassandra on how many body parts had been pierced between them, but neither one of us wanted to ask, let alone see.

"Yeah, Mrs. Smith told me to wait for you here on the front porch. She said Cassandra had gone back to Los Angeles for a few months," Billy said as he walked through the front door. "She sure wanted to know who I was; I think she's afraid I'm a bill collector or something like that."

"Who did you say you were?" I stared at him.

"I'm your old buddy from Viet Nam," he answered. "We served together in the Marines for a little over two years."

"That's right." I nodded.

"Besides, she appears pretty harmless." Billy glanced at me. "Isn't she?"

"She's a sweetheart." I opened the door to my office and ushered him in.

"Who? Cassandra or Mrs. Smith?"

"Actually, both." I cracked a smile at him for the first time. "Find a seat and tell me what this visit is all about."

During the first month that we began reclaiming the front apartment as our office, Cassandra had had a blast; she decided on the Spartan look. We knocked down half the wall between the bedroom and living room to make one big space. A bathroom and kitchen in the office appealed to us, so we left them. When clients walked through the front door to our office, they saw our big desk towards the back wall, between two windows. We kept the blinds partially closed since the major view out those windows was our dilapidated garage. A two seat sofa rested to the left of the front door, and two wing chairs against the wall to the right. The kitchen and the bathroom were down a small hallway immediately to the right. Against the wall to the left we placed our phone, fax and copy machine on two low wooden tables, a small coffee table was placed in front of the sofa with some magazines scattered on it. In front of the desk, Cassandra had placed two straight backed wooden chairs which were much more comfortable to sit in than they appeared. None of the furniture matched, but I thought that gave it a certain charm. Cassandra said she would think about it and get back with me about buying different furniture, which meant she liked it the way it was.

"When do I get to meet Cassandra?" Billy plopped into one of the winged chairs. "Can you turn off that music?"

"What?" I had turned on the office stereo.

"I can't concentrate with all that caterwauling." Billy shot me a disgusted look.

"That's opera." I gave him a sour expression but pushed the off button.

"So, when do I meet your girlfriend?" Billy asked again.

"Not for a while." I sat behind the big desk we had bought desk at a used furniture store six blocks from our house. It appeared to have begun its life in a nineteenth century hotel lobby, and stayed there for years; I think we did a nice job in restoring it. Cassandra had the left hand drawers, I had the right, which left the center drawer for supplies.

"Maybe after we get married she can meet you," I replied.

"Married?" Billy sat up in his chair. "Now, that's new."

"She finally said yes, right before she left," I beamed.

"That changes a few things," Billy sounded serious.

"I know." I nodded. "We need to discuss it."

"It'll have to wait until after this job I'm here to tell you about."

Billy didn't want to talk about it; I didn't see why not.

"I'm getting married to my partner, and she's going to remain an active collaborator in the detective business," I insisted.

This was my new rallying call, and I was going to use it as often as needed to get his attention.

"I hear you," Billy acknowledged. "We can discuss it later."

"She's good at what she does." I kept on. "She works well with me and she's saved my ass more than once."

"Are you going to invite me to the wedding?"

Billy didn't want to talk about it then, I guess he had to talk to his superiors first.

"Don't press your luck." I relaxed a bit more into my chair. "Why are you here?"

"Well, there's been a change in plans." Billy leaned towards me. "Is this place safe?"

"If you mean are there any bugs here, no," I answered. "If you mean we can leave our doors unlocked, no."

"Well, I checked for myself before you came home." Billy patted the outer right pocket of his top coat.

"Right," I acknowledged.

I figured he had already done that; we were safe from prying eyes and ears.

"You need to go to San Francisco tomorrow at the latest, and then on to Hawaii." Billy reached into his inside coat pocket to pull out a fat envelope. "I've got your tickets and other stuff in here.

"Why the change of plans?" I picked up the envelope he had tossed onto the desk in front of me. "I thought I was headed back to Germany, something about background information on three British citizens living in Hamburg."

"Things have changed, North Korea is more of a problem for us right now than Russia is," he said.

Billy stood up, as if he couldn't sit still, he then stopped himself, pushed a wooden chair close to the desk, then sat down in it.

"The NSA picked up transmissions from a freighter sailing under an Indonesian flag about three hundred miles off the Hawaiian coast. It'll dock there to drop off and pick up cargo containers, then head on to Los Angeles," he added.

"I think I'd like Hawaii better than Hamburg."

43

All of a sudden I got more interested.

"Funny thing about Hamburg."

"What?"

"That freighter is based in Hamburg," Billy replied. "Not a damned thing to do with why we were sending you on the other thing, but strange anyway."

"Synchronicity rules our lives. Anyway, what was the transmission the NSA intercepted?   I bet it wasn't a happy birthday greeting for grandma. "

"It was coded and meant for the North Korean National Security Bureau." Billy shook his head.

"Their secret police?"

"Right." Billy rested his forearms on the desk, staring directly at me. "The best translation of that message was that a computer scientist is somewhere in this country who is going to deliver something to their agent on that freighter."

"I guess you don't know who either the agent is or the scientist is." My next few weeks might be full.

"No, and no." Billy nodded; he didn't crack a grin. "That's your job to find out who both the agent and the scientist are."

"Why not let the FBI take care of this since all this is taking place on US soil? I assume the scientist is a citizen." I thought those were good questions.

"Don't be an ass, Benjamin, will you."

"Kind of snippy, aren't you?"

What did I do to him recently? Maybe something else was going on I didn't know about.

"Sorry," Billy sighed. "It has to do with turf wars back in DC. The election cycle is in full swing and that has a lot of people worried about their budgets, and their jobs. Besides, the FBI still has its own problems. In these post-Hoover days I'm beginning to wonder if they'll ever recover."

"Our agency has its own problems too, so why are you guys paying me to do this type of stuff inside the country?"

He still hadn't answered my question.

"We have enough intelligence to believe that the North Korean agent will contact an intermediary here in the states to set up a money transfer and a meeting with the scientist either in Canada or Mexico. Except for the scientist, they're all foreign nationals. Besides, if we let the FBI take it, you know they'll fuck it up, so you're the man for the job."

"What job?"

"All you have to do is find out who the agent is on the freighter. Then, you'll follow whoever you have to until you find the American scientist, it should be straight forward. Find out who the contact is, then shadow him until he leads you to the American."

"What then?"

"That depends." Billy shifted in his chair. "If the meeting takes place in this country, you'll contact the FBI to arrest them. If it takes place in another country, you'll hold them and contact us for an extraction. We kind of think the action will be in either Canada or Mexico."

"So, how much?" I asked. I hate to be mercenary; no, I don't.

"Has your rate changed?" Billy leaned back in his chair.

"No."

"Two hundred a day plus expenses."

"When was I put back on the payroll?"

"Yesterday." Billy slapped on a mordant grin which told me he was tired of hearing about my cash flow problems. "I've put you on for a minimum of three weeks this time."

"It's not much, but it pays for the fried chicken." I grinned back at him. "Hey, maybe I can buy Cassandra a ring with the extra money."

"Everything I told you is in the envelope, plus other details." Billy pointed to it. "Please burn all the non essential pages after you read them."

"Like I don't know that." I sighed. "What's my cover story?"

"Lloyds of London hired you as a loss prevention investigator looking into problems for the owners of the freighter." Billy tapped the desk next to the envelope. "Papers and letters of introduction are in there."

"What about communications?" I asked.

"You're on your own until you get into Long Beach." Billy leaned back in the chair. "You contact our people there and we'll set you up with everything you'll need."

"Will you be there?"

"No," Billy answered, "I have six other operations going on during the time you'll be alone on this cruise."

"Life is so tough for the highly placed." I laughed; I always liked teasing him as he moved up the food chain.

"Not so highly placed," Billy said quietly. "If I were, I'd be a political appointee and wouldn't have to work at all."

"Who owns the freighter?" I asked.

I wanted to change the subject; I could tell the upcoming election was stressful for him. My guess was that the party in power would shift and that meant a whole new bunch of political appointees to break in.

"A German company out of Hamburg owns the holding company which operates this and ten other freighters," Billy said. "Only three of them, including this one, sail under the Indonesian flag. But, the German company bought the insurance policy for it."

"What nationality is the crew?"

"The officers are German, all the rest Asian."

"Good."

"I'll get in touch with you in three or four days." Billy stood up.

"How about lunch?" I also stood. "This place has some great food spots."

"Where? Your tie, or in Atlanta?"

"You always were a barrel of laughs."

. . . .

"Mr. Katz ." Mildred Smith glanced at me as I stepped out the front door with a single suitcase in my hand. She was a short woman, in her mid to late sixties and pleasant. Her husband had died about four years ago and she had moved into our building before Cassandra and I took possession of it. Her eyes must have been blue, but now they just looked gray, like her hair. Babies are kind of shaped like the Pillsbury Doughboy, and

I have observed that as people push into old age they also resemble the Doughboy; Mrs. Smith was no exception. I made a mental note to continue to work out until my death at age 100.

"Are you leaving to visit your friend in California?" she asked.

"Yes, I am," I quickly replied.

That sounded like a good reason to me. I got the impression that she didn't approve of us living together without being married.

"That was a nice man who came to see you yesterday," she said with a motherly tone. "He was pleasant to me."

"Sometimes he can be nice," I said, with a chuckle. "He and I were friends in the Marines. We fought in Viet Nam together and we have been close friends ever since."

"Oh." She looked at the porch floor. "He told me that yesterday."

"We write to each other sometimes, and we visit when we have the chance."

I didn't know what else to say; my investigator self wanted to wonder why she was so curious, but my human self told me to shut up. She was a nice old lady, but this wasn't her concern.

"What does he do for a living?" She sounded even more curious, maybe her soaps were repeats today. "Is he a private investigator like you?"

"No," I chuckled. "He's not that adventurous, he works for some insurance company, I'm not sure which one. We don't talk about work that much when we get together."

That's my story, and I'm sticking to it. I felt a slight twinge lying to the nice old lady, but that's my job.

"Well, say hello to Miss Pales when you see her."

"I'll do that." I smiled and nodded. "I should be back in less than a week."

6
Off to see the wizard.

At least I could see Cassandra when I got back to Los Angeles from Hawaii so I called Cassandra right after making the flight arrangements and she sounded happy to hear that I was making money, and it even sounded like she would be happy to see me in person too.

I had known Billy Sullivan since the end of the first year I was in Viet Nam; it was good to see him again. He was my captain, at least he became so after I transferred to Special Operations. After the war was over, when he moved up in the Company, he brought me along as a contract officer. Ostensibly, I was hired to do background information gathering only, using my cover as a private detective. I'd be hired by legitimate companies to do investigations in foreign countries, but I was also working for the CIA, gathering information on people, organizations, or governments. I know it may appear a bit obvious to foreign governments that this private investigator could be a United States spy, but, believe it or not, they thought me less of a spy than the average US businessman; so far my cover worked like a charm. My pay was laundered through the legitimate companies so no one would know who I was working for. Sometimes they'd send me in for more intensive work, but that wasn't too often. I was a contract officer, part-time. I was not supposed to be assigned to any covert operations, nor was I supposed to be assigned to any military operations. I was promised that I would work only three or four background cases for them a year. That actually worked out to six to ten times a year. The five or six times I had gone to headquarters at Langley, I had been impressed with the size of Billy's office; well, it wasn't a cubicle which must mean something.

....

48

Too bad I didn't have enough time to explore Hawaii, it zipped by me on the brief cab ride from the airport to the seaport. Its island landscape reminded me of Southeast Asia, what I had glimpsed during my flight out after I mustered out of active duty. It all felt like a lifetime ago. I didn't have time then to explore this beautiful place; maybe later.

Today, I found the right dock without any trouble. Out the window of the office building which was my check-in point, I could see five large cargo ships docked in a line; the ship I wanted was the smallest of the five. On each ship, a large multi-story structure rose from the main deck, somewhere aft. I assumed that was where all the crew lived and ship operations took place. I saw confusing varieties of configurations on all the cargo ship decks, but common to all of them, a tall structure as well as one to four large cargo cranes rose from each main deck. The cranes reminded me of sailing ship masts for some reason, although I knew better.

"Can I help you, sir?" The tall, lanky clerk in front of me wore a bright orange shirt with a name tag on it; over some dirty jeans, and a pair of ratty sandals. Now, this was a uniform I could respect. He looked a little exasperated that I had stood silent in front of him for longer than twenty seconds.

"Yes," I cleared my throat. "My name is Benjamin Katz, and I'm an investigator for Lloyds of London."

He nodded, unimpressed.

"I need to speak to the Captain of the freighter, Veracruz," I persisted, noticing his unchanging expression. "The insurance company has sent me as a loss prevention investigator and I must accompany this freighter from here to Long Beach."

"I'll call the Captain now." The clerk picked up a phone and dialed.

. . . .

"Here are the documents from the company." I handed my papers to a smartly dressed man standing in front of me in a cramped hallway in front of his cabin. "Both from Lloyds of London as well as the owners of this ship."

"All well and good," The captain replied with a hint of suspicion. He opened the door to his cabin for me to enter. A tall, muscular man, he appeared to be in the preliminary stages of middle age; his muscle mass was broadening, gravitationally slipping a bit and his short cropped hair was beginning a disappearing act.

"I'll go over them in detail later, as well as contact my employer to confirm them," he added.

Located five levels above deck, the captain's office was well appointed with dark oak furniture. His desk, big and solid, was void of clutter except for a vase with three cut orchids that shone over the the gleaming surface. Their scent muted normal industrial port smells in the background but mixed in with them, background aromas of body odor, burning engine oil and diesel fuel dominated. The bright red and dark orange blossoms were reminiscent of the tropical port where they no doubt had come from. But who had bought them, or did he have an admirer in Hawaii?

To the right of the captain's desk stood a floor safe, larger than I'd have guessed necessary for a freighter. On the left a doorway led to his bedroom suite. Some furniture was visible through the open door as well as at least two more large windows. A ceiling high wardrobe stood next to a combination lock gun cabinet that looked big enough for twenty four rifles, at least; what he kept in that monstrous locked cabinet was a mystery. I notices the lack of music, all anyone could hear was the mechanical noises. The ship's engines were now making a low thumping sound, probably going enough to generate electricity. Occasional loud noises emanated from the docks, and two of the large cranes on the ship could be heard moving cargo containers around on deck.

Captain's name was Wolfgang Krull, quite the German name. He stood about six feet tall, and a bit over two hundred pounds, about forty five years old. His hair jet black had turned about half white, missing from his forehead halfway to his cowlick. He obviously worked as hard as his crew because he appeared muscular underneath the crisp white Captain's outfit. His appearance was as German as his name.

"I haven't done this type of job too often, and I won't be anal about it at all." I leaned back in my chair as he hovered about the cabin, finally settling near the window in front of me. "All I'll need is the cargo manifests for this trip since you left Hamburg, as well as the crew manifest."

"Anything else?" He sounded annoyed.

"Just a place to stay, also I need to look at all the containers." I studied him. "I'll count them for now, I won't look inside."

"You can't open the containers."

"Oh?" I stared at him.

"They all have a seal on them and only a government official or the recipient can break the seals."

"I understand."

"You should be thankful we're a small freighter." He kept his calm gaze on me, without revealing anything by his expression.

"This ship looks big enough to me." I looked out the large window in his cabin.

"We're a medium displacement ship," he answered. "We can deliver cargo to the smaller ports."

"Excuse me?"

"We have cargo cranes so we can off or on load cargo by ourselves, and our requirements for docking are less demanding than a larger ship."

"I see," I said. "You do have a cabin I can use until we get to Long Beach, I hope."

"We have one free cabin." Wolfgang relaxed a bit. "This ship runs with two passenger cabins and one is empty."

"Who has the other one?"

"A couple we picked up in Hong Kong." He sat on the edge of his small desk, near the window. "They're with us the whole way back to Hong Kong. We usually have one or both cabins full year round with passengers who have the time." Wolfgang's expression didn't tell me a thing. "They're good company for the officers most of the time."

"I'd also like to interview the crew." I studied the Captain, everything about him was noncommittal so far. "So, is there someone who could act as a translator for me?"

Ah, to have the free time for such a trip, maybe when I get rich and quit my real job.

"All of the officers speak English, and the cook can translate for the rest of the crew." He stood up. "But right now, I have to prepare to leave port so why don't you settle into your cabin until we get to open water, then we can work out the details."

....

"I'm sorry, Mr. Katz , but I have to take your weapon; the Captain insists that you leave it in the safe in his office while you are at sea with us." It felt like the chief engineer was also the chief of police.

"I guess that would be all right." I pondered the possibilities. "I assume no one else is armed on this ship."

"Not unless there's a problem." The engineer shook his head. "We have an arms locker but only the Captain and I have keys."

"What do you have in that locker, if you don't mind telling me."

"Oh, no sir," he said pleasantly. "We have twenty HKs. But, as I said we never let them out of the locked cabinet."

"That's a lot of fire power for such a small ship. What would make you unlock the gun room?" I just had to know.

"Pirates." He looked somber.

"Pirates?" I asked incredulously. "I didn't think they're so much a problem since Bluebeard."

"You would be surprised." He leaned towards me as if to tell a secret. "Smaller freighters like ours are a prime target for pirates in the Southern Pacific, especially around Indonesia."

"Really?" I had read some intelligence about that, but hadn't paid that much attention to it.

"Yes." The engineer nodded. "Two of our HKs are full automatics."

"You have machine guns on this ship?" I was finding out all sorts of good things from this man.

"We keep them locked up all the time, unless we need them," he answered.

"Have you ever used the machine guns?"

"Oh, yes." He nodded. "Several times."

"Not in this part of the Pacific, I hope." I gave him a concerned expression.

"Oh, no." He shook his head. "This entire stretch of sea is safe."

"Actually, before we got sidetracked by pirates, I was asking about anybody on board who has personal weapons."

The engineer thought for a second. "The Captain has a some guns because he collects antiques, and he likes to shoot skeet over the side while we're at sea."

"I guess I don't have a choice." I unloaded my revolver and handed it to him. "But, be careful with it."

The man took my gun and ammunition. The Asian man in the next cabin came over and introduced himself, Yoshihiro. We shook hands. He stood about five foot six, with short salt and pepper hair. He was dressed in formal casual wear, tan slacks and a pull over shirt, which he wore as if it were a business suit. He appeared to be in his mid fifties, quite fit and full of energy.

"My wife, Maiko, and I are on our dream vacation," Yoshihiro said. "We own an import export business in Hong Kong and we have always wanted to bum around the world on a freighter for a month or two."

I motioned for him to come into my cabin. I thought the Japanese were reserved people; Yoshihiro is a Japanese name, but this guy wasn't reserved at all. Smiling, he sat down on the only chair in my room. We were cramped. The Captain's cabin was a mansion compared to the sardine can I was assigned to. I wondered how big the other officers' cabins were.

"So, how long have you been on board?" I asked

"We got on in Hong Kong. I guess that was three weeks ago, but I've lost track by now."

"I suppose that's part of what you're paying for."

"It is indeed." Again, he grinned and nodded. "Are you with us for the rest of the trip?"

"No." I shook my head. "I'm only here until Long Beach."

"Oh." Yoshihiro looked carefully at me. "That's a short vacation, isn't it?"

"Regrettably, this is work for me." I shrugged my shoulders.

"Work?" He continued to appear puzzled. "Do you work for the shipping company?"

"No," I replied, "I'm actually a private investigator working for the insurance company."

"Is there a problem?"

"No, it's a regular thing they do to protect their liability in ships like this one," I paused for a second, "I'm actually a loss prevention investigator."

"Oh, I see." Yoshihiro appeared to be processing what I had said. "I guess Lloyds of London doesn't want to go broke."

"I suppose not."

How did he know the company? I guess there aren't that many insurers in this market, and he did say he was in the import export business.

"Dinner should be ready now." Yoshihiro stood up. "I must find my wife soon, she likes to walk the entire perimeter of the ship several times for exercise twice a day."

"I guess I'll see you at dinner." I stood up to see him out. "Oh, where's the dining room?"

"Two doors down from the Captain's cabin, on level five, you can't miss it." Yoshihiro turned back to face me. "That's the officer's mess; the rest of the crew eats at the general mess on level two, but we get to eat with the officers."

"Better food, I hope," I said, as Yoshihiro hurried down the hallway and out a door to the main deck.

7
All you can eat

All the living quarters on this ship were piled into the seven story structure near the stern of the ship, the top level was entirely devoted to ship operations. While the Captain's cabin faced aft on the fifth level, passenger cabins were on the second level facing to the port.

I was able to fumble around the four levels below the main deck only briefly before I went to dinner. Most of the area below deck held cargo containers, but some spaces were devoted to other things. The largest space, of course, held the engine rooms while the extra spaces on the bottom two decks were devoted to storage, maintenance and a large machine shop. Apparently being stuck in the middle of an ocean because of a missing engine gizmo wasn't an option, so the ability to construct said gizmo from blocks of metal in a machine shop was a good thing.

The next level up contained the food stores and kitchen, the floor closest to the main deck held the laundry and more storage areas. Surprisingly, none of the crew minded me wandering around. The Captain was right, none of the crew spoke a word of English and my limited knowledge of their languages didn't help that much. Other than 'who the hell is he?', I couldn't tell what they were talking about.

On the fifth level, the officers' dining room was about as big as the Captain's cabin. Since this room was in the center of the ship structure, more or less, it had no windows but several bright fluorescent tubes overhead lit every corner. A table of solid blonde wood which could seat ten stood in the middle of the room, partly covered with a bright white linen cloth. I noticed that the table was clamped to the floor on all five feet. Only five people were there; I was the sixth person for dinner. The table cloth was somewhat tacky, by design, so that in rough seas the plates would stay on the table a little longer than Newton's laws might dictate.

The Captain sat at one end of the table, and the Chief Engineer sat next to him on his left, against the back wall of the room. Yoshihiro and his wife sat on the other side of the table from the engineer, and a man I had not met sat next to the engineer. Before us, mouthwatering food filled the table. Roast beef, neatly sliced, hot and steaming lay next to a second meat dish, some typical German concoction of sausage and cream sauce, pungent and full of rich odors. A bowl of creamed corn, another of peas, a third bowl of cooked carrots, and a large platter of potato pancakes completed the choices for this meal.

"Come in, come in." Wolfgang exaggeratedly motioned for me to sit down. "Meals are a joyous time on this ship."

"Mostly because of the Chef." Yoshihiro stood to acknowledge my entrance to the room. He bowed quickly then sat back down, his wife silently followed suit.

"This is my beautiful wife, Maiko." Yoshihiro nodded at his wife who smiled and looked at the table in front of her. She was pleasant looking, fifteen to twenty years younger than her husband.

"I think you know most of us here." The Captain said.

He introduced his medical and communications officer, Jonathan Bruer. I nodded towards the man, who was average height, but large, close to two hundred and fifty pounds. Both he and the Engineer were dressed in black pants and stiff white shirts. It was barely a uniform, but compared to the rest of the crew they were quite dressed up.

"That appears to be an unusual combination, medical and communications combined?" I inquired.

"I like to think of myself more as a technology officer." Jonathan was the first German on board I had heard with a German accent. "I keep all the electronic gear in good order, as well as attend to any medical needs. For my first two years of university, I was a pre-med student, besides, I had medical training in the army."

"Please sit down and taste some of Cook's food," The Captain insisted. "You need to try some."

The food was as good as he promised. For what looked like a dumpy freighter, this was the best cooking I had ever tasted. The greasy looking sausage dish tasted good enough to ignore what I thought were its ingredients; I planned to never ask.

"It's good to have another passenger, even if it's for a short time," The engineer hesitated, apparently searching for something to say.

"How many officers are there on board?" I might as well start asking questions like a real detective.

"Other than those at this table, we have four more officers," he answered quickly. "We take turns on duty so you should be able to meet all of us by the time we make port in California."

I nodded. I couldn't stop myself from digging into the food. My nose was guiding my fork towards the roast beef. I noticed that the others were also silently eating, so I didn't feel so bad following suit.

"So, you're a private detective?" Yoshihiro interrupted my second bite of potato pancake.

"Yes, I am," I mumbled through the savory potato pancake. What was that herb? Was it tarragon?

I drank a short sip of the white wine placed next to me. Boy, that was good too.

"I now work out of Atlanta, but I also have an office in Los Angeles," I offered. "I lived on the west coast for years but I moved to Atlanta last year."

"It must be exciting," Maiko piped up. She had a stronger accent than her husband, but her English was perfect. Her accent, which differed from her husband's, sounded familiar, I couldn't place it.

"You must tell us some of your adventures," Maiko added.

"It's not all that exciting," I continued talking, a fork full of beef inches away from my mouth. "Most of what I do is leg work for major corporations; the work is dull, but it pays well." I stuffed my mouth, thinking this may be worth it for the meals.

"The cook says you brought a big gun on board," Maiko persisted in not letting me eat in peace.

"Force of habit." I swallowed the scrumptious food. "You never know when someone who wants to hide from a problem might start shooting at you."

"Do you get shot at often?" Wolfgang all of a sudden got interested in the conversation.

"Once is too often," I quickly answered. "By the way, Captain, I'd like to meet the cook tonight if possible."

"Why the hurry?" Wolfgang frowned.

Did that request piss him off? Maybe he didn't like me not answering his question and changing the subject, maybe I was rude.

"Well, first of all to thank him for the food, and second because he can tell me about the rest of the crew, since he can understand them." I chomped down on more of the good stuff.

"I think I can help you when we're finished." The Engineer said pleasantly. "Cook likes admirers of his work."

"Great." I nodded as I sipped more of the wine. "If I could also visit you tonight for a favor?" I moved my eyes to Jonathan.

"What?" He sounded intrigued.

"Not much." I shifted to a non-work topic. "My fiancée lives in Los Angeles and I'd like to get a telegram to her so she can meet me at Long Beach when we land."

"Sure." Jonathan chuckled at my request, it must have been much more harmless than he expected. "That would be no problem at all. After dessert, we can go together to the radio room."

I eagerly agreed. Maybe I could find something interesting there.

"So, you are trying to avoid telling us about your adventures." Maiko returned to her question.

Like her husband, she was acting more outgoing than the Japanese stereotype. A few inches shorter than her husband, she appeared trim and athletic, her smile disarmingly charming. I closely studied her face; I couldn't see any wrinkles, her skin was smooth. If her husband was, perhaps, fifty five, she had to be close to thirty. That was not too strange, my guess was that his business was profitable.

"Well, maybe some of my more domestic cases would be of more interest to this dinner crowd." I cleared my throat. "My firm handles a lot of pre-divorce cases."

"What is that?" Yoshihiro slowly asked.

"A husband, or most likely a wife, seeking proof that their spouse is cheating on them."

I looked at everyone's faces. Yes, they were all following my conversation now; sex always seems to interest everybody. No one would like to hear about the majority of divorce investigation dealing with digging up hidden assets for the lawyers to fight about, that's all too dull and all too common to make a good story, but unfortunately that exact task fills most of Cassandra's and my time in those cases.

"So, what do you do?" Yoshihiro continued.

"My partner and I usually take turns following the spouse and note who he visits, and when he visits them, if possible, we also take pictures." I quickly finished off the last of my roast beef.

"Oh, that sounds racy." Maiko glanced coyly at her husband. That look she gave her husband let me know that at the least she wasn't Yoshihiro's first wife.

"Sometimes it is," I said. "Last month my partner got a whole roll of pictures of her client's husband having sex with his secretary in a small wooded area off the sixth green of a public golf course."

"Working on his putting game?" The engineer laughed out loud. The joke was too predictable, judging by the lack of laughter around the table.

"Anything else?" Maiko asked.

"Well, just one more." I turned to see a man enter the room, pushing a cart of desserts.

"You're in luck." Wolfgang stood. "Cook is here."

"Hi." I stood and pushed my right hand towards him. "My name is Benjamin, and I would like to tell you how much I enjoyed your cooking this evening."

"I can never get enough compliments, thank you; please continue."

The cook was a short man, around five foot four. He was lean for a cook, and had a full head of jet black hair, neatly tucked under a short white chef's hat. He sounded as if he might be from India or Pakistan, but he didn't have the right accent for either of those countries.

"Well, you shall be heaped with compliments from me as long as I sit at this table." I grinned at him.

"Thank you again."

He continued smiling as he loaded the table with plates of puddings and pastries while removing the empty plates. Last, he placed a stainless steel bowl of freshly whipped cream in the center of the table.

"Sometime early tomorrow I'd like to talk to you about the crew," I said, right before he left the room.

"Sure." He looked at the Captain. "So the Captain told me; maybe right after breakfast?"

"That would be fine," I said.

"We can talk while I stack the breakfast dishes into the washer." The cook left the room.

"What about our next story?" Maiko asked.

"I guess that one would involve the husband who hired a detective to find out who was following him," I said.

"Who was following him?" Yoshihiro asked.

"I was following him." I studied Maiko's expression. "His wife hired me to follow him and find out who he was sleeping with."

"Oh." Maiko quickly glanced at her husband, then back to me.

"He owned a chain of sporting goods stores in greater Los Angeles, and he wasn't sleeping with only one other woman; he had three women he was taking turns with, besides his wife."

I glanced around the room. Still, they were all interested.

"When he found out his wife's detective was tailing him, he didn't direct his anger at her, but at me."

"What did he do?" Jonathan asked.

"He went to one of his stores, got a hunting rifle and waited in his car for me to leave my office."

I finished my flan, which was excellent flan; it wasn't too soupy and the texture was perfection.

"He then proceeded to chase me with that rifle for the next ten minutes, shooting at me eleven times."

"Obviously missing you," the Captain said, grinning slightly.

"I'd hope so." I nodded. "It was a Four fifty eight Winchester Magnum. If he had even nicked me, I would still hurt."

"Did he hurt anyone else?" Yoshihiro asked.

"Luckily, no." I shook my head. "Although that's a loud rifle and I'm sure today some people have a hearing loss due to that little episode."

"How did you stop him?" The engineer asked.

"What?" I cocked my ear towards him.

Most of them thought for a second, then chuckled.

"Sorry, sometimes I can't help myself," I added.

"Did the police catch him?" the engineer asked again.

"No," I answered. "I finally wound up shooting him in his foot so he'd drop the rifle which I was able to get to before he could pick it up again."

"What did you do then?" Maiko asked.

"I knocked him over the head with the butt of my revolver so he'd sleep until the police showed up."

"How long did it take for them to arrive?" Wolfgang was caught up in my story.

"From the time he first started shooting at me, it took twenty five minutes for the police to arrive." I shook my head. "Keep in mind, my office was downtown, and a police station was less than a ten minutes walk from there."

"Why did it take so long?" Maiko asked.

"Well, I think it took a while before anyone called them, but I also think they didn't think it was that important."

"A wild man shooting a rifle on a crowded street?" Yoshihiro exclaimed.

"I take it you've never been to Los Angeles before." I smiled; I liked to pull people's legs.

"I may wait right here on the ship when we dock, also." Yoshihiro appeared somber.

"Yoshihiro said that you two owned a business in Hong Kong." I said, to change the subject. I might as well start my subtle questioning, after all I was seeking an Asian spy, maybe.

"Oh, yes," Yoshihiro quickly answered, putting a hand on Maiko's thigh. "We own an import export business there."

"Are you both from there?" I asked. "Your name is Japanese."

"Yes," he answered. "Both our families come from there, my brother is running the business while we are on vacation."

"Our families are Japanese, but we've lived in Hong Kong for many generations," Maiko added.

"What do you sell?"

"We sell arts and crafts from the mainland," Yoshihiro said. "They sell well in your country. We import ceramic, wood and stone carvings, and some jewelry from China, then export it to Europe and America. It has been a good business for us."

"Well, Mr. Katz , do you want to send your telegram tonight?" Jonathan asked. "I need to get moving now because I have a lot to do before I get to sleep tonight; my watch starts at five in the morning."

. . . .

Jonathan quickly navigated the passageways to his small radio room one level up from the dining room while I followed closely behind. The room was crammed with electronic equipment, almost covering two large desks. One desk held a large quantity of radio equipment. Jonathan must be an amateur radio operator because he had several transceivers for the forty, twenty and ten meter bands in addition to the marine band radios. I remembered that my report had said the North Korean transmission was an upper sideband on the quarter meter band. The antenna would be small, and could be hidden anywhere, so I scanned the room for such a transmitter and didn't see one, although it could have been hidden in plain sight. The other table surface was devoted to a Radio Shack TRS-80, model two computer, and an array of peripherals surrounding the television like computer which seemed a bit too much for a freighter. Jonathan obviously liked technology, so it might be him.

Everything appeared to be in perfect order, the German psyche was in full sight. The only thing posted on the wall was a calendar with scenes of the Motherland; at least it was the West German Motherland. Book shelves rose above the equipment on three walls. I kept scanning for anything unusual, as Jonathan searched through three of the shelves to the right of a small porthole.

"Damn." Jonathan shook his head. "I must have left the log book in my workshop."

"Do you need it?"

"Sorry to say, I do," he sighed. "You wait here, I will be back in a minute; don't touch anything."

I nodded agreement and he rushed down the hall; his workshop was only a few doors down, at the other end of the narrow hallway so there wasn't much time.

My eyes caught a series of red bound books near the top of the shelf next to the door. I leaned in and pulled one out, glanced quickly at it, then pushed it back where it had been. I had seen one exactly like it before in Germany, only it was East German, a Stasi code book. It was an old one, older than I had seen outside of CIA headquarters; I thought I was after North Koreans, not East Germans. And, now that I had a clue, I noticed three other ranges of thin black books near the red ones. I quickly pulled one of the black books, opened it and then stuffed it back where it had come from; this was a Russian code book from the late forties. What the hell was this, a research library for old spies?

Jonathan darted out of his cabin with a large ledger book and rushed back towards the radio room. I was out in the hall by then so I didn't get a chance to see any more of the unusual books, but they looked like code books from a variety of countries. Not many units of either the East German or Russian intelligence use actual books anymore for coding and decoding, besides, codes that old had been broken long ago; who were these people on this freighter?

"Now, what is your fiancée's address?" He opened his log book and pulled a pen from a cup jammed into a small open space on the table in front of him.

I gave him Cassandra's address and name, as well as the time the ship was due to dock; he sent the message immediately.

Cassandra's dad had decided to take a job in Paris for a few years, but they kept their California house in Huntington Beach because they wanted to retire there. Cassandra was living there, high on the hog with a nice view of the Pacific and three thousand square feet of living space for one person.

"Tell me, Jonathan, have you noticed anything strange on this ship?" I might as well act like my job was to investigate lost cargo.

"Like what?" He appeared to be confused.

"Like empty cargo containers being on loaded or off loaded?" I postulated, "maybe two or more different crews doing the loading at one port, at the same time?"

"No." He still sounded slightly confused. "I couldn't tell if the containers are empty when they're being loaded, but they would throw the balance of the ship off if they were, and I haven't noticed that at all."

"What about the loading crews?"

"I don't pay attention to that." He shook his head. "You'd be better asking the Captain abut that."

"Sorry." I shrugged. "I have to ask these questions, it's nothing personal, just business."

"I understand." He nodded.

"I couldn't help noticing that computer." I pointed to the TRS-80. "I looked at that exact model for my office back in Atlanta. What are all the extras you have?"

"Not that much." He glanced up at me. "I ordered some extras for the system and I was able to pick them up in Hawaii when we docked."

"So, what comes with the system?"

"The main unit, two 184 kilobyte floppy drives, and all the memory I could fit into it, forty eight kilobytes." Jonathan appeared quite proud of the whole thing. "It came with the dot matrix printer in the package I bought."

"What's the box next to the keyboard?" I didn't recognize it.

"That's the biggest thing I added." Excitement crept into his voice. "That is the Winchester Drive, it can store five million bytes of data; that's amazing for something so small."

"Do you use it much?"

"The Engineer and I are playing with a network." Jonathan said happily, obviously pleased at finding a new audience. "I installed Unix on the Radio Shack system, and that was no small feat. You should visit him and see the TI 980 system he has in engineering, now, that's a computer."

"That might be more interesting if I knew anything about them." I stared back at him.

"We think it's fun." He didn't know where to move the conversation. "I think the small personal computer will be big in the next ten years or so."

"I suppose so."

I didn't want to get into a technology discussion with him at the moment. So he had a hobby, I was more interested in where a communications officer on a crappy freighter could get all the money needed to buy that stuff, not to mention why he had all those code books.

"You said you were looking at this computer for your office." His voice rose with interest.

"Yes," I did ask him, so I suppose I'd have to keep talking. "I thought we could use it to keep track of cases and clients, maybe we could do our books with it too."

"You certainly could do all that," he sounded excited. "This system is fabulous, and I understand there is office software you may be able to adapt."

"I'm sure that's true, but the price tag sort of stopped me," I admitted. "I thought I'd wait for awhile and see if the prices drop."

"They might." The conversation was becoming awkward again. "I don't think so, though. I think the speed and memory will increase so you'll get more machine, but the prices won't drop, at least that's my opinion."

"It's still a lot of money."

65

I remembered the price quote of six grand for the basic system with one extra floppy drive which was a lot of cash for a fancy typewriter and file cabinet.

"I bet you'll change your mind in a year or two."

"Maybe, thanks for sending the message for me."

I walked out the door, and down the stairs to the main deck, maybe I could look at the ocean and the main cargo deck by moonlight. It was raining hard when I opened the door to the outside so I closed it quickly; so much for the walk tonight.

. . . .

I still didn't see how they could stuff a shower, sink and toilet into such a small space. I guessed it wasn't that different than what they have done in sleeper cars for rail passengers; at least I didn't have to take a shower on deck. I had started settling into the surprisingly comfortable narrow bed when I heard a dull thumping coming from one of the walls of my cabin, the wall I shared with Yoshihiro and Maiko. Rhythmic bumping can only mean one thing; I missed Cassandra.

Maybe they didn't mean to speak so loud, but in the passion of the moment and all, I could hear talking in the next room. True to my profession, I placed my ear on the bottom of a water glass left in my room; the other end if the glass was, of course, against Yoshihiro and Maiko's wall. I knew I recognized her accent; they were both speaking perfect Japanese and her accent was from the northern islands of Japan.

Three years ago, I had met a man who worked for the Japanese Interior Ministries whose accent was different from his colleagues. We had a half hour discussion on the different accents within his country. One never knows when some bit of trivial information can help, like right now I knew they weren't born and bred in Hong Kong since the Japanese from Hong Kong don't have that Japanese an accent. Oh, well. It's off to bed I go, alone.

8

All's quiet on the water front

I woke up sometime around dawn and took instant note that breakfast wasn't for another thirty or forty minutes. While I waited, I walked around the cargo deck and made a cursory check of the containers stacked on deck. It appeared as if there had been a fog the night before, either during the rain or right after. Remaining fog this morning had mostly lifted as I emerged on deck and noticed breaks in the clouds. The sun shone in patches on the undulating ocean; making bright and brighter spots one the shimmering waves. The salty sea air smelled different in the Pacific than it did in the Atlantic, at least for me it left a more metallic taste in my mouth. The water was a different shade of blue and green too; idly I wondered why.

I paused by the railing for a second and stared out at the ocean. We had enjoyed a calm journey until now. But as I watched, the seas grew rougher in the brisk wind that often arrives in early morning. It blew from the south west, stronger and stronger as I stared out at the ever larger waves.

"Good morning, Mr. Katz ." Maiko whooshed past me in a power walk. "Beautiful morning," she shouted as she rushed towards the stern of the ship.

"You look invigorated, my dear, for some strange reason," I muttered to myself as I stared at the towering stacks of cargo containers piled on the main deck.

Finally I made my way below deck. The ship carried even more containers down here, eight rows of twenty by twenty foot containers up to four high. The containers were tightly packed with two passageways from side to side. If checking each and every container were my real job, I might have considered jumping overboard right then.

On, ever onward I mumbled as I slowly walked from big box to big box, rapping on the ones I could reach with an ear held to the side. One might be able to tell if a box was empty by the echo from the knuckle rap, but did I care? I pulled out a notebook and began writing down the numbers and other markings on the containers, with a notation of the degree of fullness I thought my rap indicated. At least the ship held only a finite number of those large cargo containers; what a life.

By climbing up a series of ladders I made my way to the top of one of three steel structures, massive cranes, rising from the main deck. They used these cranes to move around the large cargo containers, with an inner stairway leading to the control room for each crane. I took the ladders on the outside of the center crane since I liked the view, and I was feeling adventurous. At the top, the spectacular view felt a bit precarious, especially since the wind was picking up even further and the sea was churning more than it had since I came on board. I usually don't get seasick, but maybe I shouldn't push it too far. This must be what climbing a mast was like in the good old days of sail boats. Flogging, scurvy, and no women went along with the days of sailing ships, so I guess I should count my blessings and not yearn for the good old days under sail; well, this wasn't a mast anyway so I shouldn't worry.

I moved back to the ladder leading down to the main deck and began descending. What was that smell? Sewage? It smelled like sewage as I looked around for vent stacks, guessing that as the source, but I didn't see any. It was hard to tell where it was coming from, and I hoped it wasn't coming from one of the containers; what would that delivery be like?

Down the ladder was a more difficult trip than going up; maybe I shouldn't use the word trip when discussing ladders? The view from the top was worth it, though. I had copied down most of the container numbers I could see, so I guessed I could rest for a while.

"I believe it's time for breakfast." Maiko sped by me on a subsequent tour of the deck. "If you liked dinner, you simply must try cook's breakfast."

. . . .

"So, what brought a fine chef like you to sea?" I inquired. I never was good at doing small talk with a sailor; I

68

missed Cassandra for these delicate operations. Get serious, I missed Cassandra for a whole lot more than that.

"Not so smooth with this conversation, are you, Mr. Katz ?" Cook quickly stacked dirty dishes in the large steam cleaner.

"You noticed." I half grinned. "Okay, I'll try it another way, your breakfast was better than your dinner. I've eaten at the finest restaurants in Europe, Asia and America, and your cooking is the equal of the best, so why are you here in this floating boxcar?"

"The Captain likes my food; he pays me well." Cook stopped loading the washer for a moment and studied my face. "I translate for the rest of the crew, I take care of them since they don't speak the same language as the company, or the officers. The Captain pays me well for that in addition to cooking, so altogether I make more than some of the officers."

"I guess that answers some of it." I leaned against the sink, across from the dishwasher. "What's your name? Where are you from?"

"Just call me Cook, everybody does, why do you ask?"

"You speak several languages from the Indonesia area, as well as German and English," I observed. "I wondered where you were from."

"I was born in India, near Calcutta." Cook again stopped loading the dishes. "My parents moved to Jakarta when I was ten, and I learned all the languages by working with a variety of people ever since, languages are easy for me."

"It sounds like you had an interesting childhood."

"So, what do you need to know?" He finished loading the washer, then started it. Hissing jets of steam screamed so loud that we walked to the other side of the kitchen where at least we could hear each other.

"Well, how long does a crew last on this ship," I hesitated, searching for another way to say it. "Among the crew, how many have been with this ship for more than one tour?"

"Oh, hell," Cook sighed. "No one but the officers lasts more than one trip around the world, half of the crew doesn't make it that far."

"What do you mean?"

69

"A lot of the men get homesick, drunk, arrested or any combination of the three." Cook shook his head as he glanced down at the counter top, then back at me. "We pick up a few and lose a few at almost every port. A lot of them worked here before and we pick them up where we left them the last time through. I guess if their jail term is up when we hit port, we'll take them back because they know the peculiarities of this ship."

"How long have you been with this ship?"

"This will be the eighth time around the globe for me." Cook seemed happy with that. "I don't know how much longer I want to do it, but the Captain keeps raising the amount he pays me, so I just stay and stay."

"Have you noticed anything strange about this ship?" I asked.

"Why?" Cook sounded concerned. "Tell me what the insurance company thinks is going on and I'll be truthful in confirming or denying it."

"It's nothing." I searched for something to tell him. "They want to cut down on losses due to mistakes or fraud in lost cargo."

"So, you think the crew is stealing cargo and replacing it with empty containers, or ones filled with rocks?"

"You tell me." He was the only one concerned with me as a legitimate insurance investigator.

"Judging from the conversations among the crew, there isn't any funny business going on with them." Cook relaxed a bit. "All they talk about is where the best whores are in the next port, and how to avoid getting robbed after they get drunk and laid."

"Normal stuff, right?"

"Right; no secret conversations, no stalking about the ship after dark, and no strangers on board at port." Cook sounded emphatic.

"All right." I looked around the kitchen which was well stocked with utensils, each with its special place. "What about the officers? Do they seem to be a good bunch to work for?"

"Mostly." Cook's face took on a less forgiving expression. "I like the Captain a lot, but the rest of them act standoffish."

"You say they have been with this ship for a while?"

"As long as I've been here."

"Strange," I mused out loud. "Most freighters change officers when they reach home port."

"Not this one." Cook scanned his kitchen; he was proud of his domain. "I guess they like this ship and the company must be happy with them."

"I guess so." I glanced at my watch. "I suppose I'd better get to the Captain's cabin, he's expecting me."

....

"Here are copies of the manifests you asked for, Mr. Katz ." Wolfgang tapped a short stack of papers on his desk, then leaned back in his chair which squeaked loudly as his weight pushed it back. "Tell me, what do you expect to find?"

"I don't know." Still standing in front of his desk, I picked up the papers.

"Please, sit down." He pointed to a chair close to the front of his desk. "Join me in a beer?"

"It's only eleven in the morning." I sat down.

"Just thought I'd ask." He studied me.

"The engineer tells me that you shoot skeet off the deck."

I glimpsed what I could see of his face. I had to squint slightly since I was also looking out the window directly behind him; the sun had completely come out and was shining brightly.

"Yes, I do." He smiled. "Do you shoot?"

"As a matter of a fact, I do." I had found something we both liked. That was useful.

"What do you shoot?"

"Well, If we're talking about shotguns, I have a Parker Brothers in twenty eight gauge, but I'd never consider shooting that one on the range." I grinned at him. "I shoot a Ruger Red Label in twenty gauge normally; it's a new model, but I like it a lot"

"Wonderful." Wolfgang smiled broadly. "I have three Parker Brothers, one in twelve one in twenty eight and one ten gauge. Do you hunt?"

"I used to." I shrugged my shoulders. "I guess I don't have time to any more."

"Have you ever gone hunting for dangerous game?" He studied me as if I could be a friend; he tried to be cautiously relaxing.

"No, I haven't, not unless you count man as a dangerous animal, which I do."

"Well." The captain sounded unnerved for a second, then righted himself quickly "You should try big game hunting sometimes."

I guess this was his expensive hobby, like the electronic toys were for the communications officer.

"Have you been hunting lately?" I asked.

"I went on an elephant hunt in India not eight months ago," he affirmed. "I'm having the ivory made into decoration for a carved sea chest."

"Oh," I said, "what do you shoot on these hunts?"

I thought big game hunting in India was illegal, unless you were able to bribe someone.

"I have a beautiful Holland and Holland double rifle in four seventy nitro express." He got up and leaned on the edge of his desk. "Would you like to shoot it?"

"I'd love to." I thought for a second. "Do you reload for that rifle?"

"Oh, no," he sounded insulted by the question. "I buy factory ammunition for it when we stop in England. It's not that hard to find if you know where to look."

"I'd love to shoot skeet and try the Holland and Holland."

Factory ammunition for an extinct weapon? That had to be expensive. What is it about this crew spending fortunes on their hobbies?

"Then, you must join me this afternoon, I shoot off the stern."

"I'd love to."

I had to force myself not to start making up 'shooting off my stern' jokes. That was a lot of money in guns he rattled off, unless those Parker shotguns were the Japanese knock offs, but somehow I didn't think they were.

"About the other stuff," I continued.

"Yes?" He answered quickly.

"I'll look at all this paperwork and write a quick report tonight." I smiled almost to a wink. "There isn't anything else I should know, is there?"

"Not at all, Mr. Katz ." I didn't think that man could smile any harder, but he did. "I like you, you're a nice man after all."

"So, we dock tomorrow?"

"Yes." He stood, noticing my twitching to leave on a good note. "We'll be in Long Beach by three next afternoon."

"Good." I got up. "This'll be a easy twenty five hundred."

"Is that how much they pay for an investigation?" He sounded surprised.

"Yeah." I grinned again at him as I reached for the door. That wasn't exactly true, but it sounded impressive. "Now you see why I like these jobs. A relaxing trip on a ship, most of the time there's nothing underhanded going on and there's lots of easy money."

"Life is good, right?"

"You hit the nail on the head, my friend." I shook his hand before I walked down the passageway to the exit.

"See you at four on the fantail," he said as I walked through the door to the stairwell.

Outside the exit to the main deck were three wooden deck chairs, lined up facing the ocean. The overhang was deep enough to shade the chairs. Yoshihiro was lounging in one of them wearing shorts and another short sleeved pullover shirt, again a bit on the formal side for a vacation at sea on a freighter.

"Where's Maiko?" I asked as I plopped myself in the chair next to him.

"Oh, she's painting up by the bow. She took that up right before the trip and she brought a bunch of her art supplies with her," Yoshihiro said, pointing in the general direction of the bow. "She's painting the dolphins that run with the ship this time of day."

I made the appropriate social noises while my mind threw up a brief image of Maiko throwing gobs of paint at the fish as they leapt from the waves. I know, not that kind of painting.

"Do you want to talk to me alone?" I asked.

"Yes," he did sound surprised. "I do; who do you work for?"

"Lloyds of London." I didn't change my expression.

"I don't think so." He carefully scanned me.

"What makes you think I don't?" I asked. "Do you work for them too?"

"Not exactly."

"Well, guessing by your accent, and especially Maiko's accent, I'd say you were both from Japan, not Hong Kong."

"Yes." He looked harder at me.

"I'd also say that you probably work for JETRO, the Japan External Trade Organization," I paused briefly to emphasize my palpable cleverness . "If I had to guess."

"How did you know?" His surprise let me know I was right. He couldn't be a real spy, what we call an industrial spy sent here for some reason as yet unknown to me.

"That's not why you're worried, though." I was about to either make him jump off the edge or greatly relieve his mind.

"Why?" He stuttered. "I mean why do you think I'm worried?"

"Maiko's not your wife." I patted his shoulder. "She's most likely your mistress you took along on this government sponsored junket, but I wasn't hired by your wife or your employer to snoop on you."

"What?" He stammered again.

"Don't worry, I don't care at all about your personal business, " I said reassuringly. "I'm only here to find out if thieves are on this ship."

"Oh." Yoshihiro sighed and relaxed a bit, just a bit. He looked away from me, and out into the waves.

"Are you here for the same reason?" I asked; he didn't answer. "Maybe we can share a bit of information. After all, I leave this ship tomorrow and I have to write a report before then. You could be a great help to me, and it won't cost a thing since I won't tell your secret to anyone."

"How did you know?" Yoshihiro glanced at me briefly, then again stared at the ocean.

"Last night, when I was telling about my exploits with unfaithful husbands both you and Maiko appeared a bit too interested in the stories, and a little embarrassed."

At his crest fallen face, which he was quickly changing into a deadpan, I added, "Remember, that sort of thing is my business, and I've learned to read people in these situations." I allowed myself a knowing smile, short of wise ass territory.

"I don't think anyone else suspects anything, so you and Maiko can continue to enjoy your vacation."

His expressionless face managed a silent rebuke for me. Then he decided to cooperate. "The crew is fine, except when they hit a port, then they're a bunch of drunken bums." However, the officers are up to something, I don't know what yet for sure, but I have an idea."

"Are they stealing cargo?"

"No, not that at all." He leaned towards me. "If you are investigating theft for Lloyds of London, you can report that they do not steal their cargo, nor would any of the officers tolerate anyone stealing it."

"What, then?" I asked.

"I don't know." He sounded tentative.

"Do you have a theory?" I asked.

"Have you noticed the book collection in Jonathan's radio room?" He turned and looked at me; maybe he knew more than I thought he did.

"You mean the code books?"

"You saw them too."

"Yeah, East German and Russian code books."

"You should ask him to show you the rest of them." Yoshihiro glanced at me like I was a dunce.

"The rest of them?"

"Yes," he said, smothering a laugh. "He collects them, they're all from the late forties and early fifties. Jonathan is quite proud of those code books, he trades for them all over the world. Some of them have to be worth a fortune, and I think some of them are not exactly unclassified. He has a collection of old Soviet propaganda posters that's the best I've ever seen, most of them go back to the nineteen seventeen revolution."

"Oh."

I was almost speechless. Well, back to the drawing board; maybe Yoshihiro was the spy after all, a spy afraid of being caught with his mistress, but I still didn't think so.

"The question is how you knew what they were right away." Yoshihiro was puzzled. "Something tells me you're not an insurance investigator after all."

"But, I am. I think it's rather obvious what the books are once you look at any page." I appeared as sincere as I could. "Besides, how many spies chase after unfaithful husbands and crooked ship's captains?"

"I guess not that many, but why are you here?"

"I am what you see, a paid snoop for an insurance company." I grinned again at him. "But, I am curious about the real story here; I have to know what's going on whether I report it to the insurance company or not, it's sort of a game with me."

"I guess before you leave, I'll tell you some of what I've learned up to now." Yoshihiro carefully studied me. "It isn't what I was sent here for, either, but I guess I have the same love of the game you do."

"Don't forget," I said. "I get off this ship around three tomorrow."

"I'll see you in my cabin right before we dock, don't worry." Yoshihiro closed his eyes and lay back into the deck chair.

I found a large room on the third level with a wide window facing towards the bow. Most of the ocean view was blocked by cargo containers, but lots of sunlight still poured in. It had a pool table, a ping pong table, four pinball machines and several broad tables, this was the recreation room for the crew which, at ten in the morning, was empty so I was alone. As I spread out the cargo manifests on the table, I compared the container numbers to the ones I had noted on my walk around the deck, placing a check by those.   All the containers I had seen were on the manifest so I added the numbers that I had missed so that I then had a complete list in my notebook. I could wander around the deck and in the cargo holds, checking off the other numbers to make the crew think I cared about the cargo. What I wanted to do was hunt for a possible hiding place for a radio transmitter.

. . . .

"How often do you do this?" I lifted the muff of the hearing protector up so I could listen to the answer.

"No so often." Wolfgang handed me his shotgun. "All the shells and clay pigeons take up a lot of space in my cabin as it is. Here you try it, I'll operate the launcher."

I killed about a dozen clay birds before I noticed the Captain becoming a bit anxious. It was his toy, his hobby but I was shooting better than he had.

"Wow." I handed the shotgun back to Wolfgang. "I have forgotten how much a twelve gauge kicks." I rubbed my shoulder after he took it back.

"Yes." He cradled the gun in his right arm as he patted his right shoulder with his left hand. "That's why I wear this shooting jacket with a shoulder pad sewn into it."

"Speaking of kicking." I stared at the expensive double rifle resting in an aluminum carrying case with a foam insert in it.

"Be my guest." Wolfgang handed me a box of cartridges. "Would you like a target?"

"What?" I asked.

The captain pulled out an empty wine bottle with the cork stuffed back into it.

"No, thanks."

I shot the hefty double rifle only twice and it kicked much harder than the shotgun had, so my shoulder complained loudly after the second shot. I could only imagine how bad the kick would have felt if I had shot it sitting down at a shooting bench. As I handed the rifle back to the captain, I noticed that it had extensive game images engraved into the metal; it was quite a beautiful rifle. English double rifles are a rare find since most of them were built around the turn of the century when manufacturers were changing from black to smokeless powder, and the market for them was quite small. I guessed this rifle might sell for ten thousand, maybe more since it was in almost perfect condition.

"Are you done?" Wolfgang asked.

"I think so. This is actually quite a life, you know." I stared out into the churning water off the boat's stern.

"I love this life," Wolfgang agreed. "I don't think I'd be truly happy anywhere else."

"Have you done this all your life?" I leaned against the railing and looked at him. "I have this mental picture of you learning the sea when you were a teenager and working your way up to Captain."

Wolfgang chuckled for a second as he thought out his answer. "Actually I worked in an office until I was thirty; I was an engineer who designed mechanical systems for large ships."

"I never would have guessed that." I was a bit surprised. "How did you get here?"

"I've always loved the ocean." Wolfgang shifted a bit, moving the shotgun to his left arm. "I got my first ship by knowing somebody who knew the owner, and I worked my way up to this ship in a few years."

"What about the rest of the officers?" I pressed, maybe a bit too much. "Cook told me that all of you stay together run after run, isn't that unusual?"

"Not if we all like this ship, and the setup we all have here." The Captain became a bit agitated. "If we go on to other ships, it's hard to set up a skeet range, or drag along large collections of junk. As long as the company is happy with our profit, they let us stay here, where we can all be comfortable."

"Like I said, I'm a little jealous of it all." I almost believed what I was saying. "It's so peaceful, no one to bother you most of the time; I'd love a setup like this, most people with half a brain would."

"I'll take that as a compliment." Wolfgang appeared to accept me as an admirer.

"I meant it as a compliment."

"Well, I must clean my guns and wash up before dinner. With all this salt in the air, I have to keep them all spotless and well oiled." Wolfgang began walking towards his cabin, then turned to face me again. "My cabin is air conditioned and my gun cabinet is humidity controlled, but this sea air can be devastating if I don't clean and oil them right away."

....

"How long will we be in Long Beach?" Yoshihiro pushed two blintzes onto his plate as he looked at the Captain.

"We have to wait for a shipment of transformers." Wolfgang sipped his wine. "They wired us that the shipment will be two days late in arriving at the dock, so we will wait for it."

"They're heavy, so we have to delay loading the rest of the cargo on the ship until they come," Jonathan added. "I suppose we'll also have to rearrange the containers on deck to accommodate the heavy load."

"I guess you may have three or four days to play in Los Angeles if you like?" The Captain continued.

"What's good to see?" Yoshihiro looked at me. "You lived there, is there anything to do in Los Angeles other than being chased by armed criminals?"

"There's all the Hollywood tours, there's a whole bunch of fine museums. The selection of restaurants and live entertainment cannot be equaled on this coast." I thought for a second. "There's lots of tour companies who will tailor where they take you to your interests."

"Maybe you could take us a few places." Yoshihiro glanced at me, his expression didn't say anything. "If you have the time, that is."

"I suppose I could give you a quick tour of a few places." I guessed he wanted to talk to me off of the ship. "What are you two interested in?"

"Hollywood," Maiko spoke up quickly.

"Sure." I glanced at Yoshihiro, then at Maiko. "I guess I could take you two on a couple of studio tours."

"What about the rest of us?" Jonathan asked.

79

"You want to see the movie stars, too?" I wondered what was behind his request. Maybe he just wanted to keep an eye on me.

"Why not?" Jonathan shrugged. "I've been here several times and have never had the time to sight see."

"Anybody else?" I glanced around the room. For this meal all ten seats were filled; Cook had also joined us, sitting down to eat.

"Not me." Cook shook his head. "I already have my tour of restaurants picked out."

"I think I'm staying here." Wolfgang swallowed a forkful of pork. "Someone needs to make sure the ship is still here when all of you get back."

"So, I guess it's just the four of us, then?" I asked the group.

I looked at Yoshihiro, he didn't mind, at least he didn't say anything then.

9

Katz' call

All that is what brought me to this moment in the silent cabin. I've been arrested for shooting someone before, but on those occasions I actually did shoot someone. It was always in self defense, so I always got set free eventually, but this time it felt different. First of all, I didn't shoot anybody, secondly, I didn't even want the man dead, I needed him alive to help me figure out who was who on this boat. Now, not only wouldn't I be able to question Yoshihiro, but I would be dragged from here with no chance to scrutinize the people I was sent to observe; damn.

Wolfgang had the engineer tie me up in the dining room; he assumed the police would take me away before dinner was served. The crew didn't want to miss Cook's last meal before he was scheduled to take off on his tour of fine eating establishments in the greater Los Angeles area. They not only tied me to a chair with rope, but they also handcuffed me as well; I thought it odd that they'd have handcuffs. Someone hovered outside the door guarding me, but I never could figure out who it was. Whoever it was had one of the HK rifles from their armory, I knew this because I could see the barrel every once in awhile as the guard came close to the open door.

I sat in silence for about thirty minutes before the police arrived. After they showed up, I listened to several conversations between the Captain and a police officer before anyone came in to see me. Among the heated discussions, I could make out the captain shouting that he had a schedule to keep and he couldn't wait more than thirty six hours in this port. I thought I remembered him saying earlier he would be here three days. I couldn't understand the policeman who was speaking quietly, I guess the cop didn't want me to hear his answers to the captain's many questions. A key question of the captain's was why they

81

didn't take me away right then since I was a cold blooded murderer. That sounded a bit too much like the captain knew who actually did kill Yoshihiro, at least that was a clue for me. I supposed the cop was salivating over an easy murder case, one with me as the murderer.

"Well," a large plain clothes officer spoke as he walked into the dinning room. "Benjamin Katz , I thought you left the west coast."

A forensic team came with the investigating officers. I could see them scurrying around with the evidence bags every once and a while past the open door to the dining room.

"You have me at a disadvantage." I smiled at him. "You seem to know me, but I don't recognize you."

"I don't know you personally, only by reputation." His voice sounded a little too surly for my taste. "My name is John Billups, detective John Billups from the Long Beach police department."

"Good to meet you, John." I rattled the handcuffs behind my back and shrugged.

It was a friendly show that I wanted to shake his hands, but couldn't.

"You may not think meeting me is so great, Mr. Katz ."

"Please, call me Benjamin."

"All right, Benjamin." John took in a deep breath. "You have the right to remain silent, anything you say may be used against you in a court of law. You have the right to an attorney. If you cannot afford one, an attorney will be provided to you by the people of Long Beach, do you understand that?"

"Before you ask." I nodded. "I understand that, and I do want to make a phone call."

"We can do all that once we move you to the holding tank." John pulled a chair up and sat down right in front of my face. "Are you sure there isn't something you want to tell me before I throw you in jail?"

"I didn't kill Yoshihiro." I let out a breath, then continued. "I don't even have a gun, the captain has mine in his safe."

"Yes." John nodded. "He gave it to my partner."

"Wasn't fired, was it?" I was as emphatic as I could be, without acting like a wise ass.

"No." John noticed two men pass by the open door. "That doesn't mean you didn't have another one; you did bring a suitcase or two on board."

"I only brought one suitcase on board, and I only carried the one pistol on this ship." I nodded. "Maybe if you look hard you might find an automatic without my fingerprints on it around somewhere."

"How do you know he was killed by an automatic?"

"I didn't hear a shot, so it had to be an automatic with a silencer."

"We're tossing your room right now for it." John stared at me. He was enjoying his job, I could tell. "Do you wanna come clean now?"

"Not if I didn't do it."

"We'll see."

"Am I charged?" I asked.

Another detective appeared at the open door; he had a small thirty two caliber automatic in a plastic bag in one hand, and another bag with a silencer in it.

"Where?" John looked from the man holding the pistol to me.

"In Katz' cabin."

"Well." John stared at me. "I guess you are charged."

"What with?"

"Second degree murder for now. We'll see about other charges later, after we're through with the investigation."

John untied me, took the handcuffs off, and replaced them with his.

"Look," I called to the detective. I needed the cops to keep tabs on the rest of the crew while I was away in the slammer. "If I didn't kill that man, then someone else on board this ship did. Are you going to keep an eye on them while you're beating me with a rubber hose?"

"Don't tempt me, Mr. Katz ," John sighed again. "I don't think this crew is in any danger of disappearing."

"You underestimate them, detective," I insisted. "I think you should restrict their movements until you're sure I did it, which I didn't."

"I think we have the right killer." John looked intently at me. "You were here, you had the means; all we have to do is find out why you killed him."

"At this moment in time, all you have to do is let me call my lawyer." I had to get a message out somehow. "This is a formal request from your innocent suspect for his lawyer."

....

As I was pulled down the plank to the dock and the awaiting police cars, all with their bright flashing lights screaming, 'we caught the bastard', I saw Cassandra trying to talk her way in to see me; this was a good sign. She could help me get my message to my contact in Los Angeles. Although I had several possible means to get word to my government friends, I had to pick the least obvious if I wanted Cassandra to do it for me.

"Listen, John." I pulled back my handcuffed hand to stop the large detective. "That's my partner down there. The good looking woman trying to get through the perimeter." I nodded towards Cassandra. "If you let her talk to me now, I'll be a lot more cooperative with you."

"Do I hear confession?" John asked.

"No, you hear cooperation." Gees, I said I wanted my lawyer, why would I confess?

"Okay." John turned towards the gaggle of cops surrounding Cassandra. "Frisk her, keep her purse then let her come over here."

"Thanks," I said to the detective. Maybe Cassandra could make the phone call for me, I had to get word to Billy soon.

After Cassandra handed the cop her pistol, the female policewoman gave her a thorough going over, grabbed her purse then gently shoved her towards John and me. I enjoyed seeing her, maybe a bit more than I should have considering my present state, but I hadn't seen the love of my life in a while.

"What the hell is it this time?" Cassandra's expression hardened, her eyes narrowed as she glared at me in handcuffs.

"It's good to see you, too."

I leaned out to kiss her, but she wasn't in the mood for that.

"What did you do?" she irritatingly asked. I guess she was still pissed about the intense frisking.

"Nothing," I insisted back. "They have arrested me for murder, though."

"Murder,." She slowly sounded out the word.

"I didn't do it, and they don't have any evidence to prove I did, so I need to arrange bail and get our lawyer."

"I know the drill." Cassandra sighed. "What were you working on?"

"The insurance case." I gave her that, 'don't push me too hard' look. "You remember, Lloyds of London hired me to check into shipping losses."

"Right." She pretended to remember something about the job. "The high paying, low risk job?"

She did remember that much, I actually liked that bit of sarcasm. I'd have used it too, if the roles were reversed.

"Turns out it wasn't too low a risk, right?" I raised my eyebrows and shrugged.

"Right." Cassandra didn't seem too happy, but I think she was glad to see me.

"Something else," I quickly added. "Could you call a dry cleaner here in Los Angeles and ask if my suit is ready?"

"Say, what?" John interrupted me. "I don't think you'll have to worry about a suit, we have all the suits you'll need for a long time at the jail."

"Really," I repeated, staring at Cassandra who gave me a barely perceptible nod.

"Can you loan her some paper and a pen?" I could tell the detective was somewhat mystified by all this. "Your minions took all her stuff."

"Sure." John shrugged as he tore off a page from his notebook and handed it and his pen to Cassandra.

"Okay."

Cassandra didn't know why, but she did know the call had to be made. She wrote the number on a piece of paper which she then folded in her left hand. She put her right hand on my left arm and quickly kissed me. I could see the wheels turning inside her head, she wasn't stupid; she knew that phone call wasn't about some damned clothes, and she knew that number wasn't our lawyer. She turned and walked back towards the herd of cops on the dock.

"Wait a minute," John called for a uniformed officer with a radio. "Check out this number and tell me what it is." He scribbled down the phone number I had given to Cassandra.

"It's a dry cleaners in central LA," the officer answered after a few moments.

Cassandra turned and stared at me again, she was mulling over all this. The number was a real dry cleaners, and the cops could stake it out for then next decade and see nothing more than a dry cleaners. The trick was that the phone was tapped for this week only and my friends were listening for my call.

"Call them now and leave a message so you can pick it up tomorrow," I said, catching Cassandra's eye.

She kept a straight face as she turned away and continued to walk towards her car. The cleaners would even have one of my suits there, waiting for whoever showed up to get it.

"You're such a clotheshorse." She paused to get her stuff from the woman cop.

Cassandra knew something else was going on. She would do what I asked, but I knew I would be given the third degree from her as soon as I was out on bail and I wasn't looking forward to that.

"I want a good suit to go home in."

"I can almost guarantee you won't go anywhere tomorrow." The detective shook his head. "Unless you get arraigned tomorrow, then you'll only go to court."

A short distance away, Cassandra turned to look at me from beside her car. I saw that she was troubled by all this; she had to wonder what the hell was going on. I had to get permission to tell her soon, or she might decide not to trust me and I couldn't let that happen.

John sounded exasperated; he and his partner, Sam, had taken turns trying to get me to confess for the past two hours. "What about all that cooperation you promised?"

"Where's my lawyer?" I asked. "You know, questioning me after I ask for my lawyer isn't kosher," I added.

"Like I said, your shyster hasn't gotten here, you must not be one of his favorites." John leaned into my space. "And, I know the rules better than you do, so shut the hell up about what I can and cannot ask you."

"He's not one of my favorites either, but I pay him well," I admitted. "Has anyone else come down here to see me?"

"What?" John leaned back in his chair. "What makes you think anyone cares about you, except us?"

"I have lots of admirers, John. I'd like to have you as a friend too." I knew I couldn't stall much longer, they would soon tire of my rambling and dump me in a cell for a few days.

"I don't chum around with murderers." He slapped the table with his palm.

"I'm not a murderer and if you'd let me out for a day or so, I could prove it."

"Not likely." John rolled his eyes and gave me a loud sigh. "Like I've been saying for hours, you aren't going anywhere other than jail for a long, long time. I'd be willing to bet a month's salary on that."

As he finished speaking, the door opened, to reveal four men in suits hovering outside. One of them motioned for John to join them.

"Maybe your ass is fried now, Benjamin." John appeared happy at the thought.

"Or, maybe not," I had to add; I kind of guessed what was next.

"What the fuck is going on!" I heard John shout outside the door.

The door opened again, then two men entered and sat next to me, one on a side. I didn't recognize either of them. The man to my left unlocked my handcuffs, while the other man flashed an FBI badge at me.

"My name is Conner, and this is Bernstein." Neither one smiled.

"Langley got your message," Bernstein whispered.

"This is pure bullshit!" John was in a heated argument with his lieutenant as the two agents pulled me through the squad room. John's partner, Sam, moved directly in front of the three of us.

"John's right, this is pure bullshit and we're not going to let this go easily, I don't care what the brass says," Sam spoke in a low, angry tone. "I know this scum bag killed that Japanese fellow."

"We don't care." Bernstein leveled a stare at Sam. "These are orders for us as well as for you; we're going to follow ours, and I strongly suggest you follow yours."

"Listen," I interrupted, looking at the two agents at my sides. "I promised I'd cooperate, so I am. I'll do it quick."

"Are you sure?" Conner gave me a cautious expression.

"It won't hurt, and I promised." I looked at Sam, then spoke quietly and quickly. "That guy who was killed was an agent of the Japanese government. The German crew is smuggling something in and out of Asia, Europe, and here, it may be drugs. They were afraid the Japanese agent caught them, so they killed him and planted the gun in my room. Search all the cargo containers and I'm sure you'll find lots of stuff that shouldn't be there. And, while you're doing that, you might find a reason for one of them to kill the agent."

"You're full of crap," Sam whispered.

"If I were you, I'd search the cargo like he said," Conner replied. "He may be a dumb ass private dick, but he usually knows what's going on, that's one reason why we're taking him away."

"Trust us, he's not that full of crap," Bernstein added. "Usually."

We left quickly. Billy Sullivan was waiting for me in a large black Suburban.

"What took you so long?" I was a bit peeved, especially at the dumb ass private dick comment. "I think the man we want is the cook from that boat, is he still on board?"

"No." Billy shook his head. "Besides the woman, he's the only one who has left the ship."

"Why are you here anyway?" I looked at Billy. "I thought you had more pressing cases that would keep you out of Los Angeles for the next week or so."

"Leave it to you to get arrested for murder." Billy wanted to grin, but held it back. "What's a poor middle manager to do?"

"Cut the crap, something else brought you here."

I didn't feel like getting a hard time about the past six hours, it wasn't funny. At least it wasn't funny yet; maybe in five years I might smile about it.

"You have to remember, Double O Seven is a fictitious character, and the license to kill isn't real." Billy re-grew his smirk. "At least not for you."

"I'm not Ian Fleming either." I briefly glanced out the window. "Why are you here?"

"A case from France sort of spilled over into yours." Billy took in a deep breath.

"How so?"

"We think the scientist is going to deliver a set of encryption keys to the Russians that could compromise almost every covert operation in Europe." Billy stared directly at me.

"So, it's that serious now."

"Yes."

"Where did Maiko go? It must have been devastating for her." I wondered aloud.

"She went to the Japanese embassy in LA."

"Good." I took in another breath. "Where is the cook?"

"Right now, he's at the Four Seasons enjoying a better meal than I've had in the last two years," Billy answered.

"I take it he's being followed rather closely," I asked. Billy nodded. "I shouldn't get near him yet, I added, "since he thinks I'm still under arrest."

"Do you think he set you up?" Billy asked.

"No." I thought for a second, "I think the Captain set me up. I think he bought the insurance story, but he was afraid I might talk to the Japanese agent, and then put one and one together and bust his smuggling scam."

"So, he killed two birds with one stone." Billy agreed.

"I'd like to see Cassandra."

"Is this the time she meets me? You know if you two do get married, I think she'll figure it all out. I suppose your official request should get higher priority," he said. So, Billy appeared to have thought this out, he must have felt the time to confront the 'Cassandra' issue was now.

"We live together now, and I'm sure she suspects something." I thought my request was high priority.

"Why is that?" Billy was surprised.

"That phone call to the dry cleaners in the middle of the night wasn't suspicious?" I shook my head.

"Maybe it was." Billy looked at me. "But, doesn't she trust you?"

"She does," I sighed. "But I always tell her the truth, especially when I get arrested."

"Yeah." Billy looked out the front windshield. "I suppose you've never been arrested in this country when we've had you on assignment."

"I have to do something soon," I insisted.

"I could tell her something." Billy turned around to face me. "Management has given the go ahead to recruit her, so I guess it's all right to tell her something."

"No," I quickly replied. I knew tonight was the time to do this thing. "I need to tell her."

"You want me there?"

"Alone, please."

10

The hare and hound

"Hello, Lepus Detective Agency, Fred Lepus speaking," Fred cleared his throat. He had been napping in his office with his feet up on the ratty metal desk in the back of his office. While his full-time secretary and some time girlfriend, Cathy Rumson, was out of town visiting her mother for a week or so, Fred was indulging himself more than usual. In Cathy's absence, Fred liked to think of his time as free time; he slept more often during the days, played more during the nights. The problem with such a schedule was that cash flow dwindled.

"Mr. Lepus," a male voice on the other end of the phone said, then paused. "I need to hire you for a job."

"That's why I'm here." Fred snapped to mental attention, at least as much as Fred Lepus could.

He had no paying job for the last month, and he needed new tires for his car, even the spare was bald.

"I need you right now," The caller said nervously, his voice slightly shaking.

"Now is fine." Fred felt a rush of greed. "I don't have a pressing case ongoing right now."

"Good," The man said. "Can I see you today?"

"Sure." Fred pulled a pad of paper from the middle drawer in the old desk, along with a pencil. "You could come to my office if you like."

"No," The man finally replied.

"Okay." Fred tapped the pad with the tip of the pencil. "Where?"

"Can you meet me at an office?"

"Sure, where?"

"A lawyer's office?"

"Sure, which one?"

"Livingston and Associates."

"I know them." Fred relaxed into his chair. "I do work for them."

"I know," the man on the phone said. "That's where I got your number."

"I see." Fred didn't want to bite the hand that feeds. "What do you want me to do?"

"Nothing that hard." The man sounded a little less nervous. "I need a place to hide out for a day or two and have a meeting with an associate without anybody knowing about it."

"I have to ask at least some questions about why." Fred didn't want to get into anything that might land him in jail.

"It's not illegal, or anything."

"Then, what?"

"My wife." The voice trailed off for a second. "My wife is going to file for divorce, and I need to talk to my lawyer without her knowing about it. She's been having me followed."

"Ah." Fred was happy; there would be no police trouble from this.

"I have a lot of money I inherited, and I don't want my wife taking it from me," the man added, all in a rush. "You have to find a safe place for me and my lawyer to talk in private."

"I think I know just the place." Fred thought quickly.

"Great," The man said. "Can you meet me tomorrow, sometime in the early afternoon will be best."

"I thought you said this afternoon?" Fred was confused.

"I know," The man muttered, "I just remembered, I can't do it today."

"Tomorrow at lunch will be fine," Fred cleared his throat. "Finding a safe place won't be cheap, you understand."

After a five second pause, the man answered, "Yes, how much?"

"How long will you need this safe house?"

"Not more than three days," he answered. "How much?"

"I think five hundred will work for the place, food, and protection." Fred was grinning so much in anticipation that his jaw hurt.

"Five hundred will be fine."

"Can you make that in cash?" Now, Fred's heart was racing, he could buy four new tires, not retreads and he'd have plenty of folding money too.

"I think I would prefer paying you in cash anyway."

"That will be more than fine," Fred quickly agreed, the man had already hung up.

11

As best as I can remember

It was a little after nine at night as I stood on Cassandra's front porch to wait for her to open the door, shifting on my heels and looking around; it was an almost perfect moment. A crystal clear sky settled above my head, well, maybe one ot two small clouds darted by in the sky. However, some pollution hung in as a low haze since I knew there had to be more visible stars than that. I have to admit, the smog has gotten better over the years, but it's still persistent and annoying. I didn't recognize the scent of any of the countless flowers which filled my nose; I never have been that good at guessing botanical odors which is not a skill that's high on my to learn list. The temperature was a pleasant seventy two which is not bad for late August. Ah, I could hear Cassandra trundling towards the front door. As she peered through a small diamond glass pane in the center of the door, I could see her shocked expression.

"How did you get out?" She managed a smile for me. "Our lawyer is on a fishing trip. His office said they were sending a messenger up to get him and it would be seven in the morning before he could possibly make it there."

"I didn't escape, if you're worried." I sounded nervous; I was nervous. "Can I come in?"

"It had to do with that number you had me call, didn't it?" Cassandra stepped back as I came in the foyer. "I left your message on their answering machine."

She was both cautious and upset; I couldn't tell which at first.

"Can we go sit down?" I asked. "And, it's a dry cleaner, and, I do have a suit there."

"Of course," she said, flatly. She stepped into the living room, wrapped in a terry cloth bath robe. I hoped she was naked underneath, it had been a long time since I had seen her.

"I'd like to assume our lawyer sprung you ahead of time somehow; are you ready to tell me what this is all about?" she asked.

"Sort of." I hugged her and gave her a long kiss.

She hugged and kissed back for a while, but she didn't act like her heart was in it. I slipped my arm under the robe and around her waist; she was naked. She let go of me and stepped back two steps to better focus on me.

"Don't be cute this time, Benjamin."

She sat on a large sofa in the expansive living room. I had only been in that house a few times before, but I remembered that large glass wall facing the ocean. A raised floor surrounded the furnished area, making a true conversation pit. Only one step difference separated the raised area from the sunken living room, but it created a noticeable effect. Most of the sofas and chairs were arranged so the guests would have a view out the window.

"What I mean is, I do owe you an explanation," I said with a sigh.

I stared out the window into the darkness, struck by the moonlight reflected off of the Pacific Ocean in the distance. I could see a thousand pinpoints of lights from all the ships near the shoreline; her parents' house was parked near the top of a hill about two hundred feet above sea level with a commanding view of lower neighborhoods as well as the beach and the ocean.

"I'd hope you'll explain this one to me." She relaxed a little. "I was headed for a hot shower and bed."

Boy, did that sound good. First the truth, maybe at least most of it.

95

"Do you remember what I told you about my experiences in the Marines?" I stood, then paced a bit in front of her; too much adrenaline.

"How's that connected to being arrested for murder?" She tightened the sash on her robe. "Look," she sounded upset, "I need to get some clothes on if you're going to get into a long thing right now."

"I won't be long, I promise," I said, but she ran down the hall and into her room to change anyway.

I had barely enough time to wander to the large glass wall and begin to stare at the dark expanse of ocean before Cassandra ran back into the room. She had hastily thrown on old jeans and a plain white tee shirt which hung loosely over her chest.

"I feel better." She sat back down on the end of the sofa.

"Let me do this," I nervously babbled on, so I wouldn't chicken out.

"Okay." She didn't know what to make of all this yet. "I don't remember much about your time in the Marines because you never told me much. I asked you about all those medals you have in that frame you keep in the back of our closet, but you never did tell me."

"I fought in the regular Marines only for six months, then Captain Sullivan took me out for Special Operations because I showed promise."

"Promise?"

"I was semi-suicidal at the time," I replied. This was feeling difficult, but I couldn't stop.

"Remember, I was still dealing with my mother's death, and I directed my anger outwards. I tend to like myself too much to beat up on myself, at least for longer than a minute or two." A defeated sigh slipped out from me. "I liked getting into fire fights, and I fought like a maniac most of the time."

This wasn't coming out like I wanted.

"I was young, and invincible, at least I thought I was invincible."

"Right." Cassandra's expression had turned slightly impersonal, she was getting analytical on me.

"Billy wanted someone who performed like me for the operations he was in charge of," I quickly added.

"Is that Billy Sullivan, the same guy who finds jobs for you?" Cassandra looked critically at me. "Isn't he the one who got you this insurance company job you're supposed to be on right now?"

"Yeah."

"What type of special operations?"

"Special Operations." This was making me a little more nervous than I had thought it would. "The kind that the CIA is involved with."

"Are you telling me you were a CIA operative? Are you working for them now?"

She stood up from the sofa, then sat back down with one leg folder under her, hunched up slightly with an unbelieving expression on her face.

"No." I chose to ignore the second question for now. "I was a marine grunt, I just worked for them."

"Hey, wait a minute." Cassandra's face brightened, as if she had just discovered sliced bread. "All those overseas jobs; you're working for the CIA right now, aren't you?"

"Well." I wanted to get to that sticky point later in the conversation. "Can I continue my story?"

"You are, it makes a lot of sense now, that bullshit story you told me about the first time you met Fred Lepus."

"Oh, that." I didn't want to go off on a tangent, this was going to be bad enough for me anyway.

"Is he in the CIA too?" Cassandra pondered that for a second. "He can't be."

"No, he can't be, and he isn't!" I felt disgusted at even the thought of that idiot working for the CIA.

"It all makes so much sense," she repeated. "Why didn't you tell me sooner?"

"I'm trying to tell you right now."

"So, tell me."

"It all happened when I was on a mission with Billy Sullivan, it was only my third mission for him."

"In Viet Nam?

"No, that was the problem, we weren't supposed to be there."

"Where, Cambodia?"

"Worse, China."

"What?"

Cassandra bolted up off the sofa and began to pace, she was soon on the other side of the room from me, as if to get some distance. I had kept all this from her for several years, and now I was dumping all this information on her, all at once.

"We had American troops on mainland China? Are you telling me the truth? What the hell were you doing there?" Cassandra retorted, her voice rising.

"It had nothing to do with the war in Viet Nam," I spoke slowly.

I knew she had been opposed to the war there; she marched in several anti-war demonstrations. I sort of agreed with her, but this had nothing to do with that, at least not directly.

"We were sent there to extract a Chinese scientist from over the Cambodian border, then move him quickly back into Cambodia. From there we'd chopper him to Viet Nam, then fly him to Japan, and then here." I tried to calm her down a little. "It was supposed to be a simple little extraction mission."

"Well, will you at least tell me how the hell this relates to your showing up here instead of being in jail?" She stood still, her hands on her hips. "You still work for the CIA, don't you. I know you do, so don't lie about it."

"Yes," I reluctantly answered, "I need to tell you my way, though, please."

"Okay, you went on this simple mission to China and I take it something went wrong."

Cassandra let her hands fall to her sides as she let out a breath. I could see that she was forcing herself to breath calmly.

"Fifteen of us started the mission. When we picked up the scientist we were sixteen. Captain Billy Sullivan was in charge, and I was the second ranking noncom."

I might as well be honest about this, even though I don't like to relive it, ever.

"They set us all down by helicopter right on the Chinese border near the Mekong River. We were in Laos, not far from Burma; none of us should have been there, but the Chinese have agents in this country, even right now as we speak, so it's all part of the game."

"I get the picture." She sounded exasperated. "They spy on us, we spy on them; that part's okay."

"Anyway."

"Didn't a gaggle of Americans stand out?" Cassandra interrupted. "I mean all of you in Marine uniforms and loaded down with M16s and gear?"

"We wore peasant clothes and I carried an M14 because I was the sharpshooter; the rest of the troops carried AK-47s. All but Billy and I were Asian-Americans and each spoke a different dialect from the region so we could blend in better if we needed to."

Memories had surfaced now and maybe if I did this fast it wouldn't be so bad for me. After the initial debriefing, I have always refused to go over that mission in detail in my mind or with anybody else, I can compartmentalize it better if that way.

"Besides two of our faces not looking right, we could pass at a distance for the locals. Anyway, we went up the Mekong river ten miles into China where we met the scientist. We traveled at night, it took over six hours to make the ten miles. The Chinese intercepted a radio transmission from our extraction crew and pinned them down for thirty minutes in Laos before they killed them all; four choppers were blown up and eight men died in Laos. We got one transmission from them in code telling us we were on our own."

"What was the B plan?" Cassandra sat back down on the sofa, her expression was intense.

"Plan B was to head up the Mekong River, at least close to it, staying away from the population. We were supposed to then cut into Northern Burma and radio for an extraction. If we had to, we would head to Bhutan, then to India."

"How far was it? Didn't you have transportation?" Cassandra asked.

"It took ten days and nine nights, and we only had transportation part of the way," I sighed. "We ran into several army patrols along the way and had to scramble off course to get away. The problem with plan B was that a lot more civilians were around than we thought there would be. We lost nine men in the three firefights we had with the Chinese Army right before we were able to scramble out of their country."

"Nine of your companions dead?" Cassandra's anger and disbelief had started to dissipate. "What did you do with the bodies? You couldn't take them with you, could you?"

"We had to strip everything off that might identify them, and leave them there," I sighed. "All of us had to fight the urge to bury them or drag them along with us, but, as you said, we couldn't take them with us, so there wasn't enough time to do much else anyway. Our mission objective was to deliver the scientist to the United States, and that's what we had to put first."

"I suppose since the dead soldiers were Asian, the Chinese wouldn't necessarily know what country they were from." Cassandra put her hand on my leg.

"It didn't matter." I picked her hand up and held it briefly, then let it go. "They knew their scientist was missing, and we all assumed they knew the U.S. was responsible. So, after the first firefight, the Chinese Army started searching in earnest for us. Probably three hundred regular army troops were looking for us by the time we managed to cross the border out of China. Billy came up with the idea of finding drug traffickers and paying them with the gold we took with us."

"Gold?"

"British gold sovereigns are good everywhere in the world, and we took about a hundred of them with us," I said. "It's common practice, and it saved our asses. The drug smugglers drove us into Burma, then tried to steal everything we had left, including the Chinese scientists since they figured out he was the most valuable thing we were carrying. That gun battle lasted two days and attracted the Burmese army."

"What about the extraction in Burma?" She asked.

"By that time we had no radio, and no way to contact any of our people for the extraction."

"Would the Burmese government be any help?"

I guessed the stress was showing on my face, it's easy to gloss over a pitched gun battle verbally, but not emotionally.

"No." I shook my head. "They'd have turned us over to the Chinese Army. By then everybody important in the region knew about us, and that the Chinese would pay a lot for our hides and even more for the scientist. We had to then fight what was left of the smugglers as well as a ten man contingent of the Burmese army. We were able to kill most of the smugglers; we guessed that perhaps five men were left when the smugglers quickly headed out of the mêlée. Most of the Burmese headed after them, leaving two soldiers to take care of us."

"How did you get out of that?"

"Most of my friends who were left, died in the fight with the drug smugglers."

I needed to quit soon or I'd be all too depressed for a long time again. It had taken me the better part of six months to get over that fight. At least I could sleep again, I don't know if I'll ever be able to forget it.

I continued, "We hid, and left our dead buddies for the two soldiers to find. All we took from our dead was all their identification and some of their ammo. The Burmese soldiers stripped them of everything else and finally left to join the other Burmese troops. That was the hardest thing to watch, the hardest thing I ever had to watch. Only Billy, the scientist and I got out alive; we made it to Tashigang, Bhutan, where we were met by another extraction team to fly us out. The terrain we had to cover was the damned Himalayas. It was hard going."

"Sweetheart." Cassandra looked like she was about to cry; hell, I felt like it too.

"It's all right now." I hugged her, harder than usual.

"Why did you tell me that?" she finally asked.

"That was the worst mission I've ever been on; that's the one I had to tell you, to get it all out of me, all these things I've held back from you, all in one horrible story."

"I'm glad you finally told me." Cassandra sunk the side of her face into my chest. "I love you, but."

"What's the but about?" I sort of demanded.

101

"That war story tells me a lot about you that I didn't know, I mean part of what made you the man you are today, but it doesn't tell me why you're a spy," Cassandra answered thoughtfully.

"That answer might take a little longer." I collected my thoughts. "I guess I'm still trying to decide why I took up that occupation."

"Maybe we should have that discussion now," Cassandra softly said. "I'm still here, sitting next to you because I love you, you have to know that."

"I love you too and that's the reason I'm telling you all this, but I need to finish." I lifted her face and implored her with my expression to let me go on.

"Finish it? There's more?" She looked up at me like I was a bomb about to explode. "Go ahead."

"In spite of that miserable China mission, I found that I liked the work I did for Billy Sullivan," I said. "It was serving my country, and I enjoyed the excitement of the missions. I was able to use not only my military skills, but I also had to use my regular old wits to keep myself and my buddies alive; a lot like I do in our present job."

"That sounds like you." Cassandra briefly grinned.

"I got a field promotion to Lieutenant, and they insisted that I stay in the reserves when I mustered out. The rest of the world, including you, thinks I'm long out of government service. But I'm not."

"So, what are you? Are you still a spy, or are you a detective?" She shook her head.

"Not all the time." I anxiously smiled.

"Can you explain that?" She blinked rapidly. "This is getting stranger and stranger."

"I'm a contract agent, my nonofficial cover is that of a detective." She didn't understand. "I don't work directly for the CIA, I'm a contract officer. I don't get a paycheck from them, I'm not on a normal Langley personnel list, but I do work for them from time to time. When I do a job for them, they pay me as a private investigator as well as paying me reserve pay."

"So, that's why you get those overseas assignments working for banks and big companies?"

"Right." I shrugged. "I'm a captain now in the reserves and that's how they list me unofficially. On DOD paper, I'm a reserve officer in the Marines. The long term benefit is that I'll be eligible for a military retirement when I'm old and gray."

"Something to look forward to, I'm sure." Cassandra relaxed a little as she began to pace in front of me.

"And, I was on one of those jobs when I got arrested."

"Is that how you got out?"

"It pays to have friends in high places."

"Although this is complicated." She sat down on the sofa, "I'm a bit miffed at myself for not figuring it out before; all the clues were there, but I never put it all together."

"You would have eventually." I smiled again. "You were getting suspicious of those overseas jobs I wouldn't take you on."

"I know." She nodded emphatically. "I was determined that those jobs would stop as soon as I finished school."

"That part of our relationship." I thought for a second. "The part of our relationship where I head off to France or Germany without taking you along or at least tell you the real reason why, that's over; from now on you'll know everything."

"Is there anything else you want to tell me?" She stared at me like I wasn't Benjamin any more, for a second, then she smiled quickly.

"Nur, daß ich Deutsch sprechen kann. Ich kann es gut, auch sprechen"

"You speak German" Cassandra's eyes opened a little wider?

"Y Español, también. Anche parlo l'italiano abbastanza per andare d'accordo completamente bene, de même que parlant en forme de français un natal. Hva passer ikke inn i resten av dette taler Norsk, I gjetter ikke alt gir perfekt mening."

"Was that last one Norwegian?" Cassandra sounded impressed.

"It was," I agreed.

"You're turning out to be one damned bundle of surprises. " She didn't sound happy. "Can you tell me about this job you're on now?"

"I want you to know one thing that isn't a surprise, and that hasn't changed, is that I'm in love with you and I want to marry you."

"But, who are you?" A worried looked flickered over her face.

"I'm still me." I reached out to her, she let me take her hand. "It's these little details about my life that I'm telling you now that you didn't know; the real me you've known for a long time."

"Okay." She squeezed my hand. "Let's get back to the question I asked you, what's this job you're on right now?"

"You mean the job that we're on now?" I looked right into her eyes.

"Hey, you're not getting me involved." She bolted back up. "They assigned me to a class for the quarter and I start teaching next Tuesday. Besides, I'm not a spy, I'm a private investigator. What's more, I haven't even decided if that's what I want to be when I grow up."

"I thought you liked working as a detective?" I was surprised. "You like the variety and excitement, as well as working with me, I thought so."

"I do." She took in a deep breath and let it out slowly. "This is a lot to take in all at once."

"I'm sorry." I continued to hold her hand, she was still letting me. I guessed that was a good sign. "I was planning to tell you soon, but this whole case I'm on blew up and that moved my time table up."

"When were you planning on telling me?"

"As soon as I got permission to." I sat back into the sofa some more. "As long as I work for the government, they're the ones who make the decision to let me tell an outsider what I do for a living."

"I suppose so," she sighed. "But, I'm not exactly an outsider."

"That's my point too." I nodded. "I've been in negotiations with them to let me talk to you for six months."

"Obviously, they agreed, since you're talking now."

"Exactly."

"What about my class I have to teach?" She was coming around, maybe she'd agree to work with me.

"It's Tuesday, you have a week with nothing to do, and it shouldn't take longer than Sunday to finish the whole job." I snuggled closer to Cassandra.

"I suppose I could get someone to take notes for me; I was supposed to go to a big meeting of all the new instructors tomorrow." Cassandra hugged me. "I'm always easy when it comes to you."

I wanted to tell her everything but I had to wait until Billy had all the background work done; there wasn't that much more I was keeping from her anyway.

We were both startled by the front door knob loudly turning and the dull thud of a body pushing it open. Billy and his companions barged in the front door.

"I hate to break up this homecoming, but I thought I'd better interrupt you two before it became embarrassing."

"Why didn't you lock the front door?" Cassandra looked up at me.

"Because I'm stupid?" I didn't let go of her.

"I have to agree with you about being stupid." Cassandra leaned towards my ear and whispered. "I need to get a bra on, this is awkward."

"As soon as there's a chance, make a run for your bedroom, I'll lay down some cover fire for you." I softly stroked her bare arm.

She smiled back at me, then glanced at the three other men, now sitting together at the dining room table in the next room. "Who the hell are those three?"

"The one on the right is Billy Sullivan"

"I'm glad to finally meet you." Billy stood up and grinned at Cassandra.

"Who are the other two?" She asked.

"These are Conner and Bernstein," Billy answered.

105

"Who's who?" Cassandra asked.

"It doesn't matter," Conner answered.

'Okay." Cassandra's eyes darted quickly from Conner to Bernstein.

"What's happening?" I asked.

"Your cook has made contact." Billy motioned for me to join him at the table. Cassandra followed me.

"She's helping me from now on," I said as Billy studied Cassandra for a second.

"Fine." Billy moved his gaze from the floor to me. "But, we're not paying you any additional for her help."

"That matters less than the problem you and I have been discussing." I looked back at Billy. "You know the paperwork that seems to be stalled, I've told her everything."

"I hate to interrupt all this, but we got a tape of the cook's conversation at the restaurant," Conner said, to move our attention to more pressing matters, at least to him they were more pressing. "The next meeting will be in Washington, DC."

"Is it with the target?" I asked.

"We don't think so," Bernstein answered. "But, there can't be too many more links in this chain."

"You two will have tickets for a flight to National by the time you get to the airport." Billy noticed that Cassandra looked happy.

"Let me arrange someone to take notes for me tomorrow." She ran down the hall towards her bedroom. "I'll call the lawyer and leave a message for him not to bail you out tomorrow."

"Are you sure?" Billy sounded concerned, but I wasn't.

"As sure as I can be," I whispered. "I'm serious, she's a package with me from now on."

"Are you sure?" He repeated.

"Damned sure, sure as a heart attack. She's gotten me out of too many jams to ignore her value as a partner, I'm sure you've already done a background check on her anyway."

"She's good as gold as far as that's concerned but a lot of other details need to be attended to." He was thinking more than he was telling me. "Good luck, and I'll be in touch in DC in a day or so."

"Are you going to pick up the cook?" I asked.

"Not yet." Billy shook his head.

"His ship will not be going anywhere after those cops search it and find the drugs or whatever," Conner added. "So, I guess he'll stay here for a while since he's no longer needed."

"Do you think the encryption keys are the only thing they're up to, and do you think the North Koreans are in on it?"

"Why?" Billy asked. "Don't you?"

"No, I don't." I slowly shook my head. "I can't pin it down, but the North Koreans don't belong in any of this."

"So, you think it's the Russians?" Bernstein asked.

"They're the old standby for everything, but I'm not sure yet."

I wasn't sure of anything except that the crew of that freighter were up to no good.

"I got someone to take notes for me." Cassandra walked back to the dining room. "So, this thing had better be over in a week."

"What about my pistol?" I asked.

"We couldn't get it for you," Bernstein said. "Maybe in a few days, but not in time."

"Can you get weapons for both of us in DC?"

I was particular about what I carried, Billy knew that.

"Not one like you carry, but I can have a forty four with a holster for you at your hotel right after you check in," Billy answered.

"Don't forget Cassandra," I added. "She carries a small three eighty."

"No problem." Conner wrote himself a note. "We'll have some cash and clothes for you too."

"Pack." Cassandra's mind raced from thought to thought. I only hoped some of those thoughts were kind towards me. "I need to pack."

She ran off down the hall to her bedroom.

"The plane leaves in two hours." Billy reminded me.

"She'll be ready sooner than you expect."

107

12

The box rebellion

"Do you know how many pissed off city attorneys and judges are in Long Beach this time of night?" John Billups glanced at his partner, Sam.

"Right." Sam looked out the side window of the police car at the hulking Veracruz. "It's not night any more; if you haven't noticed, the sun is coming up."

"This involved a German shipping company, the Indonesian government and the U.S. State department," John continued.

"It shouldn't have," Sam sighed. "It's a murder investigation in our jurisdiction and they called us, not the other way around."

"Whatever," John grunted. "We have the search warrant, five cops and two dogs so let's do this."

"You're pissed that the FBI took Katz away from us." Sam got out of the car.

"You're damned right I am." John glared at his partner.

"Well, they did, and there's nothing we can do about it right now." Sam started walking towards the crowd of cops and dogs. "Let's find out if there's any drugs on this ship."

"Do you see that man near the gangplank?" Sam pointed.

"I think this won't be a surprise, do you?" John walked away from their car towards the ship.

"There's three of them making a break down the gangplank," Sam shouted, "Stop them!"

"I'll call for more backup," John barked as he raced back to their car.

. . . .

"I have to protest this whole thing." Wolfgang stood his ground on the main deck. "This is not your area of responsibility. This ship is registered in another country, this isn't even your country on the deck of this ship."

"Is this an embassy?" John stared at the captain.

"Of course not, but this is the territory of another country," Wolfgang insisted.

"Unless this is an embassy, and you're an ambassador, this ship is part of the city of Long Beach and I can serve this search warrant, and I can throw the whole lot of you in jail if you try to stop me," John glared at Wolfgang.

"I will protest this with my consulate, and I will have you fired," Wolfgang insisted.

"Fine, fine." John pushed the captain out of his way. "Protest all you want, but stay out of our way while we go over your ship."

"What are you searching for?"

Wolfgang changed his position, his voice lowered and sounded more accommodating.

"Read the warrant I gave you." John turned to look at Wolfgang. "I don't have to tell you anything. Just keep in mind, a murder took place on this ship."

"And you have the man who committed the murder," The Captain insisted. "What else is going on? Do you think some of my crew carry some drugs?"

"Maybe." John glared at Wolfgang.

"Who told you drugs were on my ship?"

"A little murderer bird told me."

John motioned for the two dogs and their handlers to come onto the main deck.

"Who?" Wolfgang looked surprised. "Katz ?"

John ignored the captain as he motioned for five police officers to head towards the living quarters. "Search all the spaces in that area. The dogs will go in after they do a quick run through the cargo spaces."

"You believe what Katz said? Anything he said?"

Wolfgang walked quickly to keep up with the detective.

"I don't." John turned and stared at the captain. "But, the FBI thinks he knows what he's talking about, so we're here."

"The FBI?"

Wolfgang was to be stunned for a second. John made a mental note of his reaction.

"The FBI makes you nervous?" John studied Wolfgang. "Why would that be?"

"They don't make me any more nervous than you do," Wolfgang said, awkwardly. "I mean all these police rummaging through all our personal materials is enough to make anyone nervous."

"Why?" John pursued the question. "If there's nothing illegal here, nothing to hide, why should you be nervous?"

"Well." The captain thought for a second. "If one of the crew has stashed away some marijuana that we don't know about, that could cost this ship and our company a lot of money."

"Listen," John carefully said. "If all we find is a few personal stashes of pot, I promise we'll be out of your hair as soon as possible, and you can go sailing off in a few days."

"Fine." Wolfgang fell silent for a while. "That's all I was worried about."

"If you have any more concerns, please talk to my boss." John pointed to a shorter man in a suit walking towards them "His name is Henderson, Captain Henderson."

"Billups," The detective captain spoke to John. "Is this the ship's captain?"

"Yes, he is." John stepped aside. "I need to help these guys search, if you won't need me."

"I don't think so," Henderson replied. "You can go ahead, the captain and I will wait right here together."

"Hello, sir." Wolfgang extended his right hand. "My name is Wolfgang Krull, I am the captain of this vessel."

"Hi." The police captain shook his hand. "Everybody calls me Henderson. My first name is Edwin, but I never did like that name, so call me Henderson."

"Well, Henderson." Wolfgang looked around the main deck, noticing at least twenty policemen on his ship, and ten more on the docks. "How long do you think this will take?"

110

"I'm not sure."

"Has your department ever searched a freighter before?"

"Yes, yes they have." Henderson turned to face Wolfgang. "The last time it took four hours, so I suppose we should be out of here at least in another three, maybe sooner, unless we find something."

"There's nothing to be found on my ship." Wolfgang took in a deep breath. "Nothing illegal, that is."

"Sir." A uniformed police officer ran to the captain.

"Find something?" Henderson asked.

"Barney did it again," The officer sounded quite proud of his dog. "We had to drill through an inner container, but we found uncut heroin."

"Barney deserves a steak dinner for this." Henderson smiled.

"Barney?" Wolfgang looked confused at the captain.

"Barney Fife is our best sniffer dog." Henderson glared at the ship's captain. "He's the best in the state, I'd bet a month's pay on that."

"We don't check our containers when they're loaded on the ship," Wolfgang spoke rapidly. "They are locked and sealed before we load them."

"Maybe you should have taken a more active interest in what you let on your ship, since you're going to be arrested for it." Henderson nodded at the uniformed officer who pulled out a pair of handcuffs.

"Do you want to take in the rest of the crew?" The officer attached the hand cuffs to Wolfgang's wrists.

"I think that would be the right thing to do." Henderson studied Wolfgang. "Maybe one of them might be willing to talk to us about all this and what it may have had to do with the murder on this ship."

....

"So, maybe Katz was right." Sam stared at his partner, John, looking for a reaction.

"Maybe." John didn't change is sour expression. "These German guys were into lots of stuff, weren't they."

111

"As soon as the captain called in the customs folks, this case had to get complicated," Sam observed. "Did you see that case of old ceramic jars? That guy from customs said that if they were all real, they might be worth a million or so."

"About an eighth of those cargo containers below deck had smuggled shit in them." John stared out the front windshield of their police car. "I wish they hadn't thrown us off the ship so soon, I'd like to see what they found in the Captain's cabin."

"Whatever it was, the FBI sure sent a lot of men in there." Sam started the car. "It had to be worse than the six cases of surface to air missiles we found in one of the container boxes, I wonder what it was."

13

Have it your way

"Are you sure I can trust those guys to lock up my parents' house?" Cassandra asked.

She settled into her seat. This was a early morning flight and we were both showing our lack of sleep.

"Hey, how can you doubt their honesty." I tightened my seat belt. "After all, they put us in first class, didn't they?"

"That doesn't attest to their honesty, just to their expense account." she smiled back at me.

"It's so good to be back with you." I kissed her briefly.

"I know," she sighed. "I love you, and I've missed you too."

"Well, in December you're finished with school." I grabbed her hand.

"I can head off before Christmas," Cassandra said. "I give the final the last week of class."

"Really?"

I mentally made a list of places we could go on vacation with that much free time around the holidays.

"I thought you could go with me to Paris to visit my parents over Christmas week." Cassandra said quickly, as if she wanted to get that suggestion in before I said anything else.

"Paris?" I asked. Paris with the love of my life sounded fine to me, but with her parents?

"Tell me about the case." Cassandra squeezed my hand tightly, she wanted to change the subject.

"Simple," I whispered into her ear. "The NSA intercepted a message in a North Korean code stating that someone was to meet a computer scientist to receive classified information. We have to intercept this meeting and find out who the scientist is, and stop the transaction."

"The NSA?" Cassandra needed some clarification.

"National Security Agency," I answered. That's the agency that monitors communications all over the world."

"Including here?"

"Here too."

"What scientist, and what information?" She asked.

"If they knew that, they wouldn't need my help." I tried not to look self-important.

"Well." Cassandra considered whether she should hit me or not. "Anything else?"

"Yes," I sighed. "I don't think the North Koreans are involved. I think if they are involved at all, they may act as a go between for another country, maybe the Russians like Conner said."

"What makes you think that?"

"First of all, nothing was as it seemed."

"Go over that again?" Cassandra asked.

"I got that impression when I was on the freighter. I guessed that the officers were smugglers since they were able to invest in expensive hobbies as well as the fact that they all stayed on the same ship year after year without a break." I settled into my seat some more. "The captain probably had several hundred thousand invested in a gun collection, and he could afford to take an illegal hunt in India; that junket had to cost him tens of thousands in bribes alone. The communications officer had a twelve thousand dollar computer as well as a huge expensive collection of old code books."

"Code books?"

"To each his own." I shrugged. "Some people collect stamps, some collect dolls, others collect old code books."

"That does sound like a well off crew on that freighter." Cassandra arranged herself in her seat so she faced me.

114

"I didn't get to know any of the other officers, but I bet they were also rich from all the smuggling."

"So, what do those smugglers have to do with the spy you're seeking?" Cassandra stopped herself. "Never mind, that was a stupid question."

"The man who was killed was a spy of sorts, and I never did find out what he was looking for, or what he found." I tried to relax as our plane took off. "Maybe he was searching for smugglers, but I don't think so."

"So, what else was there?"

"The cook is a criminal of some kind, or at least a messenger for the smugglers," I said. "So, maybe the Japanese agent knew something about the cook that could help us, see what I mean? Most of the officers on that freighter were smugglers, but the real problem for us was someone else, doing something else. "

I spent the next half hour telling Cassandra all about the rest of my few days on the freighter.

"So, where's the mistress of the dead man?" Cassandra asked.

"Billy said she went to the Japanese embassy." I thought I saw where Cassandra was headed. "Why?"

"She also might not be as she seemed."

Cassandra was good at this game.

"I assumed if she went to the embassy, she'd try to get back to Japan as soon as possible." I shrugged. "But maybe not. Besides, why didn't the cops nab her as a suspect?"

"Perhaps you should have someone ask at the embassy to see why she went there," Cassandra said. "And, ask the cops about why they didn't grab her; the mistress is always a good suspect in a murder, at least as far as I'm concerned she is."

"Are you trying to tell me something?" I leaned into her a little more.

"Not necessarily." Cassandra patted my shoulder. "But, her association with the dead man isn't that clear, is it?"

"The two passengers both acted as if she were his mistress and he was worried I would spill the beans to his wife somehow." I tried to remember as much as I could.

"He might have been genuine." Cassandra sunk back into her seat, leaning her head on my shoulder. "But, instead of him being the one in charge of that relationship, the woman may have set him up to get onto that ship, then to keep an eye on him for some reason."

"But if she's the real courier, then who are we chasing?" I thought for a second. "No, I still think we have the right person. I saw the notes from the conversation the cook had with our fugitive, it has to be a meeting with a computer scientists they're setting up."

"I didn't read any of that." Cassandra was fading, both of us were tired. "Did the cook mention a computer scientist by name or occupation?"

"Not exactly."

I sensed that she was headed somewhere else. Working with a partner can be a benefit, she sees things differently, and sometimes clearer than I do.

"There might be something else going on with that woman." Cassandra yawned. "I need to try to get some sleep."

"Me too." Yawns are contagious.

"When I have enough rest to think again, you and I will have to have a conversation about this bombshell you threw at me." Cassandra patted my leg as she tried to get comfortable in her seat.

"Sure," I answered. "I've wanted to tell you for the past year, but they wouldn't let me."

"What changed?" Her eyes were closed.

"We're getting married, and I will not continue to work with them unless you know about it."

"I'm glad for that, but we still need to discuss a few more issues."

"Like what?" I closed my eyes. "Who will be my best man?"

"No," she whispered. "Like, will I still be your partner in all your jobs."

"I knew I fell in love with you for a good reason."

"I'll take that as a yes."

"Yes."

116

I had used the National airport metro station since it opened up in nineteen seventy seven. The Doubletree hotel nearby was relatively new. The only demerit I could give the place was the incessant, mind deadening music that droned in the background. Why couldn't a high class hotel play classical music in the public areas? Well, at least it wasn't the Grand Old Opera.

First class air, a first class room, now what was to become of my low class opinion of government jobs? It was a pleasant blip I supposed. I handed our key to the hotel bellman who led us to the elevator.

"That was a nice touch," I whispered to Cassandra. She was holding my hand. "Billy booked us here as man and wife." I held her hand.

"He also sent along some early wedding presents," The hotel employee whispered.

"You're not a bellman, are you?" Cassandra stared at the man carefully.

"You're not a real bride, either." He looked ahead as the elevator reached our floor.

"Is Mr. Sullivan reachable yet?" I asked him as he opened the door to our room.

"Not for another hour or so," he replied, "maybe around lunchtime."

"We'll most likely be out looking for our target before then." I glanced at my watch, the local time was nine thirty in the morning.. "Could you give him a message?"

"Sure thing."

"Tell him to locate Maiko, the mistress of that dead Japanese agent."

"Sure thing." He dumped the suitcases. "Be careful." He left and closed the door.

Cassandra grabbed one of the suitcases, threw it on the bed and opened it.

"That's the best thing about doing one of these government jobs." I opened the other suitcase. "You get a lot of first class backup."

"I swear this looks like something from your collection." Cassandra held up a small automatic pistol.

"Let me see that, please." She handed me the pistol. "It is from my collection."

"At least they sent one of my shoulder holsters." Cassandra dragged it from the suitcase. "You know, I had a hell of a time finding a holster that would fit a woman and not look too obvious."

"Not that many women carry concealed weapons, you know." I glanced at her.

"This gun's a little smaller than mine." She took it back. "I remember seeing it in your safe."

"It's an older Beretta," I said. "It shoots the same as your Walther, but I guess it's smaller and easier to hide. If you're interested it's a model 1934 Beretta."

"It shoots, doesn't it?" She looked at me and grinned. "I could use a better selection of clothes now, that means shopping."

"Maybe later."

"Deal." She strapped on the holster and stuffed the extra clip in her coat pocket. "I guess I don't want to know how our guns got here."

"It's probably not that hard to figure out." I pulled out my Smith and Wesson in it's shoulder holster. "I strongly hinted that he have someone break into out apartment and get our stuff."

"That's a comfort." Cassandra pawed through the contents of her suitcase. "This is all my stuff, I don't think I like knowing some burley spy has fondled my underwear," She sighed loudly. "You don't suppose any of our neighbors saw these guys in our apartment, do you?"

"Probably not." I thought for a second. "They might have come in at night when everyone was asleep or they could have come in during the day as a repairman or the pest control guys."

"I suppose." She shrugged her shoulders. "I guess they know what they're doing."

"Ah, here's the presents." I pulled out an eight and a half by eleven envelope and dumped it onto the bed. "Lots of cash and information, just what I wanted for a wedding gift."

"So, what's the information?"

As Cassandra sat on the edge of the bed, she turned to face me.

"I think the person we need to catch here is Anthony Zimmer, he works at Livingston and Associates, a law firm here."

"Not THE Livingston, I presume?" Cassandra wanted to smile, but didn't.

"Maybe an associate."

I slowly shook my head; lame jokes are sometimes not worth it. Not that I pass them up, but there's a note of embarrassment to them.

"The keys to a rental car are also here so I guess we go now. It says our car is in the parking garage, it's on the third level, space fifty nine. Are you ready?" I asked.

"Hey, an hour's sleep on a plane in the past twenty four," Cassandra said. "You bet I'm ready."

"First, I'd like to take a quick shower." I looked around the hotel room. "I haven't had a decent shower in a few days."

"In that case, do you mind if I join you?" Cassandra coyly pulled out a change of clothes from her suitcase and lay them on the bed; the change of clothes wasn't the only thing that got laid on that bed.

. . . .

"Say, this is a nice car." Cassandra slipped into the passenger side of the new Lincoln.

"A bit big." I adjusted the wheel and the seat position. "I think it's Billy's idea of another gift."

"Why, what do you usually get?" Cassandra pulled papers out of the envelope to read while I drove.

"A compact POS." I glanced at the address in front of me.

"Do you know where you're going?" Cassandra asked.

"Get on US Fifty and stay on it heading to Dulles. The office is right off Fifty, before we get to the Town and Country Golf club," I replied.

"I have to comment on all these top secret stamps all over everything here." Cassandra paged through the papers in her hands.

"That means you can't ever talk to anyone other than Billy and me about this stuff."

I turned on the radio and began to look for the classical station. I knew they had several in this town, and I was determined to find one of them; I had to cleanse my auditory palate real soon or I would go crazy.

"Are all our cases going to be this kind of stuff?" Cassandra put the papers in her lap.

"No." I drove the car out of the parking garage. "Just a few snooping assignments a year, it's not that bad."

"I guess I'll have to take your word for now." She returned to reading the papers. "This Anthony Zimmer person is sort of a legal secretary, not a lawyer."

"What else? We should be there soon."

"He's a naturalized citizen," Cassandra read. "He immigrated ten years ago, and became a citizen only two years ago."

"What country did he come from?"

"Germany."

"More of those Germans." I looked at Cassandra. "Coincidence?"

"Maybe." She scanned some more papers. "These documents say that they suspect this unknown scientist of wanting to sell encryption keys." She glanced up at me. "What are those? Some sort of algorithms that allow somebody to read an encoded message?"

"Exactly, sweetheart."

I knew she would fit right into this job.

"Those keys must be important." Cassandra ignored my last comment.

"Must be." I focused out the front windshield. "I think that's the office building up ahead on the left."

"That's not a big parking lot they have," Cassandra said. "Maybe our car would stand out there."

"You think so?" Sarcasm doesn't fit me that well. "Maybe we could park in that shopping center right after it, then walk there."

"I'd better lock all this stuff in the trunk." Cassandra gathered all the papers together.

"No." I pointed to the page on the top. "All the pages with that top secret stamp need to be separated out."

"Okay." Cassandra started separating them. "Why? Do we have to eat them?"

"See, I'm not the only sarcastic one."

"You were due."

Cassandra handed me the pile of top secret stamped pages.

"Do you know all the important stuff on these?" I asked.

"Most of it?" Cassandra sounded worried. "I didn't know I had to memorize it."

"You didn't." I looked out through the front windshield. "Just so you remember it for the quiz coming up later."

"One of the talents that's gotten me through grad school is my photographic memory, " She said. "Now what?"

"Hand me the briefcase in the back seat, it's a paper shredder. Not exactly high tech, but effective."

"Paper shredder?" She stared at the strange container in the briefcase.

"Sort of."

I opened the rectangular metal box, slightly larger than the papers I put into it. I closed the box, securing it with four wing nut like fasteners. I then pushed a red button on top of the machine and placed it back into the briefcase.

"All right, what does it do?" She couldn't contain her question.

"Acid melts the paper so there's no way anyone could reconstruct what was on the pages, let alone the paper itself." I motioned for her to get out of the car. "But, the rest of that stuff we do need to lock in the trunk, including the paper melter."

Cassandra pointed to the office building while I locked the trunk of the car.

"You saw the guy's picture." I started to walk towards the lawyer's building. "We wait for him to show up or leave, then tail him."

"So, we stay near our car?" She asked.

"Right." I pointed to a bench near the edge of the parking lot. "I thought we could sit there for a while."

"Do you see that car that pulled into Livingston and Associates?" Cassandra pointed.

"That beat up old rust bucket?" I noticed that it did seem familiar.

"Lepus!" We both exclaimed at the same time as Fred Lepus got out of his car and ran into the building.

"What's that mealy little worm doing here?"

I was a little pissed seeing him there, mostly because I didn't like him. I had run into him for the first time a few years ago while I was on a brief assignment here. Fred Lepus was a lazy, fly by the seat of his pants private investigator who had stumbled into a high profile case Cassandra and I had worked on in California. His mistakes almost cost the life of our client as well as his own.

"He's not all that bad." Cassandra patted my shoulder. "Maybe he's working a job for one of the lawyers."

"Think again." I pointed at Fred and Anthony Zimmer rushing out the door and diving into Fred's car.

"Maybe you're right," Cassandra said as we both raced back to our car.

"The world isn't small enough to explain this to me," I stammered.

I quickly pulled our car out of the parking lot.

"I see him, just keep driving."

Cassandra gave her full attention to Fred's rust bucket car.

"Which way?"

"Looks like he's headed back towards DC on Fifty." Cassandra stared in Lepus' direction. "What're those two up to?"

"Can I please beat the answer out of Lepus when we get him alone?" I was half serious, well, maybe more than half serious. I didn't like the prospect of him screwing up another case we were on, especially one we were doing for the CIA.

We followed Lepus for about ten miles, I kept our vehicle about three car lengths behind his most of the time and Lepus never noticed he was being followed. I never could figure out how this inept detective could keep talking customers into giving him money to investigate anything, let alone doing it for more than five years.

He merged onto the Beltway and headed north, still with no idea I was behind him. Lepus took exit eleven and headed towards McLean on Dolly Madison Boulevard. What a name; I'd hate to have a business, let alone a house on a street that's so lame. He turned south on Great Falls, then took a quick left onto Chain Bridge, into a residential area. What was he up to? He took another left, right across from a bunch of athletic fields then pulled in front of a row of middle class houses.

14

A Hare's breath away

"What kept you so damned long." Anthony Zimmer jumped into Fred Lepus' rusty fifteen year old finned throwback. "I've been waiting in my office for two hours for you to show up."

"Keep your shirt on." Fred started up his car and buckled his seatbelt. "I got here didn't I?"

"Yes, but not in good time," Anthony complained. "You're late."

"No time like the present, and for the time being, you're in good hands for sure. Like I told you yesterday, I'm used to cases like this." Fred proudly sat up straighter in his seat as he maneuvered his car onto US fifty and headed east.

"I got a call from you yesterday that said you needed to hide out from your soon to be ex-wife's lawyer." Fred looked at Anthony. "It was your voice, wasn't it you?"

"Yeah." Anthony leaned back in his seat. "It was."

"I know you, don't I?" Fred carefully studied the man next to him. "I remember seeing you in the office when I do jobs for those lawyers, I saw you the last time I went to pick up my check."

"I can't say I remember you there," the man replied. "But a lot of people go through that office."

"Why didn't you use one of the lawyers you work for?" Fred was paying attention to the traffic which was beginning to build up more. "If you don't mind my asking?"

"I like to keep my personal and professional life separate."

"I see," Fred agreed politely. "But, I do work from time to time for your law firm, so in my case you're not separating work and home life, but mind you, I don't mind and I certainly won't say a thing to the lawyers you work for."

"Sure, thanks." Anthony looked out both sides of the car, then turned around to see the traffic behind them.

"What're you looking for?" Fred asked.

"Are we being followed?" Anthony sounded nervous.

"No." Fred laughed as he looked into his rear view mirror. "I've been a professional investigator for close to ten years now, and I can tell when I'm being followed, and we're not being followed."

"Are you sure?"

"Do you want me to drive around for the next hour and see if anybody follows us?" Fred was annoyed with this person questioning his abilities. "I'll do that if you want, but the results will be the same. No one is following us now, and no one will be following us in an hour. If you want to kill an extra hour, I'll do that, but I'll charge you for the extra hour and the gas."

"Never mind." Anthony looked out the side window. "Just get me to the house."

After a few minutes of silence, Lepus had to say something, "How long do you think you'll need the house?"

"Why?" Anthony had been carefully observing other vehicles as they drove through congested traffic.

"No reason, just curious."

"I have to hide out for a few days, but not more than three."

"The owners will be back in two weeks, so you can stay there longer than three days if you like." Lepus was eager to please.

"I don't think it will be longer than three days," Anthony replied.

"Will you be alone?"

"Why?"

"Nothing," Lepus answered, "If you plan on having any wild parties, I should warn you that the neighbors might call the cops."

"No wild parties." Anthony chuckled; that was the first time today that Lepus had seen him smile. "I guess the only person who'll be there will be my lawyer."

"Is he coming today?" Fred asked.

"Maybe late this evening or early tomorrow," Anthony answered. "We are going to decide on a strategy, then, I guess I'll have to go on and do it."

"Is the divorce that bad?"

"What?" Anthony spun his head to face Fred. "I'm sorry, I was thinking about something else. Yes, the divorce, there's a lot of money involved, and, well, you know how complicated it gets when there's a lot of money involved."

"Yes, I do," Fred replied. Doubts entered his mind; how could a legal secretary have a lot of money? Zimmer said he inherited it, but if the family was that rich, why is he a legal secretary? Maybe the wife was rich, but then again, why would he work?

"Speaking of money," Fred continued.

"Right." Anthony pulled an envelope from his inside coat pocket. "Here's the fee we agreed on."

"Thanks."

Fred took the envelope and tucked it under his rear end.

"It's all in cash, like you asked for," Anthony said, with satisfaction.

"Thanks." Fred patted the envelope with his free hand. "We're almost there."

"These are nice houses." Anthony stared out the window. "What does this friend of yours do?"

"He runs an electronic retail store in Alexandria." Fred turned down the final street. "He and his wife are in Europe for a vacation, and like I said, you've got two weeks to use the house."

"Does he mind?" Anthony asked.

"As long as you don't trash the place, he'll never know you were here." Fred smiled as he parked in front of a house in the middle of the block. "Leave it like you found it and don't make any big messes."

"What's that car doing behind us?" Anthony stared at a black Lincoln driving around them.

"It's probably nothing." Fred looked at the car as it pulled into a driveway a few houses down.

"Do they live here?"

"Most likely they do." Fred opened his car door. "Let's get into the house quickly before the neighbors get too curious."

"Sure." Anthony quickly followed Fred into the house.

"Maybe it would be best if you keep a low profile while you're here." Fred closed the door behind Anthony as they both walked to the back of the living room."

"I was planning to do that anyway." Anthony glanced around the room.

"The neighbors shouldn't be a problem," Fred assured him. "The owners told them that a friend would be coming around to water the plants, fill the bird feeder in the back yard and feed the fish."

"It should be fine then." Anthony nodded. "I'll even do all that crap for you."

15

Reunion

Cassandra had been quiet for several minutes; I wondered what she had been thinking, but didn't ask. I pulled into a driveway four houses down from Lepus' rusted hulk.

"We'll stay here in this driveway until he goes somewhere, then we'll turn the car around and park on the street," I said.

"Turn that radio down, everybody in the neighborhood can hear that thing," Cassandra insisted. She nervously glanced at the dashboard, searching for the volume knob.

"He must be pretty dense if he hasn't seen you by now." She shook her head. "Or maybe he has, and doesn't care."

"I'll go with the dense assessment."

We watched Lepus and Anthony Zimmer walk quickly from the car to the front door of the house. Lepus paused and looked carefully both ways before he unlocked the house door. He stared right through the car Cassandra and I were in, but didn't notice us looking at him.

"He didn't see us?" Cassandra sounded dumbstruck.

"He is consistent."

A few moments after Lepus and the man walked into the house, I pulled our car back into the street and parked it behind Fred's car.

"Maybe his eyesight is bad," Cassandra mused. "I've never seen him in glasses."

"I never thought about that," I mused. "I assumed the windows are tinted well enough."

Cassandra unbuckled her seatbelt. "What do we do? I say we waylay Lepus when he leaves."

"You read my mind."

The houses, in what appeared to be an upper middle class neighborhood, appeared to have been there for twenty years or so. All the houses were all red brick, or half brick and half clapboard; all were two stories. The front stoop of our subject's house had plantings around it which were head high and quite thick. I've never been interested in plants, or I'd have known the scientific name of the large green shrub I hid behind, but I don't think it ever matters.

The temperature was already in the upper eighties but the humidity was civilized so it wasn't that unpleasant out there. The dirt was fairly dry, it looked as if it hadn't rained in a week or so. Burrowing down in my shrub, I couldn't help but notice the stale smell of rotting leaves and mulch under the plantings, too bad no blooming plants were nearby to moderate the odor. It could be worse, my shrub could have been the bathroom for the family cat.

"I'll wait on the other side of the door," Cassandra whispered as she headed to the other large green shrub. "This kerria japonica will hide us just fine."

The wait wasn't long; Fred Lepus opened the door not five minutes after Cassandra and I settled into our hiding places.

"Remember not to answer the phone, let the machine answer." Fred was talking to Zimmer. "I'll come by here once a day to bring you groceries and take the trash bags away."

"No," Zimmer said. "I'll call you if I need anything."

"Suit yourself, make a list of everything you eat or use, so I can replace it."

"No problem," Anthony Zimmer replied.

As soon as Fred shut the door, I rose from my hiding place. Fred was shocked to see me, or maybe he was stunned to have a large revolver pointed at his head.

"I think we need to become reacquainted, Fred," I whispered, motioning with the barrel of my revolver for him to walk to his car.

"What the hell are you doing here?" In a split second he ceased to be shocked, and shifted into irritating annoyance.

I put my index finger to my lips to quiet him but Cassandra was less subtle; she pressed her pistol into the middle of his back and pushed him towards the car. I quietly sneaked a peek into the front window, to observe Zimmer slowly walking back towards the kitchen, oblivious to our small commotion on the front porch. I guessed he was more interested in what was to eat in the kitchen, which saved me from having to deal with another pesky complication right away.

"Get in the car," Cassandra whispered loudly to Fred as she spun him around; his posterior bumped against the rear door to his car.

"You too?" Lepus scanned Cassandra from her legs to her breasts where his stare moved up to her face. "At least I don't mind you pushing me around."

"Get in the car," Cassandra insisted a little louder. She didn't hate Lepus, but I could see the boob staring pissed her off a tad. Lepus slid into the rear seat of his old car, stopping to shove a small mound of trash onto the floor to make room for himself and Cassandra. I sat down in the front passenger seat and looked back at Fred.

"We don't have time for a lot of bullshit, so tell us why you brought Anthony Zimmer to this house?" I asked.

"I don't know what the hell you're talking about," Fred stammered. "I'm here watering the plants for a friend of mine."

Cassandra poked her finger into Lepus' chest. I guessed she was going to try the good cop – bad cop thing on him. "We followed you and Zimmer here from the Livingston and Associates office."

"No, you didn't." Fred pushed Cassandra's finger out of his chest.

"Yes, we did." I glared at Fred. "You never could tell if someone was tailing you. Tell us why you're hiding that man and we'll be gone, so you can get on with whatever penny ante job this is."

"I don't do penny ante jobs like you two," Fred sounded truly insulted.

"You also never manage to check out the clients before you get involved," I sharply observed.

"Like, what do you mean?" Fred shrugged.

"Like, Zimmer is involved with drug smuggling and murder."

"No way," Fred said, smothering a gasp. "He's a legal clerk."

"He was in Los Angeles two days ago meeting with a man from Indonesia, they worked a deal. Besides running drugs, the Indonesian's also involved in the murder of a Japanese cop."

130

I let that sink in; I knew he didn't like complications of any kind, especially violent ones.

"You're bullshitting me, right?" Fred looked from me to Cassandra and back to me.

Cassandra shook her head; he paled.

"You can keep all the money he gave you to hide him, all we want is some answers to help us with our case," I added. Money was almost the only thing on this guy's mind.

"How much is it worth to you?" Fred grinned nervously. "I know you have to be working on a good case if you can fly from coast to coast on short notice."

"I won't beat the crap out of you, that's about all I can offer," I replied. I didn't flinch, giving him my best poker face.

"I need more than that," Fred called my bluff.

"Okay, then," Cassandra interrupted. "Then, I won't beat the crap out of you either."

"Right." Fred smiled at Cassandra. "Like you could."

Cassandra rapidly raised her small three eighty pistol over her head, to aim the pistol butt at the left side of Fred's skull. I had to keep from grinning, Cassandra would not have actually hit him, but he didn't know that.

"Shit!" Fred fell to the side of the car away from Cassandra. "What're you doing!"

"I'm getting damned sick and tired of your jerking us around." Cassandra now pointed the barrel of her pistol at Fred's nose. "Tell us what we want to know or I'll ventilate your brain."

The safety was still on, and I didn't remember her chambering a round anyway.

"Damn it, you two never were a lot of fun." Fred cautiously moved Cassandra's barrel from his nose with the index finger of his right hand.

"All he wants to do is use this house for a day or so. He said he was hiding from his wife's lawyer and he needs to stay low and meet with his lawyer before anybody finds him," Fred reluctantly added.

"And, you believed that?" I asked.

"Sure, why not." Fred still sounded nervous. "Besides, he paid in cash up front."

"But he's not hiding from the wife's lawyer," Cassandra retorted. "He's hiding from the cops."

"Hey, don't press your luck." Fred glared at Cassandra. "Maybe you'd better beat it for now."

I was already a little tired of dealing with Fred. Besides, like the last time I met him, he was clueless.

"Why should I?" Lepus asked.

Fred was counting the ways he might horn in on a reward or a fee, I could sense that quite well. Fred felt his rear pocket, the envelope was still stuffed in it.

"Because we'll tie you up and throw you down the nearest sewer," Cassandra retorted. She winked at me when she said it; I was happy she had found something fun to do today.

"No, no you won't," Fred insisted. "I smell money in this, money for me."

"I smell the cops in this." I shot Fred a grave look. "Cops for you."

"You wouldn't." Fred sounded cautious.

"We don't care about Zimmer." Cassandra pushed Fred towards the door on his side of the back seat. "He's not an important source, we'll give him to the cops for the smuggling charges."

"I think you'd better get back to your office and let us contact the police to report him." I opened Lepus' car door. "Don't you think that might be the safest thing for you?"

"Maybe you're right."

Fred looked at Cassandra with a modicum of dislike.

"Pleasure meeting you again, Fred." Cassandra slapped Lepus on the back as she followed him out onto the street.

"Screw you and the horse you came in on," Fred hissed back at her.

"Speaking of the horse I came in on." Cassandra smiled at Fred. "Did you know Benjamin and I are getting married?"

"It's a small wedding," I quickly added, "family only."

132

16

No rest for the weary

"I think we should find a spot to hide out and keep an eye on this place to see who visits our friend in there." Cassandra reached for the passenger door on our Lincoln.

"Wait, you drive, I have to get in touch with Billy." I motioned for her to get in the driver's side.

"And, how do you propose to do that without a phone?" She walked over to the driver's side. "I don't see a phone in the car."

"When we work for the government we get to use some nice toys." I slipped into the passenger seat. I opened the glove compartment and took out a Zippo lighter.

"You don't smoke, do you?" She started the car and looked closely at the lighter.

"No." I pulled the top and bottom of the lighter. It expanded into a four and a half inch long transceiver. "It's not the most up-to-date, but we part-timers don't often get the latest gadgets. The microphone is on the bottom and the earphone is on the top. And on top of that, it's a secure transmission directly to the communications center."

"Well, if we aren't Maxwell Smart and his shoe phone," Cassandra chuckled as she pulled up to the end of the block.

"Wait here, Agent 99."

I asked that a team be sent to wait and to grab whoever Anthony Zimmer met with; I didn't think he was the person Billy wanted me to find. Cassandra and I were booked on a flight later that night to take us back to Los Angeles, but first we had to meet with Billy Sullivan.

"While we're waiting for the seventh cavalry, can we talk about this thing?" Cassandra turned and gave me a serious expression.

"So long as we keep an eye on that house, I don't see why not." I got out of the car quickly and retrieved the attaché case from the trunk.

"What was that for?" Cassandra quizzed as I got back into the passenger's seat.

"Just keep an eye on the house," I requested. I rummaged around the attaché case for something. It was there, I pulled out a small rectangular box with two switches and one light on top. It had small dark plastic windows on all four sides, as well as the top.

"What is that?" She asked, staring at the box.

"It'll tell us if somebody is listening to our conversation." I sat back down in the front seat of the car. "I understand they have a smaller unit now, Billy told me that it's a lot more sensitive too.

"How does this one work?"

"It sends out a high frequency wave which will be reflected from any parabolic listening devices nearby." I nodded towards the device for emphasis. "It also can detect radio transmissions emanating from a six foot radius, and it can detect laser transmissions."

"Laser transmissions?"

"If someone shoots a laser beam at our window, they can pick up the sound vibrations of our voices from the windows."

"Right," Cassandra said slowly, she didn't immediately believe that. "Are we safe?"

"As long as that red light doesn't come on, we can talk safely." I placed the box on the dashboard. "So, what did you want to talk about?"

"This CIA thing." Cassandra looked at the house, then back at me. "I've heard lots of bad things about this country's intelligence community. I study politics from an academic's perspective, and I've heard lots of bad things."

"I have, too," I agreed.

"Well, like what?"

"The CIA was formed after World War Two," I said, cautiously.

"I know the history," She interrupted.

"Both the Russians and the U.S. took the cream of the Nazi scientists and spies into the heart of their intelligence communities," I continued.

"Yes," she said. "Our rocket program was all Nazis in the beginning too."

I sighed as I skipped even more. "MK-Ultra."

"That sounds familiar." Cassandra glanced down at the seat for a second, then looked up at me. "Something about mind control?"

"It was more about experimenting with drugs and other techniques to control an enemy to make them do what you want without firing a shot," I replied. "All that might be a good thing, until you add that our government used our own soldiers and citizens for the experiments without their direct knowledge; they did the same thing with radiation."

"That's not right."

"No, it's not," I agreed. "Cutting to the chase, that's what some of us in the agency fight against whenever we can."

Cassandra stared at me.

"But, like any governmental agency, the CIA is run by politicians and as long as they can get away with something slightly wrong, they will," I added.

"So, what's the upside?" Cassandra visually checked the house, then returned her attention to me.

"You'll find out that there has been this big war going on for the past fifty or sixty years that nobody knows about except the folks in our business and a few others," I said.

"The cold war hasn't been going on that long," Cassandra observed.

"The uneasy peace after World War One, World War Two, Korea, Viet Nam, the Mid East, and so many twentieth century skirmishes, combined to form an ongoing, partly hidden series of conflicts. between power centers. World War One was the leftover hot spot from Europe's nineteenth century conflicts that had lasted for thousands of years. Mostly, the twentieth century battles have been fought well below the public's radar, but they're real; people like us fight and people like us die in the struggle."

"That sounds like a recruitment poster." Cassandra wrinkled her forehead. "Simplistic history."

"You asked what the upside is," I replied quickly. "The so called cold war is still a war and I for one am proud to be fighting it for my country."

"What?"

"Do you like this country, and the level of freedom here compared to other places in the world?" I asked.

"Well, yes."

"Are you willing to fight to keep it that way?"

"I see your point," Cassandra sounded thoughtful.

"All the negative things attributed to the CIA need to be stacked up against the good it does. As long as more positive things get accomplished, I'm happy and can live with the negative," I said. "Not that I like the negative, nor that I condone the negative, but more often than not the negatives are political decisions. The Agency provides information to our political leaders to make decisions, and some of us don't agree with those decisions, but it's not our job to make policy. Besides, the other side does worse, it's sort of like fighting fire with fire."

"Speaking of platitudes, two wrongs don't make a right," Cassandra replied. I could tell by her expression that Cassandra didn't like the simplistic nature of my comments so far.

"This is a war, not a game played by a bunch of civilized gentlemen," I insisted. "Mutually Assured Destruction suggests that we won't blow each other off the map, but meanwhile we fight fierce battles for political and financial territory beneath the headlines."

"Financial?"

"You bet." Ah, she was listening now. "I'll wager you didn't know part of the reason for the war in Vietnam was for control of the multi billion dollar drug trade."

"I can see that," Cassandra sounded thoughtful, I could see the wheels turning in her head. "I don't buy that as the only reason, though."

"My point is," I interrupted her train of thought, maybe I shouldn't have told her that yet. "Just like the wars that went on in Europe for hundreds of years, our East-West conflict is as brutal and the stakes are as high. The main difference is that the history books will never publish most of the important battles, nor the heroes of those battles."

"I see your point, I guess."

"I can do this job well, I think you can do it as well, or maybe better than I can." I smiled at Cassandra. "We have the skill, so I feel we should contribute; given the brutality of the other side, do we have a choice?"

"On a more personal note," Cassandra interrupted. "I think this job is way too cool to pass up anyway."

"Why?" I laughed, and I agreed.

"Think of us as an old couple in the retirement home," she sounded serious. "Think of all the exciting things we'd have done, and all the places we'd have gone, and all the stuff we'd have seen. Living a safe quiet life is fine, but not fine for me."

"You bet your ass," I laughed again.

This was the woman I'd fallen in love with.

"I will be betting my ass," she finally said. "But, it's going to be worth it."

We had talked for no more than ten minutes when a white van pulled onto the street and parked across from us. The van had a plumbing company logo painted on the side, and it looked as battered up as a company van should be. The driver nodded at me, then I started our car and drove away.

. . . .

Most people didn't know the size of the Langley complex. The road leading to it was a divided highway with two guarded entrances at which you had better produce the proper identification. To get into the main building you must pass through several more check points, at least one of which the casual visitor won't even see. Once inside, even the rodents are monitored. For people like us, there's more than one way to gain access without going through the more public entrance; after all, the whole purpose of setting me up as a simple detective was to disassociate me with this place.

"Gees, Benjamin." Cassandra pulled my sleeve to get my ear closer to her mouth.

"You'll get used to it." I nodded towards a desk ahead of us. "I have to sign us both in."

Cassandra waited patiently six feet away from me as I signed in. I motioned for her to come to the desk and sign in too. Billy was expecting us, so our wait was short this time.

"Here clip this badge on your chest." I handed her a visitor's pass. "These will get us to Billy's floor."

"I mean, walking right into the CIA building in Langley and going up to meet the boss, even if we did have to use the back entrance," Cassandra excitedly said, perhaps getting too wrapped up in the situation. "Getting in as a visitor wasn't that hard, either, but it's not the same. You signing in as Mr. Smith was strange, but all those guards let us right on in; this is too cool."

"Not to change the subject, but I did love seeing you strong arming Lepus."

I did, although I was kind of jealous, I wanted to do it. Maybe I could do it later, sort of a Christmas present to myself.

"You did catch onto the good cop – bad cop thing quickly," she said.

We were silent until we got to Billy's office on the third floor.

"We're here to see Mr. Sullivan." I took note of the receptionist, secretary, or whoever was parked behind a small desk in front of Billy's office.

"Come on in here, you two," Billy's voice boomed out of his office.

"We don't have too much time for chewing the fat," I said as Billy pulled three chairs towards the front of his desk.

"It won't take long," he replied to Cassandra. "You'll make your flight on time."

"Do we have first class tickets again?" Cassandra sat in the chair closest to the window.

"Since when did you get a secretary?" I asked in a teasing tone.

I sat next to Cassandra as Billy took the third seat in front of the desk.

"I'm a section head now," he beamed.

"Oooh, movin' on up to the big time." I grinned back.

"What's the deal with that Anthony Zimmer guy you sent a team to look after?" Billy's pleasant expression turned serious.

"I don't think he's the one that sent the message in North Korean code." I glanced around the room. "I think the mistress, Maiko, was the one."

"What makes you think that?" Billy looked intently at me.

"Just a hunch, actually, it was Cassandra's hunch first." I pointed in her direction. "My hunch is based on who Zimmer hired to find a meeting place."

"Lepus?" Cassandra broke in.

"Right," I agreed. "That dweeb is a dead giveaway that Anthony Zimmer isn't a high grade spy, but a go-between for the drug running Germans on the Freighter in Long Beach."

"If Zimmer is just a drug bust, I'll call the FBI to take over surveillance." Billy leaned over to his desk and made himself a note. "I take it you two will be searching for the Japanese woman."

"You bet." I noticed that Billy still kept the three photos of his wife and son on his desk, one picture was on the left and two on the right. He appeared older in the newest photo, but his wife didn't. His son was now about ten years old. The picture of our old squad hung on the wall behind his desk.

"Have any of your people kept an eye on the woman?" Cassandra asked.

"Yes," he sounded a bit uncomfortable. "But we lost her yesterday."

"Another reason to think she's the one we want." I looked out the window. Billy must not be that important a section head, his view still sucked.

"Did she go to the Japanese embassy?" Cassandra was also scrutinizing Billy's office.

"They didn't know who she was," Billy said, letting out a sigh. "We found out that she did go there and the security

139

cameras clearly show her walking in the front door and talking to the receptionist, then walking around a bit and using the bathroom."

"But?" I already knew the answer.

"But, she isn't even a Japanese citizen, at least not by the name on her passport." Billy shook his head. "They did some looking for us, and there's nothing in their database on her, nor in ours."

"I take it even you now think that we should search for her?" I asked.

"Not only you, but now the local cops want her since they now think she's the shooter." Billy looked at me, then at Cassandra.

"Why do they think that?" I answered my own question, "I bet her prints were on the gun, Cassandra was right."

"Right," Billy agreed.

"Benjamin." Cassandra glanced at her watch. "What do you want to do about lunch?"

"Is this a subtle hint to take me to lunch with you two?" Billy smiled at Cassandra.

"I suppose it's not that subtle." Cassandra glanced at Billy, then looked at me.

"Whatever." I shrugged my shoulders. "As long as it's included in the expense report, I'll even buy his meal."

"I'll drive," Billy interrupted. "You two could use some down time and I don't think four or five hours will matter that much."

"What about our stuff at the hotel?" Cassandra asked.

"I'll have your things sent to the airport, and we'll return the rental car." Billy scribbled down several notes.

"You think of everything," I commented.

"You two will have to come for a barbeque with Pamela and I when this is done." Billy's eyes quickly darted to the picture of his wife on his desk, then back to Cassandra.

"I'd love that," Cassandra said to Billy. "I want to find out the real dirt on Benjamin, the stuff he hasn't told me yet."

"I'm afraid that, besides this, there isn't much, he's actually pretty dull," Billy replied. He was so diplomatic, at least he was trying to be.

"Well." Cassandra didn't quite know what to say. "This whole CIA thing is a lot, you know."

"Did you do the paperwork on her?" I asked as we walked out of his office.

"Yes." Billy looked at Cassandra, then smiled broadly. "Congratulations, you're part of the family now, that is, if you want to join us."

"What does that mean?" She wanted me to say something.

"You're approved to be a contract agent for the CIA." I carefully watched for her reaction. "I guess the most important thing is that they'll start to pay you for your time now."

"That's a consolation," Cassandra said slowly. She looked quickly at Billy, then back to me. I couldn't tell what she was thinking, yet.

"I know the place for lunch," Billy said. He handed several notes to the woman outside his office, then asked her to make several phone calls for him.

"Where?" I asked. "Not that place near the capitol you always went to when I was here last."

"Probably," he sounded confused. "Which one were you thinking of?"

"Bullfeathers."

"That's the place," Billy answered. It was a relatively new place for him and I think he liked it because it was near the capitol and he could overhear all the congressional staffers blabbing the latest gossip; once a spy, always a spy, I suppose.

"Come on, let's go," Billy insisted.

. . . .

"So, who do you think that woman works for?" Cassandra and I stood on the sidewalk while Billy spoke to the waiter.

"We don't talk cases in public," I bent over and whispered to her.

"Sorry." She looked at me. "I guess I need a manual of dos and don'ts."

"They said if we sit outside we can grab a seat," Billy said.

We surveyed the tables spread around the front entrance. The restaurant was on First Street, south of the Library of Congress Madison building and within sight of a Metro stop. Even though it was late summer, the temperature was still pleasant. A light breeze blew from the west and the sky was partly cloudy. I knew why Billy took us here; this place was a favorite for the junior staffers from Capitol Hill. They liked to impress each other and their dates with how important they were, so, with so much self absorption around, we could have a conversation and not be listened to that carefully.

Following Billy's lead, Cassandra walked to a table more near the sidewalk than the restaurant.

"I wanted to talk to you about some details." Billy held a chair for Cassandra.

"Me?" She sat down, looking a little confused; I had told her not to talk business.

"Yes, not the case, but you." He sat next to her. "About your work for us. This is provisional," he began. "You need to go through a training course before it can be permanent."

"Training course?" Cassandra sounded overwhelmed, but reluctant to show it. "Like the girl scout camp my folks sent me to for five summers?"

"I don't think so." Billy noticed her mental state and kept the conversation as light as he could. "This one is coed."

"That might make it more interesting." Cassandra glanced at me and winked.

"Hey, wait a minute," I chuckled. "You're almost a married woman."

"How long is this camp, and when does it start? It can't start until after January."

"It starts the middle of next March, and lasts for at least six months," Billy answered. "I know about your school, and your deadlines and we want you to finish. If you need a week or so off for something, that can be arranged."

"You keep track of me?" She was upset.

"We didn't care that much until Benjamin told us we had to." Billy said frankly.

"What do you mean?"

"I told them six months ago that you and I would probably get married," I hesitated. "At least within the next twelve months."

"Maybe sooner." She smiled again at me as she reached under the table and patted my knee.

"I also told Billy that I wanted to work with you." I looked at Billy, then back to Cassandra. "That's when I made the request official."

"You made an application for me without telling me?" She didn't sound that mad, well, just a little.

"Sort of," I didn't speak loudly, but I think she heard me.

"What does 'sort of' mean?" She persisted.

"He initiated a security background check on you, and sought permission for us to recruit you," Billy interrupted.

"That wasn't so hard to say." Cassandra smiled at me again, ambiguously.

"I kept having trouble with the right way to tell you about my real business," I added. I was glad I could be honest now, she patted my knee again. I can be so insecure at times, but I knew she still did love me.

"Of course I want to join the team, or the government, or whatever you call it." She looked at Billy. "What do I have to do now?"

Billy opened his attaché case and pulled out a stack of papers for her to sign. "You'll be a contract officer, just like Benjamin, you'll be a part-time contract officer. You'll get paid based on an annual salary of thirty four thousand six hundred dollars."

"That's a lot of money for a first job." Cassandra looked at the top page. "Why?"

I was interested too, because, not that that should bother me, she might make more money than I did.

"We assume you'll be finished with your doctorate, and we pay higher for PhDs, especially when they have knowledge in areas we need." Billy glanced at me, maybe to explain more to me than to Cassandra.

"Areas like what?"

"What's your dissertation about?" Billy asked easily.

"Economics of Theocratic Governments in the Arab World." Cassandra nodded. "All of a sudden I understand."

"Me too." I glanced at Cassandra.

"Can I go over these and sign them later?" Cassandra gathered all the papers and handed them back to Billy. "Give them back to me after we eat lunch."

"Sure." Billy put them back in and closed his attaché case. "If you could finish signing right after we have lunch, that would be better."

"Nothing like enough time to decide the rest of your life," Cassandra replied, frowning slightly.

"We can have them for you before our flight leaves." I glanced at Cassandra, who gave me the slightest nod. "That should give you a few hours to read them."

Billy agreed, and he paid for lunch. All three of us got up and wandered off towards the Capitol building.

17

Just one more little thing

"Mr. Lepus?"

"Yes." Fred leaned back in his chair. His secretary wouldn't be back for another few days, so he was alone and his last client had been arrested by the FBI for unspecified charges, so Fred Lepus was always happy to speak to a prospective client.

"I'd like to hire you to pick up a letter for me," the voice on the phone said, it was a woman's voice.

"I charge more than postage, you know," Fred replied flirtatiously.

"This is a important letter, and it needs special attention." The voice remained bland, businesslike.

"I can give the letter special attention for a price." Fred stayed cheerful, he always needed some more income.

"You are working for someone named Anthony Zimmer." The woman had a slight accent; Fred thought she sounded foreign, maybe oriental.

"Not anymore." Fred sat upright in his desk chair. "He was arrested late today."

"Arrested?" the woman asked. "What for?"

"I don't know." Fred shrugged. "The FBI doesn't consult with me about their cases."

"FBI?" The woman quizzed.

"Yeah, the FBI," Fred reiterated. "They called me because Zimmer had my card in his wallet. They felt it was their duty to tell me he was arrested and that they are sending an agent around to see me in the next few days."

"Okay." The pause on the other end of the phone lengthened. "I think you should go out of town for awhile."

"Who are you?" Fred finally asked. "His lawyer?"

She must have something to do with the divorce Anthony told him about. Lepus had assumed that Zimmer's lawyer was a man, but the lawyer might be a woman. Katz might also be right and a divorce had nothing to do with all this. But, as long as a paying client breathes, there is a way. How much money was this case all about?

"No," she quickly answered. "I'm a business partner of his."

"What business?" Fred demanded. He smelled money, but he also got a whiff of trouble. "He was a legal assistant at a law firm here."

"We had a business arrangement," she answered. "You are the person he hired in Washington, DC?"

"He hired me and paid me in cash." Warning bells were going off in Fred's mind. Business partner, baloney; if she wasn't the lawyer, maybe she was a girlfriend looking for something. Maybe that something was money and maybe Fred could get a piece of it.

"Didn't he give you something to deliver in person to a resort in Mexico?" The woman's voice had an edge.

"I guess he was arrested before he could give it to me." Fred was salivating about the possibility of another large envelope full of cash.

"That's a possibility," the woman continued. "Maybe he hid it for you to find."

"That's possible," Fred thought quickly. "Maybe it's in the house I hid him out in."

"Is that where the FBI arrested him?" The woman asked. "Yeah."

"I think they would have turned that place inside out looking for evidence," the woman said thoughtfully. "Don't you?"

"They probably did."

Fred fell back into his chair, finally realizing he'd have to straighten up his friend's house before they came back from

146

vacation. Maybe he might have to even make repairs to it which could cost him money, money he had already spent on five new tires for his car.

"Maybe he left it somewhere else for you to find?" The woman's voice sounded a little desperate.

"Maybe he did," Fred thought quickly. "What if I do find it?"

"If you do." The woman took a long pause. "I'd like you to deliver it to me."

"Where, and how much?" Fred didn't waste time in establishing his concern.

"Baja California, and three thousand dollars."

"Three thousand plus the airfare and other expenses."

"Fifteen hundred wired to you today, and two thousand when you deliver the envelope," The woman answered quickly.

"Deal." Fred smiled again. He'd have done it all for three thousand, maybe less. The woman proceeded to tell him the exact location, a resort in Baja California, near Ensenada.

"Wait for me at the bar by the swimming pool. I'm five foot three, and Oriental and I will be wearing a one piece black bathing suit. We will exchange envelopes there," the woman continued.

"I get the two grand, you get your envelope." Fred nodded.

"That's what I said," she snapped.

. . . .

Some hours later, Fred Lepus muttered to himself as he opened the front door of his friend's house.

"I don't care what the sign says." He gently tore the police and FBI seal on the door. The sun had set an hour before and the lights from the street were bright, lighting up the front porch quite well. But no police or FBI agents were in sight, all official cars had long since gone from the neighborhood. After he turned the living room light on, Fred looked around the room. The FBI were not as heavy handed as he had feared. Most of the inside looked the same as he had left it the day before.

The contents of the desk in the hallway was tossed onto the floor, but that was all in a single area. Fred tossed piles of paper back onto the top of the desk. Opening each drawer, he randomly stuffed things into them; maybe his friends wouldn't notice.

The bedroom was another story, every stitch of clothes was strewn on the bed and on the floor. This would take more time than Fred wanted to spend so maybe he could talk Cathy, his secretary, into fixing this right after she got back from vacation, maybe. So far, he hadn't seen any real damage; that was a plus, at least.

After looking around the rest of the house, Fred decided that the FBI had searched the house quite carefully, perhaps the envelope wasn't there. At least he could feed the fish and water the plants.

After tapping a few globs of fish food into the tank, he filled up the watering can and proceeded to water the indoor plants. Right before he left the house, he remembered the outdoor bird feeder. The seeds were in the garage, and he was supposed to fill the feeder every third day. Fred sighed as he filled the empty coffee can with wild bird seed. He'd have to do a lot of explaining to his friend, Bernie, and especially to Bernie's wife about the mess he made of their house. He could save out a thousand from the three thousand he might get from delivering the envelope and give it to them. First he had to find the envelope. He was going get more money that he thought he would for delivering the envelope, so sharing it with Bernie for trashing his house might not be a bad idea; but, first he had to find the envelope.

As Fred contemplated his misfortune with Bernie's house, he unscrewed the top of the bird feeder, mentally making fun of its alleged, squirrel-proof hanger. Then he noticed a white paper lining in the bird feeder itself which was strange. Why would someone put a liner in the bird feeder? White liner? It was the envelope!

Opening the white number ten envelope, Fred stared at the single sheet of paper folded within it. Nothing but a series of numbers and letters in two columns of ten characters each stared back from the page at Fred. Each number consisted of combinations of ten numbers and letters. What the hell was this? Maybe it was a code telling where tons of money was hidden or maybe it was the formula for a new diet pill.   What did all that matter, the piece of paper alone was worth thirty five hundred bucks.

18
South of the border

After lunch, all three of us walked to the Capitol Grounds. Not many people knew its existence, but the Botanic Garden lies behind the Capitol building on Maryland Avenue, a few blocks up on First, the same street as Bullfeathers, with park benches scattered around. Billy and I wandered off and talked about a variety of unrelated subjects while Cassandra sat on a bench and read the documents; she has always been a fast and careful reader.

"I have to talk to you about all this money," Billy said. He stopped under a large tree. From here I could see the capitol building, Billy stood facing towards the street.

"You mean the profit from selling the Los Angeles business?" I was going to be a pest about this; it was not their money, it was mine.

"You know damned well it's about that money." His reluctant tone showed that Billy didn't want to talk about it. I think he agreed with me that it was my money, but his boss had probably set a fire under him about it.

"Who paid for the business to start with?" I began. "Did the Company put a dime into it?"

"Well, actually we did." Billy took in a deep breath. "Besides, if we hadn't set you up as a private investigator, you wouldn't have the business to sell."

"It wasn't that much, and who's to say that I wouldn't have become a private investigator anyway?" I glared at Billy. "I kind of like the business. If I wasn't a spy, I'd probably be an investigator anyway, for the excitement."

"We can't have a field agent getting rich off of the phony businesses we set them up in," Billy muttered.

"And, Armand Hammer is a pauper?"

"That's different, and you know it, he was rich to start with."

"Besides," I retorted, "you guys didn't set me up in anything." I was on a roll. "All you did was suggest that I get a

150

job as a private investigator. No one paid for an office, or even the pistols I carry, I paid for everything myself, well everything except the training and credentials."

"That, and you paid for the rest on the salary we pay you for working for the government."

"The most you have ever paid me in a year is seven thousand dollars." I wasn't going to give up. "Last year I made a hundred and twenty one thousand from Cheshire Katz ."

"Not all of that was yours."

"After taxes, expenses, and Cassandra's cut, I got forty two thousand," I said. "Your part was a little over twenty percent of the whole. Enough to pay the rent, food and clothing costs."

"What rent? A client gave you that building free and clear." At least Billy was listening to my argument.

"Are you saying you want me to give the building over to the government?"

"No, no, I'm not saying that."

"But, you want me to give all the money I get from the sale of the Los Angeles business to the government?" I wasn't going to give up.

"I never could get anywhere arguing with you," Billy said, exasperated. "Let's skip any more useless discussion, and just get to the bottom line."

"So, the bosses have already made up their minds?" I had been counting on that rather large nest egg for the future.

"This went all the way to the Director's office." Billy looked serious, deadly serious.

"The politicians got involved?" I was worried. "This has got to be unfair."

"Not really." Billy patted my back. "Most of us were on your side even though the Director wanted you to turn over all the cash, plus the building in Atlanta."

"Just a damned minute, half of all that is Cassandra's and she wasn't an employee when we accumulated all those assets."

"That's what we argued," Billy said quickly. "It was a heated argument, but the final deal is this; you get to keep the building in Atlanta, and one half of your share of the profits from the sale. Cassandra gets to keep her entire half of the profits since she wasn't in the Company when you both earned the money."

After a second of considering, I agreed. "I guess it's the best deal possible."

"You have to be more careful about all this in the future." Billy looked straight at me. "You two can earn as much money as you want to from the detective agency, but you should not build a large operation again."

"Don't worry, I don't want to," I agreed. "It's too much trouble, and eats up way too much time and effort."

"Exactly," Billy agreed. "That's another point I wanted to make, you have to be able to travel anywhere in the world whenever we need you to, and if you have to take care of a big operation in Los Angeles, or Atlanta, it will be a hindrance."

So, their agenda wasn't as bad as I thought it might be. All I wanted was the Company to be fair about it, and I sure wasn't ready to fold over the whole money thing. We started talking about baseball and in less than a half an hour, Cassandra walked up to us, still standing around under the same tree. She handed all of the papers to Billy, indicating that she had signed them all.

....

Billy did indeed give us first class tickets for the flight back. I think it was due more to an overbooked third class section than anything else, at least we could sleep most of the flight back; more butt room does have its advantages.

"I think we're ready to land." I gently tapped Cassandra's shoulder.

"Where?" I think she was a lot more tired than I was.

"Los Angeles."

"Right." She turned her tongue around her mouth several times. "I feel like crap."

"But you look beautiful to me."

I kissed her cheek, figuring morning mouth had taken effect.

"Thanks." She wanted to say something else.

"What?" I asked.

152

"All those things I signed." She leaned closer to me. "Did you have to sign them too?"

"I did," I answered.

She hadn't said a thing to me since she had handed Billy back all the signed papers that afternoon so I assumed she was processing everything and it was best to let her do so.

"According to what I read, I can't even tell my parents where I am when I'm working for the government." She shrugged. "I guess that's okay with me, I can understand all the need for secrecy and everything."

"You're having trouble with it, though?"

"It'll take some getting used to," she paused to consider. "It's all quite a commitment. In a lot of ways, it's more of a commitment than a marriage."

"You are starting to see what I was going through for the past year."

"What do you mean?" Confusion passed rapidly over her face. "Like wanting to tell me and to marry me?"

"Yes to both." I grinned at her. "I had a hard enough time keeping all this a secret from you while we were dating and living together, but since you agreed to marry me, I had to push the government to agree to change your status."

"What would you have done if they didn't agree with you?" She asked.

"I don't know," I replied. "I never thought about another possibility, it would have driven me crazy."

"I love you." She kissed me.

"What do you want to do first?"

"Want to take a shower together?" She teased me.

"Race you home."

. . . .

"Who should we talk to first?" Cassandra rubbed the towel on her hair, then set it down on the sink and grabbed the hair drier. "You know what I think."

"Talk to the Long Beach cops?" I asked as I slipped on a clean shirt.

"That's what I thought." Cassandra nodded as she blew hot air over her hair.

153

"At some point I'd like to talk to Mark too," I said.

Cassandra and I had only seen Mark Hatton, my friend on the Los Angeles Police Department, twice since we moved back East, although she had gone out with Mark and his wife since she came back here for the quarter.

"That would be good too." Cassandra pulled on her slacks. "You two haven't seen each other in a while," she continued. "What do we tell Mark and the Long Beach cops we are doing? I mean we can't tell them the truth, can we?"

"Not hardly." I sat on the edge of the bed to put my shoes and socks on. "I guess we're still working for the insurance company since they're responsible for the wrongful death on the freighter."

"But, shouldn't the insurance company let the cops solve it? It's an active murder case after all," she said, playing devil's advocate.

"It's part of the wonderful Cheshire Katz service." I smiled as I stood up, ready to venture forth.

"I suppose so," Cassandra said, unconvinced. "The cops will still be pissed off about us messing in an active murder case, especially one so fresh and one with you as a primary suspect."

"And, this is unusual for us how?"

"I see your point." She checked to make sure she had her pistol and extra clip. "Is this the reason you stick your nose into cases you shouldn't, or at least the cops say you shouldn't?"

"Not always." I thought for a second. "Sometimes I feel the need to solve a puzzle because it needs to be solved, it may not have anything to do with our other job at all."

"But, when it does?" Cassandra asked.

"Like now?"

"Like now," she agreed.

"You'll learn that when the government wants us to work a case, we try not to pay attention to what the local cops say," I said. "That can prove to be a huge problem if the local cops aren't in this country."

"What happens then?" Her face had gotten grim all of a sudden.

"When you go for training at the Farm, they'll tell you all about that circumstance." I didn't want to get into the finer points of our jobs right then, we didn't have enough time.

"The Farm?"

"That's what we call the training center," I said. "It's in Virginia, not far from headquarters."

"What's it like?"

"You'll do fine there," I assured her. "I thought it was fun."

"What will I have to do?"

"You'll learn all about shooting, explosives and close quarter fighting."

"No wonder you thought it was fun." She shook her head. "Shooting stuff and blowing things up."

"There's more to it." I lost my grin. "You'll learn all the rules you have to operate under. They'll teach you how to become a better observer, and how to survive in all kinds of situations. You'll learn the company line and you'll meet all the bosses and find out what they do. Also, you'll learn some of the company secrets."

"Like the secret handshake?" She teased me again.

"Sort of." I handed Cassandra a small wad of hundred dollar bills. "Here, you take some more of this."

"Do we get to keep what's left?" She stuffed the money into her bag.

"I always do." I counted some of it as I stuffed the bills into my pocket. "It's expense money, they pay it all up front."

"So, what's the exact deal they have with you about pay?" She asked.

Questions, questions, Cassandra is big on details, especially this kind, although I didn't have the heart to tell her about the money argument I had had with Billy. I suppose I'd have to tell her before we closed the Los Angeles deal, but not now.

"I get our going rate plus expenses." I looked around to make sure I didn't forget anything. "All that money is channeled through the company they have me working for. I'm also put on

155

active military duty and paid active duty pay with a hazardous duty rate tacked on, at least most of the time."

"Hazardous duty?" Cassandra asked carefully.

"Like the soldiers in a war zone." I nodded. "A higher rate, plus no federal taxes on it."

"That sounds right," she agreed. "So, what do you do for all that, usually?"

"Agents like us are supposed to find out stuff," I answered. "We're supposed to gather information about whatever they tell us to and report it back to our handler. They have analysts to pull together all the information gathered and make sense of it."

"That doesn't sound like what we're up to now?" She cocked her head to one side.

"It's in our job descriptions; they often ask us to do other duties as described."

"What the hell does that mean?"

"If they need a job done in the field and don't have enough full-time operations officers free to do it, they can and do ask us part-timers to do it," I replied. "There's a lot less of us field agents gathering information than there used to be, it's been that way since Watergate and I don't like it."

"What kind of other jobs do they ask us to do?" She furrowed her brow. "They never would ask us to kill someone, or something like that, would they?"

"Not us," I replied. "That's called wet work, but we're just the ones who gather information. Sometimes I've been shot at, and I've had to shoot other people, but I've never been, nor would I accept being an assassin."

"Me neither," she said with certainty. "So, in reality, we're spies who go around spying and getting shot at?"

"Sort of like private investigators, right?" I asked.

"I guess you're right." She thought about that for a second.

"The detective front was their idea in the beginning," I said. "After a year or so, I liked the job, it was never dull, and it gave me a chance to meet a lot of interesting people. Even if I had never worked for the government, I might well have been a detective anyway."

"Several of the reasons I like the job too," Cassandra agreed.

"Then, you'll like working for the CIA even more," I said. "It's like the detective job you like, but there's a lot more traveling. Plus, when we're on a government job, we get lots of perks."

"I'm looking forward to it." She grinned at me. "You say they'll only pay me when I'm actually working for them, but that's only two or three times a year?"

"They pay your government salary when you're on the job for them. If we decided to work for them full-time, then we'd be on their payroll." I took her hand, I needed to touch her again. "They told me it would only be two or three jobs a year, but in reality it's been seven to ten a year. Since the jobs are no more than half time at best over a year, you're right, we couldn't live on that small amount. Most of the money we live on comes from the regular detective jobs. For each one of the jobs the government send us on, there's a background cover story for us."

"Like working for an insurance company?"

"Right." I nodded. "And, the insurance company sends us a check for the time we spend on the job."

"Is it the insurance company's money?" She asked.

"Do you care?"

"Sort of."

"No, they launder the CIA's money," I clarified. "But, the insurance companies like my work and they hire me for real jobs which pays their real money. And, from now on, they'll hire both of us for those non-government jobs."

"So, we're more investigators than spies?" She asked.

"No, we're contract operations officers first, we use our detective agency as a cover."

"I don't exactly get it," she said, confused.

"A lot of the officers who gather information have cover jobs," I said. "Most of them are businessmen who travel abroad frequently. Some others are journalists, photographers and the like, most of those occupations are suspect from the start. Hell, our government suspects most of the foreign press corps, as well as most businessmen from other countries. Would you believe the commies try to send businessmen into our country, can you believe a communist businessmen? Although most of the agents from Russia come into this country as trade delegations and diplomatic officers."

"I get that," Cassandra said. "All the time I read about Russia catching all those businessmen and throwing them out of the country because they're spies."

"That's exactly why the CIA came up with the investigator cover for me," I said. "It's our job to pry into all sorts of places we shouldn't; people, and countries, expect us to do that."

"So, they won't immediately jump to the conclusion that we're spies." Cassandra smiled. "I get it now."

"In answer to you original question, we get paid by the CIA for our work, and we get paid by regular customers, and we get our two hundred and expenses through cover jobs while we're working for the government." I felt like telling her more, I don't usually have a safe audience to share this with. "We're not like real operations officers, those guys are in the field all the time and go from one project to another, so do the full-time contract officers. The government makes up a background story for them that isn't too deep."

"What do you mean too deep?" She asked.

"If anyone spent enough time looking into their background, it would be obvious that they were a government agent. The business background, or whatever, wouldn't hold up too well. Dig into their background in this country, and no one outside the CIA would know who they were, or what they did for the past five years or so. But, dig a little deeper and it might become obvious that they were more than their cover indicates. Whereas, for us, we're private investigators, and everybody who comes in contact with us knows that and will testify on a stack of bibles that we're legitimate, no matter how deep they might dig."

"So it's the strong basic background that we're after."

"Right," I agreed. "Most of the countries I work in know me only as a detective, and they leave me alone for the most part."

"And?" She asked

"And what?"

"And inside this country?"

"We can work in this country without raising too many alarm bells."

"What's the down side?" She asked. "Besides the obvious stuff."

"When you take the training, you'll see it all."

"Give me the highlights."

"Well," I began. "the first thing that slapped me in the face is the isolation of the whole thing. I mean, you're supposed to detach yourself from friends and family since that could be a weakness the enemy could use. People you meet are looked on as possible assets. Like, you're an asset to me to be used for an advantage in a project. If you become a liability to the project, you're expendable. I never did like that, and don't do it unless I have to."

"When do you have to?"

"When your life depends on it, and when the integrity of this country is at stake," I answered. "But, I've found that there's more than one way to define asset."

"I can see moral uncertainties abound in this line of work." Cassandra was gazing seriously at the curtained wall behind me.

"In my opinion, bankers and stock brokers find themselves in more moral dilemmas than we do." I have thought about this to myself for years and I was glad to be having this discussion with the woman I loved.

"I imagine if I were ever to be assigned to a project to assassinate some political leader or overthrow a government, I might have serious internal problems, Billy knows that and keeps my assignments less ambiguous," I continued.

"What's the advantage to being a part-timer?" She asked.

"Well, the first thing is that we can make more money," I replied. "I guess the second advantage is that we can have a life outside of government service."

"What do you mean?"

"Look at Billy," I said. "He's a career officer with the CIA so he doesn't have many real friends outside the business, and that business is premised on never trusting anyone. He's active on one high profile project after another, almost everything he touches is a headline international news item sooner or later. After thirty years of that, how is he supposed to retire? His entire working career is filled with stuff he can't even tell his wife."

"I'd explode," Cassandra emphatically said. "He can't tell his wife? If we go to their house for that barbeque, what the hell do we talk about?"

"He was making small talk, we'll never go to his house and socialize with him and his wife." I shook my head. "She knows where he works, but that's about all."

"I couldn't take that." Cassandra stared at the floor. "I could never take that."

"I know." I put my hand on her arm while she was still looking at the floor. "I insisted on remaining only part-time; five to ten assignments a year I can't tell anyone about is enough for me."

"Me too." She raised her eyes. "I like your attitude about this."

"It's not all that bad, and I feel good about what I do at the end of the day." I put my hand on her cheek.

"Then, I think I might like working for them after all." She opened the door and walked into the hallway first. "It's what I like to do, plus there's a retirement plan."

"So, you plan to stay in the detective business when you're finished with your degree?"

Her acceptance of what we had discussed so far was making me fell hopeful.

"Probably, I'll do the government work for sure since I signed all those papers, but I don't know about the regular detective business yet." She turned to face me; she sounded thoughtful. "But, I think I'd like to look for at least an adjunct position somewhere around Atlanta."

"I guess another part-time job in academia could also work." I thought for a second. "I have a feeling the CIA might be calling on you for more than field work."

"You mean they'd want me as an analyst for problems in the Middle East?" Cassandra nodded.

"Given the troubles of the moment, I'd count on it," I agreed.

"So, I might be gone from the detective agency for long periods?" Cassandra said slowly. "That would negate holding a teaching position."

"I guess it would." I didn't want to be too negative. "But, the detective agency can afford to be put on hold for a period of time."

"So, part of the downside," she said, after a moment of silence. "The detective business is for show."

"Not so much." I almost believed that at times myself. "All we have to do is be believable at what we do by doing what we've done together for the past few years. As far as you've known, that's been reality, besides, we're selling the Los Angeles branch."

"I suppose the CIA didn't want us to have a huge detective business, did they?" Cassandra asked.

"No," I sighed. "We have to be able to move quickly, and dragging along a large detective operation might make us too inefficient."

"I guess we'll never be that rich," she said wistfully.

"That depends on how you count being rich." I glanced back at her. "We might clear a lot of money on this Los Angeles deal, I call that a nest egg."

"I suppose," she sighed.

"Billy wanted me to give the profit back to the agency since they feel the government set me up in it." I supposed then was a good a time as any to tell her.

"Like hell they did!" Cassandra protested. "You set Cheshire Katz up with money you got from that lawsuit."

"My point too," I said. "They finally agreed and are letting us keep most of the money."

"Isn't that big of them." Cassandra pursed her lips. "How much of it?"

"You get to keep all of your half, and I have to give them half of my half."

"So, they take a quarter of all of it." Cassandra pondered that for a second. "What about the house in Atlanta?"

"We get to keep that all for our little selves." I felt good saying that, I knew she was becoming attached to that place.

"That still sounds a little like paternalistic big brother to me." Cassandra was still counting up the missing eggs from our future nest.

"You have to understand, the government feels they have the right to run a large portion of our lives." I put my hand on her shoulder. "We have agreed to this."

"I know," she reluctantly agreed. "All this has been running around in my head for the past twelve hours."

"What?" I asked.

"What motivated me to sign all those papers earlier."

"What did?"

"I could be dismissive and say patriotism, but that's not entirely true." Cassandra looked at the floor, pensively.

"I've been doing this longer." I slid my hand around her shoulder. "I came to this line of work through the military, if I hadn't taken this turn, I'd still be in the Marines. But, sometimes, I don't know why I do this."

"What do you mean?"

"Don't worry, that sentiment is only a fleeting one," I sighed. "Sometimes, like when I get arrested for murder, I wonder why I made these choices in life."

"I can see that," Cassandra agreed. "But you have to look at the big picture."

"Big picture?" I echoed.

"Sort of like delving into an endless sea of chaos and wondering what one person can do?" Cassandra looked up at me. "Struggling against indifference is what makes me want to stay with Cheshire Katz instead of teaching freshmen

162

somewhere, the same thing made me sign all those contracts yesterday."

"Doing something, acting on something," I said. "Teaching makes a difference too, don't dismiss that part of you."

"I know it does, but this job feels like I'm doing more to make a difference in the world." Cassandra studied me. "Like you said before, this is what I can do."

"So, you're staying in the detective agency?"

"I'll figure all that out later." She moved back in front of the mirror and began arranging herself.

"Just remember, none of this goes outside the two of us and Billy." I looked at her in the mirror.

"Like you said earlier," she said somberly. "Nothing is as it seems."

"I've gone to a lot of trouble to show you what everything is. I've taken a long walk out on this limb to show you everything," I said. I don't know if my expression conveyed it, but I was drop dead serious; heart on my sleeve, life in her hands serious.

"Why?" she asked

"Simple," I answered. "I love you."

. . . .

"John Billups, this is my partner, Cassandra Pales. Cassandra, this is detective Billups." I was going to be on my best behavior with the police, especially since they might decide to arrest me again.

"What the hell do you want?" Billups didn't sound too happy to see me. I wasn't in handcuffs, so for me it was starting off great.

"Is there any news of the Japanese woman?" Cassandra jumped in. She can get away with more than I can, especially with male cops; go figure.

"If there is, what makes you think I'd tell you."

John glared at Cassandra, not like he would hit her, but not friendly either.

"Because she's not only the most likely suspect in the murder, but she's also the most likely suspect in a major cargo theft ring, which plagues the company that owns the Veracruz," Cassandra answered.

She can make this crap up better than I can lots of times, I was glad to see her getting back in the swing of all this.

"I repeat my question, why should I tell you?" Billups softened a bit and gave Cassandra's body a quick once over before looking at her face again, she had him on a hook. Are all of us men this easy? Yes.

"You want her for a murder charge, we want her to keep the insurance company from paying out obscene amounts in claims," Cassandra sounded happier. "The way I see it, this can only help you since we'll turn Maiko over to you if we find her."

"Maybe." Billups paused, she had him.

"You've got two high priced private investigators working for you as well as the insurance company. We get the money only if we turn her over to the cops and she takes the blame for it."

"I got a message from the cops in San Ysidro," Billups reluctantly answered. "She was spotted headed to Baja."

"Thanks." Cassandra smiled and patted John on his shoulder, leaving her hand for a second before pulling it back.

"Customs is supposed to get back to us within the hour to let us know if she did cross." He grinned at Cassandra, it was like I wasn't even there.

"I'll bet she did cross," Cassandra purred. "My partner and I will be in Baja within the next few hours, maybe sooner."

"I guess I hope you two can drag her ass back up here." He still hadn't looked at me. "Good luck."

"You're good at this," I whispered in her ear as we left the police station.

Cassandra patted my back. "I'm glad you appreciate my talents."

"Let's head back home and pack up."

"Don't you want to talk to Mark?" Cassandra asked.

"No time now." I rushed to our car. "Maybe I can stay a little longer when we finish this case, I could hang around you, and see Mark and Mary."

"Does your lighter work on this coast?" Cassandra looked down at my pants pocket.

"Sure does." I contacted Billy Sullivan who wasn't surprised that Maiko had run to Mexico. He wanted us to follow and had a few ideas where to look. He named a tourist town on the coast, not far from Ensenada.

. . . .

"I'd like to speak to Agent Dixon."

Detective John Billups shifted the phone from his left hand to his right. John was proud of the contacts he had acquired in his many years on the force. He could expect results from this cooperation, he at least hoped.

"One minute," A woman's voice replied.

"Hello." That was Dixon's voice, John recognized it.

"This is Billups," John said. "Katz was here."

"What the hell did he want?"

"He and his partner were asking about the Japanese woman," John replied. "I told them I thought she was headed to Baja."

"Good," Dixon said. "Katz' partner sure is one fine looking woman, isn't she."

"She is a beautiful woman," John said. "I think she and Katz are living together, you know."

John had known FBI Special Agent Dixon for about ten years. Dixon was a good field agent, and a fair man, but, he did have a weakness for beautiful women which was why Dixon was usually either in the middle of a divorce, or looking for the next Mrs. Dixon.

"Damned shame," Dixon regretfully said. "We'll put a tail on them right away."

"Are you sure Katz doesn't work for you guys?" John was still mad at two FBI agents pulling his prime murder suspect away from him.

"And, what about those two supposed agents that took Katz out of here?" John added.

"I told you that I don't have a clue about those two agents. No one here has heard of them, but that doesn't mean they aren't legit." Dixon took in another breath. "Maybe those two were from another agency, maybe the DEA or customs, after all, they did find drugs and stolen fine art stuff on that ship."

"What about Katz ?" John asked again.

"Like I said, Katz is a private investigator," Dixon grumbled. "I've done all the digging I can from here, but all I can find out is that he's a private investigator. He's got a damned good reputation and an even better track record at solving cases, did you know that?"

"I don't care about that. If he manages to locate the Japanese woman, you'll give her to us." John didn't like being teased, at least not yet.

"After we question her, like I said," Dixon said cautiously.

"You tell me one thing," John insisted. "Why do I have the feeling that you mean something else."

"That woman may be into stealing national secrets," Dixon said in a whisper. "I didn't tell you that, but you're my friend, and you've been a big help in all this."

"So, she may never come back to Long Beach, right?" John sighed.

"Maybe not," Dixon cleared his throat. "I've got to get going and set up the tail on Katz ; I'll be back in touch as soon as I can."

19
What's up, dolt?

"Are you sure you don't want a fancy new bathing suit?" I ogled Cassandra, then looked up at the entrance to the hotel. "Maybe we could stay an extra day here if we pick up the woman early."

"Maybe later." Cassandra extricated herself from the taxi. "I have to get back and teach my class in a few days."

"All work and no play." I stretched right after I exited the small taxi. "You know what they say."

I paid the driver in American dollars, since that's all I had.

"Like this is a vacation anyway." Cassandra shot me a dirty expression. "Let's get in there and change into something a bit more tourist like."

"Like a bathing suit?" I wickedly grinned at her. "A nice fire engine red thong bikini?"

"Okay." She looked up at me and smiled. "Are you going to wear high heels with that?"

"Not a pretty picture, you know." I smiled back at her. "Besides, that thong thing in my butt crack is damned annoying."

"Now you know how I'd feel."

Our destination resort rose to three stories in sections, with lots of private single story cottages scattered around its perimeter. The complex was set into the dunes of a broad sandy beach, almost every structure was painted a light earth tone, making the buildings and grounds seem brighter, more cheerful in the warm sunshine. A three story hotel, filled the middle section, cleverly designed to convey luxury. Near the broad, grand entrance, an excess of hotel employees half walked, half ran, in all directions, each with a purposeful air. Glass walls marked out the main lobby and showed off an Olympic sized large pool glistening in the background.

Several small clothing shops lined an indoor boardwalk in the hotel, where Cassandra and I found appropriate vacation

167

clothes, tan shorts, and silk shirt with subdued floral pattern for me, and a sexy green two piece swimsuit with a matching short skirt for her. We walked out of there in new sandals; Casandra bought a good sized white tote bag at the last minute.

On the way up to our second floor room, we were the only two people in the elevator.

"I don't know anything for sure, but I have the feeling that all this relates to that crooked crew on the freighter," Cassandra finally spoke.

"What do you mean?" I waited until we walked into the hall to reply.

"Maybe this case covers a bunch of drug smugglers, and that's it," she added. Cassandra opened the door to our room.

Luxurious touches decorated this space also. A large balcony overlooked the beach and ocean. Walls and other flat surfaces were painted a subdued pastel pink. Most of the furniture wicker, even the headboard. Hanging from the four bed posters, ruffled semi-transparent sheets of white cloth completed the overstuffed effect. The cleaning staff had put a small vase with a single orchid or some such flower on one of the bedside tables, Its scent permeated the whole room, better than any room deodorizer, and a lot more pleasing to the eye. With its view of the ocean, the huge sliding glass door dominated the whole room, reminding me of an old movie set. As we entered, I half expected Lauren Bacall to walk out of a nearby bathroom door, followed by Bogie.

"Why can't there be two plots in this thing?" I was curious; maybe Cassandra was right.

"Like I said, I don't know anything for sure, but I feel that it's all about smuggling, not buying secrets from an American scientist."

Cassandra closed the blinds and took off her clothes and pulled on the bathing suit. I do like watching this, it's been too long, at least it seems that way to me.

"So you think this Japanese woman is employed by the German crew?"

I took off my clothes and put on the tourist attire I had bought.

"Don't ask me why I think the Japanese woman worked for the Germans." Cassandra pulled the skirt over her bathing suit. "But, yes I do."

"Well." I happily looked at the love of my life. I stared at her; she looks great in almost anything, or even better in almost nothing. I do digress at times, well more often lately.

"Why don't we go out there and look for this woman?" I asked.

"Before we go out there, I have to apologize for what I said before." Cassandra stood directly in front of me.

"What?" I feigned, but I remembered it.

"You're right." She took in a deep breath. "You did kind of go out on a limb to tell me everything."

"You're worth tree climbing." I put my arms around her.

"It's a lot to absorb in a short time." She hugged me. "The regular cases are stressful, now there's getting married, and finishing my degree, then there's the whole thing about telling my parents about the wedding in addition to all the new stuff I can't tell anyone about."

"I know." I kissed her. "Take it one day at a time and it won't be as overwhelming."

"Says you." She kissed me back.

I didn't want to go looking for any bad guys, I just wanted to stay right there with her.

"By the way, do you mind if I remove that tag on your shorts, or is that some kind of a fashion statement?" She asked me.

. . . .

Cassandra and I settled into our lounge chairs, both of us glad we had brought our sunglasses, as we positioned ourselves so we could see both the swimming pool and the beach. Soaking in the cancerous rays and sipping on mind numbing alcoholic beverages, we looked like any other vacationing couple; what a life. It does beat chasing a cheating husband or thrashing a confession out of a cheating accountant. At odd moments, life is good.

"Benjamin." Cassandra patted my arm. "Over there." She nodded to her left, near the poolside bar.

"Oh shit," I hissed the rest of that breath out between my front teeth.

"Oh shit indeed." Cassandra pulled down her sunglasses and looked at me. "Maybe I was right about all this, maybe this is all about just the smuggling."

In front of us, snuggling his ugly ass into a bar stool, was Fred Lepus. True to his stealth discernment abilities, he was clueless to the fact that we sat twenty yards from him, staring at his backside. Approaching middle age, perhaps forty years old, maybe a bit less, Lepus wore a loud green, red and blue flowered Hawaiian shirt and light olive drab shorts one size too large for his frame. There had to have been three dozen pockets in the knee length short pants he wore. He could have spent more than a buck fifty on foot wear, he was wearing flip flops. He had let his hair grow a bit since I last paid attention to his appearance, maybe he was going to try a comb over for his growing bald spot. His hair was becoming whiter around the fringe, and with the extra length it flew up in large white tufts as the breeze blew in off the ocean.

"Why don't we keep an eye on him," Cassandra mused.

"When you're right, you're right," I agreed.

We didn't have to wait long. Lepus sat at the bar for no more than ten minutes nursing a large drink the whole time, one of those concoctions that was topped off with a large paper parasol. I mentally chalked that up to his being out of his element, not on being gay, but, one never knows. Maiko strolled up to Lepus. She was wearing a black one piece swim suit, a broad brimmed straw hat, extra dark sunglasses and a light flowered wrap around, tightly hugging her hips. Sitting down next to Fred, she quickly became engrossed in conversation.

"Do we go up to them now, or do we wait?" Cassandra whispered to me; I was facing away in case Maiko looked towards us.

"You follow her after she leaves Lepus since Maiko knows me and not you," I replied. "I'll take care of Lepus."

"If they leave together?" Cassandra asked.

"You still follow them alone." I shot a quick glance at Maiko and Lepus who both were still in conversation. "I'll follow at a distance to back you up if you need it."

"Sounds good to me."

"I think she knows I'm here," I whispered into Cassandra's ear.

"Why?"

"Just a hunch; it's not like we're hiding or anything. She's an operative from somewhere, I bet my life on it now," I whispered. "I'm going to get up and leave now."

"Do we try to take the woman back to the US?" Cassandra touched me as I got up.

"I think we have to." I sat back down. "Maybe not us, but at the least, we need to get the Mexican authorities to do it."

"They'll do that?" Cassandra turned to look at the two at the bar.

"If we put the request through the FBI, they most likely will," I replied. "All we want is to get the woman back to Long Beach and into jail there."

"How long after we call will the FBI get here?" She asked.

"Not long," I whispered to her. "Didn't you notice them tailing us ever since we left Huntington Beach?"

"Not really," she sounded surprised.

"That huge black van behind us?"

"No."

"Five cars back when we stopped at the border?"

"No."

"The clincher was that they didn't even slow down that much when they got to the crossing," I said. "The guard waved them by."

"I need to pay more attention."

"That's something else they teach you at the Farm, besides blowing things up," I chuckled.

"But, seriously, folks," Cassandra insisted. "What do we do when one or both leave?"

"I take Lepus, you take the woman."

"Now?"

I got up and wandered away from the bar, back towards the hotel lobby.

Maiko stood up from her bar stool and began to walk away. From my vantage point in the lobby, I clearly saw her tuck a white envelope into the left side of her bathing suit, near the waist of the wrap around she was wearing. Fred remained at the bar, finishing his drink, and not looking like he wanted to pay for another. He slowly turned in his seat to stare out towards the beach; it was obvious he was scanning for the best looking women in the briefest swimwear. Maiko had quickly walked back into the hotel and Cassandra just as quickly followed her as I hastily left the lobby to avoid being seen. I walked around the pool and approached the bar from the opposite way Fred was looking, he never noticed me as I sat next to him.

"Would you like another queer drink sir?" I spoke in a loud voice right into Lepus' ear.

Lepus let out an indignant snort, and I swear I heard a small chuckle from the bartender.

"What the hell do you mean by that?" Fred spun and faced the bartender who pointed to me; all expression drained from his face as he stared at me.

"You don't recognize your old friend?" I pulled off my sunglasses; it still took a second for Fred to place me.

"I ought to pound your head into this bar," Fred stuttered, lunging to his feet.

"Maybe you should reconsider and join me in my room for a friendly conversation."

I stood up next to him. He's five foot seven in his flip flops. I'm six foot one in bare feet.

"Fine."

Fred Lepus fumed the whole way up to my room not saying a thing, other than a few discernible curses muttered under his breath.

. . . .

Maiko almost immediately knew that Cassandra was following her, she was also well aware that I was sitting by the pool, and that Cassandra had been with me. To make sure, Maiko led Cassandra from the lobby down a first floor hallway,

172

pausing briefly by a door leading to a small conference room. Cassandra, recognizing the ploy, walked by, casually looking at her and the room.

Thinking quickly, Cassandra took the first right available, an exit back onto the pool area. She opened the door, then let it shut, but remained inside the building, motionless, listening for any sound from Maiko.

Maiko also remained motionless, listening for anything from the short hallway leading to the pool, and for Cassandra, who she guessed was still there. Cassandra was carrying a large tote bag and Maiko wondered if she could have a pistol in it.

Most of the space in the tote bag was, in fact, taken up with Cassandra's Beretta model 1934 automatic pistol. Even though the Beretta was smaller than her Colt, it still gave some heft to her bag.

Maiko considered her options; she decided to walk back towards the lobby and perhaps lose her tail with the crowds there but it didn't work. As soon as Maiko started walking, she heard footsteps behind her, and a quick glance over her shoulder confirmed that Cassandra was there.

Cassandra kept the distance between them to no more than twenty feet as she considered her possibilities. If she grabbed her in the lobby, it would be too much of a commotion; she wasn't a cop after all. Maiko knew Cassandra was on her tail, so she certainly wouldn't go back to her room and wait for her. Even if she did, it would be a trap and she could get shot.

Maiko made a quick turn from the lobby towards one of the restaurants, pausing at the center of the main hall leading into three different dining areas. She looked into the far left corner of the hallway, then back at Cassandra closing the gap. In that far left corner was the entrance to the one dining room that was only open for supper; it was dark, and no one was there so Maiko rushed towards that room.

Pausing long enough to see the direction Maiko had darted, Cassandra cautiously followed her. Not seeing anybody as she peered down the dark entrance to the room, Cassandra listened to scuffles from sandals quickly moving on carpets coming from the back of the dark room. She ran towards them, catching a blur out of the corner of her eyes; Maiko was headed out a back exit, but where did that door go?

Maiko hadn't a clue as to where she was headed, she only hoped she could lose whoever was obviously after her. She ran as fast as she could to the door at the end of the service hallway leading down to an outside exit, perhaps the door workers used to take trash to the dumpsters. It was locked and the glass in the door was only a small mesh reinforced ten inch square sheet. Through the small glass window, she could see the rear of the complex, and the garbage dumpsters. The heavy metal door was locked and she didn't have any tools, no gun, nor a knife; Cassandra was now blocking the only free exit.

What to do, what to do, Cassandra thought about the next few seconds. Would she have a gun, would she fight? Answers came quickly as Maiko marched deliberately towards her. Apparently, since no shots had been fired, Cassandra might be able to avoid a gun battle. Cassandra secured a one handed grip on her bag, leaving her other hand free as Maiko stopped five feet from her.

"Who are you? Why are you following me?" Maiko demanded.

"I want to know what that bizarre looking man gave you at the bar by the pool." Cassandra braced herself for a fight while Maiko assumed an aggressive stance. "You're too clumsy to be CIA, and you're too stupid to be KGB, so who are you?" Maiko began to lean backwards on her left leg.

"You're a suspect in a murder in Long Beach so I don't think you have the right to speculate as to exactly who I am."

Cassandra guessed she was about to be kicked. Still holding the heavy bag ready, she dropped both her hands to her side and prepared to duck whatever came at her.

"Fine, have it your way." Maiko snapped her body mass backwards, and lunged her right foot at Cassandra.

Cassandra saw the move a split second before it came, so she fell to her left knee as she heard a rush of air as the foot passed inches above her head. Pushing her fingers tightly into her palm, Cassandra bolted from her crouching position and slammed her right fist into the first target she could acquire, Maiko's right ribcage

Maiko knew she'd missed Cassandra's head half way through the foot stab so she tried to move the foot in a downward motion to at least strike the top of Cassandra's head. As Cassandra stood upright and struck her, Maiko righted herself, preparing again to knock this bothersome woman down.

Before Maiko launched another attack, Cassandra knew she'd have to do something drastic; she wasn't trained at close quarters combat yet, but this woman was. Grasping the short straps to her bag with both hands, she swung it in an upward arc towards Maiko's head as she lunged again at Cassandra. The sack connected, hitting Maiko on her right jaw, forcing her to fall limp and crumple slowly to the floor. Cautiously, Cassandra checked the traces of blood drooling from the left side of Maiko's partially open mouth; she was still breathing so Cassandra pondered her next move.

....

"Why are you here meeting with that woman?" I closed the door to my room.

"What woman?" Fred plopped down on a chair, staring out on the beach. He didn't look at me. "Your client must be rich, what a view."

"Forget the view." I was annoyed. I had already set out the small device for detecting bugs on the dresser nearest the window and the light wasn't on.

"The Asian woman who spoke to you at the bar, who was she?" I asked again.

"What can I say." He stared out the window. "Women can't leave me alone. it's been like that this whole vacation."

"What vacation?" I pressed. "You're here on vacation like I am, right?"

"Who am I, you're personal travel agent?" Fred looked at me for a second, then returned his stare out the window. "How was I supposed to know you'd pick the same vacation spot I did."

175

"That woman is wanted for murder in Long Beach." I pulled a chair in front of Lepus and sat down in it, facing him. "Do you want to be arrested for aiding her escape?"

"I'm not helping her do anything." Fred pulled his chair sideways so he could see the beach again. "Besides, every time we meet, you tell me my client is wanted for murder, why am I supposed to believe you?"

"Because I'm always right, and you're not." I moved closer to him. "Who paid you to find her, and why?"

"Anthony Zimmer paid me five hundred dollars to deliver an envelope to someone at this hotel. He told me that person would find me if I sat at that bar," Fred replied. "I didn't know a murder was connected with this case."

"I told you so, you idiot." Did Lepus ever tell the truth the first time you asked him anything? A rhetorical question, anyway.

"Zimmer and that Asian woman are involved in the identical smuggling plot. The cops want the woman as a suspect and Zimmer as an accomplice," I said.

"Like I said before, why should I believe you." Fred stared at me. "It's not like you're my friend and have my best interests at heart."

"Well, you're right about that." I moved my chair away from him a little. "But, it's true none the less."

"Murder," Fred said the word slowly. "Really?"

"Really."

"So, what're you going to do?" Fred asked.

"I'll do what you should have." I took a slow breath. "Turn her over to the police, to keep me from getting on the wrong side of some pissed off cops. Unlike you, I want to keep my license."

"Okay." Fred returned to gazing through the window "I'll go home now; I did the job I was paid to do, and no one can fault me for that."

Cassandra burst through the door to our room, it banged against the wall with a loud thump. She was dragging the unconscious body of Maiko behind her, grunting as she pulled

Maiko into the middle of our room and dropped her. Both Lepus and I stared at this show.

"What happened?" I asked.

"You two are stupider that I thought." Fred stood and stared at the body in the middle of the room. "If you're afraid of some grumpy cops, you guys have gotten yourselves in for a lot more trouble than that."

"Like what?" Cassandra was still puffing from the extended body drag.

"Look." Fred pointed to the unconscious body in front of him. "There's more than one crime family in this world."

"What the hell does that mean, Fred?" Cassandra moved closer, causing Fred to start fidgeting.

"This woman belongs to a far more dangerous mob than you've ever seen."

"Who!" I almost shouted at Lepus.

"Before I came out here, I asked around." Fred took in a deep breath. "My friend said the Asian countries have a mob, too. I understand that even some North Koreans and Chinese are members of the gangs. This resort is a favorite of theirs, and I assumed that she was part of some Asian mob." Fred began to almost sputter as he tried to contain his fear. "This woman has to be working for them and I was only supposed to give her an envelope. My friend in DC told me a little about those organization and I believe him because he knows foreign mobsters in this country who will kill for the right amount of cash." Lepus was out of breath.

"What have you gotten yourself into?" I couldn't contain my smile.

"Not me, you idiots." Fred glanced from me to Cassandra. "Look what you've gotten yourselves into."

"We have detained a murder suspect." Cassandra pointed to Maiko, still out cold on the floor.

"No, you pissed off a syndicate capable of doing anything, least of all killing all of us," Lepus said in a panicked tone.

Fred moved towards the door to the hallway. Cassandra had quietly slipped her pistol out of her bag.

"I don't think you'd better leave now."

"Like hell I won't." Fred reached for the doorknob. "All she saw was me giving her the envelope, and the rest of this is all you and your partner. I'm in the clear, I'll stay alive."

Cassandra slowly walked to Fred who was still focused on me, thinking I was the one to stop him. She hit him in the back of his head with the butt of her pistol.

"You've been busy this past few minutes." I sat in the chair by the window. "What's up?"

"Well." Cassandra sat on the edge of our bed. "First, this bitch decides that I'm following her too closely and tries to kick my brains in. The tough part was dragging her here. Luckily I found enough back hallways to avoid large crowds, but the couple in the elevator was a little suspicious."

"I should call someone to take care of all these bodies, I guess." I went for the phone to leave a coded message for an extraction while Cassandra hogtied both Maiko and Fred Lepus with the curtain pulls.

"I left a message for the FBI to call the local police and pick these two up within an hour." I sat down on the edge of the bed next to Cassandra.

"So, do we stay here?" Cassandra shrugged. "Don't we need to get back to L.A.?"

"We have to wait here for the local police or the FBI to show up," I sighed. "It's not like I want to stay here."

"Me neither." Lepus had awakened, now struggling against the curtain cord Cassandra had used to tie him up. "Why can't all three of us take a powder and leave the broad tied up on the floor?"

"Whose room is this?" I looked down at Fred. "Besides, I think the police would like to hear from you, too."

"Let me go and I'll pay you ten thousand dollars, American." Maiko was now awake.

"Ten thousand?" Lepus almost shouted.

"Shut up!" Cassandra shouted back at Fred.

"Good." I rubbed my hands together. "We're all awake, I take it you worked for the Germans on the freighter?"

"Who?" Maiko grunted.

"You," I replied.

I helped her roll onto her back, then I leaned her up against a wall, facing the rest of us while I left Fred on his side.

"I assume that Maiko isn't your real name?" I inquired.

"As a matter of a fact, it is my real name." She glared at Cassandra.

"Sorry I hurt you, but you acted like you were trying to kill me," Cassandra said. She looked at Maiko, I could tell she was still a bit emotional about the fight.

"You're lucky." Maiko said, still glaring. "I could have killed you so easily."

Cassandra shook her head slowly, "Could have, would have, but didn't."

"You've lost that thick accent you had on the ship," I interrupted.

"Fuck you!" Maiko spat at me.

"Why did you kill Yoshihiro?" I asked.

"I thought the police had you in custody for that." Maiko looked directly at me. "Who the hell are you? I thought you might be with the FBI, but after they arrested you I guessed you weren't."

"I'm not." I needed to steer this conversation away from alphabet agencies with Lepus in the room. "I'm a private investigator in a heap of trouble, out on bond and looking for the real murderer! Why did you kill Yoshihiro?"

"What makes you think I did?" she quickly answered, still glaring at Cassandra; it was obvious Maiko had an issue with being beaten up by Cassandra.

"Well," I answered, "your fingerprints were on the pistol that killed him; even though it was found in my room, it had your prints on it."

"Maybe someone was trying to set both of us up." She turned her head to glower at me. "Did that ever occur to you?"

"It could have been that way," I continued. "But not likely since you work for criminals and Yoshihiro was a cop of sorts."

"Who says I work for criminals?" Maiko sounded surprised. "That dimwit over there?" She pointed to Fred.

I pointed to Lepus. "He's exactly who told me you were working for criminals."

Maiko leveled another glare at me. "Can we talk alone?"

"Sure."

I walked over to Fred and hauled him to the sliding glass doors that led out to the balcony. After I dumped him outside, I shut the glass door behind me, breathing a little heavy. Lepus was objecting strongly to the process, so I decided to deal with him before I faced Maiko again.

"Just a damned minute, Katz ," Fred sputtered. "That woman offered you ten grand in there to let her go."

"I'm not going to do that."

I wanted to leave, but Lepus wanted to talk. Maybe for a minute, at least long enough to make his greedy self happier.

"I want in on whatever deal you cook up with her," he insisted.

"I don't think you're in a position to demand anything."

"I'll spill everything to the cops if you cook something up with her without cutting me in on it."

"Okay, Fred," I laughed. "If I work out any deal in there, I'll give you a third."

"One third for each of us?" Fred strained to look up at me.

"Deal." I left Fred to admire all the scantily clad women on the beach two floors down and a few hundred yards away. I turned the room air conditioner to high to provide enough background noise to carry on a conversation.

"If we talk quietly, he can't hear us," I said to Maiko.

"What about the bitch?" She returned to her stare to Cassandra who moved closer to us.

"I'm his partner, so get used to it." Cassandra pulled a chair close to Maiko.

"Whatever," Maiko drew in a short breath. "I'm an agent with the National Security Bureau of Taiwan."

"One of the Mystical 110 minions?" I asked.

Cassandra was quiet, her face had gotten impersonal in an instant.

"None of us like that name." Maiko looked at me. "It's just our address."

"So why is the Republic of China interested in a freighter full of Germans?" I asked. I wanted to know if she was telling the truth about her employer, more than anything else. But, since I'd have to wait for that, she might as well talk.

"Most of the Far Eastern countries are interested in them," Maiko spoke quietly. "If your country would pay attention to the rest of the world, you might know this too."

"What were they smuggling besides dope?" Cassandra asked.

"If you don't mind." Maiko stared at Cassandra. "I'd rather you keep your mouth shut."

"All right," I said. "What were they smuggling?"

"Drugs, art, antiquities and secrets," Maiko replied. "Look, I'm being patient, cooperating here, can you at least call the Taiwanese embassy for me?"

"I think I'll let the FBI do that when they get here with the locals." I shook my head. "If you are who you say you are, you should be free by tomorrow. Besides, in spite of what you think, my partner and I are just private investigators."

"I find that hard to believe," Maiko snapped.

"Why?" I shrugged. "I don't give a damn what all this other stuff is about, all we care about is the bonus the insurance company gives us if we can move the liability for the murder as far away from them as possible."

"If they don't have to pay, we get paid," Cassandra added.

"I told you to shut up." Maiko didn't look her way.

"Look, you could be a spy for the Martians for all I care." I moved a little closer to her. "We're going to turn you over to whatever US cops show up first."

"So, what are you two nitwits planning on doing after you turn me over to the cops?" Her eyes showed she was getting angry at the prospect of not being let go.

"I suppose we'll visit the Germans and the freighter, assuming they're all still in Long Beach." I stood up. "As long as

181

someone other than the employees of the shipping line killed the Japanese man, the insurance company will be delighted."

"And, if I did it, everybody will be happy." Maiko looked up at me, trying to smother her angry expression. "Well, I didn't do it, and I can prove it."

"I don't care." I grinned a wicked grin at her. "I get paid more if you did do it."

"You piece of shit!" she shouted.

"Maybe we shouldn't wait for the police, Benjamin," Cassandra interrupted. "We need to get back there quickly before the cops let any of the crew go, or before the ship leaves the harbor."

"I'm on it." I pulled the phone book out from under the telephone and looked for a taxi service. What Maiko heard was me asking for a cab, but I was sending a coded message for us to be extracted immediately.

"If you let me go with you, I can be a great help." Maiko glowered at me.

"If I let you go, you'd spend the whole time trying to kill Cassandra." I replied. "She's too valuable to me as a partner."

"Why, thank you." Cassandra said. She pulled her suitcase on the bed and stuffed her clothes into it. She then disappeared into the bathroom to change into traveling clothes.

"What connection did you have with Zimmer?" I asked Maiko as I put my dress shirt and tie back on. Since I had my boxers on under the shorts, I didn't mind changing back into my long pants in front of this woman.

"Nothing, ." Maiko struggled against the cord binding her hands and feet. "That idiot out there didn't know exactly who he was supposed to meet so I guess he didn't know why he came out here, other than to deliver something to me."

Cassandra stepped out of the bathroom as I zipped up my pants. She gave me a quick disapproving look, then went to the sliding glass door to check on Lepus.

"What was the real cargo?" I asked.

"I don't know," Maiko sighed. "That was what I was going to find out next."

182

"Well, if we ever meet again, I'll tell you what it was, maybe," I said. "As soon as I find out, I'll know who the killer was."

"Don't you think the FBI has already found it?" Maiko asked.

"No, I don't," I answered. "If they had found everything, they wouldn't be still questioning the crew so much."

"What if they already found everything and just want to find out who paid for what?" Maiko asked.

She was trying to manipulate the situation. I could see her expression clearly, she was mad that Cassandra had knocked her out and that she was now tied up and waiting for the FBI to arrest her, even her lips were tense and churning like her bruised jaw. I knew that if she were to get loose, we'd all pay the price.

"What if, what if, what if," I said. "If that's all they were trying to do, they wouldn't be holding the whole crew, they'd be holding just the Germans."

"Well, if you are only a private investigator, you're at least thinking like one." Maiko looked at me, expressionless.

"Why, thank you," I replied.

"When do we go?" Cassandra looked away from the glass door to me.

She tossed her bathing suit in the suitcase and snapped it shut.

"When someone comes here and takes this excess baggage from us."

Good timing. A loud knock at our door echoed inside our room. I checked through the peep hole, then opened the door.

"Which one are you?" I regarded the pair in front of me. "Rosencranz, or Guilderstern?"

"You're not that funny." Bernstein wasn't too impressed with my little joke. He flashed his fake ID around the room.

"FBI, folks, everybody relax until the local cops get here and we can get this moving along," Bernstein spoke in a loud voice.

"Hell, you boys must have been real near by," Cassandra whispered to Bernstein.

"We've been here in the hotel for only an hour or so," Bernstein whispered back at her. "Billy wanted us nearby in case you two had trouble."

"No trouble from us." I smiled at the pair. "We're not the ones you want, it's them." I pointed to Lepus and Maiko.

"We'll wait for the cops." Conner walked in. "You two need to get to the airport in Ensenada; there's a helicopter waiting to take you two back to the Long Beach cops."

They were playing along, giving the room a strong hint we were civilians, for the benefit of Maiko and Lepus.

"Why were you guys nearby all this time?" Cassandra whispered to Conner.

"You've never heard of backup?" he whispered back.

"Not until lately." She looked at me, then back at Conner.

"There's the world's worst detective on the porch." I pointed to Lepus' most recent, temporary home for the past twenty minutes. "Let him explain himself to the FBI."

"What about the woman?" Bernstein asked.

"Let me go!" Maiko pulled harder against her ropes. "You'll all be in deep shit if you don't let me go now!"

"Don't let her go," I said to Bernstein. "She said she's with Taiwan's National Security Bureau. If possible, you might like to figure out if she's telling the truth. As for me, frankly I don't give a damn."

"I can think of several reasons it'd be good have that figured out." Conner looked at Maiko.

"Are all the Germans still in Long Beach?" Cassandra asked. She had gathered all her stuff together, as well as mine, while I was talking to Bernstein and Conner.

"The ship, the crew and the Germans are still in the custody of the Long Beach Police," Conner said. "Get going, you two."

20
The tie that binds

"Now, who the hell are you two?" Fred Lepus demanded as Conner dragged him back into the hotel room.

"FBI." Conner flashed a badge at Fred.

"Not so fast." Fred motioned with his head for Conner to leave the identification in front of him, Conner obliged.

"Agent Terrance Conner," Fred read from the identification. "Could you move it a little further away so a normal person can focus on it." Conner moved the badge and identification a little further away from Fred's eyes.

"This all sounds right, but I don't know for sure."

Fred looked up at Conner, then across the room at Bernstein who was moving Maiko onto a wicker chair beside the bed.

"What don't you know?" Conner asked with an annoyed twinge to his voice. "It appears to me you don't know a lot of things."

"What I don't know is how you and this expensive case and Katz are all connected."

"We're not connected to Katz , you moron." Conner pulled Fred to his feet. "We told Katz that he's out of this investigation for good. We're taking you two and hauling you back to the states to see if we want to arrest you for smuggling or murder."

"Murder?" Lepus looked at Conner as he helped Fred into a chair near Maiko. "You mean Katz was right?"

"Murder." Conner glanced at Bernstein.

"No way Katz is just a private investigator." Maiko looked at Bernstein, then at Conner. "He's more than that."

"He is," Bernstein insisted as he looked at Conner, then back at Maiko. "He's a royal pain in the ass."

"He and his partner stick their noses into places they don't belong all the time," Conner spoke to Maiko, he was enjoying this.

"You say you're going to turn us over to the Mexican police?" Maiko looked at Conner.

"No." Conner looked back at her. "I didn't say that."

"Are we going to jail?" Fred softly asked. "I didn't do anything."

"We'll let your lawyer try to convince a judge of that," Bernstein laughed at Fred.

"Where are you taking us?" Fred asked.

"Back to Los Angeles," Conner answered. "We have an airplane waiting for us right now."

"Listen, loosen these ropes!" Maiko complained. "My wrists are killing me."

"We'll put you two in handcuffs soon enough for the ride back to the States." Bernstein answered, motioning for Conner to join him on the other side of the room to discuss something.

"Who are you working for?" Maiko whispered to Fred as she leaned towards him.

"I was working for you, I suppose," Fred whispered back as he leaned towards her. "But, you haven't paid me everything yet, so I guess right now I don't work for anybody; don't think I didn't count the money you gave me at the bar, you shorted me five hundred."

"Stop wasting time with this penny ante stuff," she insisted. "We don't have a lot of time and I need to know who you work for."

"If you mean I can get out of this somehow, then I still work for you." Fred mentally reached for solid ground, he went with what he had at the moment, self preservation.

"That was one of the possible right answers." Maiko whispered.

She had already freed her hands, she then quickly shoved a small knife into Fred's right hand.

"I think we'd better not wait for the local police to get here." Conner walked back towards Maiko. "We'll get to the airplane right now and get you two back to Los Angeles."

"Lean over and we'll put handcuffs on and cut the ropes off." Bernstein walked towards Fred.

As soon as Conner was two feet from Maiko, she kicked her left leg sharply into his groin. In the meantime, Fred had managed to cut the thin cord away from his hands before the two agents began to walk towards them. As Maiko kicked Conner, Fred sprang to his feet, which were still tied together, and grabbed the bedside lamp. Before he fell onto the side of the bed, he reached out awkwardly, to smash the lamp over Bernstein's head. Fred bounced from the side of the bed, off Bernstein's crumbling unconscious body, and onto the floor.

Maiko stood quickly and with her right foot, smashed the left side of Conner's face. Conner had pulled his service pistol from underneath his jacket, but in two quick moves, Maiko knocked the pistol from his hand and plastered the heel of her right hand into his forehead. She then jabbed her left hand into his chin, causing him to slump onto the carpeted floor.

"Damn." Fred noticed Conner slip into unconsciousness. "You're good."

"Yeah, fine." Maiko turned to stare Fred directly in the face. "Now, who the hell are you working for?"

"You," Fred said tentatively.

"You're too dumb to be working for any US agency." Maiko continued to stare at Fred.

"Which agency?" Lepus sounded dumbfounded. He glanced at the floor, Conner's gun was a good ten feet from him, near the sliding glass doors to the balcony. He could see Bernstein's gun still in his shoulder holster sticking out from under his open jacket, but he couldn't get to either one before Maiko could so nothing was left to do but talk.

"You think I belong with those FBI agents?" Fred quickly asked.

"Maybe." Maiko also had located both pistols in the room. "You're stupid enough for the FBI."

Fred was still assessing his options, he needed to stall a bit longer since he didn't think that quickly.

"You mean I'm too stupid to work for you?" Fred asked with obvious nervousness. She snapped her head to nod in agreement

187

"Well," Fred plowed on, "when do I get the rest of my money for delivering the envelope to you."

"You don't." Maiko started to slowly move towards the pistol on the floor. "That bitch with Katz got my envelope, so you don't get anything from me."

"You paid me to give it to you, it's not my fault you couldn't keep it." Fred also moved towards the pistol. "So I should get my whole two thousand."

"I don't see it that way." Maiko kicked Fred in the chest, pushing him to the floor near the bathroom door before she dove towards the pistol. Grabbing it, she rolled to her side, pointing the pistol at Fred who was scrambling to his feet.

"Wait a minute." Fred raised both his hands. "I might be able to get that envelope back."

"How?" Maiko, still pointing the pistol at Fred, walked to Bernstein and pulled his pistol out of the holster.

"I've known Katz for a few years now, and I might be able to track him and his partner down and get the paper back for you."

"Are you stupid and greedy, or do you work for the CIA?" Maiko gave him a leveling stare.

"What?" Fred stumbled over his words. "Who are you?"

"Look, I don't have time to waste with a dumb ass like you." Maiko raised the pistol, leveling it at Fred's face.

"I can find your envelope for you," Fred insisted.

She was considering shooting him, but the noise might bring someone to the room.

"Maybe you are a stupid detective." She lowered the pistol. "I'll pay you two thousand more if you get that paper with the numbers on it for me."

"What?"

"Don't be an idiot," Maiko insisted. "Don't think for a minute I don't believe you looked at it."

"What were the numbers?" Fred asked.

"None of your damned business," Maiko answered. "Just get them back."

"How will I find you if I do get it back?" Fred felt a little better, it looked like he'd live another day.

188

"Don't worry, I'll find you." Maiko backed up towards the bathroom door.

"So are you going back to Los Angeles?" Fred watched as she moved to the bathroom.

"Never mind where I'm going, open the door and get out."

Maiko reached in and pulled a bath towel out. She wrapped one pistol up in it, then flopped the towel over the one she was pointing at Fred.

"Sure, no problem." He did as she said.

"I'll find you in two days," Maiko spoke loudly as Fred stuck his head into the hallway. "If you don't want to die in two days, you'd better find that piece of paper."

"Shit," Lepus muttered to himself. As he slowly closed the door, he looked both ways, trying to decide which way he should run. The decision was easy, to his left he could hear several people about to come out of the stairwell. Fred ran as fast as he could to his right and ducked into those stairs before a group of four men cautiously entered the hallway, from the other stairwell.

Inside the hotel room, Maiko was wrapping towels around the barrel of Conner's pistol, to kill both agents as they lay unconscious on the floor. She had already emptied their pockets and stuffed all the cash she could find into her bathing suit. She had pulled out the ID card from Bernstein's badge, maybe she could forge an ID with her picture on it to make traveling easier. She took both sets of keys in hopes that she could find a car.

As she checked over her preparations to make good her escape, she didn't hear the men. They got into position, then without a second's warning, two men slammed themselves against the door, crashing it open. She fell to the ground as someone shouted, "FBI, you're under arrest!"

She fired two rounds at them as they came through the door, hitting each man in the head. A shot missed her body by inches. She could hear heavy steps, running to either end of the hallway outside. Maiko emptied one pistol, shooting through the wall and into the hallway, trying to hit whoever was running out

189

there, but missed. She grabbed the other pistol, which she had dropped on the floor, and shot twice more through the wall.

The silence after her last shot was artificially quiet; no sound of people talking, no bird songs, nothing but background sounds, waves on the beach and wind in the trees. The distinct scent of burned gunpowder filled the hotel room as she ejected the empty clip and stuffed in another one she had taken from Conner. She looked around the room, noting that she was on the second floor. Maiko ran to the balcony. She stuffed the two pistols into the waistband of her wraparound skirt, tightening the drawstring as tight as she could so as not to lose the weapons. Below her, she saw a small strip of grass in front of the sidewalk. She grabbed hold of the balcony railing and flipped over the side, lowering herself so she was hanging onto the edge of the cement balcony. She then swung herself onto the first floor balcony below; luckily, no one was in that room. Maiko thought for a second, then swung over the top of the rail and directed herself so her body would land on the narrow strip of grass. She let go. As she fell to the grass, she tumbled over and rolled one and a half times.

Running around the side of the building, she almost ran into two local Mexican cops. One of the pistols fell from her waistband as she sharply halted her forward motion. Maiko fell to the ground as she grabbed for the gun then quickly raised herself to one knee and aimed both pistols at the policemen, firing them almost simultaneously. The one on the right fell immediately. The man on the left stumbled a second as he tried to draw his revolver; she fired again, hitting him in his head.

Maiko ran through the sparse but stunned crowd of vacationers, most of whom stood slack jawed watching the assault. Although the gun battles had seemed to last for an hour, only minutes had elapsed.

Maiko hijacked a car and was gone. Less than two minutes later, one of two FBI Special Agents peered over the balcony at the two dead policeman while the other agent was dialing a number on the phone.

"This is Dixon," he said. "The woman got away; two of our men are down, and two local cops are dead."

190

"Where's Katz ?" The voice on the other end asked.

"Gone," Dixon muttered. "It's been a bad day here, boss."

"Is anybody else there?" The voice on the other end of the phone sounded metallic and flat.

"Just the two strange FBI agents."

Dixon shook his head as he mentally parsed the possibilities.

"Are they alive?"

"Yeah." Dixon looked carefully at them. "Just knocked out, I suppose."

"Get them some medical attention," The voice paused. "All of them."

"Who are these two guys?" Dixon wanted to know.

"Don't ask too many questions," the voice quickly answered. "If you get any answers, you might be permanently assigned to the Arctic Circle, do you understand?"

"All too well."

21

A shot in the dark

I guess helicopters don't get the same respect as real planes. We landed at what looked like the backwater of LAX airport, our small craft lost among private and charter airplanes, along with the maintenance hangars for them; at least the number of passengers was at a minimum. A building of sorts loomed in front of us which I assumed would be our destination. Not wanting to walk the whole way, I kind of hoped there would at least be a bus to take us to the main terminal.

"Don't you think it's a little obvious that we're not plain old detectives when we make our grand entrance in a private helicopter?" Cassandra ducked her head and pulled her suitcase out of the helicopter.

"Well." I walked with her towards the small terminal. "They did take the trench coat doll with the 'spy on board' sign out of the back window for us."

"You do need to get some new material, you know." Cassandra saw Billy Sullivan stick his head out of one of the doors leading into the diminutive terminal.

"That guy was a private pilot," I said, "not an employee of Langley, so we're like any other big wig from private industry, a private helicopter is like a private jet. Besides, getting into Mexico with our pistols was easy, but getting back into the States with them through a regular check point might have been harder"

"I guess so." Cassandra opened the door. "I suppose I'll get used to it, eventually."

"Your car is in the parking garage." Billy handed me a set of keys. "E-4, slot 73. Just take the bus to the main terminal, then the shuttle to short term parking"

"Anything going on with the Germans?" I asked.

"Nothing yet." Billy was in a big hurry as he started to walk away. "The FBI have them now, and they aren't exactly from West Germany. I'm sitting in on the interrogation, so I have to be back there in thirty minutes. Get down to the ship and look for something the cops didn't find, I'm convinced there's something else down there."

"Yes, sir." I saluted as he rushed off.

After fifteen minutes of waiting, and then riding in airport buses, we finally made it to the right parking lot.

"What are we looking for on the ship?" Cassandra asked. "What the FBI couldn't find?"

"I assume the cops searched the whole ship, but maybe they didn't find everything." I thought for a second, yes, I had taken some notes while pretending to be an insurance investigator.

"Why don't you drive." Cassandra gently pushed me towards the driver's side. "You know the way."

"Sure." I thought for a second. "Where is that envelope the Asian woman had?"

"I snatched it right after I bashed her with my tote bag," Cassandra said with a grin, she got some satisfaction from reliving it.

"Where is it?"

"Right here." She patted her jacket. "Why?"

"What was in the envelope?" I had to ask, assuming that she looked at it.

"A list of numbers and letters," she replied, "probably a coded message."

"We should have given it to Billy." I spotted our car in the parking garage. "I suppose we'll see him soon, so we can give it to him then."

"Do you want to try to get in touch with him before we get going?" Cassandra asked

"No." I thought for a second. "I think looking for a clue on that ship is more important."

"Are you sure?"

"Let me see that piece of paper." I spotted our car.

"Here." Cassandra handed me the envelope after we both got into the car.

I gazed at the sheet of paper for a few seconds in silence.

"What is it?" She insisted. "A code of some sort?"

"No," I replied. "I'm sure it's not that."

"Well, what is it?"

"It's the payoff." I turned towards Cassandra. "It's the money."

"Bank account numbers." Cassandra nodded.

"Make a copy of the numbers, then hide it in your purse, or even in your underwear in case someone takes it from us."

....

"All right." I locked the car doors. "The Freighter is over there."

Cassandra looked around the parking lot. "Yeah, I remember, when you were arrested."

"I remember too." As if getting arrested for murder was forgettable.

"So, how do we get into the restricted areas?" She was still visually assessing the vicinity. "Most of the docks and warehouses are restricted."

"I still have the introduction letter for Lloyds of London." I opened the car trunk up and rifled through the zipper pocket on my suitcase, and found it.

"What about me?"

"You're my partner." I looked up from the papers at her. "You're included in all the official snooping."

"Let's snoop."

"First, I need to go to the harbor master's office and get an official pass, so if we're bothered by guards, they won't shoot us."

"That would be nice."

"You remembered to bring your pistol, didn't you?"

"I don't leave home without one, especially when accompanying Los Angeles' finest target."

....

"Sir," A pimply faced office worker greeted me. "I will need to see some more identification before I can give you a pass to enter the restricted areas." It was after six in the evening and

194

the lesser officials were in charge; this lesser official did not appear to be a fully formed adult yet.

"You have my driver's license, and here's my PI license for California." I tossed the additional card on the counter.

"What exactly are you looking for?" The youth examined the two IDs in front of him.

"As I said," I carefully began again. "The insurance company wants to locate all the shipping containers that the freighter Veracruz either had on her, or offloaded since she docked."

"That's a strange ship, all right," he muttered.

"How so?"

"Just that I've never seen so many cops buzzing around a ship like that before." He handed my licenses back. "I don't see how anything got overlooked."

"Did they check any offloaded cargo containers?" I asked.

"The records show that no containers were offloaded," he answered quickly, too quickly.

"But," I took a long pause. "At least one was offloaded, wasn't it?"

"I can't say for sure," He sounded a bit nervous. "I did hear some of the longshoremen talking about a high priced deal they lost out on."

"It was offloading a container from the Veracruz right after she docked?" Cassandra asked.

"Yes, Ma'am." Junior smiled at the pretty woman. "I didn't see nothing, but I did hear them talking about six or seven guys who did."

"Not the ones you overheard, but other workers?" I thought I knew what he meant.

"Yeah." He looked reluctantly from her to me. "The guys I overheard were pissed because they didn't get any of the under the counter bucks for moving the container off the books."

"Where could we find such an outlaw cargo container?" Cassandra asked sweetly.

195

"If a crew wanted to hide a container, I guess they might put it in the back of a warehouse, but there's a lot of warehouses around the docks." He smiled again at Cassandra.

"I guess we'd better start looking right away, then." She returned the smile.

"I should check on your insurance letter, though." The youth did remember some of his responsibilities. "I don't guess the London office would be open."

I thought for a second, subtraction after dinner isn't my specialty. "It's about quarter to three in the morning there."

"Maybe someone is at the Los Angeles office," Cassandra added.

I looked at her with a disapproving frown. Billy might not have covered all the bases with this alibi.

"Guess I could try." The young man sighed, still staring at Cassandra. "You have the number?"

"No," I said. "I took orders from the London office."

"No problem." He pulled a phone book from under the counter and dialed the number. Someone was in the office, and he was put on hold several times, this might be a problem. I'd hate to have to break into the warehouses.

"Apparently you're all right." The junior executive beamed at her as he hung the phone up. "They said it would be real nice if I let you look for anything that would help the insurance company out."

"Thank you." She smiled harder, I thought she might break her face, or something.

"Did anyone take an inventory of the containers on that freighter?" I asked.

"Sure." The young man turned and scanned a long row of folders, neatly placed in four long layers of slots about four inched wide. "A lot of the containers are coded with special numbers, so an inventory is easy. We keep a record of all the containers on all the ships."

"Could we get a copy of the list for the Veracruz?" Cassandra asked.

"All we need is the list of the container numbers, not the contents," I added.

196

"Sure." The night manager still acted entranced by Cassandra. He gazed at all of her. Then, flipping through the folder, he pulled two pages out and used a copier that stood not far from the counter.

"Thanks." Cassandra took the copies.

"I suppose you don't need the contents of them because some of them weren't accurate?" He asked.

"Right." I thought I might try for more information. "I haven't read the police report yet. Besides drugs, what were they carrying?"

"Oh, hell." He smiled at Cassandra again. "They found a couple a hundred automatic guns, lots of military stuff, and a whole bunch of antiques from China and Japan. All the containers that had the illegal stuff in them have been put on the dock right next to the ship. Nobody would say much more after they found the guns, it was kind of like they had found something that made them all shut up real quick."

"So, the cops took it all?" Cassandra asked.

"No." The young man shook his head. "Someone sent the cops away, and the FBI came in. They got that ship surrounded and won't let no one in."

He handed us passes that would give us free access to the dock area, and walked off; we were no longer his problem.

"Where do you think they might stash a cargo container?" Cassandra clamped the large pass onto her shirt.

"Maybe we'll get lucky." I pulled my small notebook from my inside coat pocket. "I wrote down a list of most of the containers on that ship when it was at sea, at least those I could read numbers off of, and the containers listed on the manifests the captain gave me. Maybe one of the containers I jotted down was the one the Germans later moved before the officials took inventory."

"Maybe."

Cassandra frowned as she spread the two sheets of inventory numbers on a small table by the entrance to the office. The night manager was watching us but I guessed it didn't matter. As we scanned the numbers, I put a check mark in my notebook by each number that also appeared on the dock master's inventory and Cassandra crossed them out. Within five minutes, I found one number in my notebook that wasn't on the dock master's inventory; I must truly live a charmed life.

"Well, you're one lucky son of a bitch." Cassandra's eyes lit up as she tore a piece of paper from the back of my notebook and wrote the container number on it.

"If we split up we might be able to search all the warehouses in the area where that freighter is docked," she added.

"I bet we need only look in the ones close by," I said. "They didn't have that much time between calling the cops as we docked and them getting here. To be sure, I'll check the ones the cops off loaded."

"Still," Cassandra insisted. "That encompasses a lot of buildings."

"Okay." I felt nervous about letting her search without someone to watch her back, but she was right. "You go all the way to the west end, I'll go to the east and we'll work our way to the middle."

"It would help if we had radios," Cassandra said. "You don't have any in your stuff in the trunk, do you?"

"No." I should have thought of them. "Maybe your lusty young friend up there has some we can borrow."

"You don't have any two way radios we can borrow, do you?" Cassandra walked back towards the young gentleman, smiling broadly. "We'll bring them back soon."

"I guess so."

The youngster walked to the wall to his right and opened a large wooden cabinet with a key from his key chain. In addition to supplies, a rack of walkie-talkies sat plugged into chargers, six units lined up on the shelf; he pulled out two and handed them to Cassandra.

"Thanks again." Cassandra took them. "You're a life saver."

"Yeah, cherry red with a hole in the middle," I whispered to Cassandra as we left the building.

"You're a real barrel of laughs, you know."

. . . .

Finding a needle in a haystack was an easy job compared to what faced us. The pile of opened containers on the dock were all on the list the night manager kid gave us which was sort of as I expected. I was off to my first warehouse where they stacked those damned cargo containers as high as Everest. Well, maybe not that high, but it would have helped to have a telescope to read the numbers on the top containers.

These warehouses were a lot more crowded than I had thought they'd be. A hospital never sleeps, and apparently neither does a major port; ships come and go all the time. Where would one hide a container? In plain sight, if I were the one hiding it, but, it hadn't been up to me to decide that. And so it went, for three hours and four buildings; no special cargo container jumped out at me. I did meet some interesting folks hauling and stacking boxes, it's quite a trick to put them all in the right order to be efficiently moved on and off ships.

The fifth warehouse, where I could hear some sounds from the far side, all the way to the back of the building, wasn't crowded at all. Not all the lights were on in the front of the warehouse.

"I finished this building, and I'm on to the next." Cassandra's voice squawked over the two way radio.

"Me too," I answered. "Going into my fifth warehouse."

"I'll be damned," I whispered to myself. The missing cargo box was right in front of me, it was on the bottom of a stack of two boxes, on the second row back from the large loading doors which were closed and locked on this warehouse.

I had to do this carefully, first things first. I pulled out my small Zippo transmitter and left a message to send a team to this warehouse soon, next, I called Cassandra on the walkie-talkie.

"I found it," I said. "Warehouse E, inside the door, on the second row, on the ground."

"Great," she answered. "Meet you there soon."

I turned the radio off. This container had to be empty; anything or anybody in it had to be long gone by now. I tapped the side of the container with the edge of a coin, it sounded empty. I began to walk around the large metal box, looking for a clue. Several painted letters and numbers were on it, other than the official number.

Looking towards the top, I again saw the regular rectangular openings. They were air holes, there had been something alive in it, maybe a man. How would he get out? I searched for a door of some kind, and upon careful inspection of the third side I saw what appeared to be a loose seam covered by a large painted letter H. I pulled at the metal seam; it moved enough to clearly see that the lower portion of the H was a door of sorts, maybe three feet high and three feet wide. The metal panel moved side to side more than up and down so I pulled it out and then to one side, nothing happened.   I then pulled it out and to the other side, I heard a quiet metallic snap. Something happened, the seam at the right appeared wider, and the metal panel slid slightly behind the left seam. This time, I pushed in and shoved the panel down. It was hinged on the bottom, so I pushed harder until the door fell into the large box.

I should have brought a bigger flashlight, all I had was a small flashlight that took two triple A batteries which threw a weak light, but it was enough to see quite a setup in this cargo box. I also saw a switch on the wall near the small opening which turned on three thin fluorescent lights high on the back and two side walls of the cargo container; I could now see all of the inside of this box which was almost as large as a small house. A large rectangular tank was welded to the top back of the area with two pipes coming down to a sink. The whole top of the cargo container consisted of black painted metal louvers. Light baffles had been positioned so that the interior lights couldn't be seen through the air holes in the top of the container. Containers were welded to almost every surface. I opened some of them; most of the larger ones contained batteries and some held food left in the smaller containers, all canned or freeze dried; trash was also stuffed into a lot of the smaller ones. It must have been close to the end of his trip, since not that much food was left.   A chemical toilet stood half way up the side in one corner, with a steel ladder welded to the inside of the container leading up to a platform which held the toilet, sink and a small shower. Below that platform were two large holding tanks, one for the sewage and the other for the drinking and bathing water.

I could smell the faint sewage odor I noticed while at sea; I bet he had an accident in there, what a system to have an accident with.   More importantly, a radio transmitter was welded into the opposite corner. This was the source of the North Korean coded radio transmissions from the Veracruz.   I sat on a small metal chair welded to the floor next to the radio transmitter. Where was the occupant of this tin hotel? Boy would I hate to travel in these accommodations, it would truly be the voyage of the damned, especially since there wasn't even a fan over the toilet.

The sound of a leather shoe sole quietly scuffing on the concrete warehouse floor made me instinctively pull my Smith and Wesson out of my shoulder holster. The trap door to the container was open, I should have shut it.

Could it be Cassandra? She'd have called my name if it were. I stayed still on the metal seat and pointed my revolver towards the opening. If I had to shoot in this closed metal box, I'd be deaf in two shots so I madly searched around for something. I pulled out the small flashlight from my pocket and stuffed the triple A battery as best I could into my left ear. I stuffed the cap of my ball point pen into the other ear; at least I wouldn't go deaf.

A hand thrust into the opening of the box. It was a woman's hand, holding a small Metallic blue twenty two or twenty five caliber automatic pistol, a classic pimp gun. I remained still as I pointed my revolver towards where her body was, unseen behind the container wall. The hand was followed quickly by a face, I suppose it was to see who I was and to fix on a target. I recognized Maiko as I hastily fell away from the hand with the gun. She fired twice quickly and I fired once; it was loud. Her bullets missed me, all I hoped in that instant is that neither of her bullets had hit the holding tank for the toilet.

22

Who was that masked man?

The ringing wasn't all that bad in my ears but I left the battery and the pen sticking out of my head while I waited. I didn't hear anything much, although I swear I could still hear the echo of my last shot. Maybe she was gone, or maybe I had hit her. I sat up, moved towards the opening, my revolver pointing the way. I crouched down and leapt out of the opening in the cargo container, rolling on my side, taking care not to puncture my head with the pen cap still sticking out of it. I looked in all directions. Maiko lay quite still next to the opening in the container, bleeding from her side. Cassandra was crouched next to a stack of cargo containers about thirty feet from me. With no one else in sight, I didn't hear anything except my own loud breathing. I got up quickly and dashed to the container Cassandra was standing next to.

"Nice earrings," Cassandra teased.

"Oh." I pulled the pen cap and battery out of my ears. "If you haven't noticed, revolvers going off in closed containers are loud, and I enjoy being able to hear your witticisms."

Cassandra pointed to the body slumped face down next to the opening of the cargo container as she asked, "Isn't that Maiko?"

"That was Maiko." I motioned for her to cover me as I went to Maiko's body; yeah, she was dead. I searched her pockets, finding nothing except another clip for the diminutive Beretta twenty five caliber pistol still clutched in her right hand, an expensive but ineffectual little gun.

"There's a whole house in that cargo box." I pointed to the container. "But, I don't think she was the one living in it, so whoever it was is still on the loose."

"So the Germans aren't the spies?" Cassandra asked.

"At least not the ones Billy's looking for." I took in a deep breath. "There's a radio transmitter in there."

"Speaking of radio transmitters, I tried to get you over the walkie-talkie. Cassandra patted her radio. "What happened?"

"I turned it off as soon as I went into the container, I didn't want anyone to hear me when I was in there."

I was still trying to calm down, with mixed results. I deliberately took long, slow breaths, keeping up the routine I had started a few minutes before, a routine that I began when I first saw Cassandra in the clear, crouched beside a box. Gun battles are unnerving, even when I don't get hit, it had also been loud, louder than they usually are.

"But you left the lights on in there and the door open." Cassandra pointed to the open hatch.

"I know," I said, and sighed.

That was careless, maybe that's why I was upset; stupidity can get me killed.

When we heard the door to the warehouse slam open, both Cassandra and I pressed our backs against the cargo container across from Maiko's body. I quickly stepped to the far corner of the container and peeked around the bend to see seven men, all in suits and drawn pistols rushing in and looking all around. One of the last ones in had a badge hanging from his belt proudly proclaiming that they were FBI so I holstered my revolver, and turned to Cassandra.

"FBI?" I said as the first of the agents spotted us.

"Put down your weapons, we are federal agents," The second man said as they all pointed their firearms at us.

"Not a problem," I calmly replied.

We both raised our hands.

"Who are you two?" The second agent asked me, flashing identification in my face.

"Benjamin Katz ." I nodded towards Cassandra "She is Cassandra Pales, my partner."

"Partner in what?" The agent who took Cassandra's pistol asked her.

"In Cheshire Katz Detective Agency," she answered decisively.

"Katz ," The agent questioning me said. "I know you, you're the private dick working for the insurance company."

"Right," I smartly answered. I kept my hands up. They had already put handcuffs on Cassandra, who wasn't too happy.

"My name is Agent Wellstone." The man motioned for me to place my hands behind my back. "You're both under arrest."

"What for?" I asked quickly

"For being in the wrong place," Wellstone answered with a smile. "A lot of wrong places."

"We have permission to be in here," Cassandra interrupted.

"With a dead body?" Wellstone pointed to Maiko. "I assume she's dead."

"As far as I could tell." I nodded. "And, before you ask, I shot her right after she opened fire on me first."

"That's your story for now, I suppose." The impatient FBI agent replied. Wellstone lost his smile. Three of the other agents had climbed inside the special cargo container, looking around.

"Maybe we should have a discussion about what you wanted with that cargo container," Agent Wellstone added.

"It is strange, isn't it," I said. "But, wouldn't you go inside it if you came across it?"

"It appears you two were looking for it, and I'd like to know why," Wellstone continued his line of questioning.

As I live and breathe, Billy Sullivan himself now came strolling into this hectic scene, maybe we could lose the handcuffs soon.

"Agent Wellstone," Billy greeted the agent.

"Yes." Wellstone was annoyed; I think he knew he was about to be told to let us go.

"Your boss wants to talk to you right now." Billy kept looking at Wellstone directly in the eye. "He's on the radio in your car, now."

Wellstone left immediately, leaving another nameless agent standing next to Cassandra and me. Billy didn't even look at us, no sign at all, he stooped down and went into the cargo container.

"Listen up, you two," the stranger next to us whispered. "My name is Agent Dixon, and two friends of mine were shot in Mexico trying to arrest that woman."

"What?" Cassandra cocked her head and looked at the agent. "Who are you?"

"I was there too, and I'm pissed as hell about it." Dixon stared at me. "One of my friends died and the other one may not make it, I want some answers."

"You're asking the wrong man." I shrugged.

"The shooting took place in your hotel room." Dixon was clearly getting mad, the veins on his neck were bulging quite a lot.

"We had checked out of that room, already," Cassandra interjected.

"I'll check both of you out if I don't get an answer, soon," Dixon blustered.

"Before your boss comes back in here, I'll give you one piece of advice." I took in a quick breath. "Whatever this is, both you and I are in over our heads. The FBI isn't in charge of all this, and I'm afraid that the actual agency in charge of all this is a lot more unforgiving than you guys are, I for one am going to forget this case and hope they forget me."

"Even if they do forget you, I won't," Dixon glowered. We looked up as Wellstone returned.

"Fine," he growled. "He can have you." He let both of us out of the handcuffs.

"Sullivan!" Wellstone shouted.

"Here," Billy answered as he came out of the cargo container.

"Take them, shoot them, I don't give a shit anymore." Wellstone handed Billy our weapons and stormed back out the door and into his car. Agent Dixon stared at us as Billy led us out of the warehouse.

"What's his problem?" Cassandra whispered to Billy as the three of us left the warehouse and headed to Billy's car.

"Inter-departmental turf wars." Billy handed us back our handguns. "They've become worse in the past five years."

"What's the deal?" Cassandra asked again. "If anything, your two agencies should get along on things like this."

"The whole FBI management structure has never gotten over the Hoover days," Billy observed. "They still think they run this country, and all the rest of us have to bow to their greatness."

Cassandra nodded silently absorbing yet another glimpse into the intelligence turf wars.

"Not to change the subject or anything, but Wellstone sounded pissed," I observed. I climbed into the back seat of Billy's car while Cassandra got into the front seat with Billy on the driver's side.

"This would make the fourth time the CIA has yanked his chain in this investigation." Billy shrugged his shoulders. "Oh well, I guess I can't complain too much."

"Who does he think we are?" I asked.

"Just plain old detectives who may have found out too much and we might have to clean up the problem." Billy smiled.

"Clean up the problem?" Cassandra asked.

"That's why agent Wellstone said he could shoot us if he wanted to." I grinned at Cassandra.

"You guys do that?"

She wasn't too happy with that last comment.

"Not usually." Billy kept a straight face. We were pulling Cassandra's leg in this particular case, but sometimes it's true. Cassandra sat tensely for a minute, ready to fight, then finally realizing we had been yanking her chain, she suddenly relaxed and looked slightly disgusted.

"That other agent back there told us that two FBI agents got shot in our hotel room after we left, what happened?" I asked.

"That was Special Agent Dixon," Billy said. "He talked his boss into letting him tail you and Cassandra to try and locate the woman, I think he's friends with a cop in Long Beach."

"Why didn't the head of the Los Angeles bureau stop him?" I quickly asked.

"He didn't find out in time," Billy sounded worn out. "I wish he had, it might have saved four lives."

"How did that Chinese woman get loose?" Cassandra asked.

"She got out of her ropes and jumped the wonder twins," Billy replied. "Both she and that odd friend of yours got away."

"He's not a friend of mine," I insisted.

"What about Bernstein and Conner?" Cassandra asked. "Are they all right?"

"Conner has a concussion, but Bernstein is all right," Billy answered. "That small woman knocked out two good officers in less than thirty seconds, then killed two FBI agent and two local cops."

"Damn, this whole thing has sort of gotten out of hand; it's good to know our guys are all right, though," Cassandra said. She sounded upset.

"This would have worked out fine if agent Dixon had gone through the proper channels," Billy sounded frustrated. "I have a feeling that his boss will have some choice words for him, as well as some disciplinary actions."

"Tell them not to be so hard on Dixon," I added. "I might have done the same thing in his situation. Besides, he did get his immediate boss to sign off on the project."

"I guess, maybe that's another reason for Agent Wellstone to be pissed," Billy said. "Do you guys think you could locate that Lepus fellow?"

"Why would we want to do that?"

The mere thought was annoying.

"Might be interesting if he could tell us what Maiko said before she shot two US agents and escaped," Billy answered.

"We'll find him," Cassandra interrupted.

"Bernstein said you got the best of that Asian agent." Billy grinned at Cassandra.

"She kicked her ass, if that's what you mean," I proudly added.

"You have to be good," Billy said.

207

"She tried to throw her foot in my face, and I moved to one side and knocked her out with my bag," Cassandra answered, slightly ruffled by the compliments.

"That Chinese agent was one hell of a fighter," Billy observed. "And, you must be too."

"What did the police and FBI find on the freighter?" Cassandra asked, changing the subject.

"The usual narcotics as well as national treasures from six Far East countries, including Japan, which is what Yoshihiro was investigating," Billy answered.

"What else?" She asked.

"Some automatic weapons, anti-tank missiles and six timing devices for fusion bombs." Billy shook his head. "And the worst part is, they were American, they were the latest design."

"How did they get on that ship?" I asked. "That freighter came from Hong Kong to Hawaii, to here, not the other way around."

"I know," Billy sounded pained. "If the devices have been on that ship since the last time they came through here, that might explain some of it, but none of the Germans are talking as of yet."

"That ship went from Germany through several European ports, England, Africa, Mid East, India Far East, Pacific, and here." I took stock of all the possibilities. "That's a lot of places to load up on timing devices for nuclear bombs."

"Like, we don't know that," Billy sounded frustrated. "We're checking each and every port for a clue right now, but that'll take quite some time."

"You know that container I found back there was the source of the North Korean coded transmissions," I said.

"So, did the Germans and whoever hid in that container know each other?" Cassandra asked.

"We don't know." Billy shrugged. "We don't know who, in fact we didn't know about the container until we heard that you two found it."

"I'll bet the Germans didn't know about the guy living in the cargo container." Cassandra thought out loud. "If whoever was in the box knew the Veracruz was a smuggling ship, they might feel safer on board because the Germans were adept at avoiding trouble, and I bet the Germans paid a lot of port officials to look the other way, but I do have one question."

"What?" I asked.

"If the Germans didn't know about the man in the box, then why was that box off loaded right after the ship docked and before the police came?" She asked. "Someone on the ship had to use one of the cranes to pick the container off the deck, or they at least had to know about it."

"It could have been lifted off the deck by a crane on the dock," I remarked.

"Even if it were, the deck crew would have to help do it," she replied.

"She's right," Billy agreed. "The crew had to know something."

"Maybe," I said. "But, they could have been paid to deliver the cargo container not knowing what was in it, maybe they knew a mystery man was in it without knowing who he was, or caring for that matter; a buck's a buck."

"Whoever he was and whether the crew knew who he was or not, he still got away," Cassandra sighed.

"You're absolutely right." I nodded. "He probably had an escape route planned once he got into Long Beach."

"What makes you think this was his destination?" Billy asked.

"He didn't have much more than a few day's worth of food and water left in there, besides wasn't he supposed to meet the computer scientist here in the States?" I answered.

"Was that woman an agent for Taiwan?" Cassandra asked Billy.

"She checked out," he answered cautiously. "But, she had dropped from sight for three months and they were afraid she was dead or compromised; now she is dead. We're going to send her fingerprints to them and confirm whether it was even their agent you killed."

"So, that actually doesn't answer the question." Cassandra turned back to me. "What was she up to?"

"More to the point, why was she in that warehouse, and how did she know to look there?" I asked Cassandra. "Did she go anywhere else in this complex before she got to that warehouse?"

"I'll ask the police and FBI after I drop you two off." Billy scratched his chin. "Finding out where else she went around here might be informative."

"That might be difficult since I didn't see any security cameras around any of the buildings I went into," Cassandra noted. "I didn't see too many security cops either."

"Did the Taiwanese government say what she was working on before they lost contact with her?" I asked Billy.

"Not exactly, but what they did say leads me to believe she might have been after the nuclear timing devices," Billy answered.

"Which may or may not be connected to the man in the metal box. I still don't know if we were on the same side or not," I commented.

I didn't like the prospect of having killed someone on the same side as me, but she wanted to kill me. Maybe if I had pressed her more in Mexico, this wouldn't have happened; stop this. She wanted me dead, and I'm not, I need to think simply when it comes to survival.

"So, what do you want us to look for now? The man in the box, the source and destination of the timing devices or the computer scientist?" I asked.

"All of it." Billy smiled. "Might as well have you two go for broke on this job."

"So, the whole crew of the Veracruz is in jail right now?" Cassandra asked, staring out the front windshield.

"No." Billy shook his head. "All the Germans are there, and most of the crew are, but some of the crew got loose before we could put them in holding."

"Was the cook one of the crew that got away?" I asked.

I never did trust that guy.

Billy nodded, "The police have rounded up most of the escapees, but the cook is still at large."

"Can we have pictures of the missing crew members, especially the cook since he's my favorite, I'd like a few copies of his picture." I asked.

"Yes," he agreed as he handed me a stack of photographs. "The cops gave me these. They're looking for the cook also, but not as hard as they should since they're convinced Maiko killed the Japanese man."

"Then they should be happy that Benjamin killed Maiko," Cassandra pronounced. She continued to ponder different scenarios in her head; I can always read her expression, at least that one.

"Somehow, I don't think so." Billy looked back at her, then at me. "I'll fix it anyway."

"So, the cook talks to someone at a restaurant, then that person contacts Lepus, then Lepus shows up in Mexico to deliver something to the Chinese agent." I covered the outline to mentally test for something, anything.

"Wait a minute." Cassandra pulled a number ten envelope from her purse. "This is what Lepus gave that woman in Mexico; we should have given it to you when we landed, but I forgot about it."

I forgot all about it, too. Dumb move number two, I hope number three isn't worse.

"Its a bunch of numbers." Cassandra looked at the paper inside the envelope.

"Let me see that," Billy said as she handed it over.

"We decided it's bank account numbers," I said.

"I'll bet they're Swiss." Billy nodded as he read them. "We can find out who they belong to in a day or so."

"It's the payoff?" Cassandra mused. "But for what?"

"All we care about is the man in the box right now." I was becoming focused on the task at hand.

"Billy." Cassandra collected her thoughts. "I'm new at this, but don't you think some of those FBI agents have figured out that Benjamin and I are CIA operatives by now? Especially that Dixon man?"

"Probably," Billy answered.

211

"Won't that be a problem for us later in this case, or in other cases?" She asked.

"All of them are under the same obligation as you are to keep their mouths shut," Billy said. "Besides, if anyone starts telling too many secrets, or becomes a problem..." He smiled. "Ask Benjamin about it."

....

"What the hell was that about?" Cassandra turned to face me. "What do they do if someone talks too much?"

"Did you read the papers you signed?" I asked. "Blabbing about who is a US spy, or telling the Russians all about how we target our missiles is considered treason."

"I read that." Cassandra fell silent.

"You get arrested, and put on trial," I added.

"The penalty can be death." Cassandra looked away from me.

"Deadly serious." I put my hand on her shoulder. "In some cases, there isn't even a trial."

"I don't like that." Her expression was bleak.

"This job still needs to be done, though," I pondered. "Besides, making our real jobs public can out every one of our CIA contacts, and for some of them, that could mean they will be killed."

"I guess you're right," she said sadly.

"We need to concentrate on this case," I said as I maneuvered the car out of the parking lot.

"What do you think the pay off was for?" Cassandra finally spoke after a few minutes of silence.

"I think it's a payoff for the timing devices." I quickly glanced at Cassandra as I threaded my way through heavy traffic. "I still want to know why Maiko was here in that warehouse. She couldn't have followed us because we had a huge head start. She knew exactly where that cargo container was."

"I bet she knew it was somewhere here, and when she saw us at the docks, she let us look for it," Cassandra guessed.

"You could be right."

"Maybe she was the outside man for the guy in the box?" Cassandra guessed.

"But that still doesn't tell us where the man in the box is now." I shook my head. "I think we can safely say that he's not in Long Beach, at least not near the warehouses with all the cops and FBI around."

"But he didn't destroy the home in the container, nor the radio transmitter, that would lead me to believe that he expected to use it as a way back home," Cassandra reasoned.

"Maybe he was working with Maiko?" I asked in a low voice, mostly directed to myself. "Maybe she was supposed to re-supply him with food and recharge his batteries?"

Charge his batteries? I remembered hearing Maiko and Yoshihiro doing the horizontal mambo in the cabin on the freighter, next to mine. Was he doing an investigation of missing national treasures, or were he and Maiko involved in a triple cross? No, only in the movies, but, maybe.

"What are you thinking?" Cassandra interrupted my train of thought.

"I was wondering if Maiko and Yoshihiro were planning on double or triple crossing one or more of the people on that ship for fun and profit." I said as I stopped at a red light. "They were much the couple on that boat. And, they also had loud and enthusiastic sex in the next room."

"It could be faked." Cassandra tried not to look at me. "Not that I ever do that, but some women who want to manipulate a man can do it convincingly."

"Thanks a lot for the ego booster." I shot her a hurt look. "Anyway, I had a gut feeling that they were in love when I interacted with them on the ship."

"Don't worry, Benjamin, I love you more than I thought I ever could love a man."

Cassandra patted my thigh, what did that mean? No, wait, I must turn my analytical brain off, and turn my primitive brain back on, it's more tolerable.

"And, I love you enough to marry you right here in L.A., before you finish this quarter," I blurted out.

I squeezed her hand. The light turned green and I started driving towards her house which I felt was a nice place to decompress and collectively put a plan together.

"Let's finish this case first." Cassandra looked back out the front windshield. "Isn't this the way to Huntington Beach?"

"Yeah, I thought we could regroup at your folk's house. Besides, it's down the Coast Highway."

"I like your thinking." Cassandra smiled at me. "Now, what did you mean by regrouping?"

23

Who's that knocking at my head?

"Why are you parking at the end of the block?" Cassandra asked.

"Because I don't trust anybody." I started counting the reasons on my fingers. "I've been shot at, the FBI thinks we're security risks, the Long Beach police think I'm a murderer, do I need more reasons?"

"No," Cassandra chuckled. "The list makes me feel safer."

"How about this." I pointed to her parents' house. "You give me the key and I'll go in the front door, and if the house is all right, I'll let you in the back door."

"I can let myself in the back door, the back door has a separate key," Cassandra replied.

All the lights were out, that might mean something since Cassandra told me she always left some of the lights on to make the house looked occupied. That never works with most burglars, but it didn't matter. Maybe Billy and his minions had turned the lights out when they locked up. Running scenarios in my head, I slowly turned the key in the lock; and even more slowly, quietly, I opened the front door. No moon was out that night, actually it had set much earlier and it was almost dawn. The hinges must be oiled, since I heard no squeaks as I slipped into the entrance hallway.

But I felt the presence of someone behind the door. I reached for my revolver, a dark shadow slammed the butt of a pistol down on my skull. Crumpled onto the tile floor of the front hallway, on my knees inside the door, I began to black out. I saw the pistol raised once more to hit me again on the head. Still trying to stay upright, I tried to pull my revolver all the way out of its holster. I was able to raise my Smith and Wesson almost high enough to defend myself; but not far enough to take any kind of an aim. I guess being hit is better than being shot.

I heard a loud crack which sounded as if someone had fired a gun. I didn't feel anything ripping me open; I did, however, feel a lot of pain on the side of my head. Did he shoot me there too? No, it was something else, my brain was fogging.

"Benjamin!" Cassandra shouted as she turned the light above me on.

"Who is it?" I grabbed the throbbing spot on the side of my head, feeling a small amount of blood oozing through my fingers.

"Lepus!" Cassandra shouted.

"Get me a doctor." Lepus was lurching around the living room holding his right arm. "You shot me! You shot me!"

"Of course I did!" Cassandra shouted. She ran to the kitchen to retrieve a towel.

"What the hell are you doing here!" I demanded.

I pointed my revolver at him as I sat on the front entrance floor. Cassandra returned from the kitchen and threw each of us a towel.

"Will you two stop bleeding all over my parents' living room," Cassandra implored.

She trotted over to me and looked at my head while I was still sitting on the tile floor.

"Are you all right?" She asked me.

"I suppose I'll live."

I looked darkly at Fred Lepus as he wrapped the towel around his upper right arm.

"But, I can't say the same about him," I grumbled.

"Let's find out why he's here before I let you loose on him." Cassandra said. She walked to his gun which was laying on the living room rug. She picked it up and pointed it at Fred while I holstered my revolver.

"Maybe we can shoot him in the back yard so I won't have to clean up the mess," she added.

"Very funny you two." Lepus coddled his arm. "I'm the one who almost lost his life in Mexico because of those careless FBI agents."

"So, the woman got away?" Cassandra motioned for Fred to move to the kitchen. "Don't tell me she tried to kill you."

"Of course she tried to kill me." Lepus attempted to sit on the sofa.

"Get into the kitchen so your blood doesn't mess up the living room!" Cassandra demanded.

"Yeah, yeah." He meandered towards the kitchen as I followed them there.

"Why are you here?" She demanded.

"Katz doesn't live out here anymore, but after a few phone calls I found out your parents had a house in Huntington Beach; I figured you both would come here eventually."

"That still doesn't tell us why you were waiting to bleed all over Cassandra's house," I added.

I wasn't that sorry about the hole in his upper arm; he had tried to crack my head open, after all. Cassandra's shot had shot cleanly through the flabby part of his upper right arm.

"You always were a wise ass." Lepus glared at me.

Cassandra gave him a wet washcloth. "Well, answer the question."

She wiped my bump with another wet washrag, ouch.

"I figured you two were onto a sweet deal with the insurance company, look at the way you guys pursued this case." Fred wiped his arm which was still bleeding, although not nearly as much as before he had tightly tied the first towel around the wound.

"My clients were arrested, and since the police and FBI are in cahoots against me, I thought I'd kind of horn in on your case and take a piece of the action," Fred went on.

"What makes you think breaking into my house and assaulting us would encourage us to give you anything?" Cassandra scowled. "Look at the back door, that idiot broke the window to get in here."

"Sorry about that." Fred gave her a placating grin. "Could I have a clean towel? I need to stop this bleeding."

"Sorry doesn't cut it." Cassandra threw another clean towel at Lepus. "I want you to pay to fix the window, the rugs and the hole in the wall."

"Wait a minute." Fred wrapped his arm in the clean towel. "You put that bullet hole in your own wall."

"Only because you were about to smash in my fiancé's head," Her voice rose in anger again.

"Yeah, yeah, maybe I was a little pissed off about how you two screwed up a good case for me again." Wincing, Lepus sat back carefully, calming down a peg.

"This isn't your case, you idiot!"

Cassandra hadn't calmed down, in fact, she was still winding up.

"In case you haven't noticed, this is an active case the locals and the feds are working on." She moved closer to Fred, appearing to be breathing fire at the moment.

"Maybe you two should calm down now," I quickly interjected. I didn't want her spilling the beans to that dimwit. As if Lepus needed to know Cassandra and I were working for the CIA; that would not go over well at Langley.

"You're right, Benjamin." Cassandra sat down in a kitchen chair, letting out a deep breath. "I'm pissed of as hell seeing you get beaten, and then at me having to shoot someone, even a moron like him."

"I know," I agreed. "Not to mention the mess in your folk's house."

She knew what she had almost said to Lepus, she knew she had to be more in control.

"Right." She slumped into a chair around the kitchen table.

"Besides." I smiled at Cassandra, then glared at Fred. "Lepus is lying."

"Am not!"

"You wanted to get the envelope back." I stared at Lepus. "Right?"

"Well." Fred looked at his wound again. "Maybe."

"Well, you dumb ass." Cassandra said angrily. "We gave it to the cops, so you wasted your time."

"You did what?" Fred Lepus sounded incredulous. "Why the hell would you do that?"

"Unlike you, we like to keep our licenses so we can keep earning a living." I looked at him, his wound was clotting up.

"If I don't get the list of numbers, that crazy bitch will kill me." Fred took in a deep breath. "Then, I won't be able to make a living at anything."

"I wouldn't worry about Maiko," Cassandra said with a wicked grin.

"Why?" Fred looked at Cassandra.

"She's dead," I answered.

"Dead?" Fred moved his stare to me.

"Dead," I agreed.

"Well." Fred searched for meaning in these events. "There goes two thousand bucks."

"That is all you care about, isn't it?" Cassandra looked at Fred, then at me, then back at Fred.

"You bet it is." Fred stood up. "I'm broke and stuck out here without a pot to piss in."

"Look." She stared at him, disbelief and shock on her face. "You're guilty of breaking and entering, assault, maybe attempted kidnapping. So why don't you tell us everything you know about the woman you met in Mexico and that guy you worked for in DC."

"So, what's in it for me?"

"I'll let you go home and not tell the cops to arrest you," Cassandra answered.

"I might even pay for your plane ticket myself just to be rid of you," I added.

"Something tells me there's still a lot of money in this case." Fred smiled at me. "I peeked inside that envelope. A bunch of bank account numbers were on that piece of paper."

"We know," Cassandra said. She glanced at me, somewhat chagrined that even Lepus figured out that those were bank account numbers.

"Maybe that woman was double crossing someone, maybe not. She was the chief suspect in the murder of a

219

Japanese agent on a freighter, so it's evidence and none of ours or your business," she added.

"I bet you two boy scouts didn't even copy down the numbers, did you?" Fred looked at me.

"If you had the numbers, why didn't you give them to the woman back in Mexico?" Cassandra asked.

"As soon as I realized that she wouldn't shoot me, I decided to get the original letter, then try to find out which bank it was in and attempt to beat her to it." Fred sounded so smug.

"What would have prevented her from shooting you at any time before or after you steal her money?" I slowly shook my head.

"Details are better taken care of when you're rich as hell." Fred looked again at his wound, which had stopped oozing blood. "Besides, I hadn't decided on exactly what I wanted to do anyway, I wanted more options open to me in the long run. Besides, she'd dead now, so it doesn't matter what she might have done to me."

"The best option in these cases is always to let the cops handle it," I said. "You live longer that way."

"I still don't see why you two didn't copy the numbers down." Fred shook his head side to side. "It's always better to have more options open in a case, especially options that might be worth millions. That many bank account numbers means millions of dollars."

"We don't like to spend our best years in jail," I replied. "Maybe you do, but we don't."

"Damn it." Fred stared at the table, still holding his arm tightly.

"You wanted the envelope so the woman wouldn't shoot you, didn't you?" Cassandra observed.

"Yeah," Fred sighed. "Didn't you dopes notice, the series of numbers on the back flap of the envelope? My guess was that they were keyed to, or part of the bank account numbers inside the envelope."

"So, you had to have the original envelope to give to her," Cassandra said, watching Lepus carefully. "And, you didn't open up the envelope for fear she would have picked up on that?"

"Right," Lepus sighed. "I held it up to a strong light and copied as many of the number sets as I could."

"We don't have the envelope and the woman's dead. You could help us find out what's going on." I offered.

"Why not." Fred looked up at me. "You are still going to buy my ticket home, right?"

"If you tell us the truth, yes," I answered.

"First class?"

"Be thankful if I don't stick you in a box and ship you back parcel post."

"She didn't tell me anything except that I'd better get her envelope back or she'd kill me," Lepus reluctantly said. Now that he'd lost any chance of tricking us out of the envelope, he apparently didn't mind talking.

"I heard the shooting, and I asked one of the bell boys and he said that woman shot a bunch of cops. I caught up with her near the airport, she had stolen some clothes, and I saw her dump two pistols into a trash can. That crazy woman rented a car to get back into the states, I talked to the rental clerk. She told the clerk she had to meet someone back in Los Angeles the next day, I don't know if that was just a story or the truth."

"Did she say who she was supposed to meet?" Cassandra asked.

"No." Fred shook his head. "Like I said, I'm not sure that story was even the truth."

"What about that Zimmer guy in DC?" Cassandra asked.

"Nothing special about him." Fred shrugged his shoulders.

I could see that his dreams of great wealth had been dashed, yet again.

"He paid me five hundred to put him up in a safe place. I didn't know about the envelope until that woman called me and told me to bring it to her in Mexico; I found it hidden in a bird feeder in the back yard. The FBI didn't find it, I did," Fred continued.

"What was all that crap about Asian gangs?" Cassandra asked.

"The woman had a slight accent," Lepus said. "I was talking to a friend before I left and he told me all about the gangs and how they liked to vacation in Baja California."

"You believe everything people tell you?" Cassandra asked with a slight smile.

"She didn't give you anything when you made the deal?" I had to bring the conversation back on track.

"No, she didn't. She told me she had to check it out and see if it was real before she'd pay me everything she had promised. We were supposed to meet an hour later at the pool, then she'd pay me," Fred ran out of breath.

I knew that was probably a lie, both Cassandra and I saw Maiko slip him an envelope full of cash back at the hotel in Mexico. It might have been only a partial payment, but with the way Lepus operated, we'd never know for sure.

"She still owes me two thousand for the drop," he said.

"I wonder if she was the original contact person for the Mexico deal, or if she took someone else's place?" Cassandra looked at me.

"Could you get our holey friend here a plane ticket to D.C. for later this morning? Use the company credit card, I suppose we could claim it as an expense," I said.

I was again feeling disgusted with Lepus. Maybe in a year or two I could see the humor in all this, but not yet.

"Right." Cassandra stood up. "I'll get some stuff from the medicine closet to stop any infections and bandage that arm so you won't bleed all over the airplane seat."

"You get his ticket and I'll call a cab to pick this piece of crap up," I added.

"What happens if my wound is serious?" Fred was hatching yet another money scheme.

"What happens if we call the cops and you get arrested?" Cassandra answered quickly. "They'll give you great medical attention in prison."

"I still think this hole in my arm is worth five or six grand, for pain and suffering."

"Let's see." Cassandra looked at the ceiling of the kitchen. "This is my house, and you broke the back window and entered without my permission, then you beat this poor guest of mine with a gun which I bet you don't have a California license for, and, you're trying to blackmail us."

"Not blackmail, just compensation." Fred smiled at Cassandra.

"I think my not pressing charges, and giving you a free ticket back home is compensation enough." Cassandra smiled back at him.

"Can't blame me for trying." Fred shrugged.

24

Come out, come out whoever you are.

"Do you suppose we're rid of him?" Cassandra sat back down at the kitchen table.

"You did put him in the cab, right?" I patted the sore spot on my head. "Keep in mind I wouldn't have been adverse to putting him in a coffin."

"Here, come over to the sink and I'll clean the matted blood out of your hair."

Cassandra turned on the faucet and adjusted the temperature of the water.

"Just a simple wash and a cut." I leaned over the kitchen sink.

"I'll have to remember to call some cleaning companies to get to those carpets tomorrow. I mopped as much as I could up with cold water, but there's still a mess out there."

Cassandra used the sprayer to wet down my hair, it was warm and it felt good to have her gently massage my lump; that started me thinking about my other lump.

"I don't want my mom to ask about large blood stains on the front carpet," she ruefully added. "Besides, we still need Mark to help find the missing man from the box."

"Good idea," I agreed.

"Don't move your head, I might hurt you." Cassandra gently dried my hair. "Let me get my hair dryer, maybe the hot air will feel good."

Her making over me made me feel better than anything else.

"What time is it?" I asked.

Cassandra was taking extra care with drying my hair. The small cut had closed up and after three aspirin, the throbbing was going away.

"Seven in the morning," she answered.

"Sometime we'll need to sleep, you know." I felt my head.

"Maybe tonight?" She looked carefully at my bump. "You're fine."

"Let's call Mark, then go meet him."

. . . .

Mark chose to meet us at his house. He didn't know about my working for the CIA, and he never would. He was, however, our best contact within the police department in Los Angeles and he'd help us as long as we didn't ask him to do anything too close to the edge.

Mark Hatton and I met as we both mustered out of the Marines. He had been an MP, and started a job as a Los Angeles Policeman right after his tour. He had tried to convince me to also join, but I had other career options to pursue. We had, over the years, remained good friends. Cassandra and I had helped him on many cases, and he has returned the favor many times. I think he wound up liking Cassandra more than me, but I could be wrong. Cassandra was a bridesmaid at his wedding a few years ago.

This time, asking Mark for help would be easy for both of us; we wouldn't ask anything difficult, and he could help to solve a local crime, although we had to steer clear of the real crime of espionage.

"It's good to see you." Mark opened the front door for us. "Say, you two look like you haven't gotten much rest."

"Actually, we never got to sleep last night," Cassandra answered. She walked in ahead of me, heading to the nearest comfortable chair in the living room.

"I guess the reason wasn't good either." Mark followed me to the living room.

"No," I answered as I sat in the sofa next to Mark. "It's the case we're working on."

"Hey, what's that mess in your hair?" Mark quizzed me. "It looks like you got bashed back there."

"You'll never guess who," Cassandra piped up.

I glared at her for dropping that hint. Bringing up Lepus might lead to places I didn't want to discuss with Mark.

"Who?" Mark sounded genuinely curious.

"That woman from the freighter, the one who the cops think actually killed the Japanese guy," I said, deflecting. "Kind of ironic, I guess."

"Yeah," Cassandra blushed slightly at her Lepus faux pas. "First she frames Benjamin, then she bashes him in the skull."

"Are you two working the freighter case together?" Mark asked.

"Well," she replied, "sort of."

"I thought Cassandra was here to go to school?" Mark sounded confused.

"Me too." Cassandra leaned back in the chair and relaxed. "But, you know how easy it is for Benjamin to talk me into a case. I have to be done by at least this Tuesday so I can teach a class."

"What's the case?" Mark asked. "I know about that murder in Long Beach, but what was it all about?"

"Lloyds of London hired me to check this particular ship out; they had been having problems with it," I replied.

"I thought there had to be a huge insurance company behind your problems." Mark looked at me. "I heard all about you being arrested; the detectives in Long Beach called me when they found out I knew you."

"Yeah," I sighed. "The insurance company wants to prove they couldn't be responsible for the death, and that the smuggling had nothing to do with the losses they have incurred for the ships managed by the owners."

"Big money?" Mark asked.

"Millions," I agreed; it sounded like a good story.

"The fee must be pretty good."

"That's why I'm here with him." Cassandra smiled at Mark.

"I thought I heard you two." Mary, Mark's wife, peeked into the living room dressed in a nurse's uniform.

"You have a day shift now?" I asked.

"Yes," she answered. "Didn't Cassandra tell you?"

"I guess we haven't had much time for social talk since I flew out here." I shrugged my shoulders. "We haven't had time for much of anything since I came out here."

"Do you guys want some coffee?"

"Yes!" We both said.

"I think they want to talk to me, Honey," Mark said to his wife.

"Sure." She turned to the kitchen. "I'll be in with the caffeine when it's ready."

"So, what do you need from me?" Mark got right to the point.

"The way it seems to be playing out is that the murdered Japanese man was an investigator from the government of Japan," I began. "He was checking out the smuggling."

"The narcotics?" Mark asked.

"There was more," Cassandra said. "They were also smuggling fine art objects, national treasures."

"That's kind of interesting all on it's own," Mark observed.

"How?" Cassandra asked.

"The Japanese government sends an undercover agent on that ship, then an insurance company sends their own investigator to that ship," Mark replied. "That must have been one hell of a trip you had."

"It was," I agreed. "And, before you ask, I didn't know about him. But, I did figure out who he was and we agreed to share information, but he was dead before we could."

"What about the woman?" Mark continued pressing.

"The woman he was traveling with is also dead, and we think a double or triple cross took place," I said.

Mark was now entranced with the story and Mary couldn't help but be drawn in too. She set our coffee cups down and sat on the recliner, opposite the rest of us.

"We suspect that one of the original crew of the freighter may be involved, but he has eluded the Long Beach police and the FBI," I continued.

"Also." Cassandra glanced my way, ready to stop if I gave the sign but I didn't. "There might have been someone stowing away on the freighter who was involved in the double cross."

"What kind of double cross?" Mark asked.

Cassandra knew where not to tread.

"We think several members of the crew were ready to sell different smuggled stuff to several different buyers," I replied. "I think some of the smugglers were getting greedy and not sticking to the agreed upon deals."

"Do you have any idea what that stowaway looks like?" Mark asked.

"Unfortunately, no." Cassandra shook her head. "But we think that the missing cook will try to contact this person because there's a lot of money still floating out there, up for grabs."

"We're going to start looking for him, but it would be a real bonus if you could put his face out there." I handed the picture to Mark.

"This guy maybe a murderer, and for sure he's a drug smuggler." Cassandra pointed to the photo of the ship's cook. "So, to arrest him would be a good thing not only for us, but for you too."

"Why haven't the Long Beach police dragged him in yet?" Mark asked.

"They think the woman companion or one of the German officers did the killing, so they haven't searched that hard for the cook." I looked at Cassandra, then Mark. "The FBI doesn't think he's worth it either."

"If you do manage to locate and arrest him, we'd like to talk to him for a few minutes though," Cassandra added quickly.

"Ah," Mark paused. "The real reason."

"Do you mind?" I asked.

"Not really." Mark studied both of us carefully.

"I hate to say this," Mary sounded worried. "But, you both look like hell."

"It's been a long week," I answered with a sigh.

"Not much sleep since Benjamin got arrested," Cassandra added.

"Arrested?" Mary asked. "What for?"

"Murder, this time," Mark answered. "But they dropped the charges a few days ago."

"You need to slow down, Benjamin." Mary glanced at both of us with a concerned expression. "Both of you do."

"The hours are hell, but the pay is great." I forced a smile.

I didn't know the Long Beach police had actually dropped the charges on me; I guess that was a good thing.

"Remember, you need to live to spend it." Mary stood up. "I have to get to work now, please have dinner with us before you leave."

"We will." Cassandra stood up and put her hand on my shoulder.

. . . .

"So, you think the mystery man will be around here?" Cassandra got out of the car.

"The North Korean code was a misdirection." I looked up and down the street. "My guess is that the mystery box dweller is Chinese. Maiko was Taiwanese, Taiwan and China spy on each other even more than us and the Russians, it's more of a serious game with them. Whether she was after the drugs, timing devices or the encryption keys, I think she was sent by her government to keep an eye on the mainland Chinese spy in the cargo container. The only two players left alive or out of jail are the cook and the guy in the box, so let's check around Chinatown and see if the cook shows up."

"If we find the one we know, we might find the other one we don't know," Cassandra agreed with me. "In my state of exhaustion, anything sounds good to me."

"In that case," I said with a grin. "I have a proposition for you once this case is over."

"I think it's the same one I have for you."

She patted my posterior; we had somewhat the same idea.

"He's a serious cook, so lets start with the better restaurants." I started walking north on Hill Street.

"Most classy restaurants aren't open at this hour of the morning." Cassandra pulled my arm. "You do realize it's that early, don't you?"

"Yes," I acknowledged. "I was planning to wait until lunch to start the gastronomic tour."

"What now?" She was tired; annoyed, and tired. "Breakfast?"

"Maybe later." I continued walking north on Hill. "Right now I'd like to introduce you to an old friend of mine."

"Who?"

"I guess we could start our own version of 'who's on first' but my friend's name is Ho, those who know him call him Albert."

It was too early in the morning for bad jokes, but sometimes I can't help myself.

"Why not." Cassandra slowly shook her head as she followed me across the street. "Who's Albert? A snitch, a spy or a cook?"

"It's all mysterious."

I motioned for her to turn left, one block from Alpine. "How so?"

She was right behind me as I walked up to a wooden door painted bright red, sandwiched between several business and from the outside did not look like a private residence.

"You be the judge." I rang the bell.

"Yes?"

The red door opened a crack, the security chain snapped tight. A beautiful woman's face peered through the small opening.

"Benjamin!" She sounded surprised.

"It's me," I greeted her. "I brought Cassandra here to meet you."

She closed the door, unlocked the chain and opened the door wide.

"Come in you two, let me get Albert."

Annie was beautiful, she was wearing a silk wrap around with brightly colored dragons of various sizes on it. It was way too thin, and left little to the imagination as Annie rushed back down the hall and into the bedroom.

"Benjamin?" Cassandra pulled my arm to turn me around facing her.

"I didn't look." I raised my right hand. "Honest."

"Right." She gave me a quick sour expression. "Who is she, Albert's wife?"

"Yes, her name is Annie."

"Benjamin!" A loud booming voice proceeded Albert from the bedroom. "What the hell are you doing here this early in the morning?"

"It's not that early if you never made it to bed the night before," I responded to my friend as he strolled out of the back bedroom and down the hall towards us.

"Come on upstairs."

Albert tied a knot in the sash to his robe. His robe was also silk, a dyed a dark royal blue with no images on it, although it was quilted and quite modest.

"Upstairs?" Cassandra followed me.

"The house is not that wide, but we have four floors to fit it all in, so our kitchen and dining room are on the second floor." Albert rushed up the flight of stairs. "I'll get some tea brewing right away, have you two had breakfast yet?"

"No, we have not."

Cassandra looked around as she slowly followed us up the stairs from the first floor, which had a narrow entrance hall leading from the front door. Just as we entered their home, a moderately sized living room lay to the left. A hallway led to the master bedroom, which took up almost half of the downstairs. with a straight staircase, on the right as we came in from the front

231

door. A small bathroom was tucked under the stairs. Hardwood floors gleamed around the edges of the many oriental rugs carefully arranged in the rooms. All furniture was Asian, maybe Chinese, and most of it looked old. A three panel carved wooden partition separated the front entrance hall from the stairs so you couldn't see the stairs from the front door.

"What do you want?" Albert shouted from the back of the kitchen. "Eggs all right?"

"Eggs are fine," Cassandra answered first. "What kind of tea are you making?"

"It's a morning blend, with lots of caffeine," Albert answered. "We don't like the taste of coffee, but we still need the kick in the mornings."

"That'll be fine," Cassandra answered.

"This place looks great, you've done some more decorating since I was here last." I looked around the dining room and into the kitchen at several large cabinets holding many fine dishes. The table was old, as were the chairs; Albert had inherited most of it from his father's family.

"Yeah, I think we're finished decorating for awhile." Albert stuck his head out of the kitchen. "What brings you here this early?"

"A case." I walked to the kitchen, I didn't want to shout.

"That's what I thought, sit down." Albert pointed to a seat at a small round breakfast table to the right of the door into the kitchen.

"What's on the next two floors up?" Cassandra followed me into the kitchen and sat next to me around the table.

"Oh." Albert looked at Cassandra. "The next floor has two bedrooms with big closets and a bath, and the top floor has two offices and another large bathroom, Annie and I work up there."

"Hi, guys," Annie said.

She walked into the kitchen and sat next to Cassandra, she had dressed in jeans and a pale green tank top and still wore her bedroom slippers; I could see she hadn't put a bra on yet, and, yes, Cassandra gave me another one of those looks.

232

"Hi." Cassandra extended her right hand. "I'm Cassandra."

"That will never do." Annie stood and hugged Cassandra. "I'm Annie and I'm real glad to finally meet you, Benjamin can't say enough nice things about you."

"You have me at a disadvantage," Cassandra said uncomfortably.

"Don't feel too bad, you're the first girlfriend he's ever introduced us to." Annie stopped hugging Cassandra and stepped back enough to focus on her face.

"Yeah." Albert cracked eggs into a stainless steel bowl. "You must be pretty special to have him bring you around to his old Marine buddies."

"I've kind of noticed that he doesn't talk about that part of his life too much."

Cassandra looked at me, not knowing how much Albert knew about my real occupation.

"Albert was my sergeant when I first got to Viet Nam." I slowly turned to lock eyes with Cassandra. "We knew each other quite well up until I transferred to another unit."

"Yeah." Albert stirred the eggs with a whisk, adding herbs; I could smell the strong aroma of dill weed. "We were buddies until he sold out to ride shotgun for the CIA."

"Hey, it was Special Operations, and I was suicidal then, anyway." I shot a quick look at Cassandra; she silently acknowledged that he didn't know I was still working for them.

"Well, I'm glad you came to your senses and mustered out."

Albert poured the eggs into a heating pan.

"I figured I'd live longer," I chuckled.

"I hope so." Cassandra patted my arm.

"Cassandra and I are getting married," I said, watching Annie; I knew she'd go ballistic and she wasn't a disappointment.

"Oh, my God!" Annie shouted as she dragged Cassandra around the kitchen, alternately hugging and trying to dance with her.

"Calm down." Albert waved his hands at Annie. "It's too early for Chinese new year."

"I can't help it." Annie let Cassandra sit back down. "I think this is great, when do you plan to do it?"

"I have one more quarter in school, then we'll get married." Cassandra grinned from ear to ear; her face at this moment was alone worth coming here.

"Hey, we're coming, right?" Albert slapped me on the back as the omelet sizzled in the pan.

"You bet." I smiled back at him. "Whenever we settle on where and when, you two are there."

"I heard something about a case?" Annie put tea cups, plates napkins and silverware on the table.

"Yes." Cassandra got up and helped Annie carry the teapot, sugar and milk to the table. "We're looking for somebody who Benjamin thinks Albert can help find."

"Do you remember that murder in the freighter in Long Beach a few days ago?" I Asked.

"Yes I do." Albert slipped the large omelet onto a big platter. "It was a Japanese citizen, wasn't it?"

"Yes," Cassandra answered.

"And, wasn't a Taiwanese woman shot in a warehouse there last night?" Albert set the platter on the table. "I heard it on this morning's news, they said the FBI shot her in a gunfight."

"It's the same case," I answered. I noted the public story about Maiko's death, I was glad my name wasn't used.

"The crew of the freighter was smuggling drugs and antiquities," I added.

"Was that all?" Albert cocked his head to one side.

"All that the cops will tell us about, and all the insurance company knows about," I cautiously answered.

"So, you work for the insurance company?"

Albert cut off a portion of the omelet and slipped it onto a plate and passed it around the table to Cassandra.

"Who pays better than they do to avoid lawsuits and obscene settlements?" I nodded at Albert.

"You are a mercenary, but a mercenary with a conscience and a sense of decency," Albert laughed. "That's why I like you so much."

"Was that enough?" Annie looked at Cassandra's plate.

"More than enough." Cassandra held her hand up towards her plate.

"So, let me see this guy you're looking for." Albert finished carving up the omelet.

"He's the cook from the freighter." I handed the photograph to Albert. "He's the only one at large now, and we think he has to be the one who can lead us to the mystery man in this whole case."

"Mystery man?" Albert studied the photograph.

I thought for a moment before I answered; I judged that I should tell him this part.

"Yes, a stowaway was hiding on that freighter, I think he was a Chinese citizen and that he holds the key as to why two people from that ship were killed and who paid to have something valuable smuggled into this country."

"You don't think it was drugs and antiquities?" Albert looked up from the photograph.

"I do think there had to be something else going on," I continued. "I think that the mystery man was involved in a second smuggling plot and that if we find him, we may find out if that plot involved more than the one freighter. Also, we'd like to prove the crew didn't murder the poor Japanese man."

"Liability problems," Albert sounded thoughtful. "Well, you're in luck."

"You recognize him?" Cassandra sounded surprised.

"He's been asking about a Chinese national the past few days." Albert glanced at me. "I think this guy he's looking for is a mainland Chinese operative, he has to be a hardcore agent for the Communist government, so you'd better watch out."

"A spy?" Cassandra hesitated, then she closed her mouth firmly.

"That's what I said." Albert leaned over the small table towards Cassandra. "I bet you didn't think your insurance case would get this serious, did you?"

"No," Cassandra answered. "But, I've been working with Benjamin long enough to know I shouldn't expect things to be easy."

"Well." Albert finished his eggs. "I heard last night this guy in the picture wants to meet your mystery man in the Korean Cultural Center on Wilshire Boulevard."

"Do you know how ironic that is?" I mused aloud. "Coupled with a Japanese national?"

Wait a minute, several synapses fired all at once; maybe something else all together different was going on here, I had to talk to Billy Sullivan soon.

"Yes." Albert nodded. "You'd better get going, I think they'll get together late this morning."

25

No rest for the weary

Fred Lepus trudged from the luggage claims area of Dulles airport to the long line of transport buses to deliver him back to Washington, DC. Although his aching arm wound had long since ceased bleeding, the wound still felt fresh to him. He had spent almost all of the fifteen hundred advance, and had come home with only a bullet hole in his arm, what a waste. Since he at least still did have most of the bank account numbers, there might be hope yet; maybe he could beat the police to the treasure, maybe.

After a metro ride, and two bus transfers, he was home. He looked carefully at his place; an older house located in a built up section of strip malls and professional buildings. His block he was still all houses, but most of them were used as businesses. He lived in a bedroom in the back portion of this house, and kept his office in what used to be the living room.

The sun had risen, but it was too early for the business on his street to open. As Fred looked up and down his block, he noticed too many cars were parked on the street. Fred checked three houses down and across the street from his office where four students lived, they always had loud parties and lots of overnight guests. He was becoming sick of all the noise and cars, so perhaps he should find out who owned the house and complain, perhaps later. Right now, he wanted to get home and clean up. His secretary and girlfriend, Cathy Rumson, should be there by now. Fred had called her from the airport and asked her to meet him at the office because he needed some sympathy, being shot isn't all that much fun.

Fred opened the front door and immediately noticed that the light by his desk was out which was strange since that light was always on, even during the day; if Cathy were here, the light should be on. Fred looked from side to side and everything looked in place, except for that shadow coming from someone right behind him in the open front door, damn.

He felt a steel barrel jab into his lower spine; not again. Before the man behind him said anything, Fred could hear a muffled shout coming from behind his desk. He also heard a loud thud, that had to be Cathy.

"Move on inside and be careful," A stern male voice behind him said.

"Sure thing." Fred raised his hands and walked into the middle of his office.

"Just keep your hands up." The man searched Fred for weapons which Fred didn't have; he had lost his pistol at Cassandra's house, the place where he had been shot, damn again.

"Is that my secretary?" Fred nodded towards the desk.

"I suppose so."

"Can you let her get up and sit down at least?"

"Why don't you pull her into that sofa."

"Okay."

Fred carefully lifted Cathy up, grimacing as he did. He could see Cathy looking at him as he scowled.

"I got shot out in California." Fred said, and shrugged.

"Mimmm suuuu," Cathy mumbled through the cloth tightly wrapped around her mouth.

"Everything will be fine." He lowered Cathy onto the old sofa under the front window.

"No, it won't," The stranger insisted.

Fred could now see the tall and thin man holding the gun on them. His face was gaunt, his expensive suit looked a little too big for his frame, he had a small scar on his right cheek, near the nose.

"What do you want?" Fred asked. He had a an idea what this guy was after.

"You worked for a Mr. Zimmer," The man said.

"Yes, I did," Fred answered. "But, he's in jail right now."

"I know he is," The man sounded annoyed. "I want the letter."

"What letter?" It was probably hopeless, but he could only think of one thing: to stall.

"You know damned well what letter," The man snapped. "You went to Mexico to deliver that letter to some woman."

"Oh, that letter. I delivered it." Fred wondered to himself how this could work to his advantage.

"That woman was a Chinese spy trying to make a little extra money at our expense." The man raised the pistol level with Fred's face. "I don't think that's a smart thing to do, do you?"

"You should be happy," Fred squeaked.

"Why?"

"That woman is dead."

"Dead?" The man lowered his pistol a few inches. "How?"

"I think some detective in California killed her, but I'm not sure," Fred spoke quickly. "It might have been the cops, but she's dead for sure."

"Dead." The man thought for a second. "Then, where is the envelope?"

"The cops have it," Fred said hastily; he didn't like the prospect of being shot again. "But, that wasn't the only copy."

"A copy?" The man raised the pistol back up. "Where is it?"

"I have it hidden somewhere right here in DC," Fred nervously answered.

"Tell me where it is or I'll kill the woman." The man swung the pistol towards Cathy, who's eyes opened as wide as they could. Fred could see a small tear forming at the corners of both of Cathy's eyes.

"I'll take you to the list of bank account numbers only after you let the woman go, right now," Fred spoke loudly.

"You know what it is?" the man looked back at Fred.

"Of course I do, and I'll bet the cops do, too," Fred answered.

"I should kill both of you right now," The man sounded annoyed again, although this time he sounded even angrier.

"No, you should let the woman go and get to the list of accounts right now, so you can get your money before the cops figure out which bank you used." Fred apprehensively nodded at Cathy.

"Maybe you're right," the stranger said.

"I am right."

Fred quickly moved to the sofa and dragged Cathy to her feet. The man didn't move but kept his pistol pointed at both of them.

"Go ahead." The man motioned the barrel of his pistol towards the front door.

"Get out of here and don't call the cops," Fred whispered. He shoved Cathy at the door, he opened the screen door and shoved her out.

"Run like hell away from here," he spoke louder.

"Mffffmm," Cathy shouted through her gag.

"Get out of here!" He shouted.

Fred turned to face the man with the gun.

"Let's get the numbers, then." The man pushed Fred towards the door.

"Then you'll shoot me and look for my girlfriend to kill her too." Fred rapidly walked past his front porch and into the sidewalk.

"That could be, but you still don't have much of a choice, do you." The man put his pistol under his jacket, still hanging onto it.

"I think I have a choice." Fred slowly opened his jacket. "Don't get too anxious, I don't have a gun, you checked, remember."

"What are you doing?"

The man frowned, a little nervously, Fred thought.

"Now that we're in public and you can't shoot me so easy, I want something else for that piece of paper."

"What?" The man was clearly becoming even more angry.

"I was promised five thousand for that paper, but I was never paid." Fred wasn't sure what he was doing, but he might as well ask for more money since it had to be worth more money than the original thirty five hundred.

"You won't get paid now, either." The man pulled out the pistol from under his jacket.

The sidewalks were becoming busy with the morning parade of workers going to their offices and the few residents going to work. At first, no one noticed anything strange, but one by one, the people nearest to them began to take note of the weapon.

"You're crazy," Fred stammered. "Someone's going to call the cops."

"I don't care." The man moved closer to Fred. "Give me the paper, I know you have it on you."

"No, I don't." Fred raised his hands.

"I'll take it from your dead body." The man raised the pistol and moved even closer to Fred, who was backing down the sidewalk.

"Don't bother." Fred plucked the piece of paper from his inside coat pocket and threw it on the sidewalk.

As the man reached down to pick the paper up, Fred bolted from the sidewalk and raced across the street. As he reached the other side of the street, barely missing a collision with a passing car, he looked back, over his shoulder. To his surprise, Fred saw six armed men tackling the stranger with the gun. Fred could clearly see the bright vests the armed men were wearing, the vests that shouted FBI from the front and back, in large block letters.

Fred almost leaped out of his clothes when someone put their hand on his shoulder. He spun around as quickly as he could, to face a woman a few inches taller than him, smiling and saying, "Don't be upset, I'm with the FBI; you and your secretary will be fine."

"Cathy?" Fred let out his pent up breath.

"She's back there in one of our vehicles, sir," The woman assured him.

"How long have you been here?" He looked up and down the street.

"Since that gentleman we arrested got here, we followed him to your office," The agent answered. "He got here before dawn."

"Before dawn?" Fred sighed.

"You walked right past us, sir." The agent cocked her head to one side. "Didn't you see us?"

26

Can the fat lady sing yet?

"Okay, you have to tell me how the hell Albert knew where the box man is," Cassandra demanded as she slipped into the passenger seat of our car.

"I don't know if the man in the box and the man Albert told us about are the same person, but they have to be connected at least," I said, thinking out loud . "Albert knowing all this has to do with the family business."

"His family business?"

"Yes."

"What is it?"

"Well, he's not actively in the family business."

"Stop the horse shit and answer my question." She was losing patience, I didn't blame her.

"His father and grandfather were the leaders of a large mob syndicate in Chinatown." I eased the car back into traffic. It probably was faster to take Harbor Freeway to Wilshire and head out to the Cultural Center.

"So, he's a mobster?" Cassandra sounded confused.

"Not at all, his father and grandfather were, but Albert rejected all that long before I met him."

"So, what does he do now?"

"He manages several non-profits." I paid attention to traffic, which was quite heavy this morning. "They are aimed at improving the quality of life for families in Chinatown."

"Like, how?"

"Health centers for children, after school care, Chinese language schools." I looked at Cassandra. "Mostly stuff for kids in the neighborhood."

"What does Annie do?"

"She's an artist," I said. "Her studio is on the top floor, next to his office. Next time we're over there you need to get the whole tour."

"She's quite beautiful," Cassandra acknowledged. "And, I saw you looking at her, you know."

"She's my friend's wife," I sighed. "I'm a healthy male, and I look, but I lust after only you now."

"What's wrong with that?" She chuckled.

"Not a damned thing," I quickly answered her. "Except, we don't have enough free time lately for lust."

"It wouldn't take long, you know." She put her hand on my leg. "For either of us."

"Tonight?"

I forced myself to think about the case.

"I liked them." Apparently Cassandra also needed to change the subject.

"Albert and Annie?" I cleared my throat. "I think Albert liked you a lot too, he couldn't take his eyes off you the whole time."

"Yeah." She grinned meaningfully. Oh well, I could see she got my point.

"I always have liked Albert." I quickly thought back on some of our exploits. "He's been a good friend since I was seventeen years old."

"So far, I like all your friends, Benjamin."

"And, you'll meet each and every one of them from now on."

"How does Albert make his money?"

"He inherited millions from his family, and he said long ago he'd give it all back to the community over his lifetime," I answered. "I think he will."

"They don't have any kids of their own?" Cassandra asked.

"No," I replied. "I don't know why and I never asked."

"What was that about the Koreans and the Japanese?" Cassandra asked.

"What?"

"You and Albert making that comment about the Koreans and Japanese being ironic or something," she said.

"Oh, that." I took a breath. "For the past few decades the North Koreans have been kidnapping Japanese citizens for some reason."

"They have?" Cassandra sounded confused. "I didn't know that."

"Outside of Japan, most people don't know about that," I said.

"Why?"

"The North Koreans are crazy," I said. "The rumors are that the North Koreans will kidnap an ordinary Japanese citizen, then use that person to train a North Korean agent to look, act and think like a real Japanese citizen so they can field operatives who appear to the rest of the world like a native Japanese citizen."

"So, you think Maiko was a North Korean agent?" Cassandra asked.

"If she was, that would change a lot of what we've thought happened on that ship."

I wasn't happy about rethinking everything, but maybe I'd have to.

"We need to get to Billy soon and ask him to look into all this," I added.

"I agree," she said. "But when?"

"As soon as we can."

It took us about forty five minutes to make it the few miles to the Cultural Center. As we drove past the building, we saw an Asian man pacing in front of it, oblivious to the many other pedestrians moving along the broad sidewalk. A few people were entering the Cultural center. The man continued to pace in front of it. He looked extremely nervous. Was this going to be that easy? One could hope so, since Cassandra had to get some sleep before her first day in class.

"Let's get a parking place away from sight," I said. "Do you see that guy?"

"Yes." Cassandra looked intently at the pacing man as we drove past. "This is too obvious."

"I know."

I pulled into a liquor store parking lot, just around the next block.

"How do you think we should take him?" Cassandra remained in the car, questioning me with her expression as well.

"First, I'm going to call for a team to meet us here." I pulled the lighter-radio from my pocket and proceeded to make the request to the communications officer on duty.

"Too bad we can't use that thing on all our cases." Cassandra pointed to the transceiver. "I'd love to have all this backup too."

"I know," I agreed. "Are you ready to go?"

"We'd better do something." Cassandra opened her door. "He looks too nervous to wait around much longer."

"I agree. Let's walk by him like tourists, you go on one side, and I'll go on the other."

I also opened my door, then opened the trunk.

"I guess we can't be subtle about this." She followed me to the trunk.

"I'll try to get his hands into these." I pulled out a pair of handcuffs from my suitcase. "You stand back and cover me."

"Should I shoot him if he tries to get away?"

She didn't sound like she wanted to.

"Well, yes." I looked at her. "If he's the spy we're looking for, we can't let him get away, anyway, aim for his leg."

"Why don't I try to get the handcuffs on him?" Cassandra shot back.

I thought for a second, "That might work better, he wouldn't expect it from a woman as much."

We quickly walked around the block, and towards the Cultural Center where the man was still pacing. Quite skinny, no taller than five six, he was also pale, perhaps like he'd been in a shipping container for a long sea voyage. Finally, he stopped pacing, and queued up at the bus stop with two other people who were waiting around the bus stop. Cassandra slowed down and took the inside track, between him and the building, as I wandered towards the curb. I saw Cassandra reach into her purse and grasp the handcuffs, seeing the shinny edge of them protruding from the lip of her purse; she was almost directly behind him.

I had to step into the street to avoid bumping an elderly Korean woman who had stepped close to the curb as I moved into that space. The possible box man was five feet away from me, and not more than a foot from Cassandra. The subject's attention was drawn to me as I stepped into the street and nodded to the older woman. She muttered an apology to me in something non-English. As the man's attention focused on me, Cassandra was able to clamp his right wrist into the handcuffs.

The man spun rapidly to his right, pushing Cassandra to the sidewalk, she held fast to the short chain between the two handcuff locks. The man partially lost his balance as Cassandra dragged him to his knees on the pavement. He slammed the heel of his left hand into Cassandra's shoulder as she turned to deflect the blow; he had aimed for her face. She snapped the other end of the handcuff around her left wrist, all this action took place in the blink of an eye.

"Don't move, or I'll shoot!" I shouted.

Two other bus patrons were staring in disbelief at Cassandra and the man wrestling on the sidewalk. Glancing up, they watched me level my Smith and Wesson at the man on the sidewalk. After a second of shock, they both fled for the the Cultural Center. Meanwhile vehicle traffic near us at first slowed, then sped by.

"Give me the key or I'll kill the woman," the man in the handcuffs demanded.

The small Chinese man had a British accent, what the hell was this? The man was trying to turn Cassandra over so he could get a choke hold on her, but she was proving to be tougher than he hoped for.

"You're under arrest!" I shouted. As if that that might help, but it wasn't much of a help as he punched Cassandra twice in the midsection. Cassandra managed to kick him three times in the shins; I could tell she was aiming for his crotch, and so could he, as he squirmed out of the way each time.

"Stop fighting!" I moved closer to the mass of battling flesh on the sidewalk. By this time a large crowd had gathered, but they stayed at least a half a block away.

As I moved closer, I saw the man reach for something in his front pocket. I cocked my revolver and moved as close as I could to him and still be out of the way of a reaching hand.

"Stop, and take your hand out of your pocket or I will shoot you!" I shouted.

He pulled out a tubular device that looked like a fat stubby pen which he squeezed causing a needle to shoot out from the end of it. Not waiting, I shot at his hand as he raised the needle in his left fist. Nothing but concrete behind his raised hand, and thankfully I was shooting round nosed lead bullets, so maybe the slug wouldn't ricochet, my brain was babbling away, unable to stop the commentary. The stranger shouted in pain; his left hand jerked violently. I saw the hole in his hand as the bullet passed through; a large bloody spot was under the knuckles of his index and middle finger. The needle device he had been holding flew towards the building, to land on the concrete fifteen feet behind him.

I cocked my revolver again and pointed it at his head.

"I will kill you if you don't surrender now."

"Fine, fine!" He stopped moving. As I had fired my revolver, Cassandra had pulled herself into as much of a fetal position as she could. Now, when she felt the man relax and stop struggling with her, she looked up cautiously. She looked at me from the sidewalk, then she appraised her adversary. She sat up, then reached for her shoulder holster.

"Don't!" I shouted at her.

I didn't want that creep to start a fight for the pistol right then.

248

"Right," she agreed.

She looked at me like she understood, then pulled her right fist back as far as she could and punched the man in the back of this head as hard as she could. He fell over on his face, dragging Cassandra with him as he pulled his right hand up to his head.

"Stop it!"

I looked into Cassandra's bruised face as she recovered, panting. She stared back at me. I tossed the hand cuffs key to her which she caught it nicely in her free hand.

Cassandra freed herself, then quickly fastened the man's left hand in the handcuff. "That's the first time I truly wanted to beat the crap out of somebody," she stammered.

I tossed a handkerchief to her which Cassandra wrapped tightly around the man's bleeding hand.

"We need to get him back to our car," I said.

I heard the police sirens getting closer.

"I know who you are, you aren't the local cops." The man glared up at me, as he struggled to a sitting position on the sidewalk.

"No, you piece of shit, we aren't the cops." Cassandra was still breathing hard.

"You wouldn't be American intelligence, would you?" He spoke in a whisper as he struggled to his feet. "Red fifteen, white eleven."

"Green thirty nine." I looked at him carefully. "That's about as lame as it gets."

"It apparently got your attention." The man shook his head quickly. "I'm MI 6," he whispered, even more quietly as I pushed him by the handcuffs towards our car.

"What the hell did he say?" Cassandra ran in front of me to open the back door to the car.

"If he's telling the truth, he's the wrong person," I answered.

I shoved him into the back seat. I managed to find a rag in the trunk and wrapped it tightly around his bleeding hand. Although the first bandage had stopped most of the bleeding, that wound had to hurt.

"Can I still shoot him?" Cassandra asked. She slid into the front seat with me, at least she was regaining some composure after being punched around.

"Not yet." I was worried about her. "Let him talk first."

"Like I said, I know you." The man looked at us. "You work for the CIA."

"No, we don't." Cassandra looked at me.

"We are not the CIA or the FBI." I looked back at Cassandra. "But, I think you'll be meeting the real FBI soon, so we'd like some information right now."

"Were you the man in the cargo container on the freighter Veracruz?" Cassandra asked, almost demanding.

She looked back and forth, first me, then him.

"I don't know what you're talking about," he said. "My name is Chauncey, by the way."

"It sounds like a strange name." Cassandra glowered at him.

"My father was British, and my mom's Chinese." He attempted a smile at her. "I'm quite sorry about hitting you and all."

"Why are you so interested in all this?" I had to ask, it appeared that a lot of countries were involved in this whole thing.

"Those nuclear timing devices your chaps found on that ship were actually ours, and I was supposed to find out who was paying for them." Chauncey looked out the side window at two approaching men in suits. "The cook thinks I'm the contact, but I'm the wrong Asian in the right place."

"So, you're after the cook?" I asked. "The cook thinks you're the buyer for the timing devices?"

"Right." Chauncey nodded. "The cook works for the Libyan government and was the contact agent for dealing the timing devices."

"Open up Katz ." One of the men tapped on the driver's side window with an FBI badge.

"He's all yours, and he's not the one we were looking for," I replied as I slowly opened my car door.

"He's ours, so we'll worry about all of that later." The second man hauled out Chauncey. "Give me the keys."

Cassandra handed the keys to the handcuffs to the agent.

"Look, there's Mark." She pointed to the large crowd of law officials gathered in front of the Cultural Center.

"Do you need us?" I looked at the larger of the two FBI agents.

"No," he grumbled. "We've been told that you're cooperating with this investigation, and we shouldn't arrest you; not that I don't want to, mind you,"

"Why, thank you," I said, carefully.

"For civilians, you sure got deep into this mess, so you'd best stay out of it from now on."

I motioned for Cassandra to follow me to see Mark Hatton.

"Look me over quickly." She pulled at my arm for me to stop. "Am I coming out of my clothes anywhere?"

She had scuffled around a lot on concrete. Cassandra turned slowly as I studied her, head to toe, a few minor rips were obvious, but nothing important was showing. She was wearing long khaki pants and a short sleeved cotton shirt with a lightweight coat over it. The pants had one large tear in the right leg from her knee to her thigh and several smaller ones on the other knee. Her coat was torn in many places on her back and near the waist on the front. A few places on her arms, and the side of her face oozed blood, but I saw no deep, profusely bleeding cuts. As she turned to face me, I lifted her shirt up to look at her stomach; she didn't stop me, instead she also looked down at herself. One hell of a bruise started to show over her left upper hip.

"How do you feel?" I asked.

"Just sore," she answered as she pulled down her blouse and looked into my face. "Real sore, a little sick, and, still mad."

"You held your own in that fight." I gave her a quick hug. "I'm proud of you."

"Ouch!" she winced. "That hurts."

"I'm sorry."

"I want to talk about this later, a lot later." She pointed to the crowd ahead of us. "Right now, let's go get Mark."

"Well," Mark said. He had seen us and walked towards us. We met him right outside the perimeter the police had set up.

"I heard about all this on the radio and I had to come down here since I knew you two were responsible," he teased.

"Are you going to arrest us?" Cassandra replied. Her sense of humor hadn't completely gone and I was glad to see that.

"Not at all." Mark shook his head. "This belongs to the FBI for some reason, and they don't want you. Although, since according to all the witnesses, you're the one who shot that poor man being arrested, I don't see why you're not in the back of their car with him."

"I learned long ago to never look a gift pass in the mouth," I cautiously answered Mark.

"Whatever that means." His expression was somber, maybe he had started to connect the dots and to realize I was more than a private investigator, but he never said anything. But, perhaps I'm paranoid.

"What abut the cook?" Cassandra whispered to me.

"My men found the cook," Mark answered. "He was trying to buy a train ticket to Washington DC from a travel agent, which was kind of dumb."

"Where is he now?" I asked.

"He's in our jail for now, and the Long Beach police are putting in the transfer papers as we speak." Mark turned around to look at the growing crowd. "But, maybe the FBI will take him first."

"They probably will," I said. "I have a feeling that something was of national interest in that freighter, and that the rest of us will never know what it was."

"Maybe." Mark looked sad for a second, then he forced a smile. "The Long Beach detective told me that the only fingerprints in the cargo container home were yours and the cook's. He thinks the cook is the one who shot the Japanese agent, too."

"That would explain some things," Cassandra said. She didn't know what to say, she must have hurt from the fight she was in.

"But, not everything." I put my hand on her shoulder. "We need to get you back to your folks' place to clean you up."

"You might consider a hospital to make sure nothing's ruptured in there." Mark was concerned as he pointed to Cassandra's partially bare midriff. He was right, we needed to get her some attention.

27

The Katz Box

It was eleven in the morning when we left Wilshire Boulevard, managing to exit before any reporters and their pesky cameras arrived. We dropped by Good Samaritan Hospital since it was on Wilshire, and not too far away. The emergency room physician wanted to take x-rays of Cassandra's innards, so it took us until three in the afternoon to get out of there. A social worker questioned Cassandra for ten minutes, they thought I had beaten my girlfriend up. We both showed our California PI license and we both told the same story about the fight in the street that morning. A call to the cops confirmed that both of us were involved in a street fight with a possible felon, but that whole scene in the emergency room made me feel bad for the rest of the time in the hospital; not because they thought I did it, but because the negative side of our work hit home. Cassandra could have been badly hurt and I knew we should talk about this sometime.

She was bruised in a few places, but the doctor didn't find any broken bones, cuts that required stitches, or a concussion. While waiting for her to finish with the thorough going over, I called Billy Sullivan and asked him to meet us at her parents' house at three that afternoon. We were late.

. . . .

"How did they get in here?" Cassandra put her keys down on a counter as she turned to me. "I might as well not lock the damned doors anymore."

"They're good at breaking and entering." I observed.

"What are all the blood stains from?" Billy pointed to the spot on the carpet in front of him.

"That's where I shot Lepus." Cassandra looked down at the front hallway. "And, that's where Benjamin bled all over the floor."

"Perhaps we should let Cassandra change into something without so many holes in it before we start talking."

I stared at the love of my life, I was happy she was all right.

"Damned good idea." Cassandra added. She looked down at her pants, and the large rip in them, then wearily trotted down the hall to her room. In less than three minutes, she walked back out in a pair of jeans and a dark blue tee shirt, falling into the sofa in the living room and looking expectantly at Billy, then at me.

"You two have been busy." Billy stood up and walked towards her. "How are you doing, Cassandra?"

"I've been better, but the doctors assure me that I'm fine."

She plopped down on the sofa next to me and looked out the picture window; the view was spectacular, especially during the daytime.

"By the way, who pays my hospital bills?"

"Since you signed the papers the other day, we do," Billy answered. "Benjamin knows where to send the bills."

"I'm sure he does." Cassandra patted my leg. The tension in her body showed that she was still as upset as I was about the whole morning encounter with the MI 6 guy.

"I heard from the FBI that you did quite a number on that British guy," Billy said.

"He got it worse than I did." Cassandra sounded a bit nervous. "I'm fine."

"I wanted to say you did an outstanding job this morning." Billy put his hand on her shoulder. "I'm proud of you."

"Listen," Cassandra turned to face Billy, speaking with conviction. "I have gotten into fights before, I have been in gun fights, and I have killed before."

"I know." Billy sat back on the sofa.

"I'm sorry." Cassandra briefly touched Billy's right sleeve. "I haven't had much sleep, and there has been a lot going on lately; I don't mind this type of work, is all I'm trying to say. After working with Benjamin for the last three years, I kind of like the work. Just because I'm a woman shouldn't make a difference in how I perform on the job."

"No, it shouldn't," Billy agreed. "And, I like your attitude, that's what I was hoping to hear."

"When it comes to official attitude, I'm one of the guys." Cassandra smiled back at him.

I could tell from that smile she was getting close to smacking the crap out of Billy, I think Billy saw that too.

"Did the Japanese government ever say what Yoshihiro was investigating?" I asked Billy.

"No," he answered. "They told us it was about the antiquities, but I don't completely believe them."

"What if Maiko was a North Korean operative?" I had my suspicions.

"She could have been," Billy pensively answered. "That way, some of it makes more sense."

"Did you get a response from the Taiwanese?" Cassandra asked.

"Yes." He looked at Cassandra, still slumped into the sofa. "Maiko's fingerprints were not the same as their missing agent."

"So, if Maiko was a North Korean agent, and Yoshihiro was tailing her to find out about some of his countryman that may have been kidnapped, what would that have to do with computer encryptions, timing devices or anything else?" I wondered.

"My guess would be that the woman posing as Maiko was after the timing devices," Cassandra said.

"Why would you say that?" Billy asked.

"I don't know," she replied. "It makes better sense than drugs or antiquities. And, hasn't the fearless leader of North Korea always said he wants the bomb?"

I could tell she was tired, almost as tired as I was.

"I suppose so," Billy said, doubtfully.

"So, is everybody from this case in detention?" I needed to change the subject.

"Yes," Billy sounded relieved to follow my lead. "The FBI has them all, even the rest of the crew was rounded up and put in various jails."

"So you think the cook was our man in the box sending North Korean codes?" Cassandra looked at me, not at Billy.

"No, I don't," I said. "The British guy said the cook was a Libyan spy after the timing devices, besides, what ever happened to the scientist with the encryption keys? That's what started all this."

"You're right," Billy said.

He took a sip from a beer he had gotten from Cassandra's refrigerator, at least he was using a coaster.

"We haven't been able to get anything out of any of the crew that remotely would tie them to the encryption keys," Billy added.

"I assume the British guy was MI 6?"

I guessed he was, but I wasn't sure.

"Yes, he is," Billy answered.

"He was after the timing devices," I said. "I don't think he even knew about someone hiding in a cargo container."

"Yeah, his government was after the timing devices only," Billy said. "Our State Department got a formal apology from their Ambassador in Washington for the whole thing. They claim all they wanted to do was to find out who stole them and plug the leak on their side of the Atlantic."

"He seemed to know me, I didn't know him, but he knew a recognition code from a few years back, did he know me?"

I hoped Billy would know the answers.

"He was on a British team that worked with us two years ago," Billy answered. "He did know what you looked like, and that you were working for us, but you never saw him before."

"Oh."

"So, the cook was an operative from Libya trying to get nuclear timing devices for his country." Cassandra was clearly still back with her original question. "Do you know the trouble that implies?"

"You bet your ass we know the trouble that means." Billy looked at Cassandra. "With your expertise, you might get to know first hand what a mess that whole area is becoming."

"That might be interesting." Cassandra leaned back in the sofa, I could tell her mind was wandering; she was into the whole Mid East thing since researching it for her dissertation.

"How about we stick to the case de jour," I interrupted.

"Right, the big sale in Long Beach was to be the timing devices and the cook was the contact man for the buyers," Cassandra agreed. "The guy in Washington was the money man, or at least the front man for the money, but Benjamin's right, where does that leave the computer scientist?"

"The only people we can't grill about the encryption keys and the computer scientist are the dead Japanese agent and the dead Korean agent, or whoever she was working for." I said. "You know, maybe it wasn't those two humping and bumping in the next room on the freighter, maybe it was Maiko and the man in the box."

"But they only found the cook's fingerprints in the cargo container." Cassandra shook her head.

"The real box dweller could have worn gloves, or wiped the place down before he left," I guessed. "You know there might have been a woman in that box, and she and the Japanese agent might have played while Maiko was walking around the deck."

"All that's possible, but so what?" Billy shrugged his shoulders. "None of it helps unless we can find that person and connect them to an American traitor. Over three hundred possible computer scientists could sell us out, and we can't keep an eye on all of them, at least not a good enough eye on them."

"What about the British agent Cassandra beat up?" I winked at Cassandra, she frowned at me.

"The FBI have him right now," Billy answered. "Like I said, I don't think he has a clue as to the encryptions or the scientist."

"Were the timing devices British like he said?" I asked.

"It looks like they were," Billy said. "They might be part of a batch we sold to them last year."

"Why don't we work backwards, then." Cassandra stood up. "You want a beer?" She looked at me.

"No, thanks." I looked up at her. "What do you mean work backwards?"

"How's the company that owns the freighter going to get it back home, or back to delivering cargo?"

She walked into the kitchen and got a big glass of water while Billy and I looked at each other in silence until she got back.

"Assuming that person wants to go back on the ship that brought him, he'll have to get back onboard somehow. If they send a new crew to sail it out, the man, or woman, in the box could sneak back on since no one knows what they look like, they might even have the encryption keys already. If you recover the spy and the keys, then you might be able to discover who sold them." Cassandra said.

She sat back down on the sofa, sipping her water.

"Why would that person want to go near the ship?" I felt a little confused. "If it were me, I'd look for another way out of town, some way that didn't have ten thousand cops looking right at it."

"Think about it," Cassandra said, intensely. "The FBI have gone over every square inch of that ship, so by the time the Veracruz leaves port, the FBI won't care about it anymore. If the mystery person wants a safe pass out of this country, wouldn't that be the perfect way to leave the country, while the cops and FBI are looking at every train, boat, plane and car leaving town."

"Hey Cassandra, good thinking." Billy turned to look at me. "You were right about her."

"What did he say about me?"

"He told me that you'd be as good as he is in this job," he answered.

"Thanks, sweetie."

She kissed my cheek. Ah, I am loved again; life is good.

"Did the company say when they'd take possession of the freighter?" I asked.

"The FBI went through the ship yesterday, they studied every square inch of it several times, as well as every container on it, or to be loaded on it. They then sealed the ship and won't let anybody on it until it leaves port." Billy said. "There's a new crew in town right now, and they're due to leave port in less than two days. The FBI, immigration and the local cops have gone over every one of the new crew with a fine tooth comb, and they all check out fine."

"What about the new cargo?" I asked Billy, who was acting like he had to make a phone call.

"I said they had checked it all out," he said. "I suppose I could get them to check it again."

"The captain did say that they were supposed to take on a load of heavy transformers," I remembered. "I wonder if a properly bribed loading crew could add on another hotel cargo box right under the nose of the FBI?"

"Surely the FBI would double check every cargo container loaded on the ship," Cassandra sounded amazed.

"They might have inspected them on the dock, and marked them as ready for loading," I surmised. "A good accomplice could easily switch another box for one with the FBI seal of approval."

"The possibilities are endless, but we'll only find out which one is right by being there," Cassandra said.

She got up and headed to the front door.

"Since the departure of the Veracruz is fairly soon, perhaps we should go back for one more look." I also got up.

"Let's go." She beat me to the front door.

"The FBI will be the back up this time." Billy headed to the phone in the kitchen. "I'll get them going."

....

260

"Will the FBI at the scene know who you are?" she asked me. Cassandra looked out the side window of our car as I drove Ocean Boulevard towards Long Beach. I guessed it'd be faster than anything else, besides I didn't feel like getting lost right then.

"The Chief of the Los Angeles bureau knows that I'm a contract worker for Langley, so I assume he'll tell his agents there to let us go if they burst in too soon. I doubt if any of the agents on the scene actually knows who we are." I looked at all the lights near the ocean to our left. "This could be an inter-departmental nightmare, but so far that hasn't happened."

"How so?" she asked.

"The CIA isn't supposed to be involved in any active investigation on US soil, especially on US citizens, we're only authorized for overseas operations. Most of the people in the CIA don't have a lot of respect for the FBI to investigate espionage in this country, they never have been good at it for whatever reason. Sometimes we do their job for them and never tell them, sometimes, like this time, we do their job and dump it on them when it's done. I can get away with this because, at least on paper, I'm just a contract employee doing a specific, fact gathering job."

She might as well know some of the nuances of her new career.

"This is a hell of a way to gather facts." She screwed up her lips as if she wanted to laugh, but wasn't ready yet. "Will we do many of these types of cases in this country?"

"Well, usually I do these investigations in other countries." I looked for at the sign indicating that Los Angeles was a mile ahead. "This one started outside the US, and they thought the deal for the encryption keys would take place in Mexico or Canada."

"But, we don't know where it actually took place, or even if it did take place," Cassandra collected her thoughts. "I think, if I am going to do these jobs with you from now on, I'd like it better if we could do some interesting travel too, not the docks of Long Beach."

261

"Some of the places I've been aren't much more scenic." Although some were, but I didn't feel like adding that, at least not until she had enough sleep.

"I guess we don't know what this person is supposed to look like, do we?"

"Neither the national origin nor the sex of the person, although I suppose they could have tested the contents of the chemical toilet and gotten a clue, but that's something I wouldn't wish on anybody."

"I thought about that too, but, depending on what chemical they used in the toilet, there could be no trace of who it was," Cassandra added.

I looked over the side of the bridge at the almost dry river emptying into the harbor, in the distance I could see the docks.

Years ago, millions of tons of sand and fill had been dredged and hauled into Long Beach bay. The man made peninsulas grew, finger like, into the water to support many docks for a multitude of craft. The interior docks attracted all the expensive sailing and pleasure boats while the other areas were allotted to passenger ships, freighters and oil tankers; lots of oil tankers, but we weren't headed there, nor were we headed out on a cruise. The whole area around the docks had fallen into disrepair lately, but the city fathers had proposed a wide ranging, expensive and long term rebuilding project, a project that was getting off the ground.

"Shall we look over the whole ship when we get there?" Cassandra asked. She was a little nervous, maybe it was that she was starting to feel the fight she was in that morning.

"I'll be willing to bet whoever it is will try to settle into another container like the first one." I wasn't sure, but it sounded logical. "I like the container theory because it's easier not to avoid being seen by the crew."

"I guess it would be hard to pass the close scrutiny the FBI gives the new crew." She nodded.

"Right, if they try to blend into the new crew, it would be easy to get caught." I turned South onto the Long Beach Freeway. "I'll bet another special cargo box was in one of those warehouses."

262

"What do you mean?" she asked.

"It would be easier to have a fresh cargo home set to go than to try to refit the old one," I said. "Besides, the old one is in the hands of the FBI right now; they'd have to plan for the possibility that the old one would be discovered."

"But, how could they sneak a cargo container hide out onto the ship with the FBI staring at them?" Cassandra wondered out loud.

"If I know the FBI, they didn't have guards around the ship, docks and staging areas, around the clock."

I was only guessing, but I thought it was a damned good guess.

"The new shipment of transformers would be inspected and the containers sealed. If the bad guys had a crew hanging around looking for a free moment, they could swap a sealed transformer filled container for a sealed spy filled container."

"I suppose you're right," Cassandra agreed. "I take it we're both assuming that this person, whoever he or she is, will be using the Veracruz to escape."

"Right." I looked for the sign to pier G and there it was. "I think that's exactly what the mystery man will do."

"You do know I kept our access badges from the other night, don't you?"

She smiled at me as I searched for a parking place in the large lot near the administration building.

"I thought you did, it's good to have you with me this time." I returned her grin; I was glad to see her feeling better, at least I hoped she was.

"And, I look forward to going along on these government junkets with you more often." She rummaged around in her large bag. "Especially when they're in Europe, or maybe North Africa, I know I'd like to go shopping again in Casablanca, or maybe Cairo."

She was feeling better. I saw a parking spot and headed for it.

"Do you still have that list of cargo containers?"

"Way ahead of you." She pulled out the two pages.

263

I nodded and opened the door, then and looked up and down the large lot; a few people were there, but many more parked cars. I went to the trunk and pulled out a few items that I might need. I checked my supply of speed loaders, and stuffed another two into my coat pocket. She tossed her bag into the trunk.

Like the other night, I noticed a lot more activity than I might have expected; several ships were offloading, or loading cargo on this complex of docks. It was about a ten minute walk to the Veracruz, which was still docked, looking precisely as I remembered a few days ago. Except, the containers on deck were different; I could be right.

"Look at the main deck, the one with all the containers on it." I pointed to the Veracruz. "At the stern."

"Left or right?" Cassandra stared at the ship.

"I'd swear a stack three containers high used to be on the left side when we last saw the ship, now it's two containers high," I said as I walked faster.

"Maybe they offloaded the real cargo, but, I guess that's a good place to start," she replied.

"The captain didn't say anything about unloading anything, only loading more containers," I mused. "That might not mean anything, but who knows."

"So, where's the FBI?" Cassandra asked.

"Beats me, maybe Billy waited to call them."

I stopped and looked all the way around the area of that dock.

"Why would he do that?"

"To give us more time to locate the box man?"

"Or, to get ourselves killed," her voice trailed off.

"No way." I shook my head. "Not now, with each of us to back the other up."

"You do have a way," she forced a laugh.

"Hold it a minute, you two," A voice shouted from behind us. A guard had finished patrolling the warehouse behind us and had stepped out to see us headed to the Veracurz.

"Let me do this," I whispered.

"Who are you and why are you here?" The guard caught up to us.

"FBI," I sternly said. I pulled out the fake ID from my left pants pocket. I'm glad I remembered where I had stuck it, or we might not have made it to the ship.

"My name is Agent Smith, and this is my partner, Agent Jones."

"Oh." The guard didn't look too closely at the ID and luckily he didn't ask for Cassandra's. "Are you guys back again?"

"We want to go over the Veracruz one more time before she leaves," I said, pointing at the freighter. "There might be some more agents out here soon, could you please tell them to come on board when they get here?"

"Sure will, sir." The rent-a-cop nodded. He gave us one more close look, then headed to the next warehouse on his appointed rounds.

"Why didn't I get a fake ID?" Cassandra asked.

"This is the Federal government here," I teased. "It takes years to make up all the fake IDs you'll need."

" Funny." She turned and walked towards the gangplank.

"That stack of containers is eight wide." I pointed to the stern of the ship as we walked up onto the Veracruz. "Let's compare the numbers and see which one is new."

"Sir," Another voice called to us. A guard was at the top of the gangplank. Of course a private guard was here, the FBI was gone, and the ship's owners didn't want the place to be sacked before the new crew got on board. This guard didn't have a uniform, but he did have a big Colt three fifty seven in a holster around his waist. Two pouches of extra cartridges hung on his right, next to the holster, and a nightstick hung over the left side of the belt; he wore that belt like a cop.

I flashed my fake ID again. Cassandra held back, three feet behind me.

"No one told me you were coming back." The guard looked at the ID. It was real, well, as real as a fake one could be.

"I didn't know we had to announce our presence every time we need to search this ship," I sounded as if I were Admiral Nelson, well, at least I wasn't Ricky Nelson.

265

"Who do you work for?" I semi-demanded.

"Why?" He sounded indignant; most rent-a-cops don't act that uppity.

"Because I asked, and I can arrest you if you don't belong here." Full frontal attack, nothing like it to throw them off balance.

"I work for the company who owns this ship." He stood his ground. "And, as far as I know, I say who gets on board and who doesn't."

"Do you have a permit for that weapon?" I pointed to his pistol.

"I don't need one while I'm on private property, sir." He glared at me. "But, to answer your question, I do have a California and Los Angeles permit to carry."

"May I see them?" I pressed.

The glowering man sighed, he stared for ten seconds longer, but pulled out his wallet and thumbed through it for the two permits which he handed to me.

I looked at them, noticing they were both issued to Wayne Larson, a name I thought I knew. Wayne Larson was an ex-cop from Venice, I recalled about three years before we left LA. He was retired early for being too forceful on suspects, I remember reading about it in the papers. He was not convicted, not even a hearing that I remembered, but he was asked to leave the force; I guess he's a hired tough guy now. No matter, he must have bought my Federal ID since I'm not being pistol whipped.

"I suppose the broad's with you, right?" Larson looked around me to Cassandra.

"Yeah," I agreed. "That's Agent Smith."

"How long will you two be here?" Wayne Larson stuffed his permits back into his wallet.

"No more than an hour." I motioned for her to go on around me. "There should be more agents arriving soon, if you could, tell them we're already here and to look for us, I'd appreciate it, sir."

"Yeah, yeah." Larson stepped aside and let me go on.

We made our way to the back row of containers. The bottom one on the left we looked at was on the master list of containers we had gotten from the administrator the other night. The one on top of it was not on the list which could mean it was a new container full of transformers, or it could be the one with our prize.

"What are we looking for?" She whispered.

"A way into it," I whispered back.

Cassandra pointed to the top portion of the container where she saw a black stripe painted all around it. The container was constructed of corrugated metal and it still had thick metal cables attached to it which met at the top, and had a big solid metal loop clamped onto them. This must be the way it's moved from the dock to the deck. The ripples in corrugated metal on the box were more pronounced than in the others. Along the top, if you looked carefully, you could see open slits; they were the air holes, like the one I saw in the warehouse.

"I see them," I softly said. "Just like the air vents in the other one, I bet they kept this second box home here for the return trip, like you guessed. They simply replace the whole container with a fresh one."

"Do you think he's in there?"

"Yes, I do."

"You know." She smiled, I could tell she was up to something. "You figured this box thing out, and you're about to tidy this whole mess up, so."

Cassandra likes to make bad jokes when she's nervous, whereas I don't need an excuse.

"If you say I have to clean the Katz box up, I'll leave you here alone to do this." I was serious.

"Never mind, then."

I pointed to a large painted letter 'R' on the side of the container facing the dock, then I motioned for her to follow me to the next cargo container up, towards the bow.

"The entrance is in the lower portion of that painted 'R'."

"How do you propose getting into the box without getting shot?" Cassandra cocked her head to one side. "It's rather obvious that a bullet will go right through that metal."

I looked up, remembering something.

"See that loading crane?" I pointed. "That one's got a weight on the end of it to help maneuver it when it's empty."

"So, you want to smash a hole in the side of the Katz box with that thing?" She pointed up at the crane. "How are you supposed to work that thing?"

"I don't know, but I have a lot of faith that you'll figure it out." I didn't like her pun anymore the second time.

"Me?" She pointed to her chest.

"Do you want to have the gun fight out here after the door is smashed in?"

"No," she disagreed. "I think one street fight a day is enough for me, thank you much."

"If you could, try to get that thing positioned without making whoever is in that box aware. The motor will make some noise, but if you don't clang about near the box, the person in the container won't be too nervous, I hope."

I looked up at the control room for the crane, it was a small room midway above center of the thick tower nearest the stern of the ship with a glass window on the front and both sides, looking out on the deck. This was the aft most crane tower of the three on this ship with a door on the back side leading to the stairway to the control room. A ladder was also welded to the outside of the tower for maintenance; that was the ladder I had used several days before to get a good look at the whole main deck.

"That's easy for you to say." She scratched her head. "I'll have to practice a little bit, I wasn't born knowing which lever makes the metal ball go up and down and side to side."

"It might have little pictures showing what the levers do, but don't actually hit any of the containers until you're ready to smash open the door on that box." I pointed back to the supposed home of our suspect.

"Stay in sight so we can signal each other," Cassandra advised me.

She plodded off towards the doorway. The path to the control room for the crane was obvious and once in the door, which surprisingly was open, Cassandra had to climb up to the control room. I watched as she closed the door after her.

As she climbed into the control room, she waved at me through the window. Enough lights were around the immediate area to see quite well on the deck as well as the crane, and its control room. I assumed the whole thing would be run by electric motors, and that there should be enough power on the ship for Cassandra to swing the hook and weight at the end of the crane into the container. I remembered the engines running the whole time I was on the ship in port at Hawaii. I bet they kept generators running all the time to power the whole ship so she should be able to run the crane with no problems.

I heard a motor whine above me as the crane moved from its position pointing towards the bow. It stopped above the stack of containers forward of the suspect one and silence reigned once again. The crane slowly swung again towards the bow, which was the wrong way. She knew it and stopped it, I guess she was trying the controls to see which direction they sent the crane. The hook and ball continued swinging a few feet; she had made it go too fast. Luckily it was above all the containers, and swung in dead air; she let it swing back and forth until it was almost still again.

A slight movement towards the bow of the ship caught my eye. I looked carefully up the main deck and didn't see anything so I looked back up at Cassandra who was wildly pointing at something I could not see; it had to be Wayne Larson. Was he paid to keep thieves off the boat, or to protect the spy in the box? That question was answered quickly with a loud shot.

Cassandra ducked behind the controls in her booth. Maybe the metal around the control room was enough for protection from three fifty seven slugs. She's a real trooper, because she took in the new situation and formulated a different plan. As soon as I saw her moving the hook and ball over top of the container with the possible spy in it, I knew what she was up to. The person in the box knew damned well he was in trouble as soon as the hired thug fired his first shot. I caught a glimpse of something on top of the cargo container; a small rectangular metal shaft popped up about two feet above the top. Damn, he

269

had a periscope in that box, how much could he see? Did he have another escape hatch in there too?

I ran towards the bow of the ship, reaching two containers ahead of where I had been. I saw Larson climbing a ladder and pausing to take aim, so I pulled out my Smith and Wesson and aimed directly at his chest. I steadied my right arm on the side of a cargo container and fired. Wayne Larson grunted loudly, slumped over slightly, then let go of the ladder with his hands. I could see his pistol fall from his hand, and bounce off the deck, then over the side; Wayne's body did the exact thing a second later.

I looked up at Cassandra quickly to make sure she was all right. She was, and she was busy lining up the hook with the large metal loop on top of the cargo container. I heard rattling coming from the container and rushed back towards it. I saw the hatch clanking open on the painted 'R'.

"Stay where you are, you're under arrest!" I shouted before I fired a shot above the hatch.

The hatch stopped moving, then I heard muffled shouting and banging around inside the box as Cassandra snagged the top of it with the hook. With a loud clank and lots of creaking from stressed metal, the cargo container began to rise from the deck of the freighter.

A loud roar emanated from inside the box. Whoever was in there had a fully automatic weapon and was firing it straight up in an attempt to halt the movement. I dove for any cover I could find, just in time too. The bullets soon came zooming out the side of the box, in search of anybody, in search of me. Cassandra pulled the container five feet in the air, and swung it out over the side of the ship, and out over the dock below. It had to be thirty to forty feet above the dock when it stopped, swaying in the silent night air. Again, bullets spewed from the other side of the box, ricocheting off the side of the ship, and the deck. If that idiot kept shooting holes in all four sides, the container might split open and drop him forty feet which would be messy. I crawled to the opposite side of the ship and away from the gunfire.

Now, I heard loud police sirens. At the moment when the whole thing was finishing up, the heroes in blue charged in for the rescue. I looked up for Cassandra and didn't see her in the control booth. I heard a clanking sound and looked towards the crane tower and saw her scrambling towards me.

"Hurry up," I shouted. "The cops are here."

"We don't want to talk to the local cops, do we?" Cassandra huffed and puffed as she turned to face me.

"All we should have to do is wait right here and let the FBI come on board." I put my right arm around her waist.

"Come this way," a voice shouted at us, coming from the direction of the gangplank.

"Who are you?" I asked, holding Cassandra back; she wanted to run towards the voice.

"It's Special Agent Dixon." I could see him now. "We have to get you both off of this ship now, before the police come on board.

"This is cutting it a little close, you know," I said to Dixon as the three of us sprinted to the gangplank.

From the deck of the ship, I could see several police cars entering the large parking lot, at the rate they were going, they'd be at the dock in minutes.

"I know, I know." Dixon led the way down the gangplank. "As soon as all the shooting started, the harbormaster called the cops."

"Where to?" Cassandra asked, looking at Dixon, as soon as the three of us had made it to the dock. By this time about ten FBI agents had reached the dock, running like hell towards the Veracruz.

"My car." Agent Dixon pointed to the first warehouse to our left. Cassandra dove into the rear seat of the car as another burst of gunfire blasted out of the cargo container hovering high above the dock. Dixon and I hurried into the front seat and as soon as Dixon got into his seat, he started the car and drove like a maniac away from the scene.

"Can you take us to our car?" I asked.

"Where is it?" Dixon slapped a red flashing light on the roof of his car.

271

"In the main parking lot." I pointed the way as he maneuvered his car between two warehouses and back towards the large parking lot.

"I know I'm not supposed to ask, but." Dixon made a sharp right turn and entered the lot, following my hand signals as to which direction to go.

"We're just private investigators," Cassandra piped up from the back seat.

"I'm not a complete idiot." Dixon quickly glanced at Cassandra in the rearview mirror. "I read your résumés on file with the local police departments, and this isn't private investigator work you're involved in right now."

"And?" I was becoming concerned.

"Don't worry." He looked sideways at me. "Like I said, I'm not stupid; I like my job and I'd like to stay out of prison, but I have to know who's in the cargo box?"

"That's the sad thing." I slowly shook my head. "We don't know for sure."

"We had a hunch he sneaked back on the ship, and we had to find out for sure," Cassandra added.

"Well." Dixon stopped his car. "Here's your vehicle; I can't say it hasn't been interesting, but I want to get back there and find out who's in the container."

28

I do, and then I don't

Billy Sullivan was waiting for us as we walked into Cassandra's parents' house, I don't think he ever left there. Three empty beer bottles stood lined up on the table in front of the sofa, at least he had put each of them on a coaster.

"You should thank me." Billy didn't get up from the sofa as Cassandra and I walked into the living room.

"And, why should I thank you?" She looked at the empty beer bottles.

"I was able to get some guys out here to clean the carpets."

Billy pointed to the now clean spots on the living room rug.

"I do thank you."

Cassandra looked down at the still damp carpet.

"They did a good job, too, it's a relief to get that done before any more time went by."

"Have you heard who was in the box?"

I sat down in the easy chair next to the sofa, Cassandra sat on the arm rest of the same chair and leaned into me.

"We didn't stay around long enough to see who it was."

"Yes, I got that phone call." Billy stood up and gathered several empty beer bottles. "How's this for a shocker, it was a Russian in the box. And the best part was that the American with the encryption keys was in the box with him."

"Really?" Cassandra sounded amazed, as did I.

"No kidding." Billy went back to the kitchen with the empties. "That was a good haul you guys had out there."

"So, we did everything you needed?" I slowly got out of the overstuffed chair and slid Cassandra down into it as I left.

"Indeed you did," Billy said from the kitchen.

"You wait here, I need to talk to him alone for a minute," I whispered to Cassandra.

"I thought you might." She looked up at me and smiled. "If you're going to talk about me, be nice."

"I don't know any other way to talk about you," I said, and headed towards the kitchen.

Billy glanced up at me as he put the bottles in the trashcan. We paused solemnly, until the sounds of glass hitting glass stopped.

"I know," he said. "What about your girlfriend, right?

"I told you months ago, she's my partner in everything." I had to make him agree.

"She's already in, Benjamin. The papers she signed have been approved and sent on." Billy patted me on the back. "I liked her tenaciousness with the British agent."

"She held her own." I proudly grinned at him. "That guy could have killed a less competent person."

"Yes, he could have," Billy agreed. He sat on one of the bar stools by the breakfast counter.

"What about that woman?" I asked. "The one who claimed to work for the Taiwanese government."

"The dead woman? We don't know who she worked for, no one's claiming her and I bet no one ever does," Billy replied.

"I'll assume she's a North Korean agent, but what was she after?" I looked thoughtfully towards the floor. "She must have known that Yoshihiro was after her and suspected she was a North Korean agent."

"I suppose so," Billy agreed. "And I bet she killed him for it."

"But, that still doesn't tell us the reason she was on that freighter," I mused.

"I'd be willing to bet that she was in it for herself, trying to take over the deal for the timing devices, those bank accounts had a total of fifteen million dollars in them," Billy said. "She was awfully interested in those bank account numbers."

"Was that all she was after?" I had to ask. "In addition to the money in the secret accounts, was she after the other stuff on that ship?"

"A lot of folks think she was," Billy answered. "I do, too. I think once she found out all the goodies that were on that ship, she decided she wanted all of it for herself. It seems to me that she decided to set off on her own to raise as much money as possible in a short as possible amount of time."

"Why?"

"That's a damned good question." Billy shrugged his shoulders. "It might take years to figure that one out."

"Do you think she had anything to do with the encryption keys?" I had my doubts.

"Maybe." Billy's expression was a bit skeptical. "That might have been her official assignment; helping to steal our secrets sounds like an assignment the official North Korean government might take on which would explain the North Korean codes being used."

"She could have been the outside person for the Russian in the cargo container," I mused. It did sound logical, but until the Russian could confirm it, we could only speculate.

"Can you imagine." Billy looked at me and smiled. "That woman had her fingers into the drugs, antiquities and illegal arms on that ship, in addition to the timing devices and the American scientist."

"Boy, if she were able to get away with all that." I thought about all the stuff on that one boat, "That would have to be one for the books."

"I suppose it would be," Billy responded. "Hell, it still is, think of all the illegal stuff that boat had going on."

"But, with her dead, I suppose we'll never know the whole truth." I shook my head. "Are you sure the Japanese agent wasn't part of any of the double dealings?"

"Almost completely sure." Billy sat on a kitchen chair. "We spoke to his supervisor, and he was completely above board. Their main concern, and the reason he was sent out on that freighter, was to track Maiko. The Japanese government is desperate to find out anything about all those kidnapped Japanese citizens, it's a real heartache for them."

"Yoshihiro must have gotten wind of the illegal cargo the Germans were carrying," I said. "My big question is how did he hook up with Maiko?"

"His boss said that Yoshihiro was approached by Maiko. The Japanese had already made Maiko's real identity, and they told him to start an affair with her," Billy said. "He said that Yoshihiro had started seeing Maiko a few months before the vacation on the Veracruz"

"I take it Yoshihiro is married?" I asked.

"For twenty some years." Billy shook his head. "I know, I know, their culture is different than ours, his agency apparently puts up with mistresses better than ours."

"What did they think he could get from Maiko?" I asked.

"They won't say." Billy shrugged his shoulders. "The Japanese think that Maiko had already decided to strike out on her own, and they thought Yoshihiro could bribe her to tell about the kidnappings and maybe get some intelligence about where the kidnapped Japanese were, or how many were still alive."

"In a way, that must have been quite a delightful assignment for Yoshihiro," I said with a half grin. "Being ordered to sleep with a beautiful younger woman for several months."

"Yeah." Billy tried to look as ironic as he could. "An assignment to die for."

"I guess you're right; have you gotten anything from the two in the box yet?" I asked.

"Not from the Russian, but the American scientist won't stop talking."

"At least something'll work out well," I chuckled.

"Yeah, we're sure the Russian's KGB," Billy said. "The FBI will handle this one the rest of the way, hopefully even they can't screw it up."

"Well, back to Cassandra," I pressed again.

"Her application was fast tracked, and she's in for sure." Billy got off the chair and slapped my back. "Personnel finished all the paperwork and got all the right signatures."

"Wow, that's great," I beamed. "Let me tell her."

"No problem, but don't forget, she has to report to us early next year." Billy pointed to the living room. "Are we through?"

"I'm through," I replied. "It's time for a vacation."

"Well, maybe not quite yet." Billy blinked a few times rapidly, then forced a laugh. "We have a problem in France, and we'd like you to do some background work on a group of American artists in Lyon. We think they might be doing a few side jobs for some bad people to earn extra money until their art starts to sell."

"Hey, I just finished a job which hasn't let me sleep in a couple of days."

"It's just a snoop job, all you have to do is hang around and keep an eye on them for a week or so. You can get all the sleep you'll need on the plane ride over there."

"I don't think so."

"Why not?" Billy asked.

"I plan on marrying Cassandra this next week, and want to take some time for a honeymoon. Since she's starting a class next week, I'll have to be here for awhile. We have to plan, tell her parents, and arrange a lot in the next week, so I can't do your job for you."

"Does she know you are getting married next week?"

"Not yet."

"What's your plan?"

"I don't know, maybe kick you out of the house and then ask her."

"That might work, but if you take the job I offered, telling her parents might be easier." Billy looked at me.

"How so? Because they just moved to France?"

"Something like that." He smiled broadly at me.

"Are you trying to tell me something else?" I stumbled around the possibilities.

"Not really."

"Not , what?" I insisted. "Does her father work for the company?"

What a revolting development that would be.

"Not any more," Billy laughed. "He worked for us when he was still in the Army, he was an analyst for European affairs."

"That doesn't count." I took in a deep breath. "Are you sure?"

"Sure as a heart attack." Billy kept his smile. "I had to tell you, I love the irony."

"What's the real reason you told me that?" I knew it had to be something else.

"He's been gone for a while, but you two might know some of the same people. He's not stupid and he might put one and one together; you need to know." Billy's grin faded.

"Is he going to be told about me?" I sure as hell didn't want to tell him.

"Maybe," Billy replied, "the brass is still pondering the whole situation."

"Are they thinking of recruiting him again now that he's in Europe?" I knew better than to ask, but that person was about to become my father-in-law.

"No comment," he replied.

Billy was serious, damn.

"Cassandra doesn't know, does she?"

Finding out first that I was a spy, then her father in one week, no, she didn't need that.

"No."

"I won't tell her." Damned right I wouldn't, she'd have to find out on her own, if ever.

"I didn't think you would," Billy laughed. "I'm sorry, but we do need you over there."

"I'm serious too, I'm getting married next week, and I won't do this next job for you." I looked at him and didn't flinch, I was serious. "Find someone else, besides, you promised no more than three government jobs a year and this one makes eight I've done for you for this year already."

"I guess we could assign someone else to it, but you'll have to invite me to the wedding."

"If you promise to get the hell out of here right now, I will."

"I have to go now anyway." Billy walked back into the living room. "I'm sorry the boys and I drank all your beer."

As I walked into the living room, I saw Cassandra, sound asleep in the large chair. She looked so beautiful, and so peaceful. I felt like a real bastard shaking her shoulder to wake her up, but I did need to propose to her.

"It has been interesting." Cassandra blinked as much of the sleep out of her as she could in the second before she sat up.

"It's always interesting," Billy said.

He paused in front of Cassandra, not knowing what to do. He started to extend his hand to her.

Before Billy could move his right hand more than an inch, Cassandra hugged him; Billy was a little surprised at that.

"I'm glad to finally meet you, I'm glad to finally be let in on this aspect of Benjamin's life. And, I'm looking forward to my new career."

"I'm glad too but, keep in mind, this is just the start of the roller coaster ride." Billy smiled, gave her cheek a peck and quickly left us alone.

"What was that roller coaster crack?" Cassandra turned and looked at me as the front door closed behind Billy.

"The agency officially accepted you as one of the family." I sat on the sofa and patted the cushion next to me. "Billy told me they all signed off on it and you're officially a spy now, although you still have to pass the training in March."

"Not a problem." Cassandra sat next to me, appearing to be fully awake. "I feel great now, life is strange sometimes. Five years ago, all I wanted to do was get my degrees and teach political science in some college, look at us now."

"In more ways than one." I wrapped my left arm around her shoulder. "Look at us now."

"What does this do to my school? To our agency?" She pulled back a bit and looked me in the eyes. "What about all the details?"

"Nothing," I reassured her. "Your deal will be the same as mine, we only do three or so government jobs a year, which in reality translates to five to ten. It means nothing in regards to your finishing your degree, that task you'll do this quarter."

"Are we full-time spies after I finish their training?" she asked.

"We aren't spies like in the movies." I shrugged. "We'll mostly do background information gathering; the job we just did is atypical of most of them."

"So we won't get shot at most of the time?"

"Are you disappointed?"

"Not at all." Cassandra relaxed onto my shoulder.

"What about this training thing?" She asked.

"It's not that bad." I tried to assure her. "Like I said, I kind of enjoyed it."

"It sounds like it could be interesting." She gently rubbed her head into my shoulder. "At least it sounds completely different from academia."

"Quite different," I agreed.

"So, what do we do in between government jobs?"

"We mostly do our usual detective stuff like chasing after the cheating husband, it's our cover. The world will forever think that we are plain old private investigators, so when we do a job for the CIA, they pay us through a multinational corporation and give us a cover story. The detective business is our NOC."

"What's that?" She asked.

"Non Official Cover," I answered.

"Sort of dull James Bond types."

"Exactly."

"It sounds like fun." Cassandra looked up at me and smiled. "As long as we're together, especially after we're married, I want to be a real part of our life together."

"Speaking of that." I hesitated.

"What?" She guessed the worst. "You're having second thoughts about getting married?"

"Not getting married, just the timing."

"What did you have in mind?" She calmed down.

"Next week?"

I kissed the top of her head, then lifted her head so I could kiss her lips.

"I'd love to, Mr. Katz ." She sounded happier than I had heard her since she left Atlanta.

"Should you wake your parents up?"

"You bet your ass I will." Cassandra sprang up and headed to the phone.

29
Guess who's knocking on my door?

Fred Lepus leaned back in the sofa in his front office, which was as old as the house itself, dirty and sagged in the middle, but if you sat on one of the ends, it was comfortable. Fred took in a deep breath through his nose; behind the faint odor of mold, Fred could smell the fresh pot of bubbling caffeine. Cathy had driven him back from the hospital where she insisted that Fred have his arm wound looked at by a doctor; she was worried about possible long term damage to his arm. Fred was worried about possible long term damage to his finances due to the high cost of a hospital visit, but Cathy insisted to the point that he went to the hospital to shut her up. Cathy Rumson trotted into the room from the back kitchen with a cup of steaming coffee.

"Here ya go, sweetie." Cathy carefully handed Fred the oversized cup.

"Thanks." Fred carefully took it with his left hand.

"So, how's the arm?" Cathy sat next to him. "How's it doing?"

"I could have told you that nothing bad happened to it." Fred sipped the drink. "Nothing important was severed, and it'll heal up fine in a month or so."

"But, it could have cut tendons and stuff and left you unable to use that arm, and you're right handed," Cathy reminded him.

"I guess." Fred wasn't in the mood to argue that much any more. "I wonder how I'll pay the bill when it comes due."

"It's a public hospital," Cathy said in a reassuring tone. "You can put off paying them for six months or more, then you can pay ten dollars a month and they can't do a thing."

"Yeah." Fred smiled for the first time in ten hours. "What're they gonna do, repossess my arm?"

"So, do ya think you could sue Katz and get some cash?" Cathy smiled back at Fred. "It's good to see you smile again, sweetie."

"Like I said, he and his bimbo girlfriend said they'd press charges of breaking and entering and assault on me," Fred answered. "Besides, if I know Katz , he'd counter sue because I smashed his head in first."

"I still think they owe you some money for helping them in their case," Cathy pouted. "It's not fair."

Both Fred and Cathy jumped up a few inches as a loud banging began on their front door.

"What the hell's that!" Cathy shouted

"Police! Open up!"

The answer to her question came rumbling in from outside the front door.

"It's open, come on in," Fred replied as he turned to Cathy. "Now what?

"Sir." A large uniformed police officer loomed over Cathy and Fred as they remained on the sofa. "We have a warrant which specifies that you be immediately sent to Los Angeles California to testify in a preliminary hearing in a case involving national security."

"That was a mouthful." Fred's attempt at sarcasm was spoiled by his stunned tone.

"He just got back from there," Cathy protested.

"I know, ma'am. We need to catch a plane in less than an hour, so you'll have to come now."

The same female FBI agent Fred had met not twelve hours before now entered his office, pausing inside the front door and looked at Fred.

"You said testify?" Fred stood and looked at the agent, eye to eye. "Does that mean I'm not under arrest?"

"For now," The woman replied, not changing her expression. "You will be in our custody while the hearing is being conducted, and I cannot say how it may end."

"Does he need a lawyer?" Cathy stood and asked.

"He'll be informed of his rights to a lawyer if that becomes necessary, ma'am." The agent turned to look at Cathy.

"So, I'm not under arrest?" Fred asked again.

"No, sir." The agent shook her head. "You're under our custody."

"I'm going with him," Cathy insisted.

"I'm sorry, Ma'am, you cannot go with us," The agent insisted. "If you could pack a bag for the gentleman quickly, you'd be a great help. Ma'am."

"Yeah, yeah." Cathy started to leave the room to gather up enough clothes and personal items for Fred to survive a few days at least. Most of what he needed was still in the suitcase from his last trip out there.

"Wait," Fred sharply said. "I want you out there."

"She cannot go with you, sir."

"She can go by herself," Fred spoke to Cathy, who had turned to listen to him.

"Get a ticket and fly to Los Angeles."

"And go where?" Cathy shrugged. "I maybe have enough money for the ticket, but where will I stay, and what will I eat?"

"Katz is staying at the broad's house; it's in Huntington Beach, listed under a Colonel Jacob Pales," Fred quickly spoke to Cathy. "He owes us that much, don't you think?"

"I hope he sees it that way." Cathy turned and trudged into the back bedroom to pack for Fred.

. . . .

"Your brother said he'd be here the day after tomorrow?"

Cassandra stretched her back as she sat up in the kitchen chair.

"Right."

I loaded the dishwasher with the lunch dishes.

"He said Trudy couldn't make it because too many of the kids have school things she has go to, but Becky would be coming out here with him."

"That's great," Cassandra beamed. "I kind of wish more of them could make it, though."

"I suppose we could try to get up to the farm sometime after Christmas," I said.

284

I wished we could go for Christmas, but Cassandra had promised her folks we would go to France to be with them.

"Yeah, speaking of my folks." Cassandra sat up in the chair. "We have to pick them up at the airport tomorrow at ten o'clock."

"Right." I looked at the ceiling in a resigned fashion

"Don't get all hinky on me now," Cassandra pleasantly warned me. "If I can get through this, you can too."

"It's going to be awkward," I said with a sigh.

She didn't know her father had worked as an analyst for the CIA, like I did. I bet he either had already or would soon figure out I worked for the Company too and that wasn't' going to be a pretty picture. Cassandra was his only child, and I'd found him to be quite possessive in the past. Oh well, he was going to be my father-in-law so I had to make the best of it.

"I know." Cassandra got up and put her arm around my waist. "I still love you more than anything, so don't worry about it."

The doorbell rang. "I'll get it." Cassandra said as she hurried to the front door.

"What are you doing here?" she gasped.

Standing in the front doorway, Cathy Rumson stared back carrying two medium sized suitcases. Her thick veneer of makeup was shifting slightly off center.

"The FBI dragged Fred back here because of that case you and Katz forced him into!" Cathy burst out crying as she dropped her suitcases with a thud.

"Calm down." Cassandra motioned for her to come in.

"I don't know what to do," Cathy sobbed as she pulled her bags inside the front door and made a bee line to the sofa, plopping down in the dead center of it. "They wouldn't say if he was under arrest or not, they hauled him away and I don't have enough for bail or even a place to stay, he's depending on me." Cathy looked up at Cassandra, then out the front window. "Hey, that's a real nice view."

Cassandra was trying to keep a grin from showing. "What's this about the case?" she asked.

"The FBI said it was a national security case and they'd keep Fred as long as it took to find out what part he had in it, and they wouldn't even tell me where he was." Cathy ran out of breath, then dramatically inhaled.

"Wait here," Cassandra said. Her mind was quickly parsing the possibilities, no way in hell did she want that woman and her strange little boss to even come close to thinking she and I were government employees. She turned to head back to the kitchen where I was waiting for her by the kitchen door.

"I heard," I said in a whisper. "I'll go back to the family room and call them right now and make sure we have our stories straight."

"That sounds good, what is our story?" Cassandra looked concerned for a second, then she looked as if she suddenly got a joke.

"Uh." I paused long enough for a mental picture to form. "We were hauled in yesterday and they quizzed us for hours. We didn't do anything illegal, and cooperated with them, and they let us go, how does that sound?"

"Pretty good for no notice." She smiled back at me. "I'll go stay with the strange woman while you make the phone call."

Cassandra walked back into the living room. Cathy had walked to the front window and was engrossed in the view.

"Are you all right?"

"This is a nice house?" Cathy turned to face Cassandra. "Who owns it?"

"My parents do," Cassandra answered.

Cathy was in her mid thirties; with a proper makeup job, she could probably pass for her late twenties, but not now after a long flight and a hurried one at that.

"This is a nice place." Cathy rocked on her feet.

"So, why did you come here?" Cassandra asked.

"Well." Cathy looked at the floor. "I don't have any money left and I don't have a place to stay out here while Fred's in custody, and, well, he sort of thought that you could put me up since it's your fault that he's in so much trouble."

"What?" Cassandra was dumbstruck for a second; this almost stranger thinks she should be a houseguest? In the middle of all these wedding plans?

"It won't be for long." Cathy smiled timidly. "Just until Fred gets out of jail, or wherever they have him."

"We have something going on here next week, and there's going to be lots of people staying in this house starting tonight," Cassandra sounded quite flustered.

"You can put me in the garage." Cathy looked hurt. "I'll sleep in the garage if there's no more room, I need to have a place to stay until Fred gets out."

"That's not the point." Cassandra regained some of her wits. "Benjamin and I are getting married next week, and, well, you'd be in the way."

"Oh no." Cathy flashed a genuine grin on her face. "I could help you, I have such a great fashion sense, I know you can't tell it from the way I'm dressed now, but with more rest and some makeup and all, I look like a fashion plate. I can make your wedding look like a million bucks, honey."

30

It could have been worse

"Hello, Agent Dixon?" I asked into the phone.

"Yeah, who is this?" He answered back

"Katz ," I replied. "You guys picked up Fred Lepus for questioning?"

A long pause lingered on Dixon's side of the conversation.

"I may have a small problem," I added.

"What?" Dixon finally answered. "And, why the hell did you call me?"

"I didn't want to go through channels for this," I quickly answered. Why didn't I? I guess I didn't want to bother Billy about this; hell, I don't know why, I just did.

"Okay," Dixon said. "We got him late yesterday and have been questioning him about his dealings with Zimmer and the dead Asian woman."

"That's fine, and you can even use a rubber hose on him as far as I'm concerned, but his secretary with the big hair showed up on my doorstep and I don't want her thinking Lepus was the only one dragged in and questioned."

"I understand." I swear I heard Dixon chuckle. "The story'll be that we brought the two of you in first and beat you with the rubber hose."

"Thanks." I was somewhat relieved.

"No problem." Dixon hung up.

I could get to like that guy, if I planned to stay out here, that is.

"What are we going to do?" Cassandra crashed into the family room as I hung up the phone."

"About what?" I looked at her. "I fixed our little story."

"That's fine, but now that woman out there wants to plan my wedding for me!" Her expression showed more panic than I had ever seen.

"What?" I was confused.

"She says we have to keep her here until Lepus is out."

"Why?"

"Because I shot him." Cassandra started shaking her head from side to side. "No way, no way!"

"Hi, you two." Cathy strolled into the family room. "So, this is where you've been hiding, you sweet thing." She winked at me.

"Hello Cathy," I verbally stumbled.

I grabbed Cassandra around the waist, sort of like a shield.

"I hear you two are finally going to tie the knot." She rocked seductively back and forth as she almost purred. "I'm jealous."

"Don't be." Cassandra glared at Cathy. "Why don't we all go back out to the living room."

"Sure thing, honey." Cathy turned around and started walking. "Have you decided where I'm staying? I wasn't kidding when I said I'd sleep in the garage."

"Didn't your dad fix up a loft above the garage?" I innocently remarked.

I looked at Cassandra as we walked into the living room; boy, did she glare at me, I felt like my head would explode any minute.

"That'd be great!" Cathy turned and hugged Cassandra, who let her arms dangle at her side.

. . . .

"I know my dad'll hate it," Cassandra spoke softly. She looked out the side window of the car as we approached the airport.

"But, what do you think?" I asked. I liked the idea, and I wasn't going to give up on it.

"I was raised Episcopalian, and I think my parents would be happier with the priest from their church out here," Cassandra replied. "But, I love the idea."

"I was raised confused, but that doesn't matter." I considered what I had just said for a second, or two.

"You said your mother's side of the family was Jewish, right?" Cassandra wouldn't let me think out my last statement.

"Right," I softly said, wondering where she was going.

"So, what religion was your father?"

"He was Congregationalist." I looked at Cassandra. "But he didn't go to church much, I suppose it was the compromise he and my mom worked out, but he never said."

"The reason I asked was I wondered about your last name. It sounds Jewish, I just wondered."

Cassandra looked carefully at me; at least now I knew what she was after.

"Is that a problem?" I was curious.

"Has it been so far?" She looked at me as if I were a tax auditor.

"I guess not," I said with a grin.

"Well." She smiled again.

"The farm came down through my grandmother's side, she married into the Katz family."

I took in a deep breath. I never have told the woman I loved this little family story.

"The surname of the original farming family was Fischer. My great-grandparents on my father's side had only one daughter, their daughter married a Katz and had only one son, my father."

"Was the Katz side of the family Jewish?"

"I suppose so," I replied. "A long time ago, but for as far back as anyone can remember, they were Congregationalists from New Hampshire; what's the point of this discussion?"

"Do you want a Jewish wedding?"

"Not unless you do," I sounded a little confused. What was this conversation about?

"I'd like to have the Reverend conduct the wedding, not that I plan to become Southern Baptist or anything." I tried again to turn this conversation around to my original request.

"So." She didn't want to let this go. "You're mother's side of the family?"

"She had only one brother. You met him, I was named after him," I said, wanting to settle this thing about who would do the ceremony. "Her maiden name was Rosenblum, both those grandparents are dead. That family immigrated in the eighteen seventies to get away from one of the wars in Eastern Germany, they came directly to New York and stayed put."

"No," she paused, "I don't particularly want a Jewish wedding, we haven't had the religion discussion yet."

"Excuse me?"

"Three things can break up a marriage," she paused for effect. "Sex, money and religion."

"What about relatives?"

"Okay, four."

"So, you decided we'd get all of those discussions in before we got married," I said, a little surprised.

"We've done all the others, so I thought we'd get the religion one done now," she cleared her throat. "It's getting down to the wire as far as talking about these things before our wedding."

"So, I suppose you don't see any landmines?" I saw her shake her head. "What about using the Reverend?"

The Reverend was a friend I had made many years ago, he was a real Baptist minister, and a fairly well known jazz singer who owned the apartment building I lived in while I was in Los Angeles. To a stranger, he could look quite menacing, but in reality he was a true friend.

"As long as he's legal, and we're married after the ceremony." She patted my knee. "He'll do fine by me."

"That's what matters most," I agreed.

I pulled into the lane for the short term parking. I hated to do it, but we had to lease a car for four months since neither one of us had a vehicle out here anymore.

"I'll call the Reverend as soon as we get back home," I added

"I hope he has better clothes than the last time I saw him," Cassandra mused.

"He has a nice set of suits, I've even seen him in several of them." I wedged the car into a slot.

"It's too bad your uncle and aunt can't make it." Cassandra got out of the car.

"Yeah," I said, regretfully. "Aunt Ruth sounded upset that we didn't give them enough notice to come out here."

"I need to meet her, she sounds nice." Cassandra looked at me over the top of our car. "Your uncle sounded nice too."

"They're sending my cousin Bernie, the doctor, out here," I added. "He gets in tomorrow morning early."

"Your brother gets in later today, right?" Cassandra locked her door.

"Right," I answered. "You can stay at home with your folks, and I'll pick my brother and Becky up."

"Don't let Dad get your goat right away," Cassandra said as we walked to the terminal. "He sounded a bit surprised by all this, so give him some room, okay?"

"Don't worry," I answered nervously. "I plan on being married to you for a long, long time, so he and I have to get along."

"Fine." Cassandra's mind had gone elsewhere, some other detail of this whole production I assumed. "The family pre-wedding party is tonight."

"Right." I nodded as I looked for the gate of her parents' flight. "I called the caterer right before we left to confirm the time and the menu."

"Good." She mentally checked that off again. "Now, the pre-wedding dinner is just going to be family."

"And Becky and Billy," I added.

"Becky's almost family, and I guess I understand you're inviting Billy." She stopped and looked at me. "I almost understand it."

"I can't quite explain it to myself, let alone to you," I sounded flustered.

"It doesn't mater." She hurried to the gate. "He's only one more mouth to feed, and it doesn't matter."

"What about Cathy?" I almost didn't want to say it, but I had to. "I asked the caterer to add one more serving just in case."

"Damn." She stopped dead in her tracks. "I forgot about the bimbo."

"We can ask her to stay in her loft and send some food up to her." I looked at her. I could see the wheels whizzing away up there.

"That might work." She shook her head. "No, that woman's social skills aren't that good, she'd never take the hint. She'd barge in anyway, so why bother; set another place at the table."

"It could be worse, you know."

I tried a smile on her; it didn't work.

31

I told you it could get worse

"That was a great meal." Jacob Pales looked at his daughter. "I've never had chicken that good."

"Thanks, Daddy." Cassandra smiled. "But Benjamin arranged it all."

"Which restaurant?" He looked at me; Cassandra's smile disappeared.

"It wasn't a restaurant." I did smile at him, I hope it didn't look too forced. "I know a private caterer in Los Angeles, and she insisted on doing this dinner as well as the wedding reception."

"Well." He looked back at his daughter and grinned again. "Whoever it was, that was one delicious meal."

"I know," Cassandra said. She wasn't about to let her father get away with ignoring me. "Benjamin has a whole slew of friends with the most unusual gifts that you could imagine. As a matter of fact, one of his old friends is a minister, and he's going to marry us."

"What?" He turned to look at me, then back at Cassandra. "What about Father Walters?"

"Don't worry, Daddy." Cassandra patted her father's shoulder. "Mom and I have already worked this out."

"As long as your mom's happy with it." His gaze remained on me, what else could happen?

"Listen," Jacob leaned over and whispered to his daughter. "I think Benjamin and I need to have that little talk now."

"Gees, Daddy," she said with a slightly disgusted tone. "You don't have to be so dramatic about it. Besides, the wedding is going to happen tomorrow anyway."

"Hey, I think us talking will be a good idea." I smiled again at my future father-in-law; the man who I thought might want to use me for target practice right now.

"Fine." Jacob slapped my back. "Why don't we go to my den, son."

At least he called me son, maybe that was a good sign.

"Don't get too comfortable there, that's my bedroom for the next four months," Cassandra insisted.

She turned to head back to the family room where all the other guests had gathered for dessert and drinks.

"You know, Benjamin." Colonel Jacob Pales settled into the wooden chair in front of a small writing desk against the back wall of what was now Cassandra's bedroom. "I don't dislike you, in fact, I kind of like you."

Was that praise? Did he mean that he liked me, or was this a preface to something worse? I sat on the edge of the double bed facing Jacob, not answering him just then, I had a feeling this was the beginning of a monologue.

"But, son, Cassandra has worked hard for this degree she's going to earn in a few months."

I could tell that the Colonel was coming completely out of his shell.

"Hell, she'll have doctor in front of her name." He looked up at the rows of photographs on the wall, most of which were of him and his friends, all in army uniforms. "What I'm trying to say is that, well don't you think it's a huge waste of her talent for her to be a detective?"

"How do you mean?"

I felt like adding 'Colonel, sir!' after that, but that might be too much.

"Well," he slowly started again. "She's going to have a PhD and you've never even been to college."

"Does that matter?" I forced myself from getting too ego involved.

"Not really," He back peddled a little. "Not for you in what you've chosen to do, but for Cassandra, well, don't you think she'd be better suited being a college teacher somewhere?"

"If she wants to teach college somewhere, I certainly won't stop her." I shrugged. "You have to know her better than I; since when could anybody force her to do anything she didn't want to do?"

"I'm thinking about your future," The Colonel continued. "I mean, Cassandra could easily make fifteen to twenty thousand teaching at a university. And, you could get a job with a large corporation in their security division." He looked at me; I didn't say anything because I wanted him to finish. "I spoke to personnel at the drug firm I work for, and for someone with your experience, I could get you a position paying up to fifteen thousand, between the two of you, you could be living well."

"Well." I thought carefully. "Cassandra owns half of our agency."

"I know," Jacob acknowledged. "She told me that over a year ago."

"Did she, by chance, tell you how much she made from the detective agency last year?"

"Not in exact amounts, but I got the impression it wasn't that much." Jacob stared at me.

"Before taxes and expenses, Cassandra made a little over sixty thousand last year." I wanted to smile at him, but I didn't dare. "If I'm not mistaken, that's more than most chairmen of political science departments make."

"She didn't tell me that." The colonel's jaw went slack for a second.

"Since she and I share everything fifty-fifty, I made the same amount."

I loved this. After we sell the Los Angeles branch we'll probably never make that much, but I still loved telling him we made that much.

"Did she also tell you that the five unit apartment building in Atlanta we live in belongs to us, free and clear?"

"No, no, she didn't tell me that either," The colonel didn't sound like he wanted to pursue my working as a corporate rent-a-cop anymore.

"As far as our financial future, sir, I don't think you need worry about us," I cleared my throat. "We save a lot of our earnings, we always have."

"I'm happy to hear the business is doing so well, but I'm a bit surprised."

"Why?"

"You see that photograph to my left?" Jacob pointed to one of the photos on the wall.

"Yes," I replied. "That looks like you in the back row all the way to the right."

"That's me," he said with a nostalgic grin, still looking at the picture. "You see that younger man in front of me?"

"You have your hand on his shoulder, right?"

"That's the man," Jacob concurred. "His name is Brad Casey, he was a captain then, he worked close to my office while I was stationed in Germany."

"Was he assigned to NATO?"

I had a feeling this was leading to a difficult conversation.

"No, son." Jacob pulled in a deep breath. "He was an operations officer for the CIA."

"Really?"

He knew what I was, but did he know Cassandra had signed up too?

"Really," he spoke deliberately. "I've been friends with Brad for decades, he retired from the Company this last year. About ten years ago, he was mentoring a young operations officer who showed a lot of promise."

"That was nice of him."

Where was he going with this? Where?

"He talked and talked about him." Jacob looked intently at me. "That young officer's name was Billy Sullivan, and I about crapped in my pants when Billy Sullivan showed up here for this family dinner before my daughter's wedding."

297

I took in a deep breath and let it out slowly, "You were an analyst for the Company while you were in the army."

"And, you're an operations officer." He continued his glare.

"I'm a contract officer." I didn't look away. "Most of my waking time is involved with the real detective business, my cover is my real life."

"Does Cassandra know?"

"They gave me permission to tell her this week," I said slowly. "She knows."

"And?" He cocked his head to one side.

"She was suspicious about all the trips I took without her," I continued. "She'd have figured it out sooner or later."

"I never told Betsy." Jacob looked down at the desk for a second, then back up at me. "I think she knew for a long time, but she never said a word. You know, it's a lot easier to hide what we do when you're in active military service."

"I suppose it is," I agreed.

"Is she working for them too?" He threw that one in like a grenade.

"Does Cassandra know who you worked for?" I answered with a bomb of my own.

"No."

"Ask her yourself." I kept looking straight at him. "Even if she were working for the Company, I wouldn't tell you, she'd have to."

"You're right," He replied, then smiled. "You know, you and me are a lot more alike than I thought we were."

"I think so too."

I stood up, hoping he was finished, which he was. He got up and began to walk with me to the dining room, and all our company.

"I have to ask one question," I spoke up before we joined the others.

I never did ask Cassandra this one, and I suppose it might be easier to ask her father since we bonded, sort of.

"What?" He stopped and looked at me.

"Why did you give your daughter that name?" I shrugged my shoulders. "She's not like the classical Cassandra at all."

The colonel smiled, looked at the floor, then back up at me.

"Well, when she was born, that little baby screamed coming out into the world." He enjoyed this story and so did I. "It wasn't one of those, 'how dare you pull me out here' screams, nor was it one of those 'man, this hurts' screams."

"Sort of like she was trying to tell you something?" I began to get the gist.

"Yeah," The colonel chuckled. "You would have to have been there, it was like she was telling us, more shouting at us, about something important, only the gods had made her unfathomable to us."

"I love this story." I grinned from ear to ear.

"Her mother is a big fan of the Greeks and Romans, and she loved the name Cassandra," the colonel said with a broad grin. "For the first twelve years of her life we all called her Cassie, but once she read the Iliad, she made us call her by her real name and it's stuck, no one in the family calls her anything but Cassandra anymore."

"Thanks." I studied my future father-in-law. "I'm glad you told me."

"One thing I don't understand." Jacob put his arm around my shoulder.

"What?"

What was he up to now?

"Who the hell is that strange hillbilly woman?"

"Oh," I didn't quite know what to reply.

This isn't that bad, it could have been so much worse.

"She's the girlfriend of someone Cassandra shot."

32
Life is good

The ceremony was over and we were Mr. And Mrs. Katz . The Reverend even shaved for the ceremony, and he wore a tux; it was all crushed red velvet, but it was a tuxedo. Becky was so glad to see him again, she clung to him for thirty minutes before she'd let him go and I know the Reverend loved it. Mark was an usher and his wife was the maid of honor; Mark didn't stop smiling the whole time and Mary didn't stop crying. My brother, the best man, kept patting my back, and I think I saw a tear or two from him; he's so happy I finally got married. Albert and Annie took tons of pictures for us and Annie said she'd pick out the best shot and make a painting of it. Cassandra's major professor showed up but I think he was a bit nervous around some of our friends, especially the undercover cop with all the tattoos and body piercings; Ellen is actually a quiet homebody type if you get to know her.

Cassandra and I traipsed back to her bedroom to change for the reception. Cassandra's mother, Betsy, was marshaling the troops back into the dining room to get their food; our wedding had been held in the back yard. While the guests were in the dining room standing in line for more of the delicious food prepared by my friend, Betsy hurried some of the volunteers in rearranging the chairs in the back yard for the reception.

"I'll get it," Betsy said loudly to a group of helpers as she rushed to the front door to answer the bell.

"Hello?" She looked at Fred Lepus standing on the doorstep. "Are you here for the wedding?"

"Well." Fred slowly looked at Betsy Pales. "I guess so."

"Come on in."

She stepped aside to let Lepus walk into the front hall and into the living room, the same living room where he was shot.

Fred looked around at the carpets for any sign of his blood, there wasn't any; he shrugged.

"Actually, I came here for a Ms. Rumson." Fred turned to look at Cassandra's mother.

"Oh, are you friends with my daughter or with Benjamin?" Betsy asked.

She looked at Fred for a while, observing that he fit with Cathy; this was a strange pair of guests and she was curious; no one had explained Cathy's presence to her, at least not well enough.

"You're Cassandra's mother?" Fred smiled at her. "You're good looking too, I can see where she gets her great looks."

"Thank you," Betsy politely answered, but she pressed on. "How long have you known Cassandra?"

"Well," Lepus answered. "I've known Benjamin for a few years now, but I've only seen your daughter a couple of times."

"On cases?" Betsy asked.

"Sort of," Lepus stumbled ahead. "The first time I met your daughter she kicked me in the nuts, and the last time I met her she shot me in the arm."

"Oh, she did?"

Betsy didn't want to pursue this with Fred, not at all. She did, however, want to pursue it with Cassandra.

"Yeah, right here in your living room." Fred pointed to the exact spot.

"Uh, thank you for sharing that with me." Betsy felt a renewed urgency to speak to her daughter. "Please, go on through to the dining room and get some food, I think your friend, Cathy, is in there."

"Thanks Mrs. P." Fred flashed a quick smile at Betsy. "I could use some free grub right now."

He darted into the dining room and took his place in the serving line.

"Cassandra." Betsy intercepted her daughter as we stepped out of the bedroom door.

"What, Mom?" Cassandra looked at her mother.

"Your Dad has had some strange friends over the years, but I think I met someone a lot stranger a second ago." Betsy put her hand on Cassandra's arm.

"Who?" I had to ask.

"Apparently, the man you shot in my living room came to the reception." Betsy looked straight into her daughter's eyes. "Do you mind telling me what that was all about?"

"Lepus is here?" I tried to hide my annoyance.

"Is he a criminal?" Betsy looked at me.

"No." I tried to calm down. "He's a royal pain in the ass." I breathed slowly, measured. "Your daughter shot him because he was bashing me over the head with his pistol."

"And." Betsy looked carefully at me. "Why was that strange gentleman doing that?"

"It was a case we just finished, Mom." Cassandra looked at me, then at her mother. "We were working for Lloyds of London on a cargo smuggling case, and Fred was trying to steal some evidence from us."

"Why was he dong that?" She asked me.

"He's stupid," I laughed, it was a nervous laugh, but that was the best I could do on the spur of the moment. "He was working for the smugglers and didn't know it; he's a poor excuse for a private investigator from Washington, DC."

"After talking to him for a brief moment." Betsy smiled at me. "I concur, he is a bit slow."

"Mom," Cassandra laughed. "I can't believe you're not reaming me out for all this."

"Well." Betsy put her hand on Cassandra's back. "First of all, it's your wedding day, and second I accept what you do for a living. I may not agree with your choice, but I approve of you and I know you'll make a damn fine spy."

"Mom!" Cassandra dropped her jaw about as far as she could and stared at her mother.

"Darling." She patted both our backs. "I may be only a housewife, but I'm not brainless."

The Author

Bob Henneberger has been writing for the past decade, working mostly in Science Fiction and Mystery, He has also written short stories, plays, television scripts and articles for professional journals. He lives in Vermont, close to Lake Champlain with his wife and several cats; not that that's an indication of anything unusual.

www.ingramcontent.com/pod-product-compliance
Lightning Source LLC
Chambersburg PA
CBHW060853250626
47159CB00008B/2718